Advance Praise for Sara Wolf's *HEAVENBREAKER*

"A genre-bending, viscerally written thrill ride with a feral heroine who will stop at nothing."

—Xiran Jay Zhao, #1 *New York Times* bestselling author of *Iron Widow*

"A seamless, captivating blend of *Ender's Game, Pacific Rim,* and the knights of King Arthur with its own innovative twists and sublimely crafted sci-fi world. A brutal, sharply gripping, full-tilt ride that will become your new obsession."

—Abigail Owen, award-winning author of *The Liar's Crown*

HEAVEN BREAKER

HEAVEN BREAKER

NEW YORK TIMES BESTSELLING AUTHOR

SARA WOLF

Entangled Publishing, LLC
644 Shrewsbury Commons Ave., STE 181
Shrewsbury, PA 17361
rights@entangledpublishing.com

Red Tower Books is an imprint of Entangled Publishing, LLC.

Visit our website at www.entangledpublishing.com.

Edited by Stacy Abrams
Cover design by Elizabeth Turner Stokes
Deluxe Endpaper Design by Elizabeth Turner Stokes
Stock art by aksol/Shutterstock, Warm_Tail/Shutterstock,
and OnlyFlags/Shutterstock
Interior design by Heather Howland
Interior formatting by Britt Marczak

Hardcover ISBN 978-1-64937-710-4
Deluxe Edition ISBN 978-1-64937-570-4
Ebook ISBN 978-1-64937-546-9

Printed in the United States

First Edition May 2024

10 9 8 7 6 5 4 3 2 1

RED TOWER BOOKS™

MORE FROM SARA WOLF

BRING ME THEIR HEARTS SERIES

BRING ME THEIR HEARTS
FIND ME THEIR BONES
SEND ME THEIR SOULS

LOVELY VICIOUS SERIES

LOVE ME NEVER
FORGET ME ALWAYS
REMEMBER ME FOREVER

For Ruth. I am the one left missing you.

Heavenbreaker is a fast-paced sci-fantasy story set in the brutal and competitive world of mechsuit combat, which includes elements regarding grief, violence, murder, suicidal ideation and acts, hospitalization, drug use, poisoning, loss of autonomy, depictions of religious trauma, classism, depictions of sex work, and drowning that are shown on page. Domestic violence and sexual abuse are mentioned off page. Readers who may be sensitive to these elements, please take note.

If you or someone you know is contemplating suicide, please know *you are not alone*. Visit befrienders.org or bethe1to.com and help save a life.

PART I

THE RABBIT

0. Ignesco

ignescō ~ere, *intr.*
1. to start to burn; catch fire

IN THE SAME YEAR, on the same space Station orbiting the green gas giant Esther, three children turn five years old.

One of them is a girl, black-haired and skipping barefoot along a steel pipe belching sulfur fumes. Weathered crosses suspended by barbed wire and half-broken holoscreens watch her journey from above, coffee and air-purifier ads winking down at her like fond parents. In one hand she holds a basket of scavenged treats for her mother—burned bread and the parts of fruits no one wants. She has never met her father, but she dreams of him.

One of the children is a boy, platinum-haired and much smaller than his peers. His coat is embroidered silver and his shoes are shiny and new, but his face is smeared with his own days-old blood and excrement. He cries and cries as his mother leads him by the elbow through the marble halls of their mansion and into the cockpit of a red metal beast. The cockpit door slides shut behind him, and he slams his fists against it, begging to be let out. He dreams of freedom, but he has never had it.

The last child is a girl with eyes as deep and blue as a shadowed lake. She's snuggled under a white-feather blanket, squealing with glee when her father pokes his head in before bedtime. By the light of a holocandle, he reads her the tale of the Knight's War on old Earth—four hundred years gone and with five billion dead in its wake—and outside the girl's window, there is only black space and silver stars and a great green planet with a white silica storm rotating slowly across its face. She dreams of great honor, and she will have it.

But then she will lose it all.

FIFTEEN YEARS LATER

1. Acies

aciēs ~ēī, *f.*
1. a sharp edge
2. a battle line

W hen I met my father for the first time, we talked about roses, the theoretical feel of rain, and the lilac perfume that used to waft from Mother as she brushed my hair. Oh, and the dagger in my father's back. We talked about that, too.

But only briefly.

Now he's dead. And I probably will be soon, too.

I inhale and turn the gold-plated handles of his sink. Under the gentle water, I scrub my hands and watch his blood circle the drain. Bit by bit, I scrape him out from under my nails.

The lights of his office bathroom are soft, steady. Nothing like the constantly flickering fluorescents of my apartment in Low Ward. In the bright light, I can see every unraveling seam in my patched tunic beneath my janitor coat disguise, every old tear Mother fixed with plastic fibers as thread.

I shiver at the face staring back at me in the mirror. It looks like Father's. Same black hair, although his was salt-and-pepper. Same cheeks set at a sharp angle.

And we both have the same thin blue eyes that look dead inside.

No. Not "have." *Had.*

A knock at the office door jumps me out of my skin, then a silken voice on the other side calls out, "Duke Hauteclare?"

My heart catches in its own beat. Father's attendant.

For a moment, my insides twist in anticipation, my breathing shallow. Is it now?

Do I die now, when he comes in and sees the blood pooling on the rug and draws a hard-light pistol? Do I die when he calls the guards and they airlock me into space to join Father's corpse? Or do I get to wait in a cell before receiving their so-called justice—an excruciating death burning beneath a plasma vent?

I, Synali Emilia Woster, have killed my father, a duke of the glimmering court of Nova-King Ressinimus the Third. After so many months of planning, waiting, watching…I've done it. All that's left now is to escape back into the alleys of Low Ward.

The attendant's voice is guileless. "Your steed awaits in hangar six, Your Grace. They've issued the twenty-minute warning, so please send your chosen rider out shortly."

Footsteps in the marble hall outside signal the attendant leaving—small miracles—and yet still my guts writhe. He's not the only one out there waiting for me. The guards, the cameras… I planned my entrance route into the tourney hall down to the minute, but with revenge burning in my blood, my exit route was only ever a vague idea.

Only now do I realize it with cold finality—there is no exit.

I glance at the sleek white riding helmet on the marble counter, a gold lion with wings gracing the visor. The flying lion is the emblem of the noble House Hauteclare—*my* House, a House I didn't know I was a part of until six months ago.

My father, Duke Hauteclare, ruled it like a despot, like all noble Houses are ruled—underhanded deals and drug rings and protecting weapons dealers. I grew up watching the noble Houses pillage and destroy Low Ward: slowly, insidiously, and then all at once when the honorable duke sent an assassin to murder Mother and me.

I survived. She did not.

My gaze falls onto the bloodstains on his office carpet, viscous and dark.

Footsteps in red, drag marks in red. I turn away, my shoulders shaking. Space lingers outside the office window, even darker. Our Station is one of the seven made during the Knight's War—a giant ark protecting the remnants of humanity after the enemy razed Earth's surface with their laserfire. The knights eventually won, but in their last attack, the enemy flung the seven Stations across the universe with some mysterious power—and so we remain here, alone, orbiting the green gas giant Esther and trying desperately to terraform it and make contact with the other Stations.

I stare at Esther until my eyes water. I don't know what to do now. My life since Mother died has been clear-cut: eating, sleeping, preparing—a list of steps I followed to the end. I touch my right wrist, the rectangle of implanted blue light blooming beneath my skin and projecting my vis into the air in a perfect hovering holograph. I tap the timer and set it for sixty seconds. One minute of weakness. That's all I will allow myself.

I clutch Mother's cross pendant around my neck until I feel it biting into my palm.

"It's all right to cry, dearheart."

I let my tears wash his blood splatter off my face. His blood ruined everything.

He killed her, and he tried to kill me. My father, my family, the man I never met, the man I dreamed about as a child, the strong and good man Mother always said he was… Why? No—I know why. I traded my body and soul these last six months to find out why.

Muffled sobs impact in my chest like half-swallowed pain, like fury, like despair. It all rises up again like a terrible wave as the blue vis digits count down starkly in the air: *Five. Four. Three. Two.*

One.

My tears slow and then stop. It's not over. I killed Father, but he isn't *really* gone. I've destroyed his body but not his world. My world was Mother, but his world was his reputation, his credits, his power and pride. He killed her for power. For his *House.* So long as House Hauteclare stands, he yet lives on.

I can't dissolve a noble House; no one save for the king himself can do that. But I *can* disgrace one.

There is no escape, but I can still die on my own terms.

Suddenly, a dim roar pierces the office walls: the arena crowd. They wait outside for the greatest show of all—a riding tourney. Only pureblooded nobles are allowed to ride in such tourneys, but I will ignore this. I am the shame they whisper of in the Nova-King's court, half Father's noble blood and half Mother's commoner blood—his bastard daughter.

And if I'm the reason Mother died, then I will be the reason House Hauteclare meets the same fate.

I have never ridden. Steeds—the giant mechsuits the nobility rides in tournaments—are not for commoners; they were killing machines designed for knights in the War.

Nobles must train from childhood to ride a steed, or they'll die in its saddle.

I swallow down a stab of fear. Like most everyone in Low Ward, I've spent my childhood watching noble tourneys on my vis. I know what they look like from the outside and only the outside. Nobles participate, and nobles spectate. Bastards do not ride. It would be an unforgivable disgrace on whichever House let a bastard like me ride.

The extra rider's suit in my father's cabinet gleams, white tipped with gold. He used to ride for House Hauteclare before his age caught up with him, and the irony isn't lost on me; now his old suit will allow me to disgrace his House once and for all. I will not die quietly. My death will be a blaze of revenge.

The massive sheaf is made of a patent leather–like material and double my size, but when I drape it over my head and press on the golden wrist cuffs, it conforms to my body with a single hiss as it snaps tight against my half-starved flesh.

I slide the pompous helmet onto my head, and in the cabinet's reflection, the opaque visor consumes who I was and turns me into what I must be.

I will hide our family's bloodstains as Father did—with white and gold all over.

2. Aureus

aureus ~a ~um, a.
1. covered with gold, gilded

I redouble my strides as I head down the tourney hall toward hangar six. I have to move fast—I lost precious minutes shoving Father's body out of the airlock. The cavernous walkway looms in cold marble and steel. The Station is large enough to house three wards—Low Ward, Mid Ward, and the Noble Ward—but the tourney hall is grander than any building on the Station save for the king's palace. As riding is the only sport approved by both the king and the church, the tourney hall is a beacon of entertainment and leisure—one of the few places commoners are welcome to spend their credits and fill the stands.

I pick up my speed as I take a left down to hangar six, following the orange lights carved in the shape of angels. How easy the nobles must have it if they can waste time making lights this beautiful. They have food aplenty and medicine enough to heal whatever sniffle they may catch, while the red pox ravages the rest of us with no end in sight. The pockmarks on my own cheeks burn—I caught it long ago and barely survived. My father's face, on the other hand, was terrifyingly smooth. Nobles never have to survive. They decide who survives.

A duke is the highest position within a House. He oversees a handful of lords, and the handful of lords then oversees the many barons who keep the rest of us impoverished, at the mercy of the aristocracy and their myriad friends in all places. They decide who lives, who gets protein rations, and who dies.

But this time, I've decided. From now on, I'm the only one who gets to decide when and where I die.

And it will be inside a steed.

I glare up at the stately banners of the noble Houses lining the tourney hall: the purple-gold dragon of the king's House—House Ressinimus—hangs more prominently than any other. Fans aren't allowed near the hangars, but a group has snuck in anyway, waiting with hothouse flowers and autograph books—real, precious paper; real, unprecious fanaticism—for their favorite riders to pass by.

"Who's that?" a girl whispers, eyes on me.

"Hauteclare's rider," a man next to her asserts. "The only House who wears a white that bright is Hauteclare."

"But…she's a girl. I thought Duke Hauteclare rode their steed?"

The man shakes his head. "Lady Mirelle Ashadi-Hauteclare rides for them now. The duke retired three years ago. His head injury in the last Supernova Cup—"

I tune them out as easily as turning the dial down on a vis. I used the vis on his dying wrist to ping this "Lady Mirelle" and told her the tourney match was delayed by thirty minutes. She will be the least of my problems.

Riding is a pure noble's profession with an entire academy dedicated to it. Steeds themselves are highly tuned, highly complex machines—and one wrong move spells the end. Despite watching the sport, I will surely make many wrong moves that end in my own death today.

Still, the court won't know I'm a bastard until they crack open the steed's cockpit and take the helmet off my dead body. The pockmarks on my cheeks will prove me a commoner without the credits to fix them, and the DNA test will prove me worse—House Hauteclare's bastard. They will be the first and only House in history to taint the hallowed world of riding.

A shiver races down my spine. This death will hurt more than the judiciary plasma-vent burning, but it will hurt them more than me.

A tall rider with broad shoulders draws my attention as he walks toward me. He's in a red rider's suit so crimson it hurts to look at. *Blood in Father's carpet; blood on Mother's throat.* A brown hawk sigil screeches over the rider's crested helmet, but I'm ignorant of the House it belongs to—there are fifty-one Houses in the king's court, and only nobles bother with memorizing the sigils of dozens of their fellow assholes.

I lift my chin. Once, I might've felt fear at this rider's sheer height looming over mine, the way their tight crimson suit highlights every hard-won muscle on their impressive body. I might've felt unease at how seamlessly they move over the marble floor—like liquid fire. *Something that big shouldn't move that gracefully.* But all I feel now is the end, pulling me in as inexorably as a gravity generator.

We draw even, and Red Rider's shoulder collides with mine. On *purpose.* I stagger, but they don't so much as raise their visor to apologize. A deep voice comes out flanged by the in-helmet speakers.

"Tipsy, Mirelle? Interesting way to start your season. Should I send you a bottle of nice old Earth whiskey? Let's toast after I beat you in a single round."

I keep silent. He circles me like a hungry dog.

"Huh—you look thinner. Been skimping on your veggies?"

My voice will give me away, but if I don't react at all, it'll draw even more suspicion. Red Rider reaches for me, and I shoot my hand out to intercept him instantly. Our palms freeze flat against each other's, and adrenaline surges hot in my stomach. He cocks his helmet, the hawk sigil's eye watching me beadily.

"Feisty today, aren't we? We've still got fifteen minutes till launch. Should we take this to the showers, just you and me?"

He tries to lace his fingers between mine, and he might be taller and stronger, but my time at the brothel digging for information on my father taught me the art of the armlock very well.

I crank his elbow back, his grunt of pain resounding as I kick forward with the momentum and slam him to the ground, pinning him beneath me. My chest heaves as I look down into his soulless black visor, my gold-white helmet reflected back at me.

The only hint of human in Red Rider is the way his broad chest caves with every shallow breath. My wrists are nothing but bones compared to his. He's so ridiculously massive that breaking this pin should be child's play, but for some inscrutable reason, he stays beneath me far longer than he needs to. A breath. Three.

The heat of his torso burns the insides of my thighs. A heat moves on the small of my back…his fingers, trying to get the upper hand. I grab and twist, slamming his arm to the ground above his head. Our helmets are suddenly too close, black visor on black visor. The feeling of a band stretching too far tightens in my chest.

He breaks first. He raises his visor just enough, the shiny black hard-light dissolving to reveal brown eyes the color of redwood—like Mother's pendant, warm and auburn and rich, with dark eyelashes.

"If you wanted me like this"—he laughs softly—"all you had to do was ask."

He's a noble through and through—pleasure-seeking, arrogant, ignorant. The sports cup does little to hide his excitement, but that excitement does a terrific job of distracting him from the impostor who sits atop him. My disgusted sneer behind my visor is the first expression I've made at another human in…weeks? Months?

The tourney fans close in around us to record everything on their vis, wrists flashing with the blue glow of a dozen projected holoscreens.

"A bodily altercation between riders before a match is a foul!" someone cries out.

"Should we call a ref?" another asks.

Ref. It's less a word and more a stab into my brain, a warning—*authority is the only thing that can stop you now.* I stand up and move off him quickly.

"No," Red Rider blurts as he hefts himself to his feet. "Don't call the ref— it's my fault. I was pretty much asking for an ass-kicking."

"But she twisted your—"

"You all saw," he interrupts the shrilling fan, his gaze holding mine. Assessing me. He continues without looking away. "I tried to get touchy-feely without asking for the lady's permission first. I'd consider her reaction justified."

He presses the button on the side of his visor and hides his eyes behind the darkness again, but like every noble who swears fealty to King Ressinimus, he's painted a blacklight halo on his forehead. With its dim blue glow, I catch the bare outline of his lips quirking into an affectionate smile—affection meant for Hauteclare's real rider, Mirelle.

I press onward down the hall, leaving Red Rider to drown in his own fans, his deep laugh scraping against my ears.

Finally, hangar six comes into view. The Hauteclare winged-lion banner undulates above in white and gold. A row of Hauteclare pit crew in bright-white uniforms bows as I walk up. The crewhead takes his goggles off, face smooth. He should be heavily scarred by constant laser-torch exposure, but I suppose the nobles pay for even their pit crews to be kept "beautiful."

"Just in time." He grins. "Ghostwinder's in fine form today, milady. Decon is ready and waiting for you."

I nod, hands trembling as I push past the crewhead. I need to get into this Ghostwinder steed as fast as possible—the ping I sent from Father's wrist won't keep Mirelle away for long. Thankfully, she must have a similar figure to mine; otherwise, I would've been discovered by now.

My eyes find the white door of the steed's hangar. Something is carved in it, embossed gently and grandly—a story, but not of the church's usual angels and demons. This is a man riding a horse, his projection spear aimed at what looks like a thousand undulating snakes. I squint—not snakes at all but *tendrils*, joined at a labyrinthine central mass, each with a row of fangs on its underbelly.

The enemy.

There are no true pictures left of them—the king's ministers insist the War razed all the databanks, and the priests echo them by saying evil's work is often difficult to see. The twisted enemy whom Saint Jorj rides against depicted on the hangar door has no real shape, fewer defining features than the typical overblown church metaphor. I've always had doubts that's the enemy's true form; history is rarely accurate and written only by the victors.

"Saint Jorj looks well today, does he not, milady?" the crewhead asks. When I'm silent, he presses. "Always comforted by him. Reminds me of the War—all those steeds and brave knights lost against the enemy. Reminds me there's a great sacrifice what came from riding and…well. I'm just honored to be a part of it all, milady."

Of course you are. The nobles gladly hand out their table scraps to keep us grateful.

I give a nod, and the crewhead presses a button on the synth-marble wall. The hangar door slides up slowly, and I walk into the bright light alone, embossed tendrils weaving shut behind me. There is no war anymore. The enemy is gone. We won. We fight against ourselves now.

I am no knight.

But I will die like one today.

3. Bellicus

bellicus ~a ~um, a.
1. of or pertaining to war
2. warlike

Hangar six is very cold.

The Station as a whole never runs out of cold. Space is everywhere around us—cold is in great supply. It's heat that matters. Heat is survival.

Once a year, the nobles cut heating to Low Ward to "reserve Station energy." They even have the gall to call it a holiday—Winterfolly. Fog gathers in the streets, and the sulfuric acid leaking from the vents crystallizes to neon spears. People freeze to death in their beds, and yet the nobles insist we should celebrate it.

All the hate in my heart has become a single blade stabbing me forward.

The fog of hangar six is thicker than even Winterfolly. I can barely see. How am I supposed to find my way to the steed's saddle like this?

"Decontamination beginning in five, four, three, two…"

A calm mechanical voice resounds, and I wince away from the blue laser that suddenly shoots toward me. It spiders out over my body, a net of beams parsing every angle—some kind of ID system. I must pass, because the winged helmet and white suit abruptly seal together under my chin. There's a searing hiss as my ears pop and adjust, and in one helmet-muted rush, the thick mist in the hangar gets sucked somewhere else, leaving only clean, white-gold marble walls behind.

"Decontamination complete. Please proceed to the saddle."

The voice is as cool as I am burning with suppressed fear. Space is not forgiving, even inside a steed. Riders die riding, but they are few and far between. During tourney season, the news reports more on riders' broken limbs and loss of brain function—but I *must* die in this steed. Not just an injury—real, final death. There is no other option; my death must hurt House Hauteclare as my life could not.

Out of the corner of my visor, I spot slick movement—a door sliding open in the marble wall. The only exit.

I have learned that when fear bites, you must bite back, or it will eat you whole.

I walk forward, ignoring my thumping heart.

The next room is nearly identical; the only difference is the circle on the ground big enough to hold three people comfortably and made entirely of black glass, bordered at the base with a glowing emerald ring. Every steed has a saddle—the seat from which the rider can control the steed. That must be it.

I step in and wait, trembling. After a moment, the ring of green rises with a rumble, thin and translucent and painting the world emerald as it closes up around me into a hard-light tube. Something suddenly splats onto the black glass next to my foot—a pale periwinkle glob—and then another and another. I catch one in my hand; it feels like the cheap med-gel one can find in any first-aid kit.

At first, I think it's oil-based because of the rainbow shine, but…the shine is from thousands of strange, shimmering silver whorls moving slowly inside. I lean down to sniff it. It's bitter, with hints of citrus. What the hell is—

A click echoes above my head.

I look up just in time to see the ceiling open and slop a wave of gel on me. I scrabble against the hard-light wall, but there's nowhere to run—the gel just keeps pouring in, filling the tube to my waist, my shoulders. If it reaches my helmet's air vents, I'll suffocate. But no—if every rider suffocated in the saddle, there'd be no tourneys.

The shimmering silver whorls writhe in the gel. They look like worms or tadpoles or cells, small and struggling to survive. Are they nanomachines? It's possible; nobles tend to keep the best technology for themselves, and steeds are only for nobles.

Even as the strange gel fills the tube up to my neck, I feel no pressure from it; in fact, I feel *lighter*, as if my body is being supported rather than weighed down. The gel reaches my visor, and in a blink I'm submerged. Bravery is not something you do, it's something you endure, and I endure until the gel seeps into the air vents in my helmet. It feels as cool as velvet on my nose and eyes. I hold my breath, but there's no air left, and I gasp open, sucking the gel deep into my lungs as I flail my arms against the tube's walls. It floods my mouth with a bitter citrus taste and dissolves instantly on my tongue, and then I swallow oxygen like air. As soon as I realize I *can* breathe in this stuff, the chest-deep panic in me subsides, and I go still. Still alive.

Still, I will get my revenge.

A muffled jolt runs through the ground then. The silvery gel blocks out everything, but the bone-shaking vibrations tell me I'm moving lower, until there's a resounding click into place.

Down comes the lightning.

Electricity blazes through my body, burning away my calm with *pain*— can't move—my lips pulling back from my teeth, my eyelids frozen open. Through my spasming vision, I see the silver whorls in the gel glow brighter and start to writhe faster than ever before, pinwheels, whirlpools—and when the pain abruptly fades, it's replaced by a feeling of *knowing*. I *know* I'm not alone.

Something's here, right next to me, hovering all around me. It's the certainty of someone standing behind you in a dream. It's the hot prickle of eyes watching the back of your head, of someone's invisible body heat looming close. Someone huge, bigger even than Red Rider. Someone not-me.

And then it moves.

Before terror can take hold, it reaches out for me gently; a featherlight, cautious touch, something I can feel in my mind but can't see—a reverse headache, a finger pressing against the inside of my skull. It feels like curiosity, but not my own; the inquisitive head tilt of a dog. It's like an invitation, an unseeable hand reaching out to me.

This is the line. This is the hairpin turn of fate I cannot see around. This is death.

"You must wait for God *to punish them, Synali."*

No, Mother. I will not.

I reach back.

In an instant, my body goes fever-hot and ice-cold, sweating then clammy, and I grow. I feel bigger, expanded, like my limbs have been stretched far longer than they actually are. My chest is the only thing that still feels normal, filled with my heavy heartbeat. I don't know what the hell is going on; all I know is that this is the saddle. All I know is that the thing in here with me is huge, and I'm small. We're different, but the pressureless gel and the electricity have…*linked us* somehow. Put us in each other's thoughts.

"Handshake complete." The cool mechanical voice reverberates in my helmet. "Prepare for immediate deployment in *seven, six, five, four, three*—"

Is this feeling…the steed? It feels like a person. My mind instantly pivots to true AI, the sort banned a hundred years ago after it rebelled. False AI is used for everything on the Station, from cleaning sub-routines to surgical machines, but true AI is illegal. Not even nobles are misguided enough to put true AI in their steeds—they want things they can control, and the true AI our ancestors made cannot be controlled anymore. That's why the king before King Ressinimus ordered it destroyed.

"Whatever you are," I murmur, "I ask only that you kill me."

"—*two, one.*"

The floor beneath our feet clicks open, and we fall.

My organs crush up into my throat, a fist punching me from inside, but weightlessness quickly takes over, everything catching on nothing, and then we free-float in zero gravity. Either the entire Station's gravity generators have failed or we're in…

The silver whorls in the gel slowly dissolve from my visor, allowing me sight again: the sight of a glass-clear darkness scattered with trillions upon trillions of cold, sharp, pinprick stars.

…Space.

Soundless, airless, lifeless—space opens to me like a horrific black flower, the center of its petals the glaring white sun in the distance. Accidents flash before my eyes—hull breaches in Low Ward; bodies sucked out into space coming back freezer-burned, mummified, and with every cavity imploded; Father's dead-warm skin peeling with frost the very moment I vented him.

No frost on my skin. Still breathing. I must be inside Father's steed.

The big feeling, the longer limbs but hot chest core… It makes sense in a twisted, fumbling way. I've seen it on the vis—nobles riding massive steeds as tall as buildings into space for their self-important tourneys. The stories are clear: four hundred years ago, the knights of the War went into space on their gigantic steeds to defend Earth against the enemy. But seeing and reading are not doing. Doing is lung-crushing. Doing is terrifying.

I am *riding*.

Well, floating, at least. I look down to see sleek, pure-white metal limbs below me—legs—and hands the same color tipped with gold on the fingers. It's like looking at my own body but made huge and too shiny.

They say God made man in his image, but so, too, did man make the steeds in theirs.

A steed is a gigantic artificial human, armored. It stands upright on thick legs and feet, with a waspish torso flaring out to a broad chest and arms and finally a helmeted head, usually with no visible eye, ear, or mouth holes—holes are structural weaknesses in space. Plasma vents dot the feet, the ankles, the torso, and the back. Every metal edge of a steed is sanded smooth, stylishly yet uselessly, considering aerodynamics are nigh pointless in a vacuum; when nobles want something beautiful, they make it so at all costs.

I slowly move farther into space as a holographic screen springs to life in front of me and hangs there among the stars in high definition, displaying two men in decadent breast coats and headsets. They sit before stands filled to bursting with a seething audience. I recognize them: the court-appointed tourney commentators.

"Welcome, one and all, to the 148th annual Cassiopeia Cup Semifinals!"

The thunderous roar of the crowd nearly drowns them out completely, but it all goes dull in my ears when my eyes find the Station. It's the first time I've ever seen my home from the outside. I know the shape of it—a metal ring lined with honeycomb projection shields the hue of rainbow oil-slick, a spire running through it like a pierced halo, and the many hard-light highways connecting the two like bright-orange spokes in a wheel, trams zipping to and fro on their underbellies.

The gas giant the Station orbits—Esther—hangs swollen and green behind it. Dozens of substations circle her massive bulk—some attached to her many moons, some free-floating, but all of them smaller, all of them slowly terraforming her surface, as they have been since the War's end four hundred years ago, when the seven Stations were flung from Earth's orbit and into distant solar systems by the enemy's final attack.

He's out there somewhere. Father.

My eyes dart around the Station, the spindle where the nobles live in its center, the thousands of solar panels facing both into Esther—*terrene*—and out toward the stars—*sidereal*. There's no sign of his corpse, no graying hair, no ruffled cuffs, no white cape. I can't see Father's body at all, but I slammed the airlock button, watched the evidence of my murder drift into nothing...so where is he? Esther's gravity wouldn't pull him down that fast.

Another holoscreen interrupts my view—the commentator's face is too happy.

"We have a fantastic clash for you today, folks! The storied House Hauteclare gears up at last against the indomitable House Velrayd—two families known for their pride and prowess on the tilt! Who will overcome? Who will fall? Only heaven knows!"

I try to wave the holoscreen away, but it doesn't fade like a vis screen. Another voice patches into my helmet with a smoky rumble—Red Rider.

"Forgive my figure of speech, but *what the flying fuck are you doing*, Mirelle? This isn't amateur hour—get to your tilt."

A crimson dot cuts through space, coming toward me. I've seen steeds on the vis, on posters, and in the hands of children as figurines, but not like this: huge and framed against the cold blanket of space and the green glow of Esther and all too big, all too *real*, coming close all too fast. *Nothing that big should move that gracefully.*

Red Rider's steed is painted like drying blood—crimson diffused by deep brown—and it's roughly the length of an entire tram. Its helmet has a beaklike protrusion on the mouth that sweeps up the forehead and over the skull as if it's the crest of a bird, and its heels have the same feather shape. For a second, I wonder where his saddle is: in the chest or the head? Where are we positioned as riders in these gargantuan puppets? I look down to my steed's titanic white chest. I must be in the torso somewhere—that *feels* central.

Red Rider jets over to me, and I watch, momentarily mesmerized, as the crimson plasma the steed produces lingers behind it like hot twin ribbons, and then the cold of space dissolves them. Eats them. Heat is survival, but only now have I realized it's beautiful, too.

Too late.

His gravelly voice on the comms is insistent. "Did your initial thrust screw up or something? Here, lemme help."

I don't need your goddamn help, noble.

No buttons in the saddle, no levers to pull—only my own body floating in gel that's now turned clear as glass. Whatever switches Red Rider uses to move his steed, I can't see them. My steed is unresponsive—I can't even twitch away as he laces our metal arms together. The sensation of him touching my elbow makes me jump—skin-on-skin pressure on *get the fuck away from me.* The feedback is exactly like touching in real life. I mentally flip him off, and surprise sizzles through me when the golden fingers of my steed's free hand mimic my thoughts perfectly. The same middle finger—the same exact wrist tilt.

Red Rider chuckles. "You wanna give me the silent treatment that badly? Go right ahead. It's not gonna stop me from helping a fellow rider out. You know, chivalry? That thing you love so much?"

I only hear him faintly—too busy closing my fist experimentally. I go wide-eyed as the fist of the white-gold steed closes, too. The delay is nonexistent—like watching my reflection move in a mirror. I'm not just inside the steed—I *am* the steed.

Slowly, Red Rider tows me to the tilt: a span of what would look like empty space if not for the floating hexagonal plates on opposite sides bookending it. I can only estimate the distance between the two plates—fifty parses apart, maybe more. In the direct middle of the tilt is the unmistakable blue glow of a gravity generator, hanging like an azure star in the stretch of black, but this one is much brighter than the ones in the Station's walls. It must be a short-range grav-gen, the sort used in the War to launch battleships and steeds alike with its slingshot effect.

When we reach one of the plates, Red Rider presses my floating body against it—his fingertips on my chest trigger instant venomous thoughts—*don't try to control me, you entitled piece of shit.* With a vicious jolt, magnetics kick in and rivet my spine to the tilt. I glare straight ahead, refusing to look at him.

"Well," he starts jovially, "I'm off. Best of luck and for the glory of the king and all that."

His steed makes a little salute—red fingers to red forehead—and then he pivots, the jets on his back and feet blazing crimson as he propels past the halfway point of the grav-gen to the hexagonal plate on the other end of the tilt. He moves easily—obviously academy trained. He *chose* academy. Noble children like him get to decide their own cushy fates while the rest of us scrape at dangerous, back-breaking jobs: servitude, welding, mining on the substations…things that break, kill, maim. Commoners are disposable, after all—the brothel taught me that. Father taught me that. He treated Mother like something to be used and then thrown away.

My anger simmers high, a fire that cannot be stopped, a fire *I will not* stop, and it burns and burns and *burns*, and strangely, I feel the thing in here with me start to burn, too, anger coursing molten all around me.

My mother is dead, and I killed my father. I'm alone in this life. I know that.

But for the first time in six months, there's the barest venting of pressure, a release in knowing something else in this universe—*anything else*—burns the same way I do.

I will go down in fire, and the flames will scar every Hauteclare on this godforsaken Station.

4. Caecus

caecus ~a ~um, a.
1. *(literally and figuratively)* blind
2. devoid of light

One does not bow in space to show respect after a match. One takes off their helmet.

If I somehow survive this match against Red Rider, I will take my helmet off in the saddle. I will be arrested and questioned, and then I will be executed. The guards will eventually find Duke Hauteclare's body orbiting the Station. House Hauteclare will cry false, but the results of my corpse's DNA test will come back true—Duke Farris von Hauteclare sired a bastard out of wedlock, and she killed him, then *rode* his *steed* in a *tourney*. Not a skirmish, not a qualifier, but a *tourney*—the most hallowed proving ground, the one place nobles can go to show the entire Station that they are beyond reproach in their honor, strength, and morals. That they rule for a reason.

It's the tourneys where nobles believe nobility is the most sacred, second only to the bedrooms where their purebloods are sired.

The only thing nobles value more than their riding competitions is their blood.

This is why Father hired an assassin to kill Mother and me. It took me months to dig and bribe and fuck my way to this truth, but it eventually rose to the surface like all scum does. Duke Hauteclare killed us because he was planning to run for the open seat on the king's advisory board. A bastard is the one true disgrace—if his rivals found out about my existence, they'd have used me to politically ruin his grand aspirations.

Mother and I were sacrificial lambs on the altar of Father's lust for power.

I feel like a sacrificial lamb magnetically lashed against this tilt, a hexagonal altar holding me still for the final blow. It rotates slowly in space, and I rotate with it, stars turning upside-down and back again. Red Rider waves to me from the tilt opposite—with any luck, he'll be punished for crossing lances with a filthy bastard like me. All I can do is wait. Space truly does go on *forever*, naked and black, but I won't let the yawning fear of it in.

The saddle's silver-whorled gel smells vaguely like citrus. It reminds me of Mother's baking—artificial lemon and synth-vanilla, things so rare we could only afford them once a year for my birthday. She loved to bake—no matter how poorly she was feeling. If I brought a parcel of mealy flour home from the scavenge pits, she'd always find the energy to get up and make something. Our oven would hum and shudder, and the fresh-baked scent would cloud our little apartment, momentarily driving out the sulfur fumes and the scream of the tram.

I swallow the hard lump in my throat. I'd forgotten. Among all the blood and death and plotting…I'd forgotten that today is my birthday.

A commentator's voice pierces my thoughts.

"In the red corner stands the illustrious House Hauteclare and their magnificent steed, Ghostwinder! Let's give a warm round of applause for Ghostwinder's endlessly bold and effortlessly graceful rider—Mirelle Ashadi-Hauteclare!"

The crowd's applause shudders through my helmet.

"Lady Mirelle has too many wins under her belt to count, Gress," the second commentator adds.

"That she does, Bero," the first commentator agrees. "We'll see if she can notch one more today. If you'll turn your attention to the blue corner, we have the relentless House Velrayd and their steed, Sunscreamer! Sunscreamer's rider is none other than the one, the only, the former child prodigy with the highest scores in academy history—Rax Istra-Velrayd!"

The applause is ten times louder for Red Rider. *Rax*. It's a terrible name—

like a dry protein bar on the tongue.

"Rax specializes in decisive timing," the second commentator muses. "But Mirelle's more of a power striker. Things could get messy, Gress."

"Absolutely, Bero, but in the world of riding, 'messy' is just another word for 'exciting.' Riders, prepare your tilts!"

The tilt suddenly spins me upright and locks into place. I blink away dizziness—it's a clear shot from me to the grav-gen, from me to Rax on the opposite side; his tilt is locked upright, too. Something hard begins to materialize in my hand, crawling piece by piece out of the metal of the steed's palm—white, long, ending in a needle-sharp golden point. I know what it is even before it fully takes shape: a lance. The enormous weapon every steed has within them—a lance made to kill the enemy so long ago, but now used only for sport.

"Let the countdown to round one begin—in the name of God, King, and Station!" a commentator shouts.

"In the name of God, King, and Station!" the audience echoes titanically. Reality seeps in with their booming voices—I know the two steeds are pulled into each other by the grav-gen, and I know it's a straight line at blistering parses per minute, the two of us passing each other barely parallel. In that moment of passing, we attempt to strike each other with our lances: helmet, breastplate, pauldrons, gauntlets, greaves, tasset…six places to hit, but only the helmet is considered an automatic win. Everywhere else is one point. How do I know all *that*? I don't. I've never cared about how this game is scored. It just spilled out. Who…?

The thing in here with me knows. It eagerly tells me everything in wordless streams of certainty; it knows we hit. It knows the two gigantic humanoid steeds then separate out into space. It knows the grav-gen pulls us around and in again like a loop, an infinity symbol, for two more rounds. Whoever has the most points at the end of round three wins. If a rider is flung from their saddle, they lose. If anyone hits their opponent's helmet, they win. The only thing allowed to touch the opponent is the lance—all else is considered a foul.

It knows all this because it's been trapped here for ages. *Trapped?* It's a machine…but I have no time to ponder this as the tilt suddenly disengages the magnetics and thrusts me into open space toward the grav-gen, which is spinning its core ever faster. The blue glow brightens—not enough to hinder sight but enough to guide me to the end. I should be terrified, but with the end so close, with Mother so close… It's been six months since I've seen her. It won't be much longer now.

I don't know how to ride. I don't know how to win.

But I know well how to grip the weapon.

The lance isn't a dagger—it's bigger. Heavier. I struggle to hold it steady, arm straining under the weight even though my human hand in the saddle cups emptiness. I *feel* it; just like Rax and his elbow touch, the lance's handle is real and hard in my palm even when it only exists outside me in space.

Swallow. Push down the fear. *Faster*, I think. *I want to ruin him faster.*

I want to see her faster.

Gold plasma suddenly bursts hot from my back vents, my leg vents, pushing me out from the tilt as the generator pulls me in. The speed lurches my guts, my heart into my throat, and the stars start to blur to ribbons; the Station melts to gray-rainbow sludge, Esther's stormy green surface blends together, and all I can see is the red steed as it nears horrifyingly fast, my white-gold lance biting forward like a gilded fang into the darkness. Rax's red lance narrows to a point in my vision too close, his steed moving in slight shifts, changing, he's somehow bracing against the massive g-forces crushing the life out of me—

We ***impact***.

Too fast to breathe. Too fast to move. A millisecond of everything sears across my mind all at once: metal, light, fire, pain.

And then black.

The next thing I sense is darkness. Death, maybe.

The end is soft and shrouded in rhythmic beeping. Can't move. My body—if I still have one—feels heavy, head heavier. Faint voices echo in my ears.

"—recovery time?"

"—months, at most. The nanomachine treatment was very—"

"What of— DNA results for the—"

"—as you asked, sir."

Something soft lands on my forehead, and then one of the voices moves close to my ear, calm as still water.

"I'll see you on the other side, brave one."

I'm not brave. I merely endure.

My mouth doesn't move, my throat doesn't rattle—I'm a prisoner in my own body. There's the shuffle of footsteps, a click of something closing, and then darkness claims me again.

—10. Aranea

arānea ~ae, f.
1. a spider

Fourteen years ago, on the same space Station, a fourth child turns five years old.

He is a forgotten child, left on a doorstep in his early hours. His hair is spun gold. His eyes are the color of ice, and they focus on the burlap dummy in front of him, the heat of a projection dagger clutched in his small fist. The hard orange light gouts and sputters from the handle, ready to strike. His instructor—the only father-mother-family the boy has ever known—jerks his head at the dummy.

"Kill."

Kill he does. Over and over again. Each time, he receives a "well done." Each time, a smile.

The boy dreams of family, and though he has one, in fourteen years he will kill a woman with black hair and kind eyes in front of her daughter, and it will be the end of this dream.

And the beginning of a new one.

5. Abyssus

abyssus ~ī, *f.*
1. *(Late)* an abyss

My skin wakes before I do—soft blankets, fluffed pillows, the air of a room gently circulating. I can *feel*. I can *think*. I can *hear* steady beeping.

I'm alive.

I bolt upright so fast, an IV jerks out of my wrist, and I stare blankly at the blood oozing over my skin. My hand juts to Mother's redwood cross around my neck—relief first, terror second.

"No," I whisper. "No, no, *no*."

This is wrong. Why am I not dead? I rode a steed and impacted and— The beeping fluctuates wildly as I rip the sheets off my body. Everything's white and smells sterile: a hospital, but not just any hospital—one of the fancy ones in the noble spire. They've wrapped me in a white gown and shoved me in this cocoon of a room to what? *Recover?* There's nothing left to recover for. Did I ruin House Hauteclare? Did they DNA test me? I can't remember, and not remembering is worse than even living.

I fling my legs over the side of the bed, and they buckle—can't walk far.

The door is no doubt guarded, but my life is not theirs to decide. I have to die. There are no sharp objects, not even a mirror to smash.

And then I see the window.

I stagger to it, and my fingers freeze over the sill—I didn't know sunlight could *be* this warm. In open space, it sears, and in Low Ward, it's nonexistent, crowded out by smog and the massive shadows of competing churches and unsleeping holoscreens. But here, it's *gentle*, like an embrace—like Mother again.

"Oh, dearheart. I hope one day you'll see the sun rise."

Real voices ring outside the room. "She's awake!"

I lunge my body up the sill, and the unfair brilliance of the noble spire hits me in its entirety—clean walkways, green bushes and blooms of all colors, sunlight captured and redirected and let free, evenly spaced buildings instead of crushed-together hovels. This is how people should live…this is how Mother and I *should've* lived. Shouts ricochet behind me.

"Stop her!"

"Get the tranq—*now*!"

Hands yank me back from the sill, but I thrash, claw, tearing at anything I can reach: clean skin, clean cloth, let me go, let me see the sun rise, *you don't get to give me mercy, I won't be kept like one of your pets*—

"Clear!"

A puncture in my thigh, and then something like hot honey rushes through my veins. They lay my heavy body back in bed and leave. My fist tries to clench, but nothing happens—only blinking, only breathing. They can stop my body, but they can't stop my mind; the last thing I remember is the red steed charging for me. Did I pass out? If I was unconscious and kept my helmet on… If the cameras didn't see my face… If I'd ruined House Hauteclare, I'd be dead by now. Burned beneath a plasma vent.

The world spins without moving, every inch of me darkening in free fall. Trapped in this hospital bed, I know only two things for certain:

One—I have failed in ruining House Hauteclare.

And two—I will not make the same mistake twice.

6. Clarus

clārus ~a ~um, a.
1. clear, bright
2. renowned, famous

R ax Istra-Velrayd stares into his teacup, the amber liquid shuddering with his mother's every frantic step over the marble floor.

"How could you not know she was an impostor?" She snarls, wringing her paper-thin hands around her own cup. "We've risked so much training you—for what? For you to throw it all away fighting some common rat who snuck in and stole a steed? You should've known. You should've stopped the match before it ever took place!"

Before the fireplace, the projected hologram of her vis scrawls blue and translucent, screaming with headlines: COMMONER COMMANDEERS HOUSE HAUTECLARE'S GHOSTWINDER, RIDES AGAINST HOUSE VELRAYD. Rax shoots a look to his father standing motionless against the wall. The shelf of Rax's many riding trophies glimmers ironically at his father's side—gold and silver up to the ceiling. As per usual, Father doesn't seem to want to say anything. Rax must clean up the pieces alone.

"Nothing's wrong, Mother. The SCC declared it a null match. We didn't lose any—"

"We could've." She snaps her eyes to him, voice cold. "You don't understand. You never do. You ride, but you don't ever *think*—we came a hairbreadth away from losing every ounce of our family's honor yesterday."

"She fooled everyone, Mother," Rax says. "*Mirelle* had no idea—"

The violence always comes in flashes. A white blur hurtles at his face, and then there's the wicked sensation of porcelain cutting into his jaw as the cup breaks on him. The pain would hurt more if it were the first time. Rax can't remember what time this is—the thousandth, perhaps. Ten-thousandth. He feels the blood drip gently down his chin and watches it drop onto the table.

"This isn't about the Hauteclares!" Mother hisses. "Duke Velrayd is asking *questions*. We cannot have him questioning us—we are reliable. We are a Velrayd barony, now, and we will remain such at all costs. You will not ruin this for us."

The embers in the fireplace flicker weakly over her face—shadowed, unrepentant. Her bodyguard in the corner shifts, waiting with expectant fingers on his baton. When Rax was younger, all it took was Mother to keep him in line, but as he grew, she started enlisting help—realizing it was perhaps unbecoming for a baroness to discipline her children herself.

Rax knows his next words will mean pain. His body aches with the phantom bruises. Still, he can't help the soft laugh rising from his lips. "I'd ride against a hundred commoners if it meant I could be free from you."

7. Vulpes

vulpēs ~is, *f.*
1. a fox, vixen
2. *(figuratively)* cunning, craftiness

Tally marks are the best way to remember time — gouged in your apartment wall if you must. One line for every day, when every day feels like the same eternity. A single line meant a time you wiped the blood off your split lip and got up again. A single line meant you ate to keep yourself alive. A single line meant you fucked a rich man three times your age for information about your mother's killer no one else would give you.

For each day in the hospital, I scratch one neon line into my brain.

Three marks. Three days. Every six hours, the nurses check my restraints. Every four, they refill my IV — a lower-grade tranq than the hot honey but still strong enough to keep my heavy limbs in place. In my fevered tranquilizer sleep, the night Mother died plays like a recording corrupted by time, skipping and replaying and skipping back again — the empty hood of the assassin moves toward her like a hungry predator in all black, and she falls to her knees, face blurred and words garbled nonsense. She begged. I remember, but I don't *want* to remember. I want to stop the assassin, but I never can. He is darkness, cold space, the devil, and as he looks at me with eyes a terrifying ice-blue, the scar he gave me in my collarbone begins to ache terribly.

I'm crying before I'm awake.

I cry without moving, until my pillow and my hair and my ears are full of salt, like the woman in God's book who looked back. I was weak with Mother—too happy and naive and soft to do anything—and it killed her. I was weak. *My softness killed her.*

Four tally marks. Five.

On the sixth day, a man arrives. Not a nurse or a doctor but someone from outside. He smells like a moth—old fabric and dust and secret darkness. He walks measuredly across the tile, his tabard and breeches plain silk but his walking cane made of elaborate sapphire and silver. He could be anyone's milquetoast uncle: middle-aged, middle height, with smooth skin and a mop of pale brown hair—a man with no hardship in him. Noble, then, but no blacklight halo is painted on his forehead. Strange…I thought they all wore that symbol of fealty to the king.

He seats himself in a chair at my bedside, slender lips pulling into a smile.

"Thank you for waiting for me, Synali." His smooth voice is identical to the person who called me "brave one." "It must've been terribly hard on you."

I sit up straighter; nothing good comes from the sort of person who knows your name without asking for it first.

"Apologies," he says. "I've been told your tranquilizer should wear off soon and you'll be able to speak. Can you at least blink?"

I do. His smile widens, teeth surgery white.

"Let's say one blink for yes and two for no. That way our conversation won't be quite so one-sided. Agreed?" He interlaces his fingers on his knee. It's the expensive rings on his fingers that beget realization: I have been kept alive so I could meet this man. *He's* the reason the hospital didn't hand me over to the vent. And that makes him my enemy. Though, whoever he is, he clearly has power—and power always proves useful.

He repeats himself patiently. "Are we in agreement, Synali?"

Blink once.

"Wonderful. Allow me to be frank—you murdered Duke Farris von Hauteclare by stabbing him with his own ceremonial dagger. Do you regret this?"

Blink twice. I expect anger or disgust, but his smile is gentle.

"I see. That bodes well." He inspects the silver head of his cane. "After your patricide, you vented the duke's body out of his office airlock, stole his rider's suit, and then rode House Hauteclare's steed in a tourney against House Velrayd. And not just any tourney—the Cassiopeia Cup Semifinals. The nobles were absolutely *furious*."

A pleased twinkle moves through his thin gray eyes. I open my throat and croak something impossible to understand, but he interprets quickly.

"Oh, you were decimated by House Velrayd's rider. Untrained as you were to withstand the g-forces, you were thrown from the saddle on impact, and—as you were unable to deploy your helmet cushion—your skull fractured on the metal innards of the steed. The doctors say it's a God-sent miracle you survived, even with the nanomachine treatment I ordered."

Miracles for *me*? Nanomachines for *me*? Why bother? I'm a murderer, a bastard—I am nothing anyone values.

The man leans back in his leather chair. "All of what I just relayed to you occurred two months ago."

I choke. I've been in this bed for *two months*? No—*no*, it was six days! I counted. I kept a tally.

"You regained consciousness a week ago." He answers my spiraling thoughts coolly. "Two months ago, I ordered your nanomachine treatment done. I even managed to keep your murder of the duke a secret; to the rest of the Station, he died of natural causes—heart attack, I believe. I don't remember precisely what I had the investigating officers write when they recovered his body."

My groan becomes a single stumbling word. "Wh-Why?"

"I have a favor to ask in return."

"I won't…sleep with you, y-you noble fuck. Just kill me."

The man's face goes slack, and then he laughs. All his pale lines and thin folds crease into one sun-riddled moment of pure amusement—the most concentrated emotion I've heard from him yet.

"Those sorts of favors don't interest me." He calms enough to speak. "Nor am I interested in killing you."

"I want to die—"

"I know precisely what you want," he interrupts. "One does not murder their father and then make an inexperienced tourney ride intending to trot on to a happy life. If one wished to survive, one would try to escape after their deed, yet you did no such thing. You were ready to die for it. You wanted to hurt House Hauteclare, even if it meant your death."

The way he talks…he's unmistakably noble-born. His eyes meet mine without softness. Where there once was joviality, there's now only steel. He knows who I am. What I was trying to do. It curdles my insides to be known so plainly.

"Who are…you?" I manage, throat burning.

"You may call me Dravik. I'd like for you and I to work together."

"Why should I?"

"Because the ruination of House Hauteclare cannot be accomplished by you alone."

A snarl works over my limp mouth, but he continues.

"Please don't misunderstand me; a duke's bastard daughter riding, and his murderer besides…the Nova-King's court would've been furious at House Hauteclare. Your plan would've done the trick very neatly but not very thoroughly. A flash in the pan, perhaps two months of bastard rumors, and Hauteclare would pay off the proper people to bury it. I have a more permanent method in mind."

I lean off the pillows. "P-Permanent?"

He knows he has me, because his smile this time is patient. "The Nova-King's court consists of fifty-one Houses. They've merged and split over the centuries, but none of them has been dissolved. *Ever.* The king won't allow it, you see—they are his sources of power. They orbit him like planets, providing to him as he provides to them."

"I know all this—" My voice gives out.

"You've heard of the Supernova Cup, I assume?" His doesn't.

I blink once. The Supernova Cup is the tourney of all tourneys on the Station, coming around once every decade. As ignorant of riding as I am, I know whichever House wins the Supernova Cup earns great favor with the king, and his favor means power, money, influence—everything the nobles endlessly scheme and backstab one another for is handed on a silver platter to whomever wins the Supernova Cup. House Hauteclare—with my father as their rider—won last decade, and I grew up with their banner plastered in every ward and their barely disguised extortion and pillaging on every corner. The powerful Houses enter to cement their supremacy for the next ten years, the weaker Houses enter to reverse their fates, but *everyone* enters.

This Dravik man can't possibly—

"I wish for you to ride for my House in the Supernova Cup, Synali. And in exchange, I will dissolve House Hauteclare."

My heart leaps into my throat. "F-Forever?"

"They will be forgotten. Their deeds, their history, their honors—all of it will be erased."

He's mad. A beginner cannot win a cup like that. No one can dissolve a House save for the king. Dravik's eyes don't waver as he offers me his hand. If he's lying, it's one spectacularly expensive lie—my hospital bills, covering Father's murder for me. He's taken a huge risk keeping me alive. If he's telling the truth...

"You can't dissolve a House," I insist.

"A plan is in place." He says it as if it's an explanation in itself—a stalwart truth.

"Don't give me hope, Sir Dravik," I croak. "I don't want to hope—I want to die. I want to rest and to see my mother again."

His gaze crumples strangely, painfully, as if he's seen someone he knows well. The ludicrous idea of House Hauteclare wiped off the Station forever hangs like golden fruit in my mind. I hesitate, glaring at his outstretched hand. For the last six months, the feel of another person's skin has meant nothing but pain. I look up at him.

"Can you promise me rest?"

The beeping of the machine slows, my heart begging for the answer.

"When it is done," he begins. "I give you my word I will bring you rest."

A stalwart truth.

I reach my hand out, callused palm gripping his soft one.

8. Novicius

novīcius ~a ~um, a.
1. new, fresh

The noble spire spins slowly in the very center of the Station's ring, growing closer outside the window of Dravik's hovercarriage. The quiet hum of our engine insulates us from the bustle of a hundred more hovercarriages sluicing down the orange ribbon of the hard-light freeway, their driver's seats empty as programming guides them.

"I've never taken a hovercarriage before," I say. "Always more of a public tram person."

"Your life from now on will feature many firsts, I imagine." Dravik chuckles, tucked into the corner across from me with his cane over his lap. He wears no blacklight halo to mark him noble beneath his mouse-hue bangs, yet he has a private hovercarriage—a very expensive one, if the interior detail of powder-blue lilies on silver inlay is any indicator. The smoothness of the fine linen bliaut he gave me to wear out of the hospital slithers over my skin—too nice compared to my burlap tunics. The woolen shawl is broad, with no moth-eaten holes. The soft leather boots fit *too* well—far different from the plastic-woven sandals I'm used to.

"I see one major flaw in this grand plan of yours," I say. "I have no rider training."

"This will be remedied," Dravik agrees offhandedly.

"Going to send me to the rider academy and put me in class with the children?"

"No need. I am a former rider. The Supernova Cup is in two months—more than enough time to teach you what I know."

My brows shoot up. So he is a noble. Or...*was*? "Is that where your injury came from? Riding?"

"No." He taps his fingers on his right knee. "This was more...personal. You, however, have no such injuries, and if we train you correctly, it will remain that way."

"You make me sound like some animal," I snarl. His smile is perfectly calm.

"Would you not become an animal to get your revenge?"

I snort and lean back in the seat, arms over my chest. He makes rider training sound easy, but I've been asleep for two months—my body is weak. Even if I miraculously manage to grasp the intricacies of riding, going up against nobles who've been in this game for years—if not decades—is a losing battle. They have technique. Experience. I have nothing. Dravik could choose any skilled noble rider who graduated from the academy to ride for him, so...

"Why me?" I ask.

Dravik taps the side of his leg. "I cannot ride, and you cannot hope to destroy a House. We each have what the other wants."

"That's not what I asked."

"Your mental handshake in Ghostwinder's saddle went very well; you have a talent for it. Riders often experience nosebleeds and fainting their first time."

"You could go to any academy first-year for that. Is it because I'm desperate, easy to manipulate?"

"No."

"Is it because I hate the nobles?"

"No."

"Then *why*?"

The quiet thrum of the engine. The tinkle of the sapphire-studded tassels swinging from the hovercarriage roof. Sunlight catches in the gemstones, refracting rainbow over the soft man as he gives me a softer smile, a no-answer sort of smile—an answer he can't give or won't give—and I realize then I'd be a fool to trust him. This whole thing reeks of manipulation and control. I stand up. Sensing my movement, the carriage slows to a crawl automatically.

"Open the door," I demand.

"Synali—" Dravik starts.

"I said open the goddamn door!"

He doesn't move for his wrist. The carriage controls might be linked to his vis and his vis only, but everything on this Station has an emergency redundancy—even noble transportation. I find the button tucked below the handle, and I reach a single finger for it—

"Do you truly think your father killed your mother on his own?"

Dravik's voice freezes my hand in place.

"Seven," he says. "Seven other members of House Hauteclare voted to take her down. They each coerced your father or otherwise helped to find, track, and kill your mother. It was a group effort. Noble dealings always are."

My ears ring, my mouth thick with iron sand. The family helped him. The dagger across Mother's throat touched more palms than just the assassin's. I grip her cross pendant. Hard. *Harder.* The hovercarriages outside pass us in screaming lights. An eternity passes before I find my voice.

"These seven… You're certain they were involved?"

"Without doubt," Dravik asserts. "I verified each one carefully during the two months you were recovering. I will provide you with evidence of their guilt, should you so require."

For a moment I almost *wish* I could doubt this strange man. I wish he was wrong, but I know in my bones he isn't—of course they'd all want Mother and me dead. They are a House. They are *together*. It was *all* of their honors on the line, not just Father's.

I collapse back in the seat, and the carriage lurches into motion. For once, Dravik wears no smile. "I had hoped to wait until we were at home to discuss the conditions of our contract, but…for every round in the Supernova Cup you win, I am offering to kill one of these seven nobles. Should you win the *entire* Supernova Cup, I'll erase House Hauteclare itself."

Suddenly, the impossible golden fruit sprouts lesser, far closer fruits all around it.

"How will you—"

"Connections. People, places, things—none of which you need concern yourself with. Your only concern will be riding." He sees the unsurety in me. "Do you think me not capable of disposing of them?"

I glare at my palms. "I think you're capable of your end, but mine…less so."

His face breaks into a smile again. "I never thought I'd see the day when one of Hauteclare's blood would choose humility. Brave one—you drugged a janitor, snuck into a highly guarded tourney hall, deceived a rider, hijacked a steed, and stabbed a duke to death. I know crime lords in the Under-ring who have done less."

"Riding is different."

He looks wistfully out the window. "I suppose it is."

Our carriage dips into a black tunnel and emerges onto the silver wash of artificial moonlight bathing every gilded building and cobblestone road. I've always seen the noble spire from afar like a hateful miniature, a conceited dollhouse, but now fountains pour water in elaborate antigravity spirals over my head—up, across, and between buildings until the sky is braided with them. Nobles traipse the sidewalks in amber-studded corsets and holograph parasols and elaborate wooden masks. Twisted little creatures hang on their arms—monkeys, dogs, all of them bred beyond textbook recognition. Muffled music ricochets from quartets with real whitewood instruments on every other corner, and jesters in neon-lit caps and butterfly-incandescent suits flit and flip among the loose crowd.

No beggars, no molerats or thin dogs feeding on trash, no ragged moths choking on neon lights. No blood on the roads. No filth, no vents belching yellow sulfur. Everything's ventilated, perfumed, sheened in holograph and precious wood and the sound of music and water—*clean water*, the sort people die for in Low Ward, stab each other for—it's here, and it's made into *art*, made so their little pets can run through it and they can laugh at the sight.

My fury blitzes past itself and crash-lands into nausea.

"Fascinating, isn't it?" Dravik asks, the lights dancing in his eyes even as he holds out a plastic bag for me. I claw at it. Someone outside laughs. A band begins to play. The joyous music tries and fails to drown out the sound as I retch.

I n the time it takes for the nausea to subside, our hovercarriage turns onto a quieter road, away from the music and dancers and perfumed crowd. We wind up a rise lush with green grass and white trees (*real trees, like there were on Earth*), sleek marble noble manses peppering the hillside. The carriage stops before a great metal gate, and it swings forward as readily as a black iron maw.

"We're here," Dravik announces rather perfunctorily.

The hovercarriage glides up a hill-cut path through a garden. Unlike the other manses' verdant greenery, this one is faded, unkempt, the grass yellowed and the whitewood trees starving thin. Still…it's more empty space than I ever thought possible on the Station. Still, they're *real* trees—leaves and roots curling much like the enemy's tendrils on the hangar door. The glass-and-marble manse sitting atop the hill could easily fit fifty Low Ward families.

I clutch my bagged vomit tighter—I knew noble Houses lived comfortably, but seeing it up close burns far hotter, realer. Finally, the manse envelops us in a manicured plaza of white gravel, lined with marble statues of saints and sinners. Saint Petyr hangs on his upside-down cross in utter humility, in utter reminder of how far I've fallen.

I've allowed my life to fall into a noble's hands again.

"Welcome, Synali"—Dravik sweeps his cane around—"to my home. And your home, too, of course, for however long the duration of our alliance runs. Shall we?"

He motions me in, and it takes me two steps through the front door to smell the dust—a thick layer of the stuff covering every plush sofa, every pre-War painting. It coats even the marble floor; paths cut through where traffic treads most. Shadows choke the rooms, only a few warm lights blinking out of the very bowels of the manse. This is Dravik's smell—moths and time and that unquiet darkness. My eyes dart around, searching for waiting guards, but if he wanted to turn me in, I suppose he wouldn't've bothered dragging me to the noble spire to do it.

"I hope you'll forgive the untidiness." Dravik catches up to me. "I don't spend much time here if I can help it."

"Why?"

He pauses. And then: "Memories."

I don't know why he wants me to ride in the Supernova Cup or why he chose me in particular. I don't know if I can trust him, even. But memories and the pain that keeps you away from them—that's something I know well.

A sudden barking resounds, metallic and simulated, and I watch a shiny thing dart down the hall toward us—a robot in the approximate shape of a medium-size dog. It's made of smooth gold, but one leg and sections of its torso have been replaced with rusting, mismatched parts—doodled on with long-faded holostickers and childish laser artwork. Its ears clank against its head as it comes to a stop before Dravik's feet, wagging its rusted tail in a frenzy.

"Ah." Dravik looks down, his smile ever-so-slightly bitter. "So he's kept you alive this long, has he?"

The robot-dog barks and circles Dravik's shoes. It's strange but less intimidating than the inbred pets that haunt noble shoulders—and far less intimidating than the man at my side. I extend one slow hand to it, and it looks up at me with polished sapphire eyes, sniffing my palm warily.

"Hello," I whisper. "I'm Synali."

The dog growls, metal pulling back to reveal mother-of-pearl teeth.

"Be quiet." Dravik scoffs, then looks to me. "Pay it no mind. It's a relic of a bygone era, nothing more."

"Master."

I startle as a white wraith emerges from the gloom: an old man, his face paler than vellum and his gray hair a cloudy shock flying in every direction. He's so gaunt, it looks as if he's been eaten away from the inside—only skin and bones left. In stark contrast to his chaotic hair, his breeches and tunic are painstakingly neat and his posture is immaculate.

"You've returned, Master Dravik," he croaks with a smile. I swear I see Dravik wince at the title.

"That I have, Quilliam. Is the guest room ready?"

"Yes." Quilliam turns his papery smile on me. "Everything fit for a young miss is within. Oh, I am so thrilled to see Moonlight's End receive guests once more—"

"And the bunker?" Dravik asks.

"I recalibrated the systems myself, master. There were quite a few cobwebs, and the visitor seemed rather hungrier than usual—"

"Very good." Dravik abruptly takes the vomit bag from my hand. "Please dispose of this, then prepare a light tea. Synali and I will take it in my office."

"As you wish."

He bows and trudges away into the dim maze of rooms, and Dravik wordlessly turns in the other direction, cane rapping as he motions for me to follow. The robot-dog trots fast on his heels—as much as he hates it, it seems rather loyal to him.

"Do you usually have hungry visitors stay in your cobweb-filled bunker?" I ask, my eyes taking in every lush ancient painting we pass—Earth art. This "Moonlight's End" place is so empty and dusty and still—it feels less a manse and more a tomb.

"No." Dravik chuckles. "I'm typically better mannered than that."

"Then why—"

"You've had a very long day, Synali." He cuts me off smoothly. "Or rather, a very long two months. Let us draw up a contract and then rest for the night—there's much work to be done come morning."

He's clearly avoiding the subject. I follow him into a room—a room made not of marble but *wood*. My mouth nearly falls open. Every metal is synthable depending on what elements the substations siphon off Esther, but you cannot synth trees—they take *soil* and *space* and *time* to grow. To the nobles, whitewood and the amber it gives is more precious than gold. Dravik's office is made entirely of *pre-War* wood, old wood grown on Earth—rich, reddish stuff. It's warmer than fire, more alive than metal, sleeker than marble, with spirals winding through the grain like coffee smoke in an ember sea. It's the same wood as Mother's pendant. She loved it, stroked it like the priests stroke their gem rosaries until it was worn smooth. My thumb works over the cross around my neck idly, tracing her imprints.

"Please." Dravik motions to an armchair just before a whitewood desk. "Sit."

I do—no dust on the armrests. This must be the room he uses most. A butterfly collection hangs on the wall like jeweled candies bunched in orderly rows, and real paper books cluster on the shelves in all their expensive, outdated glory. The robot-dog lays down on a fine carpet, sapphire eyes dimming in an approximation of rest. Before I have the chance to settle, Dravik speaks.

"Your father had your mother killed."

The warmth of the room fades. I try to say something, but the words stick like swallowed ice. It's a simple sentence. It should be simple to hear, to process and put aside—it's truth—but the hounds of memory strain their leashes at it… *Blood pooling on the tin floor, the hot salt smell of it, her black hair wet with it—*

"Your father killed your mother, did he not?"

"Stop," I say quietly, *"saying it."*

The dog lifts its head at my tone and growls again, but Dravik's voice goes stern.

"Enough, you silly thing. My apologies, Synali—I'd forgotten how long the wound lasts when fresh."

Forgotten. Implying he knows what it feels like to lose his mother? I stare at him—no tells, no lip-licks or flicker of the eyes. Lesser nobles frequented Madam Beldeaux's brothel—merchant types barely related to the lowest of barons—but the higher they went in station, the harder they became to read. The Nova-King's court trains them all whether they like it or not, and it's trained Dravik very, *very* well; I can't read him in the slightest.

He pushes a blank piece of vellum across to me with his ring-drenched fingers. No vis signatures, no screens—real physical contracts, impossible to hack and harder to trace.

"Name your terms," he says. "We will each retain a copy signed by the other person. If either of us breaks the contract, we may take our copy to the police and implicate them in treason. Your treason would be killing a member of the nobility."

"And yours?"

"Attempting to destroy a House—something only the king is permitted to do. '*Assuming the responsibilities of the crown without leave of the throne,*' I believe it's called."

I snort. "Contract or not, the police never arrest people like you. You have friends in high places."

"The 'high places' shunned me long ago."

Lies again. Or the truth? It's maddening that I can't tell with him—it's like staring at a gray-eyed wall. I pick up a laser-quill from his inkwell, hovering the nib over the paper.

"I might not win. Anything. I could go out there on the first match and die."

"You won't."

"How can you be so sure of that?"

"Before she died, my mother told me stories of the Knight's War."

The quiet manse pulses silence. Dravik's gaze goes past my shoulder to the doorway, and I look back, but there's no one there. His face says someone *is*.

"The knights of the War were the greatest riders to ever exist. *Legendary*. Even in their rudimentary steeds, they accomplished unmatched feats of ease and prowess on the battlefield. Their mastery cannot be rivaled today by any modern rider—or so they say. Do you know why?"

I frown at the cold fireplace. "Because they were desperate to survive. To kill the enemy."

His mouth crinkles with a smile. "I thought so, too. But Mother says otherwise."

"'*Says*'? You just told me your mother's dead."

"She is. Fourteen years gone."

"You meant to use past tense, then."

He tears his gaze from the doorway. "No—I did not. My mother still says many things to me."

My sputter drains to a hiss. "You're a *lunatic*."

"And you're a murderer." Dravik smiles brighter. "But that's neither of our faults. Our fathers made us this way, did they not?"

He's mad, but he's not wrong. Father is why I'm here. I've used cruel men to my advantage. I've used egotistical men to my advantage. But this will be my first time using a madman.

My fist clenches around the quill. My hand makes each painful letter: *SYNALI EMILIA WOSTER*. It's fitting that House Hauteclare's death warrant is signed with Mother's last name, but the gnawing feeling of having signed my life away to a noble lingers. Dravik signs his contract as *Dravik vel Lithroi*. The surname rings a faint bell…but as I'm thinking, I'm startled by the sudden clatter of a tea tray rolling into the room. The phantomlike Quilliam comes to my side with a plate, upon which a small cake slathered in frosting and sugared flowers rests. His watery old eyes glow in the single candle flame flickering atop it.

I pivot to Dravik. "This—"

"I had much time to read your file," he says. "I was saddened to learn the day of your death would have also been the day of your birth."

I can't move. I can't do anything but breathe in the smell of baking, of wax, of memories. "I don't need your pity."

"Not pity—tradition. In this house, birthdays are celebrated." He looks up at a painting of two deer chasing each other. "They always were."

Quilliam nods enthusiastically for me to take a fork. "It's two months late, but…happy birthday, Miss Synali. I hope the taste is to your liking."

I grip the silver tines tightly. After a moment of silence, Dravik stands.

"I think Quilliam and I will retire for the night. You'll find your room at the end of this hall, by the centaur statue. Your vis has been sent the bio-key. Breakfast is at seven. We will see you tomorrow, then."

Dravik nods and Quilliam bows before they leave in cane-step and shuffle-step, the robot-dog trailing behind them. I stare at the melting candle alone. No one in their right mind would leave a stranger unsupervised in their private office. He either has surveillance or…he trusts me.

Ridiculous. This gesture of kindness is a ploy. How many commoners have I seen fall to bribery, to displays without substance? Mother fell for Father's promises to take care of her. *I know all that,* and yet still I reach for the cake as one might reach for the heart in someone's chest, and I pull a chunk out. Another. Crush it between my fingers. It's airy and delicate and refined— noble to the core. I tear it apart. Eat so fast I bite my tongue. A noise comes out of me that is neither sob nor laugh, and the taste is blood and buttercream and the realization I can't see her until it's over. Until all seven of Mother's killers in House Hauteclare have paid, I will live. I will train as an animal does.

I will devour them all.

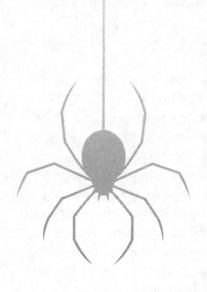

−9. Vermis

vermis ~is, *m.*
1. a worm

On his thirteenth birthday, the discarded boy with spun-gold hair was given a name by his father—Rain.

It was a word with a strange sound, and so the boy asked what *rain* was, and his father answered, "A thing that falls but never breaks." It was their own private name—the children in the assassin guild called the Spider's Hand went by colors and numbers or, if they were particularly close to one another, "sister" and "brother." To his siblings and his instructors at the assassin's guild, he was Violet-Five, but to his father—in the quiet moments they met for further training—he was Rain.

It was strange that Rain was getting extra training at all; his brothers and sisters were allowed to sleep at ten. He asked his father about this one night, and the old man put down the dagger he was polishing.

"The archons have high hopes for you."

The archons? The nine determiners of the Spider's Hand's every move? "Why? I've done nothing special. Green-Seven has completed far more contracts this year, and Red-Twelve took a baron last week—"

A flash of old fingers, and the dagger slashed past Rain's ear and into the center dot of the burlap target thirty feet behind him. His father looked to him, mouth wrinkled and dour.

"An assassin's worth is measured in neither quantity nor quality; it is measured in potential."

Rain only began to understand what his father meant two years later. What few contracts he had came sporadically and very…specifically. There seemed to be a particular noble House his killings were serving. Which House was not clear, but it had to be a powerful one—the sort that could keep an assassin of the Spider's Hand on permanent retainer.

He was jealous of his brothers and sisters at first—of their constant contracts and victories and stories of the hunt—until the funerals began. Green-Seven was riddled with holes by his prey's hard-light pistol. Red-Twelve miscalculated maintenance routines and was vented into space as she hid in the walls of a debris compactor. Every month brought a new accident, a new death. Every month brought a younger spider to take their place, just as Rain and his siblings had taken another's so long ago.

He was seventeen when the youngest of them, Yellow-Eight, died. Blood streaked down the hall of the bunker, still wet from when the webmakers brought him in on the stretcher. It was strange to see—not the blood of prey but from one of their own. Rain stared at it for many long minutes, at his reflection in the wetness, until a webmaker shooed him away.

His sister Violet-Two found Rain in the canteen, sitting alone at a table. She touched him on the shoulder, her gaze misty.

Fearing he wouldn't be able to control himself in front of her, he tried to get up, but she plunked down a glass of ale and a cup of their daily pills. Her eyes darted to the instructors eating and the webmakers posted along the walls, and he understood—as one spider understood another—that she wanted to tell him something, but the adults hated it when they speculated, and it didn't help that everyone in the Web could lip-read.

Slowly, he downed the pills and took a sip of ale, and Violet-Two didn't speak until the last instructor in the canteen looked away from them. Then she muttered into her own ale, "Everything's changed."

"Changed how?"

She wiped foam off her lips. "Yellow-Eight died under a strange contract. It's not just nobles killing one another anymore. It's not even rival merchants or corporate interests. They've started taking out contracts against commoners—well-armed commoners."

"How well armed?"

Violet-Two shook her head, and that meant *very well*. She took another slow sip. "You and the other House spiders are the only ones doing noble jobs anymore. The rest of us are being sent all over the substations to pick off... *resistance*. That's the only way I can describe it."

"Who are the prey?"

"Unionizers, philosophy parlors, Under-ring gangs, cults and atheists and black-market medics—anyone beyond the grip of the king and the church. Red-Ten and I compared notes; they all have ties to a group calling themselves 'Polaris.' Green-One thinks it won't be long until we see them on the Station proper—Under-ring first, then Low Ward."

Rain gnawed on his lip. Green-One was the best of them—the oldest, the smartest. If he said it was so, it would be so. But confusion still tore at him. "Why now?"

"I'm not sure. Green-One says they're too well organized. That someone has to be helping them."

Someone with money, she meant. No, more than that—influence and schooling, too. Someone...*noble*.

"Which House?" he asked.

Violet-Two shook her head again, but this time it was slow and fearful and unknowing.

9. Feritas

feritās ~ātis, *f.*
1. *(of animals)* wildness
2. *(of men)* brutality

I stare out the window from my new bed. *An entire room to myself.* The sunrise over Dravik's manse is artificial—pink-gold-green projected on the noble spire's shallow horizon—but it's beautiful all the same. I understand now why Mother wanted me to see it.

I open my vis and set the timer for one minute. I wrap my arms around myself, a phantom memory of a hug. Squeeze, then squeeze harder. She will never get to see this—Father made sure of that.

He tried to make sure I'd never see this, either.

Ten. Nine. Eight…

Did he hate me that much?

Seven. Six. Five…

My collarbone scar throbs. *No.*

Four. Three. Two…

If he hated us, if he loved us…if he felt anything for us at all, he would've come and killed us himself.

One.

Tears wiped. Feet on cold marble floor.

The manse halls are quiet and empty, dust swirling in the watery sun. Nothing moves but me. Nothing breathes, even as the grand family paintings and statues and gilded furniture shout about a gorgeous life. The stillness is rank and eerie as I stare up at a portrait of a green-eyed boy faintly smiling down at the nothingness around him, at nothing but bones. Moonlight's End isn't a tomb—it's a carcass, long hollowed out by a much bigger beast. My footsteps freeze at a sudden scent drifting down the hall: the warm mull of an oven. The kitchens must be nearby. If I close my eyes, I can almost taste it—bread and laughter and softness.

Not until it's over.

My contractual demands are as follows:

One—within twenty-four hours of me winning a match, one of the seven will die, and Dravik will vis me the evidence of their involvement in Mother's murder. Two—he will never require me to do anything but ride. And three—when the Supernova Cup ends, he will ensure my painless death.

Dravik has only one demand: when I'm asked who I am by anyone, I must give my full name—Synali von Hauteclare.

Because that *is* my name now.

Dravik's vis projects my birth certificate over the polished breakfast table. *SYNALI EMILIA WOSTER* has been replaced with *SYNALI VON HAUTECLARE.* My father's name and mine—*connected.* Like an uncontrollable twitch, I chuck the nearest glass of water at the holograph, and it shorts out in a shower of blue pixels. Dravik doesn't even look up from his eggs and toast, his sandy hair carefully combed over and his cravat a stark bleach white. The water pools in the center of the table as I take a seat opposite him.

"How did you get the bloodline registrar to change it?" I ask.

"How did you manage to kill your father?" Dravik retorts coolly, and the answer lingers on my lips: threats and blackmail, bleeding and bruising and drugs—*anything.* I shut up if I had to. I begged if I had to. I took the beatings and did the beatings and watched the beatings from outside my own body looking down on the bed, but I say none of that.

Dravik smiles brightly over his teacup. "Mmm. I suppose we all have our own ways of getting results, don't we?"

Through the grand breakfast room windows, that dying garden lingers, yellow grasses and sickly white trees. The smell of fresh coffee in the air is dizzying. Quilliam steps in and wipes the water off the table slowly. Why bother changing my name to Hauteclare at all? The Lithroi name would be so much simpler, draw so much less attention. Unless…

"You *want* the court to know a bastard is riding for you," I say. Dravik summarily ignores my conjecture.

"Judging by the cake's appearance this morning, you destroyed more of it than you ate. You'll need energy for training—do try to eat your breakfast."

"Will the nobles even let a bastard like me ride?" I press.

"They won't have a say in the matter. Did you like Rax?"

"Like?"

"I saw a little video of your pre-match confrontation two months ago. It's fortunate you wore your helmet, or he would have become a problem. He still may."

I scoff. "I doubt that. He seemed about as clever as a bag of metal shavings."

"One does not need to be routinely intelligent to achieve victory, Synali—one merely needs to strike when their opponent blunders. And he certainly seemed to rile you."

I don't like what he's insinuating. "I can control myself."

Dravik hums lightly. The robot-dog sits at his feet. I aim a tentative grin at it, but it puts its head on its paws and ignores me. With the table dry again, Quilliam delivers my breakfast plate piled high with eggs and meat, though I'm less concerned with the contents and more with the constant sniffing he seems to make.

"Is Quilliam sick?" I ask.

"Allergies, I believe."

"All the dust, probably. It's a lot for one old man to clean." There's a beat. Dravik didn't bake that cake—Quilliam did. "I could help him."

Dravik smiles thinly. "If you have any energy left after your full day of training, feel free."

I frown and push my eggs around on my plate. The dog cocks its head at me. *Oh, so now I have your attention?* When Dravik gets up to refill his tea from the samovar, I drop a clump of egg to the floor. The dog instantly trots over, sniffing the dust around the bit before inhaling it whole.

"Can you even taste that?" At my whisper, the dog starts to growl, but another dangled piece of egg and it's back to cocking its head curiously. I snicker. "You're so fickle."

Dravik returns, the dog skittering under his chair once more. "Quilliam will be in charge of your diet for the next two months. Our priority is to build the minimum amount of muscle required to operate a steed as quickly and safely as possible."

Rax comes to mind in all his marble-carved vainglory. The way his body waited beneath mine, tense and blistering hot... I curl my lip.

"I'm sure riding isn't entirely about bulging muscles."

"No," Dravik agrees. "But you've already proven mental compatibility with steeds—it's everything else I'm worried about. Shall we get started?"

I shovel what's left of my food into my face. Fresh meat carved from a real animal, the sort I wanted to buy Mother when she stopped getting out of bed. Meat I thought would make her strong again. I swallow at lightning speed, refusing to taste it. Wash it down with water—no tea, no sugar, no cream, no niceties.

I'm not here to be nice.

I'm here to win the Supernova Cup.

A cold steel door and a cutting-edge bio-lock guard the entrance to the manse's bunker. The long journey down the shadowed flight of stairs is interrupted only by Quilliam's sniffing, Dravik's tapping cane, and the metallic clank of the robot-dog's feet. Buried farther down than I can calculate is a room with no floor—a great crevasse bridged only by a railed walkway.

"Welcome to the bunker." Dravik motions to the featureless steel walls. There's no hungry "visitor" like Quilliam mentioned, but there is a steed: a dilapidated giant forty times my size hanging from the wall by its arms. Chunks of its colorless armor have fallen off, revealing the fiber machinations beneath like rusted threads of muscle. Rax's steed looked nothing like this—this is an old model, *ancient*, utterly ravaged to pieces by time.

I whirl on Dravik.

"Am I a joke to you? *This* is my steed? This scrap heap belongs in the War museum!"

He leans on the railing casually. "Ah, you've a sharp eye. This is one of the original A-prototype steeds—the third batch humanity ever created in their bid to win the War."

"You want me to ride something *four hundred years old*? I won't win anything in this fucking rust pile! I'll be killed in the first—"

"362 years old, actually," he corrects, waving his cane up and down the steed's broken chassis like a school pointer. "Yet it has all its component parts still intact. It might not be as sturdy as the modern models, but it's certainly quicker. And—if I may be frank—far more charming."

I crumple my fist in Dravik's cravat faster than I can think. The robot-dog starts barking frantically, invisible metal hackles rising as it snaps pearl teeth at my ankles. A waste of time—that's all this noble's ever been. I wrench us against the railing. The bunker's bottom gapes hollowly a hundred feet below, more, the steed's monolithic hanging legs disappearing into darkness.

"Should I tip us over the edge?" I hiss in his face. "End it now as it'll no doubt end later—in both our deaths? It'd be faster than this farce you've forced me into."

I feel a sharp nip in my heel through my boot, but I refuse to let go, refuse to look away from the noble who I let trick me. The dog tries to rip my tendon, my new leather boots pierced through, and Dravik says a single clear word:

"Astrix."

The teeth in my heel go slack instantly, and I hear the telltale whir of a solar cell powering down. Why shut the robot-dog down with a command? I'm going to throw us both over the edge. Dravik should fight back. The soft body beneath his embroidered vest should shift and brace and *try*, but he doesn't so much as resist. He's a calm reed in a storm; the affable smile on his face sends me spiraling deeper.

"It seems you are quite used to violence," he says.

"Did you expect anything different when you picked up a useless Low Ward girl off the streets?"

His voice goes hard. "You are in no way useless."

"Please," Quilliam pleads from the console at the other end of the walkway. "Please, miss, let us not fight—"

"Be quiet!" I snap over my shoulder. "Don't you get it?" I say to Dravik. "The nobles' steeds are leagues better than this one—they'll rip me apart in a blink. This has all been for nothing!"

Dravik laughs softly. "And it seems you're quick to despair, too."

I clench my teeth. What does his gilded ass know about despair? He gave me hope and stole it back ruthlessly with this junkheap of a steed. From afar, Quilliam murmurs something unintelligible under his breath.

"He has a point," Dravik admits.

"And what would that be?" I tilt us so far over the railing that it creaks. Not a single bead of sweat glistens on him, not a single flicker of the eyes. He's impenetrable, and I despise it. Being this close, I see it for the first time—faintly jagged pixel-shapes on the edges of his gray gaze as it cuts up to the steed. Iris surgery scars. Expensive. Painful. Loyal nobles get it to better "represent" their House and its sigil colors. He's had his eye color changed—from something else to gray.

"We won the War with these, didn't we?"

I go still, then crawl my eyes up at the steed.

This is the story the priests tell you: Satan sent the enemy to destroy us.

This is the story history tells you: We don't know why the enemy attacked, only that they did. Moving through the plentiful oceans—the closest analogue to the zero gravity of space they were used to—they wiped out three-fourths of the human population in just two decades. But then we made the seven Stations—great metal arks protected by hard-light honeycomb shields that hovered high above the razed ground. And then we made the humanoid *steeds*. The Stations saved us, preserved us, but the steeds are what turned the tide of the War from us barely clinging on to victory. The enemy was destroyed by thousands of steeds just like this one, by their valiant riders who killed and died in turn—the knights of the War.

This is the story of old Earth: Once, there were many wars. But when the enemy came, there was only one. Once, a knight must have ridden this steed.

This is the story I tell myself: Once upon a time, this steed wore the enemy's blood like warpaint.

Its gray hands droop, spindly legs fractured and twisted in their hip sockets. A crescent-shaped helmet lolls forward uselessly onto a battered breastplate. It looks wrong, broken, empty. From the depths of its gaping armor, metal catches my haggard reflection; empty, broken, wrong. Two of a kind. Seven of a kind must pay the price. There is no time to be kind.

My hand drops from Dravik. "Where's the pit crew for it, then? Surely this isn't the best your engineers could do."

The noble brushes his cravat off lightly. "They'll be here in the morning, but they require you to imprint the steed before they can work on it."

"Imprint."

"Alight in the saddle at least once," he clarifies. "Your neural handshake will be established, and the steed's system will be rebooted, as it hasn't been for 362 years."

"Where did you even find something this old?"

He gives that no-answer smile again. "As I said, your only concern is riding."

Quilliam hits a button on the console, and the hanging steed gives a shuddering screech, its breastplate parting in creaky halves and revealing total darkness within. The walkway grows a gangplank, and with a few metallic clicks, it attaches to the lip of the steed's open chest. Something chirps deep within the steed, the sound of a million volts muffled in another room. From the dark chest cavity, light rises—an all-too-familiar pale purple-blue gel shot with slowly writhing silver and contained in a cylinder as big as a coffin made for three.

The saddle.

Dravik makes an irritatingly lavish bow. "After you, Synali. That is, if you still wish to honor our contract."

The steed is huge. I'm small. It's old, but I'm young. I'm new, and the other riders will not be. I take one wary step onto the gangplank, then another—on either side of me, the bunker's abyss; in front of me, purple-blue light; and behind me, nothing but pain. I should know better than to hope. But now, framed by this strange light, its shadow struggles to breathe in me. He's given me a steed. We *could*. I *could*. Together, we might rip House Hauteclare from the world.

I slice a look back at Dravik. "There will be no honor in any of this."

He smiles brighter. "I know, brave one. But that's half the fun."

The breastplate doors slam behind me with a shuddering thud.

PART II

THE SPIDERWEB

10. Humo

humō ~āre ~āuī ~ātum, *tr.*
1. to bury

'm alone. It's dark, like space. Panic. *Don't panic*—clutch Mother's pendant and move forward.

The steed's insides smell sharp, battery acid and joint oil and that gentle citrus scent. The cockpit is bigger than I thought—the size of my scrap-metal apartment, maybe. The inherent marble smoothness of Ghostwinder is nowhere to be seen; metal juts in every direction in this steed, coarse and unfinished, with rust covering it all like dry red mold. It's just as dusty as Moonlight's End but more rotted, derelict—something still in the process of dying rather than a hopeless bleached skeleton.

The saddle waits in the center of the cockpit, gently pulsing. It's a beacon of naked periwinkle and languidly floating silver whorls, no projection barrier encapsulating it. Strange…but this *is* an old model—maybe hard-light wasn't invented yet. Gingerly, I reach one finger out and poke the surface, and while the gel ripple doesn't surprise me, every silver whorl instantly condensing at my point of impact does.

"How am I supposed to get in?" I mutter.

"Press your way in." I jump as Dravik answers over the cockpit's intercom. "The nerve fluid's surface gives with enough force."

"*Nerve fluid?* Is that really what it's called?"

He doesn't answer. I press my whole hand to the saddle. Wherever I touch, the silver whorls gravitate like a cloud of flies following a scent. All of a sudden, something's here. *Watching me.* It's stronger than the first steed, so strong I can feel its gaze fixed on the back of my head even without being electrocuted inside the gel. The cockpit feels far too small. The air feels heavy, hard to breathe, like whatever's here is *directly on top of me.*

"I—" I swallow. "I don't need a rider's suit?"

"Rider's suits are for prolonged exposure; you're simply rebooting it."

Prolonged exposure. Exposure to *what*?

Without the burn of Father's murder in my veins, I have room to hesitate… but what is hesitation if not a coward's excuse? I press on the gel as hard as I can, and it gives in one fluid gasp, pulling my whole body into it with a viscous, inescapable gravity. My heart beats into my throat, soundless pressure packing into my ears, my skin, and the something is suddenly *right here*. It hovered over me before, but now it has its hands around my neck. My breathing goes shallow, the gel like invisible oxygen to my mouth and nose, and I'm too scared to turn my head—all I can see are the silver whorls whizzing by, swarming onto every inch of my exposed skin. Why is this steed so *different*? Or is this just how it feels without a suit?

"I'm going to run the reboot current through the nerve fluid now." Dravik's intercom voice is muffled. "You may feel a brief pain."

It isn't pain; it's invasion—like water going up my nose the wrong way but in my *mind*. Like déjà vu but forced in from the outside, the watching thing goes **inside** me. It doesn't prod gently like Ghostwinder did. This isn't an open hand offered—it's filling a void. It's the dagger going into my collarbone, the vacuum of space imploding Father's chest cavity when I vented him, the unstoppable nightmare of Mother's death. It's the men in the brothel without care, without mercy (**stop**), and I feel myself go rigid, eyelids jerking open and closed, and I start to see things: White light. Beams. They cut through black space like radiant bullets—stopping only when they smash against honeycomb projection shields. A hundred silver steeds fly into my vision, zipping around space like elegant wasps, leaving no plasma trails—shining new versions of the ancient bunker steed.

And then they turn to me.

A hundred giant needles turn and aim in my exact direction. Hunters looking for prey.

They're coming for me.

A deep gut instinct stabs at me—I know those steeds are coming to kill me as readily as the assassin did. Dagger flash. Lance flash. They will end my existence. I roll, fall, spin in zero gravity, stars blurring. Worse than the fear of dying is a sharp, unrelenting fear screaming that I'm utterly *alone*. I know it. I don't know why, or how, but I know all my friends are dead.

I am the last one left.

"—is complete. Can you hear me, Synali? The reboot is complete. You can come out of the saddle now."

Dravik's voice is the knife that cuts the cord—the images and fear vanish, and my body melts away from the grip of…whatever that was. I rip myself out of the saddle, panting. This thing is a steed? No. It's a demon—a devil prying and prodding in my brain. I saw something in there…and it saw *me*. Without my permission.

I slam on the steed's breastplate, and it opens, but not fast enough. I stalk off the gangplank toward Dravik.

"Why did it do that? Is that how every steed reboots?"

He doesn't ask what I mean by "that"—which means he knows exactly what I'm talking about. He just says, "No."

"Then why did you force me into that piece of shit?"

"Heavenbreaker," Dravik says evenly. "Call it by its name."

"I don't care what its name is," I spit.

"I'm not asking you to care. I'm asking you to fight. And every fighter must know the name of their sword. *Heavenbreaker.*"

Quilliam's sniffing is the only thing that breaks the furious silence, his withered hands holding a handkerchief to his nose. Dravik suddenly motions for his manservant to follow him up the bunker stairs. Quilliam hesitates, but the dog follows, tail wagging furiously.

"Where do you think you're going?" I shout after him. "Dravik! *Dravik,* you owe me answers!"

"There are no 'answer' stipulations in your contract, Synali," his fading voice reminds me. I see red—no, Rax-level *crimson*. Quilliam toddles up to me, a roll of gauze in his hand as he kneels and reaches for my dog-bitten heel.

"Please, miss. We must bandage your wound before it becomes infected—"

"Don't touch me!" I shake him off. Quilliam won't let up, reaching for my legs still. *"I SAID DON'T FUCKING TOUCH ME!"*

My kick catches his hand, and he recoils, giving me room at last to stride furiously down the walkway. Out of the corner of my eye, I see him cradle his knotted hand and, with slow trepidation, shuffle back up the bunker stairs. *Good. That's what you get for trying to touch me. For making a vicious girl like me a cake.*

I turn and kick the railing over and over, hard enough to make my bones vibrate in pain. Damn that noble, and damn his fucking contracts! I need this machine. If I can ride it, it'll mean power even the nobles have to respect. *So, fine.* If he wants to play strictly by the rules, I can do that. I can control myself. Dravik's right—I don't have to care for it, but I'll at least use its name, if only so House Hauteclare can learn who's taken them down.

"Heavenbreaker."

It's just metal and wires and early-War tech. It's just a machine made to kill an enemy long gone. But for a moment, through the cracks in its breastplate, the silvery saddle seems to glow brighter at my voice.

I t took me eight days to stop staring at the bloodstain in the shape of Mother on the apartment floor.

Twelve days to start eating solid food again. Fifteen days for my collarbone wound to heal enough to move, and thirty days to make a plan. Fifty-two to stalk a cleaner who worked at the tourney hall, sixty to get a job delivering milk formula to said cleaner. Seventy-eight days to study the tourney hall map and guard patrols. 132 days to convince Madam Beldeaux to pay me in tranquilizers instead of credits. 175 days to spike the cleaner's milk formula and transfer his clearance to my vis and walk into the tourney hall like nothing was wrong when everything was.

It took me 175 days to fail in ruining my father.

It takes me 51 days to learn to ride Dravik's strange, broken steed.

The hardest part isn't the physical training of the first three weeks. It isn't the hours of lifting heavy weights until the world spins and I vomit, or inhaling vitamins with names I can't pronounce, nor is it the cold mornings spent running on the treadmill until my shins feel like they'll splinter.

It's the *resting*. I don't see the point of it. After putting me through physical hell with a perfect smile, Dravik digitally locks every training room in the manse so I can't use any equipment during my designated rests. Every hour is an hour the other riders of the Supernova Cup have already run through a million times over. Can't stand it. If I can't move, train, focus on something—even pain—the memories come crawling out of my cracks.

The robot-dog finds me staring at an old painting of a beautiful woman walking on Earth, in a place with more trees than sky. I can pick out the tiny metallic *ping*s of its paws from across Moonlight's End now, but my mind is drenched in blood and my own mistakes. Why did I survive and Mother didn't? The assassin attacked both of us—I have the scar to prove it. I don't remember surviving. I remember screaming, crying, being stabbed, that black hood and those ice eyes, but nothing else. The next thing I remember is staring at Mother's bloodstain on the floor, a bandage around my collarbone, and my vis saying it was eight days later.

Who bandaged me? Why do I remember the *after* so well but not the *during*? Trauma, probably. I'm smart enough to understand that, but I don't like the idea of trauma keeping my own memories from me. I don't like the idea of anything I can't control. I try to calm myself, try to reach back in my mind to that time, but…there's nothing.

There's a whine, and I feel the dog's cold nose nudging my ankle. I look down—the bandage I wrapped around my heel after its bite peeks from my shoe, frayed from all the exercise and blood-dark. The dog's sapphire eyes watch me unblinkingly, faint lights flickering in the blue depths as if its neurons are firing.

"Don't worry." I smile. "I don't blame you. You were just protecting him, weren't you? I was the same way with my mother."

Soon, I run out of paintings to stare at. Scrawling through my vis only kills so much time. The frothing tourney fans keep databases on every last rider—past and present. I memorize as many riders' faces as I can, study clips of their matches. They make this whole thing look effortless. I don't understand how the legendary knights could've been any better—steeds these days are the noble-funded pinnacle of technology, and we've had four hundred years to perfect the act of riding itself.

Names blur, but frequent ones mean stronger riders. I look up Father.

"Vis," I whisper. "Black out the picture."

Father's younger face on the holoscreen vanishes beneath a block of darkness.

Apparently, he was in the top five riders of his era. He rode Ghostwinder to countless victories and then to his two greatest achievements: winning the Supernova Cup of 3422 *and* 3432. Is that why Dravik thinks I can ride for his House—because my father was good at it? The thought makes my stomach churn.

I flip quickly to House Hauteclare's current rider, and my breath catches. The most beautiful girl I've ever seen stares up at me from the screen, her hair a sleek waterfall of chestnut and her eyes gold as sunlight, marred only slightly by surgery scars. Mirelle Ashadi-Hauteclare. She looks nothing like me; her neck is graceful and her face is a soft, symmetrical oval with flawless skin, her nose an imperious line down to rosebud lips. No wonder Rax was all over me when I pretended to be her—she's gorgeous. She's my age, but she's a thoroughbred noble. I don't know how she's related to me; a cousin, perhaps, or I might be her aunt. It appears she's good at riding Ghostwinder— good enough that she graduated from the academy a year early and people strategically bow out of facing her.

No matter how I'm related to her, no matter how pretty she is…she is the enemy.

Finally, I click on Rax Istra-Velrayd.

It's hard to avoid him on the database—he's mentioned a dozen times. As much as I hate it, his impact on the riding scene seems impossible to ignore; he was considered a child prodigy at the academy, riding in his first qualifier when he was nine. The average age for a rider's first qualifier is *sixteen*. At twelve, he won his first proper tourney in House Velrayd's crimson steed, Sunscreamer, and he hasn't stopped since. At fifteen, he faced off against Father—a two-time Supernova Cup champion—in a *friendly round of sparring*, and the match was declared a draw.

He is a threat.

He is unbearably handsome.

I refuse to look at his picture head-on, but my eyes catch flashes of platinum hair, dark quirked brows, broad lips, and redwood eyes glittering wickedly with their own permanent joke, and before the hairs on the back of my heated neck can rise all the way, I jerk my vis shut.

I don't need to know what he looks like to beat him.

I jump to my feet—I'm done waiting. If the rooms are locked, I'll run the halls.

This works until the air my lungs struggle to puff out starts to taste like mint. The lightheadedness is instant, my limbs jelly and my eyelids flickering… and then I'm groggily coming to sideways—with my head on a small pillow someone's placed between me and the cold marble floor. The robot-dog stares at me from a distance, unmoving, as if it's keeping…watch?

I check my vis—three hours have passed. *Three hours?* My mouth still tastes like mint, and my body is slept-wrong sore, and my first thought is *Dravik.* I struggle to my feet and stagger to the weight room; he's there waiting for me as per our usual schedule, wiping down the steel of a bench. He smiles happily when he sees me.

"Ah, you're awake. I thought the sleeping gas would keep you under longer."

"Gas?" I grit out. "You knocked me out with *gas*?"

"Unwillingly, you understand. You are an asset. Without proper rest, you risk injury, and any injury will delay my timeline by a significant amount."

I see red again, resisting the urge to knock over a rack of weights. "Your *timeline*? I could've cracked my head on the goddamn floor!"

"And yet it seems you did not." Dravik claps his hands in a clear bid to change the subject. "The thigh muscles are responsible for a great majority of balance within the saddle. Let's begin with a set of twenty squats and work our way up from there."

I want to argue, to scream, to destroy *something* to get him to take me seriously, but the calendar screen in the weight room looms huge and blue: six weeks left until the Supernova Cup. I *can* control myself. There's no time for anger, only execution.

"You won't gas me again," I say.

"That remains to be seen," he agrees. "If you adhere to the rules of rest."

I put a finger in his placid face. "If I do something that compromises 'the timeline,' you'll tell me. Vis me, like a normal person. No more brute-forcing."

His pale brows rise. "Will you continue to brute-force your training?"

I go quiet.

"I've spent nine years pondering over each step of this process, Synali—

almost half your life. You need not trust me as a person, but I implore you to trust the plan. If I say rest, you must rest."

"It's pointless," I snap.

"Your health and well-being may be pointless to you," he says, "but they are very valuable to me. *You* have value to me."

Something deep in my chest feels like it cracks. Dravik's eyes go soft again.

"Would you truly listen if I vis'd you my concerns?"

"I'd—" I swallow. "No. But I can try."

He hands me a weight with a smile. "Let us try together, then."

I grind out my sets. For every rep Dravik considers "successful," he taps his silver cane on the floor, the ticking like the hands of some unbearable clock. Sweat pours from every inch of my face. This isn't our first session, but it's the first time he tries to physically correct me. I startle when I feel his guiding hand around the top of my arm and the brothel fear roars up like an oil fire. I jerk away violently, the weight clenched in my fist like a weapon.

"Don't try it."

It's the first time I've seen his face surprised. "I would never, Synali."

"They always say that."

The room seethes in quiet dust and withered grass waving outside the windows. When Dravik smiles again, it's a grim, dark-steel blade of a thing, but its edge is not aimed at me.

"I suppose they do. My apologies."

11. Falcifer

falcifer ~era ~erum, a.
1. bearing a scythe

THAT NIGHT, DRAVIK VEL LITHROI finds his rider outside the kitchens. His manservant, Quilliam, is working the dough for the morning pastries with a bandaged hand, and the smell is pleasant—butter and sugar and yeast. Synali leans against the wall just beyond the wedged light of the doorway, sleeping soundly—no doubt exhausted from training. Dust and dirt smear her face, a filthy cloth clutched in her hand. A corner of the nearby floor is clean as it hasn't been for years.

Dravik watches the girl—her thin chest rising and falling—and he considers the nature of predators and the nature of those who survive them. He considers most of all the nature of those left alive and how loudly the end calls to them. Her longing for it will be her greatest strength and her greatest weakness. The knights of the War were the same; it was not their desire to survive or triumph that gave them their extraordinary riding abilities. Mother had told him quite the contrary; it was their acceptance of the end, in totality, that rendered them incomprehensible strength. In any other time, it would have been called a death cult, but in the War for old Earth, it was called a *knight's greatest honor.*

How lucky he has been, to find Synali.

How unlucky Synali has been, to have been found.

Slowly and quietly, he drapes his coat over her shivering flesh and retreats into the darkness of Moonlight's End.

12. Ovum

ōvum ~ī, *n.*

1. an egg

M ost of Dravik's training, I learn with my body. But there are two things I learn with my mind:

One—gravity is stronger than me. I cannot fight it; I can only move with it.

Two—the egg cannot break. ***The egg cannot break*** or I will fail.

Again.

And I am done with failure.

"Hold fast." Dravik's voice in my helmet barely makes it through the blood rushing in my ears. My eyes blur—the console's holograph digits strain as Heavenbreaker tears through space at 22 parses per minute. 23. 24. "Ten seconds more."

The distant stars tremble. I cling for my life to the thin surface tension of the saddle as it bulges, on the verge of expelling me. In my white-knuckled hand, I cup an egg. I tense my thighs to keep my blood pressure from dropping me into a blackout, but the g-forces still play trash compactor with my organs. My head feels heavy, as if it'll pop off my neck at any second. Every instinct in me screams to grip for balance, but the egg will shatter. *I can't.* The egg must survive this ride, or I cannot move on to the next phase of my training. It's been a week and a half of constant failure, of spiraling thoughts and clenched teeth, and though Dravik won't say it outright, I know we're far behind the timeline.

My body is one massive sweat-soaked sore under the padded gray practice rider's suit—old bruises and new bruises painting a map of my training at lower speeds. I don't know how many times I've been wrenched out of the saddle and thrown across the steed's hard metal chest cavity; I stopped keeping count at seventeen. At twenty, I started understanding—I can't resist. There is no going against the unstoppable current of gravity, but I can be **in** it, like a pendulum swinging perfectly center. Not standing firm but not fully surrendering, either… That's the only way I haven't been thrown. It's something you do, not describe; a razor-thin sliver of perfect balance. Holding for ten seconds feels like ten slow hours. Every millisecond of nauseating speed and hyper-focus scrapes at my willpower, and I clutch at the only thing I can: the pain.

"There!" Dravik barks.

I think the word *slow*, and the steed slows instantly, pale-blue plasma jets fizzing out and blissful relief washing over my body as the g-forces drop to less, some, and then none. For a moment, Heavenbreaker and I simply float in space, the massive Station and the far larger green orb that is the planet Esther our only company. Even now that it's functional, Heavenbreaker is stranger than Ghostwinder: heavier to move, harder to control, and yet it feels more… *curious*. Ghostwinder knew things—Heavenbreaker does not. The feeling in the saddle is like staring down an abyss, an empty slate voraciously watching, listening, waiting. I refuse to give it anything more than what's necessary to keep it moving; the mind invasion is still too fresh.

Dravik's voice echoes crisply. "How is the egg, Synali?"

I force my way out of the gelatinous saddle, boots hitting metal floor. The entirety of the steed's cockpit is smeared with eggshells and dried yolk from all my failures. Heavenbreaker's engineers clearly weren't paid enough—they mended the gaping holes on the armor outside but left all the dents and rust on the inside.

I release my helmet seal and tear it off with my free hand. "Broken, probably."

"Do me the favor of checking."

He's been patient. That's the worst part—that he's so patient. It'd be easier to hate the noble if he was a fly-off-the-handle type, but he's kept his composure every inch of the way, through every inspection of my smashed head, every fit I had exiting Heavenbreaker and kicking whatever ozone-scented piece of armor I could reach. When I broke down crying after eight straight days of trying, he left patiently and came back patiently.

"I'm in control of myself."

His smile was too forgiving. "Obviously."

I open my fingers slowly, the crescent nail imprints in my palm bleeding, but the eggshell is smeared with red...and *smooth*. Unbroken. Not a single crack.

I go limp against a steel wall. "I—I did it. I can't believe it."

"I can," Dravik says. "Guide the steed off the field, take a rest for an hour, and I'll meet you in the weight room for calisthenics."

On to the next part. *Finally.*

I chuck the egg at the wall, free of it at last, and pierce into the saddle fist-first again, the silver whorls in the nerve fluid eagerly welcoming me back by writhing along the seams of my graying practice suit. The practice tilt is empty save for me, a silent black arena circled by neon bands of red hard-light. I squint—something in the distance moves. Something red breaks its camouflage in the hard-light and starts coming closer.

A feather-swept helmet.

My stomach drops.

"Dravik?" I activate the intercom frantically. *"Dravik?* I thought you said I'd be alone in this arena."

No answer from him, but an incoming ping from one *SUNSCREAMER* flashes across my visor.

"Reject," I mutter. Nothing happens. "Reject, *reject*—listen to me and reject it, you piece of—"

"Hey there." Rax's voice and image come through crystal clear—his visor is let down, but his tight crimson rider's suit and helmet cover everything else. I catch his redwood eyes crinkling before I focus on his right shoulder. "Didn't recognize your steed's sig—is it new?"

Heavenbreaker's model is clearly old as sin. He's being overly friendly and forcing me into an inescapable corner in the conversation, and it feels overbearing. Stuffy. Sunscreamer floats between the arena's exit and me.

My first words to him are strained. "How long were you watching me?"

He laughs, the sound a smoky rumble. "Just got here, actually. Ditched a friend's wedding—evil, I know, but we don't get to choose when the riding thirst hits." He pauses. "You practicing for the big day?"

Yes.

"No."

He clicks his tongue. "Too bad. You got some nice maneuvers—reminds me of the academy. Maybe I'll see you next decade, yeah, Instructor?"

Arrogant. He might not speak elegantly like other nobles, but every one of his words drips their same arrogance—as if he's assuming every rider knows who he is, how good he is. Sunscreamer's posture is exactly his: languid, easy, confident.

My mouth moves when it shouldn't. "You will be seeing me sooner than that."

That laugh again—spine-tingling. "Is that a challenge? We could do it right here, if you want."

He motions around at the practice tilt, the grav-gen glowing dimly and the hexagons on either side shadowed by the two huge skeletal frames of the automatic steed dummies. I'm in no condition to fight him. I'm sweat-drenched, tired. A Dravik-voice in the back of my head tells me to ignore him. Rax Istra-Velrayd is not in the timeline.

But my body doesn't care; it just *burns.*

"Whoever does the most damage to the dummy," I say. "No lance."

This time, his laugh is incredulous. "You want to have a *punching* contest?"

"Is that too much for you?"

A beat. From behind my visor, my gaze moves to his—his curious stare like someone trying to solve a puzzle. And then his eyes smile.

"No. I'll take terrene. Give you the slight gravitational advantage."

"How kind of you," I drawl.

We jet off in opposite directions, him to the terrene side—the tilt nearest the giant planet of Esther—and me to the sidereal side, nearest to open space. Every bone in my body aches, but it's too late to back out now. I won't let any noble get away with thinking they're better than me—not even a pseudo-legend like this one. As I tap on my vis to activate the dummy on my side for Rax, he speaks.

"Mind if I ask your name?"

"Yes." I tap ACCEPT and jet softly away from the tilt. "The dummy is ready when you are."

"Straight to the point. I like that in a rider."

"What you like has very little in common with what I care for."

He laughs. "Ouch. You don't hold back."

I raise my chin. "Are you going to ride or not?"

Sunscreamer makes a facetious bow at me. Rax's holograph feed in my visor cuts out for the descent, and his red plasma jets blast hot and bright, waiting, burning against the metal of the tilt. I pull up my vis to record. Don't blink. *Watch.* Absorb it all—every ankle rotation, how he takes his starting stance. *Use him. Consume him.* I'll eat whatever scraps he's foolish enough to leave me, and I'll become stronger on them.

And then it happens.

"eat"

The word is faint but clear. I look at my vis—is someone still commed in to me? Dravik? No—that was far too young to be his voice.

"Hello?" My voice echoes around the empty cockpit.

The ribbon-tear sound of plasma against metal makes me look up—the nearby dummy's colorless white jets power on and launch it forward at the same moment Rax launches Sunscreamer. Its limbs shudder rigidly as it barrels toward the sleeker crimson steed. *Focus.*

The chest is the biggest part—easiest to hit. My eyes strain against letting Sunscreamer just become a blur of red—Rax tilts it backward, not forward like Dravik taught me. *Why? Is it because he isn't holding the weight of the lance, or...* The shuddering dummy and steed bear down on each other, the blue glow of the grav-gen making it near impossible to see. There—Rax pulls his left arm back just before impact and snaps forward with it, sending a shower of sparks and cheap metal spinning out everywhere. The wicked tipped claws of Sunscreamer's hand grip the dummy's head, and for a second, the dummy strains against him, white jets burning, and then Rax shatters the head in his hands like an eggshell.

He hit the head while moving at 26 parses per minute—a tiny, unreal target; a target difficult to hit even *with* a lance. The headless dummy, now free of its suppressor, arcs down the circuit and crashes chest-first into the tilt. It bounces and then comes to a ravaged halt. The circuit brings Sunscreamer arcing toward me, and I can practically smell the self-satisfaction in Rax's voice as his comm reconnects.

"Well?" he asks with a cock of his helmet. "How did I do, Instructor?"

My ears ring and blur out his thinly veiled insult. No database clip has ever looked like that. He didn't just destroy the dummy—he destroyed it *precisely*. He stayed back so that the momentum of his arm moving forward at the last second could be precisely controlled and propelled, like a shot from a hard-light pistol. A head hit in a tourney is an automatic win. He chose to hit the head to send me a message. Keeping a resistant stance the entire way down the tilt must've been incredibly taxing, but he's not even panting.

My mind spins as I jet toward my tilt and lock into place. How can I beat that? I can't.

Seeing his stats in a database and reading the laundry list of things he's accomplished… It's terrifying when I can see it for myself, not through washed-out old clips on my vis. *How do I do better than that?*

I can't. No matter how much I burn to…I just can't.

But that's never stopped me before.

"I guess that means you're ready," Rax says as he jets back to his tilt and the fresh dummy there. "All right, then—dummy's prepped. Give it your best shot, Instructor."

My lip curls at his patronizing tone. I think *go*, and the pale-blue jets on Heavenbreaker's back and ankles burst to life. I can feel them—gentle heat on my skin in the exact same spots, on the still-healing wound from the dog. When I rode Ghostwinder, I didn't find any switches or levers because there were none; riders don't use switches to move the steed. They use their mind. The electric current that runs through the saddle somehow links my mind to the steed's mechanics, but just thinking the word *go* doesn't move the steed—it has to be the meaning of the word, too. You have to visualize exactly how you want the movement to be.

If you're distracted, nothing happens. If you're uncertain or inexact, something sloppy or too slow happens. It's an echo of telekinesis, of trying so hard when you're a child to move a cup with your mind, except this time it's real, and the cup must be understood down to the last ceramic chip. You have to *know*, and then hit that meaning hard and clear like a bell in your mind.

More, I think. The metal of Heavenbreaker's vents squeals as the plasma blasts out against cold space. Since my disastrous first match two and a half months ago, I've never gone in a straight line before—Dravik has me on literal learning curves. The dummy at the opposite end of the tilt waits, crouched stiffly against the hexagon. The chest would be easy. The head would be hard. *How do I beat him? How do I destroy it better?*

"Synali? Are you still riding?"

Dravik's voice. *Shit*—he's reconnected.

I pin my arms to my side and lean forward into the descent, and the comms cut automatically. *Go*, I think. The speed stuffs the suit into my body, my eyelids into my eyeballs. Going straight is faster, sharper. My collarbone scar aches beneath my sweat-drenched skin. Rax fought Father and lived. He drew even. But I lost—everything. Mother. My life.

I'm stronger now.

I have to show them I'm stronger.

The blue light of the grav-gen shines like a miniature sun, brighter and brighter, and the skin of my face lifts off my skull. I can barely keep breathing, let alone lean back and prepare to strike. *How does he resist this force?* The dummy shudders toward me, a blaze of white barely held together, and for a second it turns red. *Sunscreamer.* Suddenly, this is the fight from two months ago and I'm spiraling toward my death…but there's no lance this time. This time, I won't pass out. I'm ready.

I'm too far left. *Right*, I think. I tilt, and Heavenbreaker tilts. I don't know precision, but I know destruction.

Destroy.

Through the rush of blood in my ears, I hear it echoed back at me faintly, quietly.

"destroy"

Both arms straighten out.

We impact.

I catch it. Chest to chest, ribs stabbing and lungs burning and my fingers digging into the dummy's threadbare shoulders as it strains against me. The whiplash tries to yank me from the saddle, but I bear down and clench everything—abdominals, thighs, teeth. I have a grip. I could rip it apart.

"rip it apart"

What's left of me surges through my arms, and I pull. The dummy's mindless speed grinds against me like sawblades in my torso, and the saddle's gel absorbs my scream as I give one last heave. The dummy's chassis cracks down the middle, the blasting white plasma framing its horrible blank face as it starts to bleed black oil. I feel the wet drips on my face, perfect orbs of splatter spinning through space.

Stronger.

The thing in here with me feels *closer* all of a sudden, like it's trying to help, a hand reinforcing mine. The crack in the dummy's chassis becomes a breach, becomes a ravine, wiring and gears popping out and spiraling off like tendon and tissue, and for a terrible, beautiful moment, it feels good. *Satisfying.* Stabbing Father gave me no satisfaction, but this…this giant thing torn to pieces by my small hands…

When the white plasma finally sputters out, I know it's dead.

I dislodge from its bisected body, chest heaving, something wrong with my right arm—*shooting pain*—but dull adrenaline trembles through me like fire and nectar. I lift my head to Rax, Sunscreamer floating limply just a few parses in front of me. My comms crackle with Dravik's ignored calls and my exhausted smile.

"How did I do, Instructor?"

My ears go dull, drowning out Rax's answer, and I feel my eyes roll.

Darkness.

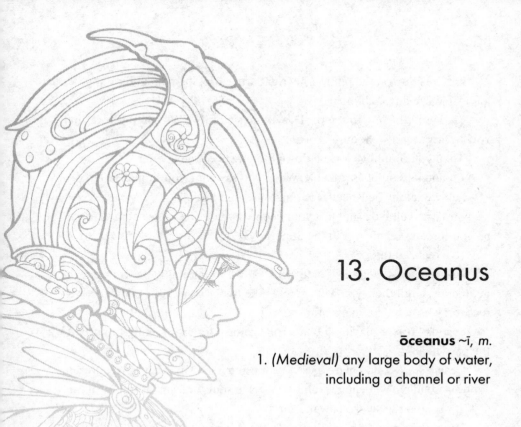

13. Oceanus

ōceanus ~ī, *m.*
1. *(Medieval)* any large body of water,
including a channel or river

I wake once I'm being carried back into Moonlight's End, Dravik's arms beneath me and his steps uneven without the cane. We pass a portrait I've never seen before—a beautiful woman with pale cornsilk hair and gray eyes, just like Dravik's. Her dress is silver and light blue, and the smile on her lips is measured. Patient.

Just like Dravik's.

I hear him grunt just before I slip into darkness again. "She weighs far too little still. Is she even eating?"

When I wake the second time, Dravik is not pleased. He keeps his face tranquil as he sits in the chair at my bedside, but the too-quick way his thumb moves over the head of his cane says everything, like a pissed cat lashing its tail.

"It was just a little extra practice," I insist groggily.

He clips his words short. "I'm more concerned with the fact you rode yourself to the point of fainting. Worse yet, you conducted all this in front of Sir Istra-Velrayd."

I try to sit up on the pillows, my right arm shrieking pain at the shoulder joint. "I learned from him."

"He learned from you, too," Dravik says sternly. "We cannot have that. You are my secret weapon."

"Then you should've locked down the practice arena better."

"I made it as quiet as possible. When you saw him, you should've left."

I glower at my bedsheets. He purses his thin lips.

"Sir Istra-Velrayd is not just your enemy, Synali—he is *the* enemy. He will be your greatest challenge in the Supernova Cup bar none."

"I've realized that."

"Yes, I suppose you have." He sighs. "Now, your painkillers will wear off in an hour. Until then, you will eat and take things slow. Your body needs to recover; your mind, perhaps more so."

I scoff. "You're playing a dangerous game, Dravik—talking fatherly to the patricidal."

Dravik stares, and I glare back. The tension in the air is cut by a clattering sound—Quilliam wheeling in a meal cart. He sniffs and smiles faintly at me.

"It's so good to see you awake, miss."

The robot-dog follows him, and after a moment of sapphire-eyed deliberation, it leaps onto the bed and curls up by my feet. I watch Quilliam's bandaged hand as it scoops porridge and berries into a silver bowl. Hurting a helpless old man—I'm no better than Father.

Rax goaded me into action. I told Dravik I can control myself, but... Shame curls up my cheeks. My eyes blearily catch on things in the room—a dresser, the dog, the faint outline of a woman hovering behind the curtains of the window in the corner. I blink. Not a woman—just a curtain waving in the simulated breeze.

I look to Dravik. "Why does my arm still hurt so much?"

He stands and comes closer to my bedside. "You dislocated it."

I watch as he leans his cane against the marble wall and reaches his hand for mine. "I told you not to touch me."

"I have to, Synali."

"To fix it?"

He looks at Quilliam, and the manservant wordlessly takes a step back. Dravik grips my hand, and as dosed as I am, I can't fight it, the feeling of skin on skin like a thousand tingling needles.

"No," he says simply and braces his other hand against my shoulder. I see *white*. He does *something*, and the pain pierces through even the tranq, a hot line of agony slicing across my forearm. I look down and gape silently—a massive red-blue bruise bulging under my skin, something hard sticking up the wrong way beneath it. Dravik's gaze is lifeless and lukewarm as he speaks.

"To break it."

For a week afterward, I think Dravik broke my arm as punishment: punishment for losing control, for not resting, for engaging Rax when I shouldn't have. My right hand is my dominant hand—everything I could do before crumbles in the after. Going to the toilet becomes more complicated. Bathing myself becomes harder. I spill and drop and break so many cups and plates. The simple act of eating with a spoon is mind-numbingly frustrating with my left hand, and Dravik watching me expectantly only makes it worse. He's just like the nobles in the brothel, like Father—breaking things because they displeased him. Just because he can.

"What, not neat enough for you?" I bite out at his glances over breakfast, every inch of my skin hot and my heart beating a furious rhythm in my chest. "You fucking did this to me."

Dravik focuses back on his newspaper. "Have you looked over the schedule for today?"

I slam my good hand on the table and stand. "You're a sadistic little prick just like the rest of them! I never should have trusted you!"

"If I were you, I'd be more careful with that," he says lightly and nods at my hand. "Considering it's the last one you have."

I grip my fork so hard, it grinds against finger bones, but somewhere between white-hot rage and embarrassment, I catch myself. That wasn't concern, it was a threat; he could break my other arm just as easily if I displease him again.

I feel like a child; out of control, unsafe. I made the mistake of trusting him even once. He's not my friend—he's my business partner. We're using each other. He's my best chance at destroying House Hauteclare. He's put-together at all times, patient, calculating, and I'm...*unraveling*.

Where is the cold girl who did whatever it took?

With my injured arm, the only cleaning I can do around the manor is dusting, and I'm not as fast at hiding when someone approaches. Quilliam catches me for the first time in the east wing's library—filled with real paper books and the scent of time. I ferret the duster away behind my back, but too late—his smile wrinkles even his bushy white brows.

"You are not required by the contract to aid me in chores, miss."

I scoff. "I know."

Quilliam smiles brighter, then silently toddles off.

Bit by bit, my sloppy eating becomes neater. I develop ways around my own left-hand inexperience, fingers in strange places, different muscles clenching. Riding is miserable—without being able to move one arm, my balance in the saddle is completely thrown off. The silver spirals congregate around my cast as if they're curious about my injury.

"I'm fine," I snap at them. "Little pests."

Like the sadistic noble he is, Dravik makes me practice the lance for the first time with my left hand—the weapon materializing as one silver length out of Heavenbreaker's palm when I think *weapon*. The knife in Father's back, in my collarbone. The knife across Mother's throat.

"You will attempt to strike the stationary dummy at the opposite end of the tilt," Dravik says through my intercom.

I close comms and snark to myself, "Will I?" Talking back to him doesn't feel safe anymore.

I glare at the fresh new dummy in the distance, its blank face cold and its stiff arms holding a massive flashing hard-light target against its chest. I grip the lance, my left fingers feeling thick and awkward. I lean against the tilt, the magnetics holding Heavenbreaker and me in place. The cockpit walls catch my eye—it's cleaner. The pit crew I've never met must've gotten paid last night.

"On my signal," Dravik announces. "Three, two, one—"

Go.

Heavenbreaker's jets burst to life, and we shoot off the tilt faster than ever before—smoother, easier, but I struggle to maintain it. I can't flex my right arm to resist the g-forces, and it's like gravity *knows* it, pulling at my right side with a fierceness and wobbling Heavenbreaker on its axis. The lance is so heavy, the extra ballast near overwhelming. It feels like I could capsize at any time—flip, lose control, and spin helplessly off into open space until my jets realign. A thing shot into space has no resistance; it just keeps *going*.

Terror grips me in sweat and panting, in the idea of crashing into a substation or being pulled down into Esther's orbit and burning to cinder. This arena is for real riders; the safety barriers only catch what's roughly parallel to the tilt. *Rax*, I think. *Like him*. Like Father's clips, like Mirelle Ashadi-Hauteclare's clips. Like the best of the best, I must remain still in the center of chaos and control. I am the one who makes every motion in the steed.

But this time, the steed makes a motion for me.

I feel something click into place inside me—*in my bones*—and like a tranquilizer dream or a controlling puppet hand, my spine readjusts into a backward lean. Not like Rax, not as true and strong, but enough that the lance feels easier to hold. My right side doesn't drag so heavily in this position. Ghostwinder never moved for me…but I wasn't in it very long. This is normal, surely, no matter how abnormal it feels.

The dummy nears. Close, *closer*, the hard-light target like a shining orange beacon trying to swallow the universe. My eyes strain against the light, my clumsy left hand grips the lance, and I pull back against the impossible gravity. I aim. I fight the weight of the tip with the weight of the handle. Imperfect balance. There's no way. There's no way I'll ever—with my right hand, maybe, *maybe*, but this…

Impact happens in a blink. Less.

I thrust.

Like every tense moment in my life, time stretches at the last second, and I see the lance hit. Scrape, really, against the very outside of the target—orange pixels scatter into space like broken water. Heavenbreaker passes the dummy, sailing onto the opposite side of the tilt.

I did it.

"I did it!" I shriek, the momentum only letting half my sounds out. Something like pride balloons in my chest…and I slip. I fall off the razor's edge between focus and unfocus, and the posture Heavenbreaker put me in collapses. The horrifying sound of metal keening and jets sputtering echoes in the cockpit.

I manage one word before the capsize.

"Shit."

The world explodes in chaos; up is down, stars and darkness whirl around each other, flashes of red and orange and green melt into one nauseating spiral as my organs drop and fall and drop again, and faintly I'm reminded of the reboot, when the thing in the saddle went inside me—spinning with no direction, propelled infinitely forward. *Jets*, **jets**, but I can't hold on to one word for long when my brain suffocates on its own heaviness. Waves of unconsciousness and consciousness weave together, and in one moment of lucidity I remember Dravik's lesson:

"A capsize is most dangerous because very few riders can regain control. A rider is only human, and space is not kind to our kind."

Why did he send me out with a broken arm if he knew the dangers? Does he want me to die? Maybe. Maybe he hates me. I hate him, too. Doesn't matter how patient he is—he hurt me.

"Syn—"

The comm rings in my ear faintly.

"synali"

My name is clear the second time—that faint, soft voice as crisp as if it was speaking in a completely silent room. I black out. Black in. Black out again. Space is everywhere, and it goes on forever, and I'm lost to it, panic like ice freezing my heart still. I can't hold on to a coherent thought, let alone a riding thought.

And then…*light.*

Shining bronze light fills my fluttering eyes… Plasma trails. *Whose?* I feel an arm grasping for me, missing, grasping again, and then the drag of my brain against my skull as all momentum slows, then stops. A noble emblem of a bronze stag solidifies in my vision, printed on a deep green-blue shellac. A breathless voice reverberates in my comms.

"Hello? You all right in there?"

I blink until the stars settle. Heavenbreaker *feels* right side up, a pressure crushed against my chest as if someone's holding me to theirs. Another steed clasps me tight—sleek blue-green armor; their helmet is slender, but the brass-brushed antler decorations jutting out from the sides are far more impressive. The nausea makes it impossible to speak as the hologram of the rider in a blue-green suit and helmet connects to my comms.

"That was a pretty impressive capsize." The voice chuckles—an older man, older than Dravik and warmer than him, too. "Let's get you back to the arena, shall we?"

"Who—" I swallow. "Who are you?"

"Sevrith." Dravik's voice reconnects. "Kindly unhand my charge."

"Gladly, old friend." The rider named Sevrith chuckles again. "Just as soon as you tell me why you're sending an inexperienced rider onto the practice tilt."

There's a silence. How does Dravik know this man? And why was he so close to the practice arena in his steed? I didn't see another hangar open in the launchpad—so was he riding around in open space? Riders aren't supposed to ride if it isn't for practice or a match.

"Bring her to the launchpad, Sevrith," Dravik insists and then cuts comms.

Sevrith turns his steed's helmet to look at me properly. "Sorry about him, kid. He hasn't changed much—still ornery and secretive. Always talking about his dreams and plans."

These two *definitely* know each other. My stomach still heaves, and I'm too afraid to open my mouth lest I vomit. I'm too sick to wrench myself out of his arms. Sevrith's jets kick on, and we make our way back toward the ring of red light that is the arena.

"Is Dravik training you to be his rider? That'd be strange—I thought he left the noble life behind a long time ago."

Sevrith speaks informally for a noble—like Rax. Dravik *left* the noble life behind? Can one even do that? *Why?* It's a life full of privilege and comfort.

Sevrith pauses. "Recessive-hand training is always tough. From what I saw, you were managing it pretty well."

I frown. "*Recessive-hand training?* What do you mean?"

"Well…you know. All riders are ambidextrous—hard to switch lance hands without it."

A gnawing dread picks at the back of my brain, working its way into my arm's cast.

Sevrith laughs and recites, "*Can't have right without switching the fight!* Surprised he's still got you training on the left. I guess you didn't do too well with the ambi class at the academy, then? I get it—those fake casts they put your good arm in get real annoying after year four."

All the clips I've studied flash through my dizzy mind at once; *they all switch hands.* Every single one of the riders switched hands when the gravgen pulled them into the infinity-symbol loop of the second and third round. You *have* to switch the lance to your other hand when you circle in the other direction, or hitting the enemy becomes near impossible.

It was right in front of me the whole time. *Every rider is ambidextrous.*

There's a "class" for it, for years. That's why Dravik broke my arm. Not to be cruel, not to hurt me: to help me. To train me like a real rider—a real knight capable of winning—but faster. The sloppy soup spoons, dropping things, all of it.

It helps me learn faster.

Dravik waits for us at the end of the launchpad tunnel, his cane glinting silver and his eyes shadowed. Sevrith walks behind me, helmet still on, but I take mine off and speed my pace to Dravik until I'm jogging. He takes slow cane-steps toward me. I come to a stop in front of him. His face is unreadable. Heavenbreaker shadows us, lying flat in the clear, massive vacuum tube looming outside the tunnel walls.

"I'm sorry," I blurt.

"It's all right," he says instantly. "It's fine. As long as you're…" His throat bobs, and he turns his back as Sevrith draws closer. "We should go."

For the first time, I follow him without hesitation. Sevrith calls out from behind us, his voice clear and visor-less, "I don't know what you're doing, Drav, but leave the kid out of it."

For once, Dravik retorts instead of ignoring, and that's how I know they must've been very good friends. "Your concern has been noted, Sev."

Our footsteps echo. The cold steel hallways of the practice arena turn into a noble-friendly foyer—white marble floors and grav-fountains and lush potted plants. The attendant behind the counter bows at us as we leave through the sliding doors. We wait on the highway stop for the hovercarriage to pull through, the Station spinning in the distance beyond the clear tube wall. The many orange spokes of the hard-light highways fetter the Station to its outer ring like a beast.

"You've done very well," Dravik says softly. "It's a difficult thing to hit a target on the first—"

"Why didn't you tell me about the purpose of breaking my arm?"

The orange hard-light glow illuminates his pale face from below.

"I think, in the end, it is perhaps better you consider me a villain."

We watch the stars turn across space-time. We've both lost our mothers. He is not them. I am not them. Whatever happens next, we must move in the same direction, until the day he brings me rest.

I look over at Dravik and smile.

"I suppose we'll be villains together, then."

14. Purgo

purgō ~āre ~āuī ~ātum, *tr.*
1. to clean
2. to purge

ONE MONTH LATER

I clutch an elaborate diamond pendant in my fist and study the skin there. I'm covered in stronger tendons and veins and scars. My fingernails no longer have ridges in them—nutrients and rest. My right arm feels freer without the cast, but the nanomachine scars are still bright and red and small as rice grains. My biceps feel stronger, flexing with muscle as I reach up with the pendant and gouge it into the marble wall. Not tally marks this time.

Targets.

White dust flirts with the hem of my blue silk dress, the robot-dog biting at the speckles uselessly. I reach down and pet its head. "Don't waste your energy, little one."

The dog barks joyfully and wags its tail.

When I'm done carving, I stand back and look at the seven circles etched in the marble wall of my bedroom—one for each fight I must win in the Supernova Cup. One for each member of a family I've never known who must die.

God made the universe in seven days, and I will unmake it in seven people.

The sniffing coming down the hall gives Quilliam away before his knock on my door ever does. "Miss? The master wishes to know if you're ready."

I close the last clasp on my bodice and look up.

"I've been ready for a long time, Quilliam."

The Supernova Cup only comes once a decade, and it is an *event*.

Nova-King Ressinimus throws a great banquet the week before the Cup begins to welcome all qualifying Houses and their riders, and no participant is exempt. I stare out the hovercarriage window, the highway slicing vermillion through the air, noble manses flashing below us in glass and marble. The royal palace rests on the very top of the noble spire as a sprawling whitewood manse on a flat green disc, waterfalls arcing over the lip and shrouding the spiretop in a fine mist. Dozens of brightly colored noble hovercarriages helix above it, orbiting like a miniature solar system as they wait for permission to land.

"Have any of the seven Hauteclares seen my face before?" I ask Dravik. He sits across from me in a fancy silver breast coat.

"I highly doubt it. Unless you showed Rax your face and he blurted a description of you out somewhere."

"As if I'd show him anything but the door," I scoff.

Dravik's smile barely pulls the corners of his lips. "A good attitude to keep."

The carriage eventually touches down and opens its doors to pleasant laughter. I step out, and the stares at my silver-blue dress are instant. Whispers swirl nearly louder than the jets on the landing pad. A futile longing hits me for the robot-dog—I miss its judgment-less sapphire eyes, its tinny bark when it tries to protect me from the dangers of dust motes and shadows. I hold Mother's pendant tight.

Dravik turns around and offers me his blue-silk arm. The silver tassels of his epaulets catch sunlight as he smiles.

"I know touch is difficult for you, but mayhap this once? As a show of solidarity."

I side-eye the nobles traipsing around us out of their own carriages. Rich. Powerful. Dangerous. They narrow their eyes at the powder blue and silver of our garments like they're unexpected dirt, filth. Something is different about House Lithroi, and the nobles seem to know it. He and I are few, and they are many.

I reach my hand out and place it on his arm.

We walk over the greenest grass I've ever seen, soft as cotton and waving in a manufactured wind. It's like a dream I would've had as a little girl after reading about Earth's bounty for the first time: manicured hedges, rows of rich dirt brimming with lush flowers and fresh vegetables and even a gargantuan creaking tree of *redwood*. Its bark is rough and its trunk the width of ten men, and it sends shivers up my spine—Earth once had millions of these. Earth was big enough, verdant enough, that a million of these could live unimpeded. It's beneath this grand red tree that the banquet lies, neat tables crowded in rainbow as the nobles congregate by House colors. Sparkling gems, bright holographic lace and feathers in hats, sparkling liquid in glasses—everything sparkles, but all I can see is the gleam of teeth.

"Aha, Drav!"

Dravik stops and I stop, and we turn to face the voice. Sevrith. He cuts an impressive presence out of a rider's suit, wiry muscles cording beneath his bronze-trimmed celadon tunic. I was right; he's older than Dravik by maybe ten, fifteen years. Time plays havoc with the crow's feet around his dark eyes and velvet mouth, and his black hair pulls back in a regal half ponytail.

"Sevrith." Dravik makes a bow, and I do as well. For some reason, clear panic shatters Sevrith's face at this, but then he melts into his own bow deeper than either of ours. When he comes up, he aims a searingly white smile at me.

"So—you're the kid, then? Good to finally meet you face-to-face."

I already know his face—I've been studying him in the database. Sevrith cu Freynille is a good rider in his own right but more famous for being a heartthrob twenty years ago. Growing up, I saw him on Low Ward's fractured holoscreens: coffee ads, contraceptive ads. Always winking.

"Synali," I say. I sense Dravik's eyes on me as he waits for the rest of the name, as we agreed in the contract. "Synali von Hauteclare."

Sevrith's eyes light up as he motions to mine. "That explains the ice. And why Drav picked you up. You must be Farris's kid."

"What do you want, Sev?" Dravik interrupts coolly. Sevrith shakes his head.

"What, are you mad I've gotten smarter? You're punting a hornet's nest into another hornet's nest by bringing her here."

"Do you intend to stop me?" I ask.

The older man looks surprised I spoke up. His smile is warm—like Quilliam's. "No. I like a little entertainment with my food. God knows these pre-Cup banquets have been boring for far too long."

I can't bring myself to glare at him—the memory of the capsize and his help is still too fresh after a month and some. He just smiles at me, the garden party pulsing around us, and then something moves on his face…beneath his nose. A nosebleed? No—the liquid isn't dark enough to be blood. *What*—

"Sev." Dravik clears his throat and motions beneath his nose. Sevrith starts, covering his face with his hand and bowing quickly.

"If you'll excuse me. Good luck in the Cup, kid. I'm looking forward to seeing what you can do when you aren't busy capsizing."

His dark eye gives a wink before he leaves, striding across the grass.

"Is he all right?" I ask Dravik.

"That's his business. Your concern for the fate of a noble is rather out of character, Synali."

He's right. Every single noble here is a potential ally of House Hauteclare—and a potential enemy of mine. "Is he entering the Supernova Cup this year?"

Dravik nods. "Sevrith is the oldest rider in the competitive ring. The seed could very well put you together. Hopefully you will have accrued enough experience by then to overcome him."

Doubt tries to squirm its way into my brain, but I refuse it. I have done everything to win. I will do *everything* to win.

Dravik beckons me to an isolated table laid with a pale-blue banner. Servants sweep it off when we sit, the silver rabbit embroidered mid-sprint deftly slithering away. The noble ladies have a special way of moving their skirts to sit, but I can't be bothered—not when the white and gold of Hauteclare glares out from the opposite corner of the garden. Seven of them sit at their tranquil table in silk and jewels, smiling with one another when they robbed Mother of her life in cold, exacting cruelty…all because it suited them. Because it would pay for more jewels.

Control yourself. A carefully tensed body like I've learned in the steed. *Focus.*

"We're attracting attention," I say softly. Dravik chuckles.

"It's to be expected—House Lithroi is something of a forgotten relic. Pay them no mind."

I look around. A table in green and black, a table in gray and orange, a table in red and brown…House Velrayd. *Rax.* I still haven't seen his face properly. I search the sitting Velrayds one by one—he was tall, but many of the Velrayds at the table are tall. I freeze as disgust creeps over me; why am I looking for him? He's an obstacle I must overcome—nothing more.

I can't help but notice one sweet-looking girl out of the many staring—her hair bright red and her clothes forest green striped with black. Her freckles crimp when she smiles at me—a curious sort of smile. Someone curious about me, instead of furious or impassive toward me…she reminds me of Jeria—a semi-friend I made in the brothel, the only one who asked if I was alright at the end of the day. The girl's smile doesn't last, as the woman next to her raps the girl with a silk fan and she whips around to face front again.

"The Solundes," Dravik answers my unsaid question. "The girl is their rider, Yatrice."

"She's my age," I say faintly.

"She is smiling now, but the Solundes are the Hauteclares' greatest allies. When they find us threatening them, Yatrice will not hesitate to cut you down."

I inhale and focus on the king. He sits at the head of the banquet, a grand gold-and-violet robe pooling around his throne. Amethysts hang at his throat, an elaborate crown of amber beads resting on his head. His white beard is braided with redwood beads, and his eyes are a deeper green than the verdant garden. Guards armed to the last hair form a crescent around the king's raised platform. His jester strides to and fro on neon projection stilts, dissipating them every so often to jump down and joke snidely in his ear, but Nova-King Ressinimus the Third does not smile.

Father wanted so badly to be by his side, he killed for it. My existence killed Mother, but the king's existence killed her, too.

"Who *is* that, I wonder?" Dravik asks coyly.

I sneer. *"His Exalted Majesty."*

"Ah, yes. Though…I called him something else, once."

My brow quirks. "And that was?"

Just then, the king's green eyes move to our table, and Dravik returns the stare in a way I've never seen from him before—completely void. Not a single scrap of emotion remains on Dravik's face. No more placidity or calmness.

Just…*emptiness*. Emptiness like a *weapon*.

Looking back, I should've known. I should've known the moment Dravik brought me into his manse, the moment I saw his iris surgery scars—the portrait of the boy with green eyes—the moment he manipulated the guards in my favor. I should've known a million moments before, but it only falls into place when Dravik's easy expression vanishes from his face, replaced with that razor in darkness.

"Father."

My head feels rusted as it turns to look at him.

To look at a prince.

15. Fulmen

fulmen ~inis, *n.*
1. lightning

"She's cute." Yavn von Velrayd elbows his cousin and points at the far table in pale blue and silver.

Rax Istra-Velrayd is really too tired to support his cousin's flirtations—no sleep this week. The nightmares have been bad lately. They've been with him since he turned ten or so, waking him at odd hours with their violently hyper-specific nonsense, but only recently have they gotten so much worse. He strains his neck to see over the courtly crowd anyway, curious, and his heart beats one moment and stills the next. The girl in the blue-and-silver dress makes the world fade, the faces all around her smearing to blurs. His cousin's a fool—*cute* isn't enough for what she is; black hair shorn tight and clean beneath her ears, no halo on her sharp brow, and her eyes bluer than the fake noble-spire sky—as the sky must've been when it was *real*. But what really takes his breath away is how she holds herself: laser-focused and bowstring-tight, like something wild, feral.

No—he corrects himself sternly—*like something hunting.*

Yavn pours himself more wine. "Those are red pox pockmarks on her cheeks. Did you know forty percent of the commoner children die from it? Guess she was one of the lucky ones."

Rax looks at him finally. "You know that off the top of your head?"

His cousin shrugs. "What can I say? I'm the type to care about my fellow man."

Pockmarks pit her cheeks here and there, but it's the circular tangle of flesh at her collarbone that draws Rax's eye most—lighter, long healed, but not very old.

Rax knows scars. He knows how they bruise, scab, heal, how they look at every stage, and he knows best of all how they're removed. Her collarbone scar is from hard-light—cauterized, forceful, angular like a blade. She wears the colors of a noble House like the rest of them but hasn't gone to a clinic to remove her scars? She doesn't even hide them with makeup or her dress—the collar dips low across her shoulders. She's the only one here unsmooth, the only one staring not at someone else around her but ahead. Odd. *Terrifying.* Maybe that's why looking at her feels like electrocution, like the saddle sending down its handshake too strong.

"What House—"

"Lithroi," Yavn answers smoothly. "I think. I remember Father talking about their silver—unmistakable in the way it shines."

Shining silver. That silver steed, the girl's voice in it, her hands tearing the dummy apart as if she were a merciless black hole or some rabid beast... He hasn't been able to forget that day for even a second. The sound of her ragged, triumphant voice taunting him has haunted his every ride since then and every shower afterward.

It's *her.*

The way she threw everything into one lunge with complete disregard for her own safety, like she was dying, like she wanted to *die*... It was unnatural. It went against everything the academy taught, everything he'd lived by in the saddle. She rode *wrong*, and yet watching it had felt strangely *right*, like music arranged in a way he'd never considered before. The rider in him starts screaming to fight her. Begging. *Just once.* The chance to see more of her, the strange new things she would do against him, how long he could toy with her before she broke, or he broke, or they both broke together—

She looks his way, icy eyes cutting across the crowd, but doesn't notice him. Every cell in Rax stands at attention when her gaze nears and falls like a wave when it leaves. He recovers with a wrenching effort.

"Not her, Yavn. Not in your wildest dreams."

"But in yours, obviously," Yavn argues, smirking. "Hey, with any luck she'll be a rider."

Rax snorts, the words running through his head too shaky to leave his mouth.

That's what I'm afraid of.

16. Indico

indicō ~āre ~āuī ~ātum, *tr.*
1. to make known, point out

"Y ou're the prince."

"Former prince," Dravik corrects me softly. "My mother was Queen Astrix vel Lithroi."

Astrix. The shutdown command for the robot dog…and his mother's name.

My brain works numbly; rumors of the queen's death circulated in Low Ward when I was a child. I vaguely remember fragments—Mother's friends coming over to whisper about a queen who *lost her nobility* and was *executed for treason.* She never had a public funeral. School shut down for the day. Neighbors blamed the rising price of bread on her death. I never heard what happened to the prince, but I knew he existed, like a distant star.

"I didn't know princes could lose their titles," I finally manage.

"They cannot, unless they give them up voluntarily."

That's what Sevrith meant when he said Dravik *left the noble life.* I stare at his soft profile, his gentle nose, the pixel scars from the surgery to hide his green eyes.

"I've had many surgeries," Dravik murmurs. "To ensure I look nothing like him. We could do the same for you, if you wish."

I catch my reflection in the tea that's been served. Thin lips, thin brows—Father's. My face has always been more his than Mother's. The idea of tearing him out from inside me for good is tempting. Mirrors wouldn't hurt so much anymore. I could look at myself with pride if I looked more like Mother.

I glance over at the white-and-gold Hauteclare table. They tried to kill me to hide their "mistake." I clear my throat.

"No. I want everyone to know who I come from."

Dravik's smile is strained but true. He said his father killed his mother. The king killed Queen Astrix? No—she was executed...but I imagine the king could very well order the execution of anyone. The new queen and the crown princess are nowhere to be seen at the banquet, but I know the queen is the sickly sort—always cloistered for her health—and the princess is still very young.

And then it hits me.

Dravik wants to get back at the king. *How* exactly, *when* exactly...none of that's clear, but *what* I am is: the pawn—the weakest piece in the game, the piece most underestimated, the piece no one sees coming. There's a game going on between the king and his son, and I've walked right into it.

But as long as we win and they lose, I will play my part.

I watch the crowd, catching many riders I've studied on the vis. Behind every face is a jumble of stats, favored maneuvers, ages and heights and weights and steed names. I must defeat at least seven of them—seven to punish the seven who killed Mother. Fortuitously, seven is the same number of matches I need to win to reach the quarterfinals—to even have a *chance* of winning it all and dissolving House Hauteclare for good.

Suddenly, a projection podium emerges from the grass just in front of the king's platform and rises up—a column for something to be displayed atop.

"It's tradition for each participating rider to give a speech at the pre-Cup banquet," Dravik clarifies.

I watch quietly. A noble girl alights on the projection podium and warns everyone she'll win. She doesn't know commoners get their throats slit in back alleys for the meager credits they earn betting on the likes of her. A noble boy gives thanks to his mother for birthing him, no matter the outcome of the Supernova Cup, but he doesn't know a commoner could keep her children alive for another month with a single gold button from his breast coat. I have but one thought, listening to them, and it's that the wolf only knows how badly the deer suffers when the tiger comes.

Mirelle Ashadi-Hauteclare finally steps onto the projection podium.

In person, she's sharper, her white-gold dress clean and bright. Her chestnut hair is kept long and luxurious, and her posture screams practiced elegance. She has Father's spine, his arrogant air. It's like he's *alive* in her.

"Mirelle Ashadi-Hauteclare—" Dravik starts.

"I know who she is."

"A very good rider, and very intelligent," he continues. "Quite prideful, but I suppose that goes without saying—the Hauteclares are all pride. She favors the tactics of the knights, honor and truth and et cetera. It shows in her matches—in my unbiased opinion, she is nothing if not dedicated, unflinching power."

"And me?" I ask. "What am I in your unbiased opinion, Your Highness?"

His smile goes sideways. "You are...*unconventional*."

"You certainly have a way of inspiring confidence."

Dravik chuckles softly. "Your enemy's greatest strength will be their weakness, too. The turtle's shell is his strength, and yet it makes him slow. The falcon's strength is his speed, but he flies too fast to see what's to the side of him. Lady Mirelle is dedicated, and that means she does not change so easily."

Inflexible, he means. It's a useful thing to know on the tilt, but there are dozens of riders standing between her and me, still.

Countless news stations flash their vis to record every speech. The riders smile brighter and declare louder and raise their chins higher—surgery, media training, all of them athletic little dolls lined up on a shelf to be ogled at, and me the newest addition. My mind starts spiraling; if I'm unlucky, the seed will pair me with Mirelle in the first round. Or worse...

The master of ceremonies introduces the next rider to thunderous applause and synth-trumpets. "Please welcome Sir Rax Istra-Velrayd!"

Someone at the Velrayd table rises: tall, bleached white-blond hair slicked back, pieces of it left loose over dark brows and redwood eyes. I still can't bring myself to look at his face for long, but his broad shoulders remain the same. He walks just like I remember—easy, slow, as if he has all the time in the world. He makes a bow to the king and steps onto the neon podium, the projection steadily rising under his crimson boots. He wears a crimson breast coat, its high collar lined with umber fur, and that grin to top it all off—free, light, *infuriating*.

"Must I bow to the king as well?" I ask Dravik. He hums idly.

"Only if you wish to. House Lithroi has earned that much, I think."

Rax Istra-Velrayd motions for the applause to quiet down, but the court ignores it, jubilant at the mere sight of him. He taps his vis to project his voice, blue glow on red silk. "Ahem, thank you. But, please—much more and we'll be here until terraform."

The crowd breaks into laughter at his pathetic joke, and he waits for them to quiet, looking in my direction. I watch only the blacklight halo painted on his proud forehead and think, *When we meet again on the tilt, that's where I'll put my lance.*

"He's one of the most talented riders we've had in a century." Dravik stirs his tea. "A formidable natural talent, some say—born with it—but I suspect it's more straightforward than that."

"Straightforward how?"

"His parents once inhabited the lowest rung of House Velrayd. The rumors say they've had him in the saddle since he was five in an attempt to raise their status through tourney. Highly frowned upon to have a child ride without first entering him in the academy, but it's not illegal. Regardless, it seems to have worked; his father was granted the title of baron by Duke Velrayd when Rax was twelve, shortly after he won the Icarus Cup."

No wonder. The idea of a five-year-old in the saddle…*I* was terrified. I can't imagine how scared he was.

Don't imagine, don't pity. He is the enemy.

"*Weakblood,*" Dravik says. "It means 'leech.' 'Hanger-on.' It's what nobles call people like Rax behind his back—far removed from the main family line and with little hope of inheriting anything of import."

"The opposite of you, then," I mutter. His laughter is made richer by the honey of the tea.

"Says the only daughter of a very powerful duke. You and I know a bastard is far worse than a weakblood."

"Why is Rax so popular if they think him a weakblood?"

"He's simply that excellent at riding. He's personable, charismatic, humorous when most nobles can't tell the difference between a joke and a distant star system. Being as handsome as he is helps, too."

I curl my lip. "What's *his* weakness, then?"

Dravik watches him over the rim of his teacup. "I'm not sure yet."

Rax finishes his speech and steps off the podium to a deluge of applause. Even the king claps, his jester doing ecstatic little flips. The excitement lasts until the master of ceremonies announces House Lithroi. The garden descends into confused glances, and murmurs choke the air quiet.

"Ah." Dravik's sunny smile defies the king's stony expression. "I believe it's your turn, Synali. Say what you will."

"*Anything?* Even the truth?"

"Especially the truth."

I rise and stride through the rows of noble-infested tables to the podium. Rax and I will pass each other in the grassy aisle. Five weeks was enough time to forget just how intimidating he is—the vis screen made him seem smaller than the towering scaffold of bone and muscle approaching me now. I keep my gaze on the king's throne. We draw even, a sizzle in the air moving ahead of him that only I seem to feel. In the redirected sun, his hair shines platinum and his dark redwood irises catch gold flakes—a futile warmth. We're too close again, too soon. Why is this making me nervous? He's just another noble.

Out of the corner of my eye, I see Rax shoot me a smile.

"See you in the arena, huh?"

My retort is instant. "Not for very long, I imagine."

We pass each other—a parting of red silk and blue silk—and then the king's green eyes are on me.

I do not bow.

Murmurs resound. The jester pretends to faint dead off his stilts, little arms over littler chest. The guards shift in their hard-light chain mail, but the king only waits, gaze riveted to my dress—the blue and silver of it. I stand on the podium, and it rises in buzzing neon. House Hauteclare watches, Mirelle sitting at their table. They all watch: the nobles, the priests, the news stations, Rax and Sevrith and Dravik. The seven who killed her. Somewhere out there on the Station, is their puppet assassin watching me, too?

I tap my vis to life. I've had time to practice what comes next.

"My name is Synali von Hauteclare. My mother's name was Gabriyll Jean Woster. She was murdered ten months ago by seven people attending this banquet."

I'm too high up to hear the impact, but I see it—stillness, hands over mouths. With those two names, they know I'm a bastard, and they know whose.

The entire court rockets their eyes to the table in white and gold, to one another, to King Ressinimus. I pull my dress farther down on my chest; stays and bra lace, but I don't care—flesh to air until it burns.

"This scar is proof: the seven murdered my mother and tried to murder me."

The crowd below me writhes, turning to one another, looking to the guards, standing up and shaking fists at me. Mirelle does not move. House Hauteclare does not move, and neither does Dravik. I can read him better now, if only in fractured increments; his eyes crinkle almost...*proudly*. Sevrith laughs and shakes his head. Rax hasn't blinked away from me once.

I will give them warning as Father never gave us.

"The seven of you have until the first round of the Supernova Cup to contact any major news outlet. You will proceed to make a public announcement on the vis admitting to your crimes in detail. If you do not do this, your lives will be forfeit."

Finally, the crowd *bursts*.

Their outrage splits the peaceful garden, and the guards have finally had enough, laser sights prickling on my skin, but I came expecting resistance—Dravik brought me here expecting resistance. He never warned me off any of it—he told me to say the truth. For a bare second, fear roars in my ears; if they shoot me now, it's over. Everything I worked for. Everything I suffered through.

My eyes slide to the former prince—*you wouldn't bring me here just to die, would you?*

A bead of sweat carves its way down Dravik's soft temple. He is not a man who sweats or cries or spits. He is contained, and yet his lips now move in a word long familiar to me, carved on my eardrums by the drone of relentless training...

"*Hold.*"

The true meaning of words was something I took for granted before him, before riding Heavenbreaker. To hold means to be patient—to wait when all you want to do is run. Endure until it's too late.

Hold, even as the universe tries to tear you apart.

−8. Exosso

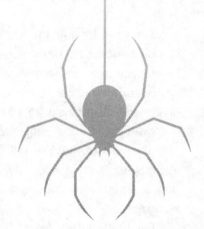

exossō ~āre ~āuī ~ātum, *tr.*
1. to remove the bones from

Through the cacophony of dancing and inebriated laughter, a holoscreen flickers above a sofa. The dust-addled man watching it snores soundly; the face of a girl with short black hair and determined ice eyes stares out at the dust den.

Rain stops in his tracks. The lights of the den flicker, though the inebriated patrons barely move in response. The smallish man in robes leading him to meet with the proprietor stops as well, his brow shooting up.

"Is something the matter, sir? It was simply one of the usual power flickers."

Rain can't look away from the girl's ice eyes. The robed man chuckles.

"Do you know her? Would you be interested in a meeting?" The vis then flickers and the camera pulls out to show the king's banquet, and the man sighs. "Ah, she's a noble. Apologies, sir—I must retract the offer."

Rain catches his reflection in a bronzed mirror and pulls his cowl farther up his face. Somewhere between slitting that mother's throat and raising the dagger to stab the daughter, he'd looked into the girl's eyes. She had his eyes, *exactly*, without any surgery scars in them, and for a moment it felt as if he was meeting another Spider in the Web, another of his brothers and sisters. His instinct overrode all logic; *could* they be blood? The Web had raised him with loyalty to his family, to those who were bound to him in this life, and he loved them more than anything. The idea of a blood family has always haunted his dreams, and there she had been—either a supremely coincidental genetic rarity or a dear part of him he'd wondered about for so long.

She'd made it, somehow, to the Nova-King's court. Rain was an assassin for a noble House, and she must've known they tried to kill her—so why return to the lion's den? Why not simply flee or hide? She would be competing in the Supernova Cup as a rider for a noble House, but for what purpose? He could not help the worry suddenly consuming him. Riding was dangerous, but the world of the nobility more so…

Rain looks up at the man and shakes his head. "Let us continue."

The man leads him through the room of languishing bodies and soft pillows, finally stopping to knock on a fine wooden door. There is a pause, the man bouncing on his heels anticipatorily.

"The boss is pleased you are willing to accept his proposal, sir—we've been forced to employ the common corporate-wetwork sorts. It's been many months since we had a man of such…*skill* in our employ."

A voice reverberates from inside the door. "Come in."

The man leads Rain into a decadent office—fine rugs and wooden shelves and great green crystalline chunks of unground dust scattered across a metal desk. The boss sits behind it, a gruff man in silks and a mercenary-mannered smile, and his bodyguards sit behind him: two on the wall, two at the door, hard-light swords and pistols bulging beneath their tunics. They took Rain's weapons at the entrance and yet supplied him with so many right here.

"The Spider's Hand at last." The proprietor motions for Rain to sit. "Please, make yourself comfortable."

And so Rain does—many times over, and with many different bloodstains, until the fine rug beneath the doorway soaks red.

17. Gravo

gravō ~āre ~āuī ~ātum, *tr.*
1. to burden, weigh down
2. to oppress or overpower

"*H*old."

King Ressinimus's voice bites down on the court's throat, and the sounds of outrage die cleanly. The guards lower their guns, the sea of red laser sights on my skin sinking as the king rises from the throne, a dour-faced pillar of gold and purple silk.

"The Great War Treaty of 3067 states the following." His voice is measured. "*A rider's personal vendetta is ratified by the knightly code of honor—chivalrie—and will not be impeded or punished for as long as they continue to ride.*"

I don't know treaties or codes, but I know a threat when I hear one: *as long as they continue to ride.*

"*Will you ride?*" hangs in the air, in the emerald stare from the man who rules the Station, whose family has *always* ruled the Station. I lift my chin.

"I will be riding in the Supernova Cup for House Lithroi."

Another ripple tears through the court, the Lithroi table the only one absolutely still, Dravik the only one smiling. He knew about this treaty. Of course he knew—he'd never send me into a situation we could not turn to our advantage.

Getting off the podium is far more terrifying than walking onto it—the path back to Dravik's table is suddenly lined with a thousand burning eyes. I manage to make it without anyone grabbing for me—such is the "breeding" and "manners" of the nobility, and for once I'm glad of it. They cannot rip my face off. They can only *appear* to *want* to rip my face off.

Dravik smiles when I sit down. "You did well."

"I did what you wanted me to," I counter.

"Is that not what I said?" His smile crooks, and his eyes wander over my shoulder. "Ah, it seems you've garnered even the church's attention."

I glance to where he's looking—a veiled woman with inky floor-length hair speaks lowly to three priests in white-and-red robes. Her dress is pale pink with a fog of cream lace that drapes over her body with ease. The woman is subtle about looking our way through her long lashes, but the priests are not.

"Talize san Michel," Dravik says. "A good rider but a far superior businesswoman. She is very devout, and she develops drugs for the nobility's recreational use on the side."

I snort. "Hypocrite."

"I'd gather that is rather the point of the church, Synali; to be a hypocrite means perhaps to one day be saved."

"Will the church be a problem?"

His smile widens. "Only if our enemies manage to make as many friends among the priesthood as I have."

The servants whirl in with trays of food then. I can feel dozens of eyes on me as I pick at roasted fish and brandy boar and fruit pastries clearly designed to impress. I can't taste any of it. Every candied cherry and gold leaf flake is a reminder of everyone I knew in Low Ward starving. The adrenaline of everyone in this garden watching me is making me nauseous.

"Dravik, where are the—"

He points to a miniature hedge maze. "Be careful. The guards can only see so much, and you now have a target on your back."

"Thank you for the reminder," I drawl as I stand. "Believe it or not, that made my nausea *worse*."

Dravik smiles into his teacup. I fiddle my way through the hedge maze and manage to unlock the hard-light watershed. The darkened orange light obscures the world outside and cuts out all sound. Two gold-etched stalls stand side by side, and I let out a sigh of relief when I realize they're both empty. Cold water against my face doesn't work in slowing my heart. I pull Mother's pendant out and rub my thumb over it desperately.

"Don't turn cowardly now," I whisper into the mirror, into the reflection of my chest scar. Seven circles. Seven matches. I can do this. They can intimidate me all they like—it will not change their fate.

I walk out of the watershed and freeze.

In front of it, in the long, lush grass, a pair of imprints lingers. *Footprints*. They look as if someone was standing barefooted, watching the watershed for a long while—the grass is indented and dark. But there are no footprints leading to the stance. Or away. No sign of life anywhere. My body goes cold.

"synali"

That soft, faint voice—the one I hear in the saddle. I hear it now, deep in my ears as if it's coming from inside me. Like a thought. Like a saddle-thought of *go* or *more* or *turn*.

"Hello?" I try.

The footprints lift, as if an invisible someone is moving, and the grass bends around new footprints as they walk off into the hedge. At the same moment, three young men in orange breast coats trimmed in ash gray round the hedge corner toward me.

My heart jumps into my throat and then settles. *Real* people. Not ghosts or hallucinations. I'm almost grateful for their sudden presence. If Dravik was with me, he'd tell me who they are, but my best guess is one, noble, and two, here to hurt me, if their grins as they swagger over are any indication. The middle one is obviously the leader—a gargantuan specimen of a noble with hands like shovels and hair like the center of a holocandle.

"Oho, who do we have here, boys?" The middle one guffaws. I stand ground—running is pointless against bullies. They quickly surround me, cutting off any escape.

"My name is Synali von Hauteclare." I make my words clear. "And yours?"

The middle one scoffs. "That's not how this works, little bastard. You don't get the privilege of me telling you my name."

"Make her lick your boots, Olric." The left noble snickers. A laugh bursts from me at how juvenile the idea is. The three of them go still, and the middle one drops his posture.

"What's so funny, bastard?"

"I've licked boots before, you know. It's not all bad." His two accomplices frown, but I smile brighter. "Is this all you brought? I'm used to far more men beating on me at once. Far meaner ones, too."

A hard yank on my collar pulls me into Olric and up, my feet dangling and my smile fading. He's at least six-five, maybe six-six, and every muscle is now evident. *A rider.* I thought they were all spoiled nobles without any real training… I didn't know— I can't breathe. If I were taller I could reach for his eyes, but he keeps me so far I can't even kick—

The sound of a hard-light pistol safety cocking back is unmistakable, and a cool voice emanates from somewhere behind Olric. "Put her down."

He curls his lip. *"Mirelle."*

I swallow lumps—Mirelle? Ashadi-Hauteclare? Saving *me*?

"Oh? I wasn't aware we were on first-name terms, Olric. I assumed that after the defeat I handed you in the Chrysanthemum Qualifier, you would know better."

Her words are icy. A bead of sweat condenses on Olric's massive forehead as he asks, "How did you get a gun in?"

"Oh, Olric. Always needing things to be spelled out for you. Whose family do you think trains these guards? Four of them are waiting just outside for you."

His two accomplices let out sudden yelps and scatter into the hedge. My collar cuts into my spine, and just as I start seeing stars, Olric releases me. My boots hit grass again, and I massage my neck as I watch him saunter into the maze, girth barely scraping through the greenery. And then…we're alone. Mirelle Ashadi-Hauteclare stands in front of me. Like Rax, she's even more *her* close up, like a pristine statue of a saint. She tucks her hard-light pistol into a holster on her impeccably white breeches and fixes me with a golden stare.

"So."

"S-So?" I croak. "Why put it a-away? Sh-Shoot me now. I'm going to destroy House Hauteclare."

The noise she makes is neither a laugh nor a scoff but something icier. Less caring. Like the noises Father made. She's so much like Father that my body trembles just being around her—his same nose, his same…*aura*. She flicks her sheet of silky hair behind her.

"You truly understand nothing, pretender."

"Then explain it to me."

"Nobles don't announce when they're going to kill each other," she says slowly, as if I'm a toddler. "They plan for it and stay quiet about it. Your little display today was an obvious bluff. The only thing you accomplished was making a fool of yourself and your defunct House."

"Then why did you just save me?" I demand. "Why not let them beat me?"

"Because," she says simply. "The Westrianis are unrestrained brutes. And a knight does not stand by and watch the defenseless suffer."

It's my turn to laugh. "You think me defenseless? And yourself a knight?"

Her golden eyes go hard. "I'm more knight than you, liar."

I stare at her, and she at me. We are both each other's enemies, and we are both each other's blood. I walk past her and to the hedge exit, pausing once before the green.

"Whatever you think of me, I'm not a liar—my father *was* Farris von Hauteclare. I will destroy our House, and our family will die."

This time, she smiles—crystal-covered and sharp.

"Let us meet on the field, then, and decide that for ourselves."

Post-banquet, the entire court lines up to say farewell to the king.

Dravik is mysteriously absent, leaving me the only Lithroi in the two long lines of nobles standing at attention on the grass. They bow and curtsey as the king passes, his violet train dragging long, and then it stops…in front of *me*. Nova-King Ressinimus pauses just before me with the excuse of waiting for his jester to catch up. He fixes his stony expression straight ahead, like a man used to looking above crowds.

"You're certain you'll compete," King Ressinimus says. In Heavenbreaker's saddle, I've learned words have so many more meanings beneath the surface, and his sizzle. *You're certain you wish to kill seven members of my court?*

"Yes," I say. There's a silence, the jester's bells growing closer. "You could stop me."

"No," he exhales softly. "If you are who you say you are, then they must deal with you, not I."

"But…I'm going to kill them," I insist. "They're your court, and you—"

His age shows when he finally looks down his nose at me, all lines and sunspots that his regal makeup barely hides. "I will not stop you, Synali von Hauteclare."

My throat goes dry. *"Why?"*

"Because long ago he gave me his warning, too. And I did not listen."

The jester catches up, and then the king sweeps away. He alights in his grand violet hovercarriage adorned with a snarling dragon, gold claws curled over its vents, and is gone.

"He gave me his warning, too."

He slips to my side when the nobles finally disperse. *He* slides into the silver Lithroi hovercarriage when it floats down to the landing zone to take us back to Moonlight's End. *He* doesn't speak until the palace is a shrunken thing through the back window.

"You did well, stonewalling Rax. And I heard the Westrianis were chased away from you by Lady Mirelle."

I ignore him. "Where were you when we were saying goodbye to the king? You left me on my own."

Dravik smiles. "I knew you could handle it."

"He spoke to me. He said he wouldn't stop me."

"The treaty he cited today was a post-War treaty, but there are pre-War treaties, too. The king cannot stop a bastard from riding. If he tried, he'd be calling the pre-War treaty into question and therefore calling every other pre-War treaty into question—including the one that certifies the Ressinimuses' right to rule. It would be opening the floodgates leading to civil war. And he knew this."

"So we used his greatest strength against him—the court."

Dravik's eyes glimmer—that proud look again. "Indeed. Humanity could not be choosy in the War about who rode and who didn't; if a rider wishes to ride—and they have access to a steed—they cannot legally be kept from the tilt, no matter their lineage or status."

"But no commoners or bastards have ridden post-War," I argue. "Or the vis would've been buzzing about it."

"Naturally—the nobles ensure the steedcraft industry is highly regulated in their favor, and all pre-War treaties are kept under lock and key. Commoners don't even know riding is an option. Bastards might, but they're murdered before they can attempt it. Occasionally, they're exiled to various substations to do back-breaking labor until their spirits die—or they do. Of their injuries, of course—no foul play involved."

His smile doesn't falter. I glance at his cane, the sapphires glimmering differently against his injured knee.

"That still doesn't explain why the king let my death threats slide," I insist.

"With no enemy to fight, an army often turns on itself. The court is no exception. In order to keep post-War peace among the various Houses, riders were granted special privileges; as long as a rider participates in a tourney, whatever 'disagreement' they have with another House is allowed. It's a duel by another name—if one House is not strong enough to meet the other on the field and defeat them, they're considered weak and therefore must deserve whatever fate befalls them."

"So?"

"So the king cannot touch you, and neither can the court. This doesn't mean they won't try, but that's why I'm here."

"I can protect myself," I blurt. He smiles.

"I know. You have been for a long while, now."

My chest winds tight and strange beneath my scar. Dravik presses on.

"Every other House will be looking at House Hauteclare to confirm or deny your bastard blood—if they confirm it, the king could strip their privileges, or better yet declare their House status null and void, erasing their nobility and disbanding them forever."

Forever. The way it rolls off his tongue tastes like golden-fruit hope, *real* hope.

"The king hates murdering worthless commoners that much?"

"No—but if the truth comes out in a public way, Duke Hauteclare's murder will be seen as a failing on House Hauteclare's part; that they couldn't control their secrets—or their bastards—well enough and therefore suffered the consequences. Again, 'twould be seen as weak, unfit. And weakness is the one thing not permitted in the Nova-King's court."

"So they'd be forgiven for killing me but not for letting me live."

His smile warms. "Precisely."

The hovercarriage passes a wasteful water fountain, the spray glinting rainbow in the simulated moonlight emanating from the round, pale hologram high above the noble spire. I feel sick—pastry and acid and the burn of the past rise like molten foam. Push it down. Move forward. This banquet was nothing but window dressing for the real thing—a pretty curtain for the imminent bloodbath. They've met me, and I've met them. They know more than me. They've won more than me. How many rounds can I even win before I inevitably lose? I've tossed and turned over that question—two? Three? I want all seven people to die. I want all seven wins. I want to win the Supernova Cup and destroy House Hauteclare forever, but if I lose even once, that will not happen.

"Even if I fail, you'll uphold the contract?" I ask the prince. "You'll give me rest?"

"You won't fail, Synali."

"Even if I fail, you'll give me rest?" I repeat, stronger. Dravik's gray eyes catch moonlight, melting.

"Yes."

The hovercarriage deposits us back at the Lithroi manse, and the moment I walk in, the robot-dog rushes over to greet us, tail wagging. Dravik ignores it, but I bend.

"Hello, little one."

Its sapphire eyes gleam up at me with simulated happiness. I stand and heel-click through the halls to the bunker door, shedding my stuffy dress and ribbons as I go. Seeing Mirelle and Rax up close has me convinced—I need to get as much practice in as I can before the Cup starts.

The cold air of Moonlight's End feels less strange on my skin these days, as if I've grown used to its grave stillness. My bare feet pad on the subzero marble. Quilliam bows as I pass, gaunt body creaking and his eyes respectfully on the floor. My practice rider's suit waits on a nearby hook, gray and colorless and imprinted with my shape, with near three-months' worth of sweat and blood. A tap on the suit cuffs and the leather-like material ripples to my naked skin instantly, sealing shut up the spine with a dry hiss.

I step out to see Dravik waiting at the bunker door, the dog at his heels.

"Does it have a name?" I ask, nodding at the robot.

"No." His word rings hard. The pearl, the sapphires, the childish laser artwork—I can see now that it's clearly a prince's dog, something from his past he doesn't want to face but cannot let go.

"Your mother's name is the shutdown command," I press.

"Of course. She made it. As she made Heavenbreaker."

I go still. "She made Heavenbreaker?"

"'Made' is not the right word. 'Conceived of' is perhaps better."

"'Conceived'? What are you talking about?"

Dravik laughs lightly and inspects his cane, and I know I'm not getting anything else out of him. Still, it's impressive—I had no idea the former queen was so good at robotics. I adjust my wrist cuffs.

"Why did the king kill her?"

His face goes minutely tight. "She tried to change things. He gave her a choice—public execution or private suicide. She chose the latter."

"Is that why you're doing all this?" I ask. "For revenge?"

I've thought about this many times before—what could winning the Supernova Cup achieve for a man like him? Is it to make a point to his father— win the greatest Cup on the Station with a bastard? Or is it something more?

Dravik's smile returns. "I want to see if we can put to rest all the ghosts that came before and all the ghosts that will come after."

I scoff. "You can't stop death."

"No," he agrees with a chuckle. "But we can make it think twice."

The prince looks down the hall then, tenderly, as if someone he cares for stands in the wedge of simulated moonlight. He does this sometimes—in quiet moments, he stares at nothing. But this time is different. This time, the dog's faded golden nose points in the same direction, at the same square of moonlight, its ears pricked and tail wagging as if it's greeting someone.

As if we aren't alone at all.

My blood runs as cold as it did in the hedge maze. Dravik merely smiles brighter.

"Good luck with your practice, Synali."

18. Quies

quiēs ~ētis, *f.*
1. repose; the rest of sleep

IN THE DEPTHS OF THE Station's noble spire, hidden far beneath the artificial ocean at its bottom, a boy watches the heart of the world move.

He's no more than thirteen, with thin legs and brown hair and a soft face. The jets of his hoverchair allow him movement, and he turns them now to make a slow circle around the foot of the gargantuan tube filled with pale blue-purple gel and millions of gently undulating silver whorls. His guards move with him, their clanking armor and ready fingers on projection swords unsettling the many scientists hunched over monitors at the room's perimeter. The tube dominates the center of the room; the silver whorls within flicker and weave among one another for three, four, five stories, the tube stretching into the seemingly infinite dark ceiling of the sub-nautical laboratory.

Something *moves* in the infinite dark, high up and around the tube, and the boy stares at it.

"Sir." A scientist in a pristine lab coat approaches nervously, the guards' hard-light visors focused on his every move. "I—I was not informed of your visit. Is there something I can help you with?"

The boy's jade-green eyes narrow imperceptibly up at the dark. "It's not supposed to be outside."

The scientist looks with him. There, hovering outside the tube and far above them in the great vaulted ceiling, is something stringy and palely translucent. It wafts as if in a breeze, making a slow spiral around the tube as its tendrils hang behind it, long and aimless. The scientist bows hastily.

"Yes sir. We're increasing the feed demand as we speak—with any luck, that will patch the problem."

The boy tilts his head slowly at the scientist. *"Luck?"*

"What I mean is…overfeeding only temporarily solves the issue, sir. It used to be years between manifestations, but in the last four months alone, we've had three. Some of us think it could be an outside stressor, but in my opinion it's most likely a matter of entropy—even suns die. There's only so much energy this core can produce before the insenescent fibrils unwind—"

The boy flicks his eyes to a guard, and the hulking behemoth moves in a blink, pinning the scientist to his own machinery with a buzzing orange projection sword against his throat.

"Sir! Please!" the man cries. "His Majesty is aware of this, and I—"

"Those who make excuses are not worthy of invoking the king," the boy says softly. The guard presses the sword so close to the scientist's throat, the collar of his lab coat sizzles black and crumbles to ash. "You will find a permanent solution."

"Y-Yes," the scientist pants. "W-We'll do our utmost."

With all eyes in the room on the boy, the wispy thing hovering far above suddenly curls in on itself and shows the beginnings of teeth on its many arms—a carnivorous flower blooming.

"I'm afraid you've misunderstood me." The boy raises his hoverchair to the scientist's adult eye level, the millions of silver whorls rising along the tube with him, following. "You will find a permanent solution, or you and everyone in this room will be feeding the core yourselves."

The scientist can only nod frantically, sweat beading his lip as the heat of the projection sword tattoos itself across his neck in phantom death. The boy nods, the guard drops him, and there is the soft hiss of jets and unsoft clank of boots as they leave.

PART III

THE HORSE AND THE STAG

19. Occipio

occipiō ~ipere ~ēpī ~eptum, *intr.*
1. to begin, start, commence

The water in my cup is sweet and clear and trembling.

I can't tell if the ripples are from my nerves or the muffled roar of the arena crowd outside waiting for the first round of the Supernova Cup to begin. The smell of makeup lingers in the dressing room like desiccated pollen. My eyes itch, heavy with black mascara, and uncountable vis screens glint in my direction, recording.

"At least the tourney hall lights aren't affected by the power outages," the interviewer says to me cheerily. "That's nice, isn't it?"

I stare at him wordlessly. We both know by the pockmarks on my face I'm from Low Ward, where blackouts and energy cuts are like breathing. He's choosing to be blithe. His gaze rests on the silver rabbit sigil printed on the pale-blue helmet at my side. It runs and runs, sprinting but going nowhere.

"You know, on Earth they used to believe a rabbit lived in the moon," the interviewer charges on.

My words come slow. "They used to believe many things—for instance, that the enemy could not be real."

He shifts uncomfortably and glances to the hovering cameramen, a room full of Mid Warders—clean nails, clean faces, whiter teeth. Well-kept dogs. I chug from the cup—real water. No parasite-ridden stuff from the community pump. No bright ochre ale made with piss for lack of grain. Just a few drops of this clean water would have cured Mother. I was so sure of it back then.

I stand and don an inscrutable Dravik smile. "Excuse me, gentlemen. I need to get to my first match."

Every ending in my life has been ruthlessly drawn with a dagger—one lodged in my father's back. One dragged across my mother's throat. One plunged into my collarbone. The last time I walked through this tourney hall, I had blood on my hands and toxic adrenaline in my every tendon. I was weaker then—less control. Less muscle, more bone. Now, each of my fingers is sharp enough to cut.

Now, I have become the dagger.

The tourney hall is all quiet marble and quieter angels carved in the lights; that much hasn't changed. It's only been four months, but it feels like a hundred. I cannot remember my father's dying words anymore, nor my mother's. What I remember are names and numbers and classifications. I remember pre-War books and post-War holograms splayed thick across my whitewood desk, holocandles burning long into the night.

Heavenbreaker is a Frigate-class A3.

My opponent's steed is a Dreadnought-class A453-171.

Their sigil flies over their hangar, a six-legged black horse on a green field. House Solunde—the red-haired girl who smiled back at me at the banquet. A swarm of people cluster around her decon chamber door, waiting for her with flowers and autograph books. For a moment I swear I see a white-blond shock of hair towering in her crowd, but then it vanishes. *Pointless*. This is no time to think about a stepping stone like him.

The blue-and-silver rabbit banner ripples over my hangar as I approach the opposite side of the hall—my alcoves devoid of life. Well, not entirely devoid—I have one fan. Dravik waits for me with a smile on and his vis pulled up.

"Your opponent is Yatrice del Solunde, daughter of Lord Jonin del Solunde. She excels at—"

"—close takedowns, so I have to be very careful of letting her into my hitzone. She has a habit of coming in better on her second tilt." Dravik gives me a rare surprised look. "I've been studying the tourney-fan database."

"So I see." He recovers. "Do keep in mind they're critics, not riders themselves—they tend to lack a grasp of key truths."

I glance around. "Where's my pit crew?"

"Come and gone. Your steed is ready and waiting."

"Strange that I've never seen them these two months," I drawl. "Not here, and not in the bunker."

Dravik just smiles patiently. "They're very efficient at what they do. Did you see Sir Istra-Velrayd on your way here? He was in the Solunde crowd."

"So that *was* him," I mutter.

"I believe he thinks a hat can hide his ridiculous height."

"As I said—he's not very intelligent."

"But he *is* dedicated."

I frown. "He won't be a problem, Dravik. I assure you that."

The prince makes no noise to indicate either belief or disbelief. There's a long silence that echoes between us.

"Did any of them...?" I ask, knowing the answer. I've used every spare moment of sweat-drenched training to watch the news for repentant Hauteclare faces admitting their guilt. He shakes his head. *None.* My scoff is a mockery of the sound; brittle.

"You were hoping differently," Dravik says.

"Weren't you?"

The prince's little smile returns. "Oh, Synali—I'm afraid this body has entirely forgotten how to make hope."

Mother's cross weighs heavy on my neck under my suit. If anything happens...

I unhook the pendant and hold it out to him.

"Keep this for me." I hate that my fingers are shaking. The prince reaches out slowly and sequesters it away in his vest pocket. "If I die, put it on my mother's urn. Charnel house Delta-6. Row 38."

"Synali—"

"Will you, old man?" I repeat harder.

That silent beat lingers again. The fifteen-minute signal blares throughout the tourney hall, and he nods.

"You know, the suit looks better on you than it ever did on me."

His cane taps a quiet rhythm as he goes. No promises, only confidence.

He's convinced I can do this. He sees things that aren't there. He's mad. But for once, I want to believe in his madness, too.

I turn and face the hangar door. The synth-marble bas-relief of the twisted tentacled enemy and valiant Saint Jorj faces me, and I face them.

Whatever happens from this moment on…

"go."

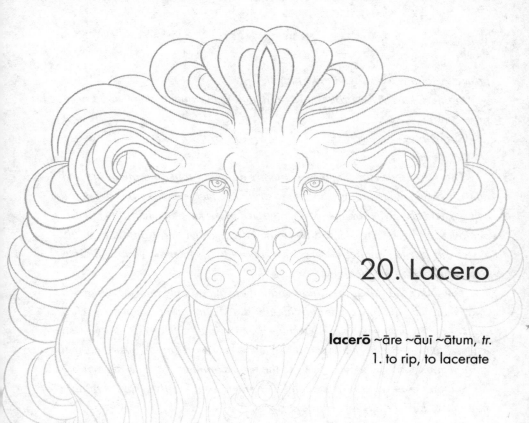

20. Lacero

lacerō ~āre ~āuī ~ātum, *tr.*
1. to rip, to lacerate

*T*he five-year-old girl—tucked snugly in her feather bed with her big
blue eyes peering over the covers—asked the most important question.
"Has anybody ever seen the enemy, Papa?"

Her father smoothed the blankets over her little feet and smiled, all crinkles
and kindness in his dark gaze. "The last people to see them died a long time
ago, sweetheart."

The girl, having just last week learned about death with a particularly
unfortunate koi, nodded solemnly. Her father put the bedtime book away and
turned the holocandle down to a bare flicker.

"But we still have pictures of them. Do you know the hangar doors in the
tourney hall and the great doors of the king's palace?"

The girl nodded, remembering marble and carvings and a man with a lance
on a horse. "A lot of scary snakes. Knight Jorj."

"He's a saint, Mirelle."

"Oh. Is that different from a knight?"

"Only a little." The father smiled around at the walls of his daughter's room
plastered in paper drawings of steeds and their riders in valiant stick-figure

poses. *"A saint is like…like God's knight."*

"Ohhh. Okay." The girl thought on it, and then pouted. *"Does God need protection?"*

"Sometimes."

"From what?"

This time, it was the father who silently thought on the marble doors and all their carvings. He thought about the steedcraft factories, the silver gel of the saddles, and about the strange royal-gold steed of the king's—Hellrunner. It was deployed so rarely, only against those the king deemed the strongest of noble riders, but its rider changed every few years—always talented young children barely older than his daughter.

The father did not always think about these things; only once he'd married into Hauteclare did more questions about riding haunt him than answers. He'd been but a boy before marriage, watching every tourney with awestruck eyes and a cheerful heart. But his daughter sought answers now, her blood buried deep in a prestigious family who were privy to the secrets of things, of the gears beneath the Station's honeycomb surface, and he remembered keenly what his mother had said to him the day he became engaged.

"The higher one climbs, Grigor, the longer the fall becomes. Do not break yourself for them."

The father stared into his daughter's eyes and knew he would break any part of himself for her. Every part. Anything to keep her safe—anything to keep the House she lived in standing and secure and strong.

And so he stopped thinking and began unthinking.

"It's time to sleep, Mirelle."

Fifteen years later, in a much-changed bedroom, Mirelle Ashadi-Hauteclare woke up.

Gone were the pictures of knights and steeds, replaced with countless medals and trophies. Books crowded her shelves—endless dull-covered books on skirmishes and the War and the tactics of riding. Only one book remained bright: a thin, well-thumbed children's book half sticking out at the very end of a shelf, a knight and shining steed painted beautifully on the cover.

Mirelle rolled out of bed and stretched, sheet of sleek hair cascading down her back. She brushed it aside—a troublesome thing, but necessary—and rang the bell for her maids. In a flurry of brushes and powders and perfumes, they dressed her—an ivory waistcoat and pale-green skirts etched in gold. When one of the maids took her hair strangely, Mirelle raised an eyebrow.

"What are you doing?"

The maid dropped the twist and locked her eyes on the floor. "I'm sorry, milady. I just thought… I've been studying the newest fashions, and I thought one of them might suit—"

"Perhaps things were done differently in the lower House in which you last served," Mirelle said crisply. "But House Hauteclare does not bow to the whims of fashion. A lady's morning hair is to be braided, and that is all."

The maid bowed deeply, and Mirelle's hair was summarily braided with strands of greenest grass and fresh marigolds from the manse's garden. She watched her vis while they worked, waiting for even a single ping. When it never came, she snorted and jumped to her feet.

"That's enough. I require food."

The maids scattered as she clipped down the hall to the breakfast salon. Her mother and grandmother sat at the table before plates of delicately fried quail eggs and poached salmon—mirror images of each other in high bouffants and jewels. The smell of lemon butter beckoned her, but she couldn't help noticing the icy quiet that fell the moment she walked in. Mirelle's stomach twisted uneasily, but she refused to let such a thing show—'twas not the Hauteclare way.

"Mother." She bowed. "Grandmother. Did you sleep well?"

"Quite." Grandmother sipped tea. For a woman so silver in hair, she held herself as powerfully as if she were queen.

"Mother?"

"Very well, yes." She waved her daughter off. The quiet stretched, neither woman asking after Mirelle's own sleep or insisting she eat or saying much of anything, really, but this was the usual. Mirelle sat, the footman approaching with her dish quickly, and considered that the two were silent for the obvious reason—the Lithroi girl from the banquet.

"They'll arrest her, surely," Mirelle tried between bites of egg. The table said nothing. So she pressed. "The king will never allow such impudence—"

"Do be silent, Mirelle." Her mother cut her off, titanium and salt. Mirelle fought the rising blush of shame—it burned to know Mother still thought her a child incapable of contributing to House politics. Nineteen was not foolish eighteen, freshly graduated from the academy and full of bravado. On top of all her riding courses, she'd made it a point to study law and jurisdiction late into the night, burning the holocandles in her dorm until dawn, and this direct threat against their House was surely deserving of being designated libel, slander—

"What was that boy's name…the one you've been talking to?" her grandmother inquired. "The Velrayd."

They'd done far more than just *talk*, but Mirelle dared not say that before mass, and certainly not in front of her elders—the last thing she needed on a Sunday was the entire house dragging her to the clinic to assure themselves she wasn't pregnant. She did her best not to flicker a glower to the still-empty vis in her wrist. He hadn't pinged her for four days—not since the banquet.

"Rax Istra-Velrayd."

"Ah yes. Quite a name he's made for himself on the tilt. 'Tis a pity he's weakblooded, or we'd more readily consider him for you."

"It's no small accomplishment to graduate from the academy as young as he did," her mother argued without arguing, adding a pile of sugar to her usual third cup of tea. "I expected Mirelle to graduate much earlier as well, but…"

Her trail-off was vinegar, and Mirelle was an open wound. Of course it wasn't enough to graduate a year early at the top of her class—perfection driven on a road already made perfect created no new paths. The family did not expect perfection; they expected exemplary, revolutionary, and she had failed in this. Rax, however, had not.

"I've heard talk he is slated to win the Supernova Cup," Grandmother said. "If he does, I suggest we consider arranging a marriage between Mirelle and one of his higher-bred cousins. It would be good optics for our House to be mated with the winner."

Mirelle twisted her napkin in her lap. His cousins were not *him*.

"Naturally, they'd accept," Mother said. Grandmother laughed softly, a rare thing.

"I'd be eager to meet the House who *wouldn't* accept a marriage proposal of ours, Ravenna."

Her laugh turned quickly to coughing, and Mother and Mirelle leaned forward. "Are you all right, Grandmother? The hospital—"

"Oh, fie on the hospital." The woman straightened, handkerchief spotted red. "I spend too much time there already—however am I to keep on top of House affairs as acting duke-regent without remaining in the House itself?"

Mirelle knew to read between her grandmother's words; "House affairs" meant the fallout from the threats that Lithroi waif made, with her nasty pockmarked face and her unbridled arrogance. Mirelle could see her now, the defiant question in her ice eyes (*"you think yourself a knight?"*), her spine straight on the podium—was the duke dying of sudden heart failure four months ago not enough? They'd barely gotten out of grieving... What right did she have, upsetting her family so? And for nothing—for *lies*!

House Hauteclare would never do something so dishonorable as murdering a defenseless commoner—it was unthinkable.

"Grandmother, you must let me help in whatever I can," Mirelle said. "Consider me at your disposal absolutely whenever."

"Oh, hush." Grandmother waved her hand. "A lady shouldn't talk in absolutes—it makes her sound desperate."

"But—"

"I will take care of the upstart." Grandmother cut her off. "You will concern yourself with riding Ghostwinder, winning us glory in the Supernova Cup, and the matter of your marriage—nothing more. That is what your uncle would've wanted from you, and it remains the best way to honor his memory."

Mirelle looked to her mother, who said nothing. The second course came—asparagus and fine ham—and halfway through clinking forks and silent sunlight, Mirelle remembered what she heard at the banquet before she intervened against the Westrianis: the traitor had said she was "used to far more men" beating her. Mirelle's mind wandered to just how different the traitor's life might've been—different in ways Mirelle couldn't fathom. This gave her the courage to ask the most important question.

"Is she really one of us?"

Grandmother and Mother swallowed their looks at each other, fluttering napkins and blank expressions beneath carefully applied rouge. Mirelle waited on slivers of glass until the butler intruded, bowing to Grandmother.

"The king's rider is here to see you, Your Grace."

All three Hauteclare women rose abruptly, and Grandmother's mouth tightened almost imperceptibly. "Let them in at once, Charlez."

Visits from the king's rider were equivalent to a visit from His Majesty himself, and he came only in the most serious of matters. Mirelle's heart lightened; surely this was His Majesty coming to promise aid in throwing the Lithroi girl beneath the executioner's vent.

The shuffle of boots preceded the king's rider and four of his private bodyguards—guards the Hauteclares themselves trained in their private schools and provided to His Majesty. Mirelle recognized some of them from the training yard visits she'd made with Father. The doorway darkened with their polished armor—gold dragon embossment and purple amethysts and projection-sword handles cold on their belts—and then they spread out into the breakfast salon.

At last, a boy came over the threshold.

His hoverchair glided near silently over the rich carpets, coming to a halt before the dining table. Mirelle kept her eyes focused and wide to get a good view of the only one allowed to ride the king's legendary steed—Hellrunner. The king chose a new rider for it once every few years, but this boy had been its rider for longer than any. He couldn't've been any more than thirteen, thin in the legs and with a face like a newborn lamb's. He looked like one of the pre-War paintings hanging just above on the wall—soft brown curls and soft green eyes and softer cheeks, a cherub, God's chosen and the king's chosen both.

Without so much as a nod to any of them—a duchess-dowager and two ladies of the honorable House Hauteclare—the boy looked right at Mirelle. He appeared soft, but something in his steady gaze knocked the breath from her.

"Are you the one?" he asked, voice barely above a murmur. Mother moved to speak, but the boy held up a hand. "Not you. Her."

Mother and Grandmother looked to her sharply, and Mirelle swallowed, torn at the attention. *"Me?"*

"You ride."

She straightened her spine. "Yes. I do."

"Was it you?"

Mirelle scrambled for something to say, something to understand. What did he mean? Why was he being so dismissive of everyone but her? Yes, he was the king's rider, but it was incredibly disrespectful to ignore—

She startled as he suddenly maneuvered the hoverchair around the dining table, past Grandmother and Mother, the vents hissing closer and then dying as he stopped just in front of her. His eyes gleamed the color of polished jade—the king's eyes. Hellrunner's previous riders had been his age, younger, but none of them had the king's eyes. The first queen was gone and the second cloistered with bad health. Surely he was not a—

"Are you the one who's doing it?" he asked her unblinkingly, and she felt the answer he was looking for was not on her tongue but on her face, in her very God-given soul. A feeling like the saddle crawled over her in slow, velvet increments—knowing and sureness—and she hardened herself.

"Forgive me, sir—I'm ignorant of what you speak."

He tilted his head like a faintly curious bird. "Do you know what it means to ride?"

The question rocketed into her chest better than any plasma jet. What a **question**. But the answer trilled itself as clear and true as sunlight, and she raised her chin.

"To ride means honor, sir."

Suddenly—like simulated sunset slipping beneath true evernight—the gleam in the boy's eyes faded.

Mirelle was overcome by a howling disappointment in herself—had she said the wrong thing? He turned his hoverchair and left the way he came— quietly, mysteriously. His guards left with him, and when the last bootstep faded, her mother turned to look at her.

"Goodness—what was that all about?"

Grandmother turned to the butler. "Charlez, what have you heard?"

Charlez bowed. "With all due respect, miladies, I've heard it spoken that the king's rider has spent the last two days visiting each noble House. He asks to see their rider and asks them the same question: *'What does it mean to ride'*?"

"A strange question," Mother mused.

"Never mind it." Grandmother shook her head. "We have much more to consider than the words of a boy barely out of the cradle."

"But Grandmother!" Mirelle protested. "He's Hellrunner's rider, the greatest steed on the Station, the strongest of us—"

"I'd worry more about the many riders you must defeat in the Supernova Cup to bring down the glory that is owed us, young lady."

Mirelle bowed her head ("Yes, Grandmother") and yet the boy's incendiary question lingered in her chest like an irrepressible ember eating sinew for many days afterward.

Do you know what it means to ride?

21. Ambages

ambāgēs ~um, *f. pl.*
1. obscure or evasive speech; circumlocution
2. confusion, uncertainty

This is what they tell you in the evacuation drills: space cannot hurt you unless you let it.

This is what I tell myself, floating inside Heavenbreaker in open space with no training fences to protect me anymore: space is a cold dragon, and it will eat everything in the end, whether you let it or not.

The Supernova Cup's tilt is farther out from the Station than the Cassiopeia Cup was, and it's far more impressive, nestled in a gigantic sphere of white hard-light like netting. Neon projection banners for every imaginable hovercarriage and air-filter and mulled-wine company trim its edges. The church's advertisement is far less colorful but just as showy: a massive LED cross suspended from the center of the netted sphere. At least the tilt inside looks the same—two hexagonal sheets of metal spaced wide and floating on either side of the glowing blue core of a grav-gen. One hexagon faces sidereal, one terrene. Red side, blue side.

I jet toward it.

The white-light net breaks open as Heavenbreaker approaches—a brief black circle like a hole in an egg—and I slip us into the arena. This is it. The real thing. My palms feel slick beneath the tight material of the rider's suit. The real arena out in space is so much bigger than the practice tilt. Hundreds of drones orbit just within the shell, camera-eyes glinting as they film every angle to project the hologram for the audience back in the tourney hall. They part for us with all the instinctual alacrity of flies in midair, and I can feel Heavenbreaker's palpable dislike of them—*too fast, too many*. For me they're ignorable nuisances, but for the steed it's an old reminder of something terrible, something like memory threatening just beneath the surface. Machines don't have memory, let alone *emotions* attached to memory. And yet…I felt Ghostwinder burn with faint anger so many months ago. I saw a memory that wasn't mine when I rebooted Heavenbreaker…a frightened memory of something like war.

The commentators' holoscreen suddenly pops into my vision. "Ladies and gentlefolk, I'm proud to give you the grandest of welcomes to the very first round of the 22nd decennial Supernova Cup!"

"We've all been waiting for this one, haven't we, Bero?"

"That we have, Gress! Ten years couldn't go by fast enough! Every noble House is trotting out their best rider in peak condition—the cream of the crop, so to speak—and we're excited to see who wins, who loses, and who—God forbid—gets injured!"

The crowd explodes in my helmet, but all I can hear is my own breathing.

"—who do you think'll win this one, Bero?"

I ease Heavenbreaker back, flat on the sidereal hexagon, and the magnets lock us in place.

I will win this one.

"On the red side, we have the mysterious House Lithroi! We rarely see this House enter a rider, and certainly not in the Supernova Cup—the last time the records say they rode at all was eighteen years ago, in the illustrious steed Hellrunner! It seems their new steed, Heavenbreaker, is being piloted by one Synali von Hauteclare—a real unknown on the scene."

"Indeed, Bero. Personally, I'm always happy to get new blood in the circuit. Let's just hope she keeps most of that blood inside her! Good luck to her, and a safe journey home."

The cameras flip to us.

Heavenbreaker looks so different canvassed by the backdrop of glittering space. Two weeks into training, the pit crew filled its broken spots; four weeks, and they polished its dull armor to a gleaming silver. At seven weeks, they painted pale-blue accents on the shins, arms, and back. It has a wasp's torso, legs slender and tucked up at the knees like a rabbit's. The shoulders sluice backward with two streamlined crescent-moon hooks, echoing the crescent-moon shape of its helmet, the smooth face below broken only by an imprint of jagged metal shark teeth on the jaw.

"And in the blue corner!" Commentator Gress shouts. "We have the morale linchpin of House Solunde, a rider famed for her brute-force takedowns and veritable mastery of the melee encounter despite her young age — Yatrice del Solunde in her steed, Voidhunter!"

I see my opponent pressed against the terrene side. Her steed looks small from my saddle, but the cameras reveal its true magnitude: three times the size of Rax's Sunscreamer. Voidhunter is made not in the shape of man, but of *titan*, with a breastplate like a fortress burnished green and striped in hard black. Its helmet protrudes like a warhorse's muzzle, square extensions on its knees and elbows only adding to its volume. And its impact. If that thing were to hit us head-on at accelerated parses per minute, we'd be obliterated…but it won't. Only its lance will.

"Seems like a bit of bad luck on House Lithroi's part, Bero — an old Frigate-class steed like that up against a much newer Dreadnought… I shudder to think of the outcome!"

"I hate to say it, Gress, but this match is shaping up to be a gruesome one."

Ghostwinder knew. It knew all the rules, but Heavenbreaker knows only practice. My mind races, and Heavenbreaker watches it from our shared mental doorway: *helmet, breastplate, pauldrons, gauntlets, greaves, tasset. Lance is the only thing that can hit; all else is foul. Three rounds. No breaks unless ref calls for a reset. Helmet strike is an automatic win. Unsaddling is an automatic loss.*

"Riders, prepare your tilts!"

The tilt rotates, and we rotate with it. Nerves hit me like a fever. Bite down like an animal — a tiger, a wolf, something long dead and long dangerous. I am trained. I am ready.

The silver lance materializes bit by bit into my right hand, heavy, but it's a heaviness I can bear now. A private comm pops up in my visor, showing the gel inside of a saddle and a green skintight suit striped in black. Yatrice.

Her helmet proudly displays the six-legged horse sigil, and through her lowered visor, her eyes no longer smile at me as they did at the banquet.

"Lady Synali von Hauteclare," she announces. "My name is Yatrice del Solunde. I greet you as one rider to another. I don't know you and therefore don't hold anything against you. But House Hauteclare is a good friend of House Solunde; I cannot allow you to stain their good name with your baseless threats and violence. On this tilt, I will be the one to protect their honor."

The blacklight halo painted on Yatrice's forehead gleams strongly. Dravik was right; I am, and always have been, the enemy. They always have, and always will, try to get rid of me. Protecting others is an honorable thing—I'm certain of that much. She thinks she's doing the right thing.

"Lady Yatrice," I say slowly. "There will be no honor in any of this."

"Let the countdown to the first round begin!" Bero shouts between us. "In the name of God, King, and Station!"

Every holoscreen wipes out of sight. The white-light net around the tilt disappears. Voidhunter raises its pitch-black lance higher.

My breathing is steady. Heavenbreaker trembles excitedly beneath me, around me. The crowd's roar echoes in my helmet like a hundred thousand bells clamoring for the beginning of the end...

"In the name of God, King, and Station!"

Just before two steeds impact, there's a sound.

I passed out too early to notice it against Rax all those months ago, but now a cry screeches around the cockpit for a split second just before our lances crash together, just as we pull even, and at the exact same time, there's a floodlight flash—*white white **white*** light filling the cockpit, and it feels... familiar.

I blink dizzily. Heavenbreaker's never cried like this, never made light against the training dummy. Is something wrong with it?

No, Voidhunter cried, too—it made light, too. *I think.* It's all too fast to be sure—the grav-gen pulling us into each other, the white flash, the sound like music played backward (*sound isn't possible in space, no air, it's coming from **inside the steed***), and Voidhunter's black lance speeds close, narrowing to a point.

I clench everything and hover on the blade edge of control and uncontrol.

Impact.

Yatrice's lance punches into my ribs dead center, *agony*, and my lungs suck in a breath on their own. Breastplate hit? Fractured ribs? It's a temporary saddle injury but it feels so real; I can't breathe enough to think or scream, but I'm still *awake*, at least.

Gravity lessens as our two steeds part and sail out into space, past the tilts, before the inevitable generator drags us back into each other. Every breath hurts like fire on the inside, and I swallow my body's urge to panic. It's all so different from the training dummy—worse. Everything hurts so much more, feels so much more real and sharp.

"This part of the round is called the rise," Dravik would say.

It would be peaceful, almost, if I wasn't being suffocated by my own rib cage.

Heavenbreaker sails into open black, and for a moment there's no opponent, no Station, no Esther. Just...*nothing*. Nothing but the pain and my own thoughts. Yatrice got me, but I got her, too; I felt it—I just don't know where.

The status screen flickers to life in my visor with the scoreboard verdict: *Red, 1. Blue, 1.* So I didn't get a helmet hit, but I *did* get her. She's heavy in her thrusts and very good at aiming them, but of course she is. This is the Supernova Cup.

The curve of the rise finishes, and I angle Heavenbreaker back, left side jets burning bright. The stars fade, the blue glow of the grav-gen drawing my eye to the green-black titan lurking beyond it.

"Remember this always, Synali: after every rise comes the descent."

I switch the lance to my other hand, just like in practice. My left hand grasps tight, more experienced. As sharp as a blade, I think the jets to maximum— *go.* **hard.**

If Yatrice is heavy, I'll be light. If she's good, I'll be better. The descent and the rise are an infinity symbol played out infinitely on the tilt, played out for four hundred years now. In the very middle of it is the only pause—the only spot of meeting between the two, that one singular moment of friction. *"Riders aren't riders simply because they're nobles, Synali. Anyone can descend. Anyone can rise. But only riders can impact."*

Yatrice draws ever closer ever faster, green jets blazing, all the weight of green Esther stacked behind Voidhunter's monolithic silhouette. The lance is too heavy, weighing on my broken ribs like a sawblade. With a cry, I wrench my other hand to hold the lance, too. Two-handed is not correct, but it takes the pressure off my pain, and I can think again. Heavenbreaker almost keels with the uneven weight, and I burn the jets as hard as I'm able to compromise. My thoughts go frantic; if we get hit like this *anywhere*, the unbalanced tension will fling me from the saddle instantly. Instant failure.

We have to dodge.

Dodging isn't illegal, but it *is* difficult. To determine what direction the opponent's lance is going and at what angle—to exert enough force to resist the pull of the grav-gen… I've barely ever accomplished a dodge against the training dummy. The flash of light between steeds—if it happens again—will only make it that much harder to see. But there's no choice. I'm past the point of terminus, and the speed is *nauseating*. Green plasma blurs the rapidly closing distance, Voidhunter's helmet in my face, and the instant I hear that melodic, eerie, backward cry—

"roll"

I release. *Everything.*

Heavenbreaker keels. The silver lance drags us down with it, and we roll violently, hitzone rotating in a split second. Yatrice can't adjust, not that fast. We spin out of control, all my organs stuffing into my nose, the flash of light, and then a tearing sensation in my leg.

She hit.

She adjusted on me! Panic sears my throat as I try to straighten out with the jets, but my left leg won't kick on no matter how much I razor-think *go*. I can't feel it anymore, and that's worse than pain. I look down in the saddle; my leg's still there, but it won't respond to even a single toe-curl. Something must've come off on the outside.

A flash of silver against space catches my eye—*there*! Yatrice ripped our leg clean off, and my animal brain screams it could be gone forever, and we spin, spin, *spin*. The status screen updates mid-rotation: *Red, 1. Blue, 2.* If I don't hit her this round, it's over. But *how*? One-legged, I won't have the jet momentum, won't have balance, won't have thrust, won't have **anything**—

I won't last to overtime. I have to hit her helmet.

I dart my eyes into space, catching the flash of silver leg again. The rise takes us close to it, and we judder in slow rotations—up is down, down is up, it's all black dotted with smearing stars as our uneven jets sputter. I reach out and grab for the leg, missing, blue metal hand stretching frantically. I can already feel the grav-gen trying to pull me back down to the tilt—after every rise comes the descent, but I can't reach, and the leg spins farther out into the void, gone forever—

"our leg"

The soft, high voice rings in my ears as clear as a bell, and this time it brings sense with it. Meaning. It's not just *its* leg, and not just *mine*—**it's ours**. I can't feel *my* leg, but if I focus, I can feel *our* leg.

return.

Nothing. I close my fist around the thought, around the spinning leg, every finger stabbing into what the word means—acid-rainy days and creaky tin doors, the smell of baking and Mother smiling when I—

RETURN.

In the distance, a new star forms—a spot of blue-white plasma blazing against the dark. The leg. It rushes to us, an arrow to a target, a child to a mother, and I suddenly *know*. It's a long shot. It's a fool's idea. Every rider's databank clip flashes in front of my eyes—normal, effective, perfect. This is nothing like that. But I have to try.

I have to *win*.

My hand darts out and grasps the flying leg. The jets on it blast hot, enough counter-momentum to stop us from spiraling out. Steady. Dizzy. I've vomited countless times before in the helmet, and I drip it out of my mouth carefully so it won't splatter and blind me. I tuck the steed's remaining leg up and force it sideways at the knee, breaking it. There's a popping noise, a popping stab of pain.

Finally, *mercifully*, we have even jets, steady propulsion along the tasset. We won't be as fast, but it'll keep us steady enough to aim. I drip sweat, panting like a cornered animal as the rib pain sears brands across my lungs. I grind the lance handle into the leg's socket, metal locking into metal. This rise isn't peaceful; every second of it is head-fuck static torture in my legs, my mouth, the sick sour smell in my helmet, and then…

Descent.

I hold the lance under my arm, try to disguise the handle-leg behind me—she must only see it when it's too late. Voidhunter barrels forward, and I lean in. Momentum, speed, g-forces peeling skin away from bone, vomit sliding in the helmet from front to back, the suit fighting to hold me together and that soft voice fighting to warn me something's wrong: *"pain wrong pain wrong pain wrong"*

The stars blur to shreds of light. Voidhunter looms. Closer. *Closer.* Wait for the light. The cry.

KrrrkRRRRR—

There.

go.

Yatrice del Solunde doesn't see it coming until it's too late. Heavenbreaker's lance blasts toward her from a lower angle—not held by my hand or thrust by my arm but propelled by the plasma jets of the detached leg. Our leg holds it, spears it forward and up with all the jetpower we have left. This should not work. This will not work. The cross glows white above us, suspended, and I use His name this once—

Please, God.

A black lance slides over a silver shoulder.

A silver lance pierces clean through a green helmet.

We blaze past each other, then come to a slow halt in space. With a wrench of pain, I remove my helmet for the cameras embedded in the cockpit walls, red-light eyes blinking from all directions. I remove it for the king, entire body drenched in sweat and misery. Vomit crusts on my neck. My makeup is running. I can't feel my leg. I resigned to give the nobles nothing—no happiness or sadness or any emotion at all (*they don't deserve that from us*)—but one corner of my lip still twitches.

A win. The Supernova Cup has the best riders in all the Station. And I beat one of them.

There was never hope.

But now the fire of it flickers to life in my chest, sickly.

22. Nihil

nihil, *n. indecl.*
1. nothing; not anything

Aman waits for me outside the tourney hall's shower chamber. Correction—a *boy*, with platinum hair and a smirk I can't look at.

"Congrats on the win." Rax Istra-Velrayd's voice rumbles. "That was a pretty remarkable maneuver at the end there."

Patronizing ass.

I shuffle past him with throbbing ribs and a sneer on my lips, my hair wet from the post-match shower and my left leg still numb. It'll regain feeling eventually like all steed injuries, but not fast enough to avoid Rax catching up to me in two easy lopes.

"Seriously. If I lost a leg in my first official match ever, I would've freaked out way more than you did—"

"A blessing I'm not you, then." I cut him off. Pain screams, but I won't let it into my voice. No weakness, especially in front of him. He laughs—*laughs*, all smoke and hot sugar—and gets directly in my way, walking effortlessly backward as I move forward.

"They've teamed us up, you know," he insists. "For the triumvirate conferences."

I ignore him, staring straight over his shoulder and willing him to trip on some crack in the marble.

"They're, like, little rooms where three riders get together and debrief about their last couple of fights to the media. I guess they thought we'd mesh together well, since we're some of the youngest in the Cup."

I crack marginally, *"'We'?"*

"Yeah." He grins. "You, me, and Mirelle."

The idea of Mirelle and me sitting at the same table makes my skin crawl. Suddenly, Rax stops walking, and I'm too distracted—I crash into his chest, and in my post-match fatigue, I can't stabilize. I tip backward, but he catches my arm and pulls me *into* him. His heat leaks through his breast coat and into my thin silk tunic, and like reflex, my head snaps up to go for his eyes—

The first time I look directly at Rax's face, it's like floating in space. Weightless, suspended in time. He *is* beautiful—to say otherwise would be a lie. The line of his proud nose and fine brow remind me of a tree: unbreakable, flawlessly arched, in perfect contrast to the softness of his mouth. His eyes really are redwood, a brown so light they burn red, framed by lashes a deer would envy.

Neither of us breathe. I hate his stare. All the parts of myself I hate—all my softness I lost, all my naïveté I sacrificed in the name of revenge—it all feels exposed at once in his eyes.

I dislodge us with a hiss. "Don't touch me."

Rax's startled face melts into an incredulous smile. "Holy shit—it really *was* you, wasn't it? In the practice arena that day. We had that little competition, and you ripped the dummy apart."

Why does he look so genuinely happy to see me? I'm misinterpreting. He's trying to disarm me—faking his enthusiasm to put me at ease so he can get away with any number of things. A feeling of total certainty grips my gut: the more I talk to him, the longer I'm near him, the more danger I'm in. I don't know why or how, but I *know* it, like I know something is in the saddle with me.

I press past him and continue down the hall.

"Wait, Hauteclare! Hold on!"

He jogs around in front of me and holds out a handkerchief, the delicate lace sort embroidered with little flowers. Handkerchiefs are intimate things for nobles. I know he and Mirelle slept together by the way he treated me four months ago in her suit. He wants to bag another Hauteclare, does he?

"I will never sleep with you, Rax Istra-Velrayd. Waste your time elsewhere."

The towering sinew of him goes still. I sidestep and continue down the hall. Sputtering echoes around the marble, then a brass-click whirl of his boots.

"It's not a— It's *tradition*. Riders wear a handkerchief under their suits, over their hearts. They say it keeps you safe."

"And they say you're one of the best," I fire over my shoulder. "But all I see is a fool."

The carved angels watch from the ceiling as I storm away. Rax doesn't try to follow me this time.

It seems the fool can learn after all.

Abouquet of white roses waits for me in my room at Moonlight's End. Father's favorite flower. The roses we spoke of when I first met him. Rage swells in my chest, but I force it down; House Hauteclare wants me angry. Anger is easy to prey upon. The robot-dog hasn't stopped growling at the bouquet since I walked in, its posture stiff and on point, like it's trying to…warn me?

Dravik knocks on my door then—two soft raps.

"Come in," I say, and tap my vis to dislodge the bio-lock. He opens the door, cane tapping across marble.

"I believe the flowers are a gift from House Hauteclare for winning your first match." Dravik picks out a rose, inspecting it closely. "Did you know? Pre-War peoples communicated by sending flowers. White roses were a symbol of purity—purity as in the bloodline House Hauteclare maintains. They want to remind you of your place as a bastard. Twelve flowers was considered the perfect number with which to show your affection, but they've sent two dozen. Even that has meaning."

"What would that be?"

The prince snaps the gold-brushed stem of his chosen rose without a flinch, a bead of blood smearing as the thorns resist. "*'I'm thinking about you constantly.'*"

"It's a message," I determine.

"It's a threat."

Not a single one of them came forward and confessed, but now that I've won my first match...*now* they speak. With teeth.

It was hopeless, wasn't it, to expect any of them would seek atonement.

"Can you smell that?" Dravik asks. My nose works faintly through my misery—a sour-apple scent. "Fairfax venom. It produces a fruit smell on contact with hemoglobin in the blood."

I look at the blood on his finger, and my stomach lurches. "The thorns are poisoned? Are you—"

"Don't fret for me. I've been inoculated with doses of the court's most commonly used poisons since birth. Fairfax is, quite literally, child's play." He chuckles at his joke, smile fading. "However, it would kill *you* in a matter of minutes. That was their plan, I suppose, but it's rather clumsy in its execution—more of a warning than a true attempt on your life."

I'm silent. Quilliam sniffs from the shadows of the doorway. "Master, I suggest we dispose of them before they can harm the young miss."

The prince nods, and Quilliam starts a fire in the hearth with withered whitewood branches from the garden. Dravik turns, offering me a thick gardening glove. "Shall we?"

Together, we throw the white roses into the fire one at a time. When it's done, Dravik holds out his hand, Mother's redwood pendant in his cushy palm.

"You should know, Synali, that none of what happened was your fault."

I take the pendant and hook it around my neck. "I didn't do anything to stop it, either."

"Miss," Quilliam starts, voice cracking from the corner. "You're too young to—"

"Too young to do anything," I finish. "But just old enough to be murdered."

The petals curl black in our silence.

My nightmare that evening is like hazy mesh—the assassin's dark hood in the doorway, projection dagger in hand, eyes blue like mine... *Why that blue?* Who is he? What could I have done to stop him? Why did I survive but Mother did not?

I jolt awake, sweating cold and staring up at the frilled canopy until three a.m. reality solidifies around me. The vis is the perfect distraction, choking on dozens of articles about my "unorthodox" win. Experts with professional-sounding suffixes analyze my every move; talk shows debate the legality of my finisher even though it's long been declared valid by the referee. Mirelle Ashadi-Hauteclare is a guest on one such talk show, all waterfall brown hair and smooth voice, her lace breast coat like ivory, her white to my black. A chessboard, and they struck first. Her voice is strong, confident.

"I simply find it strange that all anyone speaks of is her third round. It's the remarkable lack of expertise in the other two that stands out the most to me."

"Are you saying she's unskilled, milady?" the host asks. Mirelle smiles, but it doesn't reach her eyes.

"I'm saying every other rider is better. We've trained ruthlessly for years, poured our hearts and bodies and very God-given souls into riding. The Supernova Cup is a place for perfection—an unproven newcomer simply doesn't belong with us."

The audience applauds. Everything she says makes perfect sense. I despise it.

"Rumors have been circulating of riders threatening each other this tourney," the host insists. "Would you care to comment on that?"

"With the nature of human competition, some friction will inevitably occur. Yet I can attest that the noble Houses always think of fairness and honor first. If we did not, grand tourneys like the Supernova Cup wouldn't exist at all."

I swallow a scoff. The scar on my chest *"attests"* to the noble Houses' *"fairness."*

"Would you have a word for this newcomer Synali, then?"

"Yes. I look forward to our meeting, as one Hauteclare to another." Her smile says everything she doesn't: the stiff corner of her lip, letters—the flicker of her eyelashes, punctuation. Mirelle Ashadi-Hauteclare has been waiting to fight me since the day I rode her steed. She's my family. She's *waiting for me*.

She won her first match today, and Rax won his.

Rax.

The thought of his heat on my body in the dark of three a.m. isn't right. The way I stare at his winning smile on the vis feels like a poison entering my bloodstream. He is them. I am us. I cannot think of him like this—not now, not **ever**. I know lust, and I know the things it does to people. It made me, and in the brothel it remade me. Lust is a knife, and with every second I think of Rax with my fingers wandering, I allow him to wield it against me. For any other girl, he is cream and honey. For me, he is simply a nonstarter, an impossibility. One of us has to annihilate the other.

My eyes catch the seven marble circles I carved into the wall.

I shove out of bed and pad through the silent pre-dawn manse, rider's suit pulled on with haste. I exist for one purpose now—to ride. To win. To die when it's over, and rest.

"I'm saying every other rider is better."

The bunker door slides open. Heavenbreaker's nerve fluid never needs to fill the saddle—it's always filled, no decon required, no electricity to connect us.

It really was you, wasn't it? In the practice arena that day.

When I slip into the saddle, the gel silence and silver spirals seem to make the world outside disappear. My steed—Astrix's steed—welcomes me like a bored hound, everywhere and excited and irrepressible in our shared mental doorway.

"synali"

Heavenbreaker, I think back.

"ride again? go fast?"

Yes. Until the end.

23. Flos

flōs *~ōris, m.*
1. a flower, blossom
2. *(figuratively)* the best of something

R ax Istra-Velrayd's dressing room chokes on its own flowers. Vases from his admirers crowd every table, every nook and cranny bursting with blossoms. The makeup artist has to squeeze in beside his chair, angling the brush awkwardly at his face. He allows flower deliveries but makes it a policy to never read the cards that come with them — knowing keenly these affections last only as long as he wins and knowing keener he's alone on the field. When he steps into Sunscreamer, the rest of the universe falls away; the cockpit is his sanctuary, steel walls of fame and skill. The makeup artist touches his jaw, and he fights a flinch—even after the surgery, the places where Mother broke it with a crystal statuette still ache sometimes.

"You should consider getting more rest, sir," the makeup artist says. "Your dark circles are difficult to cover."

Rax smiles. "I trust your skills."

"You'll probably sleep better now, knowing your pet made it past her first round," a voice says. Rax rolls his eyes at Yavn von Velrayd, his cousin lounging in an armchair half swallowed by hydrangeas.

"She's not my pet."

"Then what is she? Because the rumors say a bastard. You don't go flying around the Hauteclare name unless you've A—got a death wish, or B—really are one of them." Yavn laughs and peers over the vis at him. "Why the long face—did she turn you down?"

Rax frowns into the mirror, and the makeup artist tries to smooth it away with cream.

"Ha! She did! My poor playboy cousin surrounded by frothing fans, getting turned down by a girl…never thought I'd see the day." Yavn smirks in that annoying knowing way of his and shoos the makeup artist before leaning in. "Forget about her. Come to my party this Friday."

Yavn's parties are secret things held in the Velrayd summer home by the artificial sea at the bottom of the noble spire—parties with rogue academics and poets and heretics excommunicated from the church—parties no one talks about afterward. Parties Rax is convinced Yavn throws just to piss off the House elders. He's sure Yavn gets away with it solely because he's a rare genius at managing the House businesses.

"I don't wanna go to your old-geezer parties, Yavn." Rax sighs. "All you do is talk about dead Earth guys."

"*Philosophers,*" Yavn corrects. "I bet she would—Synali. I might invite her. She seems way smarter than you. More sensitive to the plight of the common people."

Rax jerks his thumb to his jaw—the scar is now invisible, but the memory of the wound is still fresh in both their memories. "Kinda have my own plights to worry about."

Yavn stares, years of knowing ringing hard and true. "You should come live with me."

"And have Mother come over every Friday and ruin *your* carpet with my insides? I don't think so. It doesn't matter where I go, Yavn. It's a small Station. The family always finds me."

Slowly, Yavn nods and lowers his eyes back to his paper.

Synali's name said out loud is a razor to Rax's skin. He can't forget the way her eyes burned with hatred when she stood on the banquet podium and denounced House Hauteclare, and watching her first match was surreal. A person with academy training doesn't ride like that—like a fire is eating them from the inside out. Without a handkerchief, without defensive maneuvers—any protection at all.

The door to Rax's dressing room clicks open abruptly, but he's always ready. He cranes his head to the doorway with a smile. "Sorry, I don't sign autographs before a match. It's bad luck, and I'm the"—his eyes widen at the young boy in the hoverchair—"*superstitious sort.*"

Four guards take up places in a dressing room already crowded, cold projection swords on hips roughly pushing aside petals. Armor—gold and purple and dead serious; king colors—and Rax has never seen his cousin move faster than now, closing his vis and slinking out the door. Rax flounders for a second but only a second; he isn't Mirelle, hunting through the archive every time it updates with the tiniest bit of new info on rival riders—but he's looked at it enough. The angelic face, the green eyes, the certain ironclad composure all riders have that comes from living through impact after impact…

He quickly gets to his feet, bowing.

"You must be the king's rider. Nice to meet you, sir."

"Is it you?" the boy demands softly, ignoring decorum entirely. Rax swallows enough grace to smile.

"I'm sorry, sir—have I done something wrong?"

He can't think of anything. He doesn't want to think of the thing that clings guiltiest to him: the dream, that fragmented thing that wakes him in the night, furious and full to the brim with crystal-clear moments he's never lived—selling bread to strangers on stranger Low Ward streets, making love to people he's never met. It's a dream too real to be a dream. The older riders whisper about it as the harbinger of the end for a rider. He can't face it. He *won't* face it, not even for the king's rider.

The jets of the hoverchair sizzle over the tile of the dressing room, leaving red-hot marks in their wake, ceramic going cool and the young boy's voice going cooler. "Are you the one doing it?"

It scares him, how the king's rider doesn't seem to need to blink. Rax laughs nervously. "I'll need a bit more than that to go on, sir."

"Do you know what it means to ride?" he asks.

The question is not a question. The question is a projection sword, and Rax is paper being torn. Riding means his existence changed forever. Riding means his childhood, his terror, his only means of escape, his only protection against a world that wants to hurt him and control him down to the last hair, and finally, he manages through half-gritted teeth: "Riding is my life, sir."

The voracious curiosity in the young boy's eyes suddenly dims, *wrong answer*, and he looks up at Rax like he knows, like he *knows* knows, knows the locked-cockpit darkness Rax grew up in, the screaming until blood in his throat and the hunger and how his parents gave him scars and took them away again but this boy wasn't born yet and yet this boy **knows** as he smiles mildly—like a god who pities—and says:

"Of that, Sir Istra-Velrayd, I have no doubt."

24. Omnis

omnis ~is ~e ~a, *a.*
1. every

I once read that a hexagon is one of the strongest shapes in nature—like our projection shields. Like honeycomb. A beehive will kill their queen if they don't like her, but our beehive is a Station isolated in the void of space for hundreds of millions of light-years around. And our queen is a king.

The Station imperative is, and always has been, this:

1. Terraform Esther and establish a stable colony.

2. Using Esther's resources, create a method by which to communicate with the six other Stations scattered across the universe.

3. Reunite and return to Earth together.

This is what King Ressinimus rules for. This is what his advisory board Father tried so hard to become a part of exists for—to determine, to regulate, and to steer humanity toward reunification. This is why the commoners work and the nobles entertain. This is why tourneys exist—to distract; this is why protein rations exist—to feed. This is why no matter how many people die harvesting oxygen, no matter how scarce filtered water becomes, no matter how many excuses the advisory board gives for why the terraform is delayed and delayed and delayed again, we continue on.

We are alone. The imperative is our only hope, the only goal. It goes unspoken in every article on the vis, every sidereal window showing empty space yawning all around us; we either achieve terraform or we perish.

We try our hardest to forget this. Tourneys, booze, drugs, clubs. *Brothels*. In the months after Mother died, I kept my ears open in the brothel at all times, threshing whatever bits of information I could from wild rumor: cloistered and sickly Queen Galbrinth is actually dead; the king's scientists feed street urchins to a monster beneath the noble spire; the entire sewage-refining substation Theta-7—with all its methane gas—could be repurposed into a bomb strong enough to blow a hole in Esther; the exiled crown prince is still alive somewhere.

The last one, at least, I know is true.

Dravik spreads honey on his toast, ignoring the robot-dog begging for crumbs. "There will be some news running later today. For you."

I chew my eggs wordlessly, my forearms freshly bruised from dawn training.

"Their credits must be dealt with first, you see," he says. "House Hauteclare provides nearly all the funding for the keep and training of the king's private guard. It earns them great favor." He wipes his lip on a napkin and stands. "The weight room is yours alone for the day."

"What, you're abandoning me now?"

"If yesterday's match was any indicator, you've surpassed me. What you learn now will be on the field."

I won't let him off that easily. "Did you ever ride Heavenbreaker?"

"No. In my day, I rode a Destroyer-class A4 for a short time. Hellrunner, I believe the name was." He looks off over my shoulder.

"What happened to it?"

"Nothing. It's in the king's possession. Hellrunner is his flagship steed, as it was the previous king's and the king before that king's. It's the only steed passed down through a bloodline, a symbol of the Ressinimuses' right to rule as much as the amber crown."

"So Hellrunner would've been yours, eventually."

His grin flickers but doesn't falter. "In a different universe, I suppose it would've."

I watch his face carefully—is that what he's after? Hellrunner? The throne? Does he want me to shake the nobility's faith in the king by winning the Supernova Cup as a bastard, and then he'll swoop in to pick up the pieces? Is that what I am to him—an excuse to start a civil war?

Quilliam slowly polishes the dining silver in a corner of the room, sniffing and counting his strokes in a low murmur. "Seventy-one, seventy-two, seventy-eight—"

"Heavenbreaker is different from other steeds," I say.

"Naturally. An A3 model is not—"

"I mean *different*. It talks to me."

"All steeds have very advanced haptic feedback programs, Synali."

"A program doesn't show you memories from the Knight's War when it reboots."

There's a beat. Quilliam pats under his nose with a kerchief before returning to missing his numbers cheerily. "Eighty-four, eighty-seven, eighty-nine—"

I meet Dravik's eyes. "Using true AI is illegal Station-wide—even for royalty like you."

He knows. I know. The remnants of substation Gamma-1—scattered around the remains of Esther's fourth moon, Ruth, as a fine haze of frozen titanium and glass—know it best. Decades ago, true AI took control of Gamma-1 and rammed it into Ruth, causing a massive explosion and a wave of molten debris that nearly destroyed the Station. We almost ruined the imperative once with true AI, and no one will risk that again…unless one is a prince willing to do absolutely whatever it takes to get back at his father.

The only explanation as to why I've been hearing voices in the saddle is AI. With a true AI installed in Heavenbreaker, Dravik could make the steed stronger, but he could also turn it on me.

"I must be in total control of *something* in this plan," I say. "Or our partnership becomes a dictatorship."

The prince doesn't blink at the accusation. The two of us stare at each other, waiting for some invisible signal, for either one of us to break.

"One hundred!" Quilliam cheers, putting the silver spoon aside and picking up a fresh utensil. "One, two, three, five—"

It's not the right signal. But it's enough. The prince makes a slight bow. "If you'll excuse me, Synali, I have business I must attend to. Be sure to eat your fill."

My chair screeches as I stand up, intending to go after him, but just then my vis pings on my wrist, Quilliam's vis pinging in concert. We watch the emergency news report as it scrawls past in blue holograph: BREAKING— THIRTEEN GENTECH ENTERPRISES LITHIUM ENGINES EXPLODE ON SUBSTATIONS THETA-4, GAMMA-4, UPSILON-6, OMEGA-3; ONE NOBLE CASUALTY.

One noble casualty.

I didn't know the true worth of words until Dravik.

My heart beats frantically—all fatigue suddenly gone, all bruises suddenly bearable. I dart back to my room, the robot-dog hot on my heels. I dig in the drawers of the boudoir to find the diamond pendant and clutch it like the edge of a weapon.

KING RESSINIMUS HOLDS EMERGENCY ADVISORY BOARD MEETING OVER LITHIUM ENGINE CONCERNS. GENTECH EXPLOSIONS FORCE RING-WIDE RECALL, RAISE CONCERN OF SETBACKS ON TERRAFORMING PROGRESS.

They don't release the name of the deceased. But Dravik does.

His name was Balmoran Aglis-Hauteclare—my uncle by marriage. He had two infant twin sons—my cousins. Ten months ago, while his wife was pregnant, he gave Father the untraceable credits to hire the assassin. Dravik provides the hard evidence: encrypted message logs between the two scrawling long in my irises.

BALMORAN: *Farris, think logically—if the bitch and her pup howl even once, you'll drag us all down with you.*

Finally, finally, *finally*—

GENTECH DENIES ACCUSATIONS OF POLITICAL SABOTAGE, CUTS TIES WITH UNNAMED NOBLE HOUSE.

I walk to the wall and cross the first of the seven circles out as deep as my muscles allow, and when it's done, I collapse on the floor. Dravik did it. *He really did it.* He kept his end of the bargain like no one ever has. My brain promptly swallows the elation and regurgitates warning—*I still don't know his real goal.* If he put true AI in Heavenbreaker, I need to know.

I wait until the Lithroi hovercarriage leaves the driveway with Dravik in it to start the fire in the kitchen—green onions left on the burner. The smell is acrid, but it does the job—I hear the robot-dog alert with a shrill beep from its mouth, and Quilliam rushes down the hall as quickly as his bent posture will allow, sniffing and sniffing again at the smell of smoke. I grab a handful of the silver spoons and knives he was polishing and dart out the front door.

The hermetic Noble Ward tram is only lightly crowded. People glance at me, but I tuck away from any holoscreens replaying Supernova Cup matches, and soon they lose interest. So much of my life has changed, but the Low Ward tram remains the same. It's puerile, in a way, to be comforted by the smell of unwashed bodies, the sight of yellow puddles of sulfur, and the metallurgic foam patching the wall cracks like pinkish, bulging fungus. Low Ward *teems* with life: Garden Square is named ironically with not a single green thing in sight and packed close with shouting vendors, preaching priests, and shuffling pickpockets—and tired workers trying to avoid all three on their way home.

Waves of molerats scurry ahead of me as I cut through an alley, naked bodies and blind eyes scrambling from rusting trash pile to rusting trash pile on smell and vibration alone. Thin cats hunker on the holoscreens above, waiting for the right moment to pounce on their disturbed prey, their fur glowing green in the rays of UV sterilization leaking between buildings. The red-light district opens up on the other side of the alley, bustling with jet-powered buggies and drab gray taxi hovercarriages, flickering LED signs screaming establishment names and prices.

I swore to myself I'd never come back. And yet here I am.

My feet follow a path carved by memory, by anger, by everything swirling tight and hard in me after Mother died. It swirls still, satiated in the smallest increment by my first win and the first death. And then the neon sign of BELDEAUX'S struggles out of the others—green shutters and a vivid holoscreen replaying unsubtle still-life art—dew-wet peaches in a basket—and I lose all feeling in my hands. My breathing goes shallow. I'm surprised to see Yarnald still working the door, and by the way he raises his eyebrow, I gather he's surprised to see me, too.

"Bel's not happy," he says simply. "Hates it when people vanish for four months."

"I know. I brought gifts."

Yarnald shakes his head (*your funeral*) and opens the door for me. Perfume hits first—that sickly sweet wisteria smell covering up old carpet. Nothing has changed. The same thick green velvet curtains block out the street, the same holocandles burn mercilessly white against fake-wood patina, and the same girl sits at the glass reception desk. She smiles at me just the same.

"Synali!" She rounds the desk. "Oh my saints—is that real gold thread? Who gave you those fancy clothes? You were gone for so long, we thought you were fed to the monster under the sea! Willemina's been saying you ran off with some baron's footman this whole time, but then Helyn saw you in the Supernova Cup, and we— Should I be bowing right now? Are you a lady?"

It's better to keep this short. Keep them out of it. "I need to see Madam, Gwenna."

She pouts mightily. "Always quiet and to the point. There's no fun with you, is there?"

Gwenna looks harmless, but she's the heart of Beldeaux's. She knows more about everyone than she does about herself, but I've realized now that's the point of gossip—to worry about others until you lose your own business.

I follow her down familiar hallways, jumping at old shadows and the idea of seeing older clients, but no one's around. Busy. Each soundproof door is an invisible scar deeper than the one on my chest. I never knew what sort of day it was going to be on the other side of the door. Madam warned the other girls in advance, but for whatever reason she took special glee in watching me go in blind. Looking back, I think I reminded her of herself—driven, stubborn. She liked the fear on my face, the idea of my stubbornness finally breaking.

So when I walk into her office this time, I make sure there is none.

Madam Beldeaux doesn't look up from her papers, hard-light quill scratching relentlessly. Her office is plain, with a round window facing the street. Her vice isn't gold or gems—it's paper. It's always been paper; the scratch of it, the feel of it. The projection-proof safe in her wall is only for fine white sheets of real paper. I clear my throat. She smooths her hand over her parchment and glances up quickly, gray eyes behind grayer glasses.

"Ah, Synali. I was wondering when you'd drag yourself back here. He tired of you, did he?"

There's an instinct to shrink back, but I settle in the chair across from her desk. "He did. And then I killed him."

The quill stops. Madam's gaze lingers on the word she just finished writing—*hellbent*. Finally, she clicks her tongue and continues scratching. "This is why I couldn't give you any of the decent clients—girls like you can never control your tempers. You scare people away."

Heavenbreaker uses words like a child, but Madam Beldeaux uses them like slivers. I was too numb to feel them a year ago, but I feel them now, saddle-like, cold and biting and lodging in my windpipe. She glances up again, disinterested.

"Who put the muscle on you? No one will bed you if you look like a man."

"I want to see Jeria."

The quill moves faster, black ink shining in holocandlelight as she snorts. "No."

I stand, and to my surprise she gives the barest flinch in her chair. Her word-splinters evaporate—all of them, the old and new, the felt and unfelt—and something in me swells. Despite all she put me through, I can't bring myself to hate her. She gave me what I asked for when no one else would—a way to get closer to the nobility. She gave me a road to walk when everyone else destroyed mine. With a certain slowness, I dump my pockets onto the table in a cacophony—each utensil gleams.

"Silver," I say. "Enough to pay for Jeria's time for at least an hour."

"This is—" Beldeaux reaches for a fork, fingers working over the tines in rapture. "This isn't synth. This is *old Earth* silver. Where did you get it?"

I'm quiet, watching her do the calculations behind her glasses—how much paper this could buy, what kind, what quality. She's probably never been paid like this, never grandly and with things from real nobility, and for the first time I'm on the other side of it, and the power is heady and evil and tastes like electricity. She looks up at me, disbelieving or starting to believe, I'm not sure which, but her confusion is clear; I am a bastard the court hasn't touched, a bastard who defies them and still lives. I am no pretender, no sycophant, no pale imitation. It takes me until this moment to truly see there is no escaping my own blood.

As much as they hate it, as much as I hate it, I *am* them.

"My name is Synali von Hauteclare, and I will see Jeria—now."

Beldeaux walks me there herself, rigid steps and silence. Jeria's the only person I know who's anywhere close to as smart as Dravik—if anyone can help me break into his systems, it's her. By the way Beldeaux's leading me, I can tell she's currently in the penthouse suite, and soon enough we come across it, the door a mockery of a noble manse's, holographed over to look like redwood. The light fizzles under Beldeaux's knuckles as she knocks, leaving holes through which the plain white plexiglass shows.

"She has a client soon," Beldeaux turns to me and says. "So I suggest you speak quickly."

I raise an eyebrow. "And I suggest you delay them for as long as I need. Or do you not require my silver?"

She unlocks the door with a sour curl of her lip. I push in and close it in her face with a smile. It's a fragile thing that melts when I turn, the scent vortex of perfume and latex and silicon and sweat bearing down on my memory. It might be the penthouse "suite," but the carpet is the same yellowed dizzying pattern I forced myself to get lost in one too many times.

"Synali!" I look up at the voice—Jeria sits on the canopied bed but gets off it quickly when she sees me, the bells in her jester cap jingling. Her tunic, her shoes, her tights—all of it is a perfect mimicry of the king's jester, though made with less-expensive material. Her face is painted like the fool—whitish powder and rosy nose and cheeks. We've seen each other in all kinds of odd getups, but this one is strangest by far. She makes it work, somehow, her heart-shaped face beaming up at me. "I didn't know you were back!"

"I'm not," I manage.

"Oh." Jeria frowns, pushing wisps of brown hair off her forehead. She sees me staring and laughs. "I'm supposed to tell really terrible jokes and get 'punished' for it. It's nice to see you again."

My mouth struggles with the truth. "You too."

"I know you don't like touching." She smiles. "Otherwise I'd hug you. Nothing's really changed since you've been gone, except Willemina getting more unbearable every day, but that's just business as usual." Jeria sits back on the bed, then claps her hands. "Oh, and I finally got my sister that apartment in Mid Ward!"

I make a soft applause. "You were saving up for that for a long time."

"Yeah. She's so smart—she got into the Freynille steedcraft school on a scholarship! Can you believe that? A *scholarship*!" Jeria realizes quickly. "But you're not here to catch up, are you?"

Explaining doesn't take long—it's pulling out the backstory that's a struggle. Where I've been, what I've been doing, how I am now… I don't want to tell her. At the heart of it, Dravik and I are going against the king. The more someone knows, the more danger they're in.

Jeria pauses after I finish. "So you need a way to get into someone's vis, essentially."

"Essentially."

"Right. Well, this isn't, like, a hundred years ago—true AI is pretty scarce these days, after the purge. False AI isn't—it controls lots of maintenance stuff on the Station."

"So?" I lead.

"So, this guy could be using a false AI or a series of false AI to make you think he's using true AI. Or it could be a *real* true AI—I dunno. What I do know is all AI leave artifacts on the coder's vis. Stuff it chews up and spits out. I could make you a module that combs his vis for more complex artifacts, but it would only work if you could get into his vis in the first place."

"Personal vis are locked to bio-signatures."

"Yeah. Cracking one would take months." She ponders for a moment and then looks up, bell cap jingling mightily. "Does this rich guy have any systems in his house? Not the air or heat or gravity—but like, extraneous systems." I think back to the sleeping-gas vents I never found, the way Dravik locked all the workout equipment in the manse remotely. When I tell Jeria, her eyes light up, and she begins typing madly on her holographic keyboard.

"Perfect. I can make something that injects into his vis when it interacts with the house systems," she blurts, eyes scanning her screen rapidly. "Those usually have way less security—even if he's made his own language for it, he probably hasn't bothered altering the initial query. It validates you, and bam—you're in."

I scoff. "Remind me again why you're here and not working for the king's guard?"

"Oh, hacking's easy." She motions down at her jester outfit. "This is the real puzzle."

I feel a stab of jealousy—jealousy that this place is nothing more than a puzzle for her. It was dark for me. I was suffering. Only now do I realize the same experience can feel entirely different for different people. There's no need for jealousy or any feeling at all—this place isn't my world anymore. It's not my only weapon anymore.

"I'll send you the module as soon as I can," Jeria says through the silence.

"Thank you." I move for the door and pause on the threshold. "Be safe."

"You're the one who needs to be safe, Synali. People like this...they do bad things."

People like this. People like me. Nobles. I make my smile over my shoulder as gentle as I can.

"I know."

–7. Metus

metus ~ūs, *m.*
1. fear, dread

When he is nineteen, the things Rain kills are no longer made of burlap. There is no audience. There are surprised gurgles, sometimes a gasp, but most often there are just stunned silences. He'd aim for the groin—the femoral artery there emptying the body quicker than any other—but then they'd make noise, and so the throat would always be his territory. The skin of throats and the veins beneath were more familiar to him than the taste of bread, the feel of cotton sheets—more home than home was.

He slits a merchant's throat—the wife drugged asleep in the bed next to his red corpse—and then starts for home. Spider's Web rule four: congregating in public is always a liability. So when Rain sees Green-One standing beneath a streetlight in the disinfectant-washed late-night streets of Mid Ward, he approaches warily. Surveillance drones hum everywhere, hovering in blinking purple lights high above the tram rail and zipping between the holographic crucifixes of church steeples. It's only a matter of time before one of them makes a routine pedestrian sweep and catches them on camera.

Rain stops just before the streetlight, never once looking at the cloaked figure that leans against the pole.

"The cape makes you look *more* suspicious," he drawls. Green-One doesn't miss a beat.

"Violet-Two is dead."

Rain's blood freezes. Not *her*. She was the last of them, the kindest of them. She was his family—they had spoken of leaving the Web and starting a family on some long, tender nights. He had braced himself for the possibility, as any Spider does, but... "How?"

"Ambush." Green-One spits. "The archons used her to flush out an informant ring. Sacrificed her."

"Informant ring for who?"

"Does it matter?" Green-One snaps lava at him. "She's dead."

Rain clenches his fists, leather gloves squeaking. They are the only ones left, then, of their childhood circle. Their *family*. The others are gone, and only they remain.

Green-One exhales suddenly. "There's a noble—high rank. They're plotting something."

"Something?" Rain presses.

"Uprising."

"Against the king?"

"Against everything."

"What do you mean, 'everything'?" Rain waits, but when there's no answer he steps into Green-One. "I won't let Violet-Two's death be for nothing, Green. What do you need me to do?"

Green-One finally looks at him, hard amber in his eyes. The streetlamp above fizzles weakly and then dies. Shadows consume them, hiding them from the prying purple eyes of the drones. "Stop taking the daily pills."

"Brother, the withdrawal, and the webmakers will—"

"It's how they track us—nanomachines in the digestive tract. They lace them with low levels of dust to keep us taking them."

Rain suspected the tracking, with the way every contact knew he was coming before he stepped foot through their door, but *dust*? They'd been taking *dust* since they were children? He doesn't want to believe it, but the withdrawals that spare no one, the way none of them seemed capable of refusing the pills for long... Green-One doesn't relent.

"Every few decades, a noble reads old Earth philosophers and decides to play games of virtue. Of *change*. The Spider's Hand is the king's first line of defense. The king's allies throw us at the problem, hoping we will fix it quietly. The archons replace us with children. The Web spins faster. More die. More are replaced. The longer resistance continues, the more the Web suffers. You have to infiltrate Polaris—the rebellion. Find the noble heading it and kill them."

"But…isn't that what the archons are trying to do? If we follow their orders—"

"They're being outsmarted," Green-One says. "Deliberately misled by this noble. Wherever they send us, it won't do any good. We have to operate on our own—cut to the heart."

"I can't leave the Web."

"You can. You're the only one who can."

Rain shakes his head. "I'm not—"

"No more modesty, brother. You're the best."

Another streetlight fizzles, and a blinking wave of brownout plunges across Mid Ward. Tall, cylindrical buildings flicker—a pattern of light and shadow, communicating something and yet nothing.

Rain finds his voice slowly. "What if this noble truly succeeds at changing things? Would the suffering not be for something then?"

Green-One scoffs. "You and Violet-Two—idealists to the last."

"Green—"

"They will use guns. They will use swords. They will hack. They will construct makeshift battleships on their substations and use those. But in the end, the king will always win. He has always won."

Rain follows Green-One's glare to the flickering holoscreen of the Supernova Cup, the massive humanoid steeds racing across it, and their enormous lances suddenly seem to gleam more pointedly. Rain understands it all at once in the way a child understands reading for the first time, a new world opening before him: the king has the guards and the assassin guilds, but he has disguised his true power as entertainment. A steed could outmaneuver any warship, any artillery. The steeds are faster and stronger and ridden by nobles loyal to him.

The king *will* always win.

Green-One suddenly opens his vis to a picture of a young spider eating at the cafeteria table, smiling with brothers and sisters just as young as him. "The webmakers gave him the name Violet-Two."

Rain's stomach curls in on itself—their names recycled. Their places taken. His family hollowed out and used as shells for strangers. Through his spiraling mind, he hears the shiver in the air and whirls on instinct, projection knife thrown like a vermillion comet. It catches the wing of a surveillance drone hovering in the nearby bushes, and the drone keels violently to the ground not twenty paces away before bursting into flame.

The assassins share a wordless moment before the sirens begin, before they have to part once more.

"We are spiders, brother," Green-One says. "We make the Web. And we must protect it."

Rain isn't the best, but he is good—good enough to hide the pills in his tonsils and fish them back up again, to grit through the blistering headaches and sweat through his armor quietly. He thinks of Violet-Two and all the others of his family, dead and gone, and finds the strength to continue on. He thinks about the girl who feels like his last family—Synali, riding in the Supernova Cup. He worries: Is she all right? Will she survive? Is she caught up in these noble games as he is?

He completes his contracts over the next few weeks with hours to spare, hours he spends in the darkest recesses of the Low Ward docks. Bursting with loudspeakers and the creak of rust and the zipper-tear hum of cargo ship plasma vents, he can barely hear himself think. Thankfully, he doesn't need to hear to find Polaris, he just has to *see*—following the plastic fibers of bright red strung around beams and corrugated rooftops. They made the clues easy but the path difficult; the red strings lead not to a singular building but a series of emergency maintenance tunnels—Under-ring where there shouldn't *be* Under-ring. The Under-ring always smells the same—outdated gasoline—and it always looks the same, labyrinthine in its old Earth design, with roundabouts for ancient wheeled vehicles and pits that drop to nowhere. Like a rat in a maze, he runs, mapping it out as he goes, his dust withdrawals grinding his brain between his ears all the while.

Polaris is well hidden but still human, and he follows the faintest gatherings of hairs too long to be animal, bare outlines of dusty footprints leading him down the right tunnels. As he staggers, sweating, around yet another lightless concrete turn, he realizes his dust withdrawal serves a twofold purpose—to stop the Web from tracking him and to disguise his blade-worked body as an untrained, raw, exhausted commoner's so the rebellion won't doubt his origin.

Rain's awe grows; Green-One has thought this through down to the last detail.

At last Rain reaches it—a tunnel dark and unremarkable, until the laser sights blossom on his chest from behind barricades. Polaris. *Dozens* of them. He vis-projects the bait Green-One gave him, letters scrawling long and blue against the terse, scarred faces behind each scope:

SECURITY PERMIT LEVEL ALPHA: CARGO VESSEL H.R.M.S. *ENDURANCE*

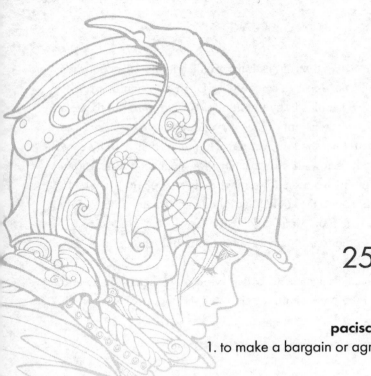

25. Paciscor

paciscor ~iscī ~tus, *tr., intr.*
1. to make a bargain or agreement; to arrange

R ax wins his second match the next morning. 3-0.
Mirelle wins hers at noon. 3-0.

In the hovercarriage to my second match, we pass the Hauteclare mansion—a monolith of marble and steel and blazingly green grass and tall, proud, well-fed white trees. Winged lions of marble guard their doors, and I stare at them. It feels real all of a sudden—*everything.*

"Is something bothering you, Synali?" Dravik asks.

"No." Pause. "Yes."

"Care to share with the class, or should I begin going down the list?"

"What did Astrix do to deserve execution?"

For a bare second, Dravik's unreadable expression flickers, then settles. "My father is a fickle man. He simply discards people when they defy him. He discarded my mother like so much chattel, and the court descended on her. They stripped her of every title, every honor, and then sent her to death."

I stare back at him. "They can do that? Dethrone a *queen*?"

"They can do whatever they want, Synali, as long as the king allows it."

The hovercarriage arrives then at the tourney hall. It looms tall in polished steel beams and a mishmash of eye-catching LEDs in every color over its crystal dome. The crowd shuffles in by the hundreds, *thousands*, all to see a tourney. To see *me*. Dravik steps out of the carriage, and the cross above the entrance doors throws its long shadow over him. His fingers twitch off his cane, then hesitate because he knows it's always hard for me, because he knows what it's like to live running from shadows, maybe. Then he opens his hand to help me down. He *could* have. He could have killed me so many times before, but he's worried about me more than anyone else has since Mother died.

The prince's smile brightens. "Shall we show them they cannot do as they please any longer?"

The cross pendant clinks against my collarbone scar. I reach my hand into his, and this time, the buzzing beneath my skin isn't so loud.

T-minus twenty minutes until my second match, I stare out from the tourney hall's observation deck. Esther looks bigger today, a white silica storm spiraling across her green face. Somewhere out there is Earth. Somewhere, there are six other Stations full of humans scattered across the galaxy. The War was the beginning of life in space for humanity *and* the end of it: the alpha and the omega. Space began all life, and it'll end all life, too, someday.

"Beautiful, isn't it?"

I'd know that voice anywhere—Sevrith. He stands to my left, his rider's suit a shimmering blue-green color with brass accents.

He's my next opponent.

When I don't answer him, he runs a hand through his coiffed black hair, eyes pensively looking out at the universe. "Looks a bit like the sea. You ever see the sea beneath the noble spire?"

"I've heard about the monsters in it," I say.

He smirks and folds himself in half to lean forward on the railing. "Could be true. It's pretty deep."

"There are no monsters," I insist. "Only humans."

"Yeah?" He quirks a brow at me. "Then what would you call the enemy?"

"They were aliens to us. And we were aliens to them."

Sevrith laughs, and before I can duck away, his large hand messes up my hair. "Underneath all those scowls, you're actually pretty soft, aren't you?"

I scowl out at the stars as I fix my hair. Sevrith just laughs again, but it dies as his eyes take in Esther.

"When I was a kid, I used to pretend the stars out there were poked holes, like we were all trapped inside a big, dark box of some sort. Like how you trap a cricket and poke holes for it to breathe."

"We don't have crickets in Low Ward."

"Shame—noble kids keep them in boxes. They make pretty sounds." I feel rather than see his gaze turn toward me. "How about you? What do you think of space?"

"I'm afraid of it."

"Why?"

Because the whole universe is full of nothing. Because there's nothing left for me. I'm going to die when this is over. Dravik can't spare me. He won't. But if he did… Where would I go when it's over? Where *could* I go? Where does a twisted girl like me fit in the universe? Everyone else is full, whole. No one wants the darkness—they want the stars.

I grip the railing. "I'm afraid it's a cold dragon."

He chuckles. "And what does this cold dragon want, do you think? Treasure? Princesses?"

"To eat us all."

Sevrith stops running his mouth at last. He holds his helmet under his arm—celadon to match his suit, brass stag antlers crawling up either side. Finally, he chuckles again. "You know, you're too young and pretty to be talking with such dourness."

"And you're far too old to consider me pretty," I fire.

"Ha! Fiercer than an alley cat. No wonder Yatrice lost."

"Yatrice lost because I was better than her."

His chuckle this time stings, and he blithely offers a familiar handkerchief in his broad hand. "Rax asked me to give this to you before our match."

I wave it away. "It's a transparent attempt at bedding me. I've no use for it."

"Is that what you think?"

"It's what I *know*, old man."

He suddenly unsyncs his suit—the pneumatic hiss startling me—just enough to reach into his hair-graced chest and pull out an almost identical white handkerchief, though his is far older, worn through with holes and frayed threads.

"I have one, too, sweetheart. It's not a gift to get you in bed—it's standard protection."

"From what? Sweat?"

"The spirals."

I pause. "You mean the ones in the nerve fluid? But—"

"For all the assurances the academy makes us"—he cuts me off smoothly—"and for all the secrets the steedsmiths keep from us, every rider knows to wear a handkerchief over their heart. We tell each other. We keep each other safe. That's the code among riders, as it has been since the War. Rax tried to tell you, and you ignored him. So it's fallen to me."

"I don't need a piece of—"

"Someday, alley cat, the spirals will take you. They take us all, in the end. The suit makes it easy for them. But a bit of cloth over the heart is enough to slow them down—enough to remind you that you are only you."

We stare at each other wordlessly. He looks lucid but sounds as mad as Dravik. I knew Heavenbreaker was dangerous the moment it rebooted and invaded my mind like a child rummaging through a sweet jar, but...what if those silver whorls are nanomachines with true AI in them? The nobles wouldn't put true AI in *all* their steeds, would they?

Of course they would—if it meant getting the upper hand against another House, they would in a heartbeat, Station rules be damned. It would then become an arms race that forced them all to have it, with or without the king's knowledge.

True AI is still just AI—a programmed brain given a machine body. It can't "take" anyone, and a handkerchief wouldn't protect against it even if it could.

Sevrith offers the handkerchief higher. "Rax is just worried about you. We all are."

Worried? No—they're worried a bastard with no academy training will win and shame them. My hand hesitates. Sevrith's voice is patient, and his smile goes light the same way Dravik's goes dark: all at once.

"Synali, we'll meet on the field as equals or not at all."

I hear his words, and then I *hear* them, the meaning beneath them—to him, this ragged thing is some kind of protection, and he won't fight someone who refuses it. For Yatrice, riding meant defending another. For me, it means winning. For Sevrith, it means balance—a fair impact.

Slowly, I take the handkerchief, the embroidered sunflower on it rough against my fingers, and he winks the wink of my childhood.

"Thanks, kid."

26. Adustio

adustiō ~ōnis, f.
1. the act of burning
2. heatstroke, sunstroke

The tourney hall's noble box hovers high above the arena stands, lined with velvet seats and servants holding trays of champagne and fresh fruit. Rax Istra-Velrayd sits in the far corner, crimson brocade on his broad chest and umber fur on his cuffs, blinking tiredly. The dream didn't spare him last night, showing him gold-haired children splashing in a fountain of a Mid Ward park. He'd ignored it as he always did, called it overactive imagination, but his hovercarriage passed that same park this morning—the same fountain—and he'd never once been there in his life.

He'd dismissed it as the years had taught him to; he must've seen it before, and his mind cobbled it together in his dream. His parents never let him go to Mid Ward or Low Ward, but he's been there, of course, on nights out with Yavn and his other friends keen to party in rags and wheat ale when old Earth brandy and fucking on redwood tables became stale. Drunken rampages are the only explanation for how he knows where the bakery by the Laurel Street church is, and how much flour it orders a week, and how to make its famous cinnamon twists—left hand over right, right hand under left and up through. It must be how he knows that in order to deliver a baby, you need to keep your pressure steady on the mother's navel and count—*one two three, push, one two three, push*—and how he knows the pink-painted walls in the butchery-district apartments are so thin you can hear your neighbors whispering about joining "Polaris."

Rax laughs into his hands and mightily rubs his face. The dream has only gotten worse since the Cup started. It gets worse when he thinks about Synali, how she rides without anything protecting her, and so he handed the kerchief over to Sevrith and prayed to a god who had long abandoned him in the darkness of Sunscreamer's cockpit.

Please, Lord. Let her take it. Protect her as no one protected me.

The nobles around Rax eat delicately and talk delicately and watch the match delicately, but when the Lithroi man walks in, they all go quiet. He sits back and watches it unfold; he doesn't know the full story between the exiled prince and the king—it began before he was born—but it echoes here and now. The Lithroi man, unremarkable in his paleness and gray breast coat, walks in slow increments to the king's seat, his remarkable silver-sapphire cane tapping thunderously in the silence. The guards tense on their projection swords, but with a flicker of the king's liver-spotted hand, they stand down. The Lithroi man stares at the seated king, but His Majesty stares only ahead—at Synali von Hauteclare.

And then the Nova-King speaks, commanding voice soft enough for only the Lithroi man and Rax, straining his ears, to hear.

"You will not win, Draviticus. Even with someone like her."

Rax feels the air go sharp, unseeable glass underfoot, and the Lithroi man smiles so big it reminds him of a hungry fox.

"'Tis not my victory I am concerned with, Your Majesty—but rather, your loss."

27. Lux

lux lūcis, *f.*
1. light
2. day, daylight

Heavenbreaker's spine presses against the cold metal of the terrene tilt, closest to Esther. I rotate my right wrist, working out the knots—silver-and-blue metal mimics me. The idea of true AI in every steed lingers in my mind. It did so much damage with access to just a substation—I can't imagine what it could do with access to hundreds of war machines. The nobles are playing a dangerous game with everyone's lives, all for the glory of their "honor." *Disgusting.*

The commentators shatter my thoughts, my helmet screen blazing to life with their velvet coats and projection headsets.

"In the blue corner, we have the unbreakable girl who'd rather break herself—Synali von Hauteclare, riding for House Lithroi in her steed, Heavenbreaker! Gress, I think it's safe to say Synali's last match surprised the breeches off us all."

"That it did, Bero—my wife's been talking about nothing else for the last few days. Let's hope she does something equally entertaining this time—for my marriage's sake!"

The crowd's laughter rings in my ears; they didn't make jokes about Rax or Yatrice. Let them laugh, then — it will cover up the sound of my footsteps.

"In the red corner stands the general of agility, the grandmaster of speed, faster in wit and in noblewomen's hearts than any rider in history — Sevrith cu Freynille and his steed, Everseer, riding for House Freynille!"

Riotous applause bursts forth.

"As a steedcrafting House, House Freynille's known for their high-end equipment, but Everseer is a step above the rest. Hot off the prototype line just three months ago, the A453-181 is reportedly capable of accelerations well over twenty-six parses a minute! And in the hands of Sevrith — well! I think it's pretty certain the newcomer's going to have her plate full with this one."

A holoscreen pops up and obscures the commentators — Sevrith, the brass antlers embossed on his helmet piercing against the black of space.

"You're wearing the handkerchief, right?" Sevrith asks. The faint white glow of his halo radiates from inside his visor. I nod.

"This once."

"*Always,*" he insists. "What of everything I told you? You have to wear it always, for your own good."

"You've made the mistake of thinking my own good interests me, old man. I'm not a *child,*" I snarl. "I don't need you to worry about me."

"Looks like he's kept you in the dark." Sevrith exhales. "So it falls to me to teach you better."

He cuts the comms. I push down the anger and ready my jets. Just because he saved me once, he thinks I'm weak, but I will show him different.

Everseer is a Frigate — a sleek minnow of a steed exactly our size. Same size, same weight.

"equal"

Heavenbreaker rings the bells of thought at me.

"equal impact"

True AI or not, it isn't wrong — with such similar weights, our impact will be determined by who moves faster. Despite being the same weight class, Everseer is four hundred years more sophisticated. It looks nothing like us: a proud chest; legs far thicker and split at the ends like hooves. The helmet is the biggest part of it — two impressive brass-brushed antlers jutting from the brow and sweeping up in grand tridents. That'd be an easy target if decoration counted as a hit, but it doesn't. It's painted that same celadon color all over like glazed pottery, like art with flesh inside.

The tilts rotate. A silver lance appears in my hand, a brass lance in his.

"In the name of God, King, and Station!"

"go"

Rabbit and stag run across nothingness, but the stag is *so much faster*—Sevrith reaches his max speed in a blink. The blue glow of the grav-gen *already* washes his armor. My heart lodges in my throat as I make frantic calculations out of fuzzy database clips in my brain; he'll reach terminus—the halfway point—long before we do and hit us at three-quarters of our tilt. Distance is speed, and on the tilt, speed is power. The more distance a steed has to run before impact, the stronger the hit, and the stronger the hit, the better chance you have to de-saddle someone and win instantly.

Yatrice was slow, but Sevrith doesn't know the goddamn meaning of the word.

I jet down the tilt at the same pace I always do—fast, but not like him. He's not giving me time to think—I have to focus on something other than speed, and my mind shrinks down to a tight pinprick. Something, *anything, hurry, it's my fault, not fast enough, **not good enough**—*

"don't panic"

Heavenbreaker says it, but it does more than say it—it *feels* it. It throws the feeling of *don't-panic* at me like frigid tranquilizer, and it wipes my mind clean enough to see the only two choices: gun our jets to their absolute maximum in a frantic bid to match Sevrith, or stay slow and try to evade. He strikes wide—I know that much from his clips.

"wide" Heavenbreaker thinks.

Dravik said it best: the enemy's strength will be their weakness, too.

We go narrow, I think.

A feeling like hot triumph flares in our mental link, and for a second our thoughts feel less like bells ringing against each other and more like a puzzle, two pieces fitting.

"go"

The descent pulls the skin from my face, pulls Heavenbreaker in on me closer, harder, heavier. Sevrith aims his brass lance right at my helmet like a needle to my eye. The blue grav-gen glow washes out all of Sevrith's color as we close in on him and as he closes in on us. I hear the faint keen of the two steeds grind louder, as if their proximity to each other is what causes that sound. I was sloppy with Yatrice, but I know now—timing is everything. If I let this maneuver go on one second too long, I'll capsize.

Stop.

Every single one of my jets dies at my thought. My gasp goes the wrong way down my windpipe as the redirected speed rips through my body—no breath left to think. No shapes, no details, only blurry colors as we spin, only my body smashing in on itself, stomach lurching. *Breathe.* I have to breathe or I'll pass out, but I *can't*; my lungs are too heavy—

There—for a moment in all the chaos, my straining eyes catch what I'm looking for. Black space.

"go"

Heavenbreaker's jets blast to life, my lungs refilling and our spine shunting parallel to the generator—our face is now facing in. We're sideways, *made narrow*. Sevrith's brass lance juts into our vision, the whole of it sliding just past our nose in horrifying slow motion. The screeching cry between steeds resounds with a bright flash of white light. I can't feel any sharp pain—we evaded the hit, but the g-forces let our lungs go far too late. My heart can't beat stronger than it—no blood flow, throat closing up, my eyes rolling back in my head.

"it hurts"

And then, all at once, it doesn't.

28. Quassatio

quassātiō ~ōnis, *f.*
1. the act of shaking

A woman wavers in front of me.

She is not a memory, nor is she a nightmare. She isn't Mother—her hair is too pale a brown, her eyes too pale; almost white, no—*silver.* Her irises are alive with a wet silver color. The blackness over her shoulder goes on forever like space, but there are no stars. Her patient smile stops wavering, crystallizes for a moment, and I'd know that smile anywhere—Dravik. Those portraits. *His mother.*

Queen Astrix leans in, whispering softly and carefully in my ear.

"do you know what it means to ride?"

And then something reaches up and drags me down.

Like breaking the surface of water upside down, my feet are pulled through a layer of something, and I float in star-studded space without fear—none of my usual terror, just comfort and certainty, and that's how I know this is not my memory or my feelings. These are someone else's. I watch it like a video, feel it like a dream. A white-gold sun much smaller than the giant one Esther orbits flashes its light over distant metal things—silver steeds zipping against the stars before coming to rest in a crisp pattern: A3s. Thousands of Heavenbreakers wait and move and rearrange themselves in lightning-quick bursts to make strict formations.

The War again. The War *again*, but I can't see the enemy at all—no snakelike tendrils, no fangs, just steeds. There's fear, but it doesn't crush me like the reboot memory, because in this memory, I'm not alone. There's another…*someone* here with me, and I know we're the only two left—only two of us facing down an entire army.

Behind the steed formation is a planet draped in beautiful blues and greens and wispy whites. The me-of-the-memory knows the name of it like a song, and the Synali-watching knows the name of it like a textbook: Earth. Faintly, I feel the handkerchief beneath my suit brush against my collarbone scar, and it takes me out of the memory—reminds me I'm real elsewhere— and my brain starts spinning.

Who is still alive who remembers Earth?

Everything shatters at that thought, the white sun fragmenting and the silver Heavenbreakers disintegrating into black, and I burst out of the memory gasping for air, ears ringing, head throbbing.

Where am I?

Reality, I think. Nerve fluid, tight suit, the saddle all around me, Heavenbreaker with me. It rings a thought at me sadly.

"miss"

Miss who? I ring back, fiercer. *Was that your memory?*

Silence.

No time to waste—I have to turn my attention forward. I blacked out, but for how long? The rise is still ushering us farther into space… I was out for thirty seconds, even if it felt like eternity. The status screen flashes: *Red, 0. Blue, 0.* Sevrith missed me, and I missed him. I saw Queen Astrix—a dead woman—and then…I remembered Earth? Heavenbreaker fought in the War, saw Earth, but machines don't have memories. The camera drones click and adjust around us, and I suddenly understand in cold clarity: *too small, too fast, too many.* That's why Heavenbreaker is uneasy around the cameras—they move like all those A3s did. But why would a steed be afraid of other…

The holoscreen mercifully pops up with a displeased Sevrith on it.

"Stop squirming, kid. You're impressing no one."

"You sound impressed," I lilt. He snorts.

"Dravik should've told you. He had a duty to tell you what it means to ride, but now it's up to me to show you."

I freeze, Astrix's question echoing: *do you know what it means to ride?* I don't. But I know what it means to win.

The rise finishes, and I max the jets—*go*—blue-white plasma burning trails behind me. The comms cut automatically for descent, and I switch my lance into my other hand. There's more pressure to hit in the second round if neither of us scored points in the first. He'll go for a hit, but he'll try to evade mine. Yatrice dodged my hit by rotating her pauldrons, the widest part of her, and Sevrith's Everseer is proportionally even wider there. He has to know that's where I'll hit. He'll dodge away, and I'll be ready for him when he does.

The cry between steeds reverberates in my bones. Sevrith's blue-green armor gleams the color of Earth. White light sparks between us, a tinder, an ignition, and the closer we draw with our steeds, the louder and brighter the world becomes. I make one last-second blink. One last-second thought.

The A3 steeds in that War memory… They were close to one another, but they never lit up like this. Never made noise like this.

Impact.

A sharp pain lodges in my shoulder, my left pauldron shattering and shards of silver armor spiraling into space. My eyes dart frantically to the status screen: *Red, 1. Blue, 0.* But I was *ready*! I was ready for his dodge, but… he never dodged at all. He didn't even move. I hit him where he never planned to be in the first place, and I missed because of it.

This is the final rise. The final descent. The holoscreen pops up again.

"When they're dead, what will you do?" Sevrith asks. He's so still it's as if his screen is lagging, brass horns on celadon helmet lowered. I swallow the lump in my throat.

"I will die, too."

His voice softens. "If all your enemies were gone, Synali, what would you do?"

He's painting me a world in which I don't die—in which rest eludes me. If House Hauteclare was gone…I'd have no reason to ride. I'd have no reason to go on. I'd be alive, and even worse, purposeless. I've hung on to the edge of the abyss all this time, but without enemies, my fingers would grow weak. A different fear than any I've felt before sinks barbed teeth into my heart with no pendant to ease it. The memory wells up—the assassin's hood, his blade, the blood, her throat—

"All that matters is moving forward," I grit out. "The past cannot be undone."

"That doesn't mean it didn't do something to you."

Silence like calamity.

"it hurts" Heavenbreaker rings.

The machine says what I can't, what I don't, what I refuse to. I have my memories. The past isn't pain—not all the time. It's the smell of baking and the color of flowers, too. The future is not pointless.

I'm just afraid of living.

Sevrith raises his lance in a perfect mirror image of mine, like balance, and speaks. "Are you ready to learn your lesson, kid?"

I raise my helmet.

"Already have, old man."

29. Relictus

relictus ~a ~um, a.
1. abandoned, forsaken

The descent.

Our two spears blaze light like comets—one silver, one brass. Sevrith sees it coming, but he doesn't adjust. Nor does he hit me…on *purpose*. The slick slide of his brass lance just over my shoulder is too well-thought out, too precise and steady to be anything but purposeful. My lance hooks in his right greave and shatters celadon, his shin twisting around itself but still intact.

Red, 1. Blue, 1.

Balance. He handed me that point. He's forcing an overtime; when two steeds end round three with equal points, the rounds continue until one of them earns a point above the other. Rabbit and stag run a race with no end. Round four. Round five. Sweat carves down my nose. Blood dries on my gnawed lips. Heavenbreaker is just a machine—a machine with memories, with feelings, with words. A machine with a dead queen inside it. A machine that remembers Earth. *Don't think about that. Move forward.*

Sevrith's experience betrays him—he expects me to keep going for a point, but I know the moment I do that, I'm finished. If I dedicate my lance to any one direction, he'll lock in, and that'll be the end of me. He might be faster and more experienced, but he's older than me, too. His lance droops on the eighth round. I pant, unbearably sweat-slick beneath the rider's suit. Trembling. *Fear.* Fear grips me—my body will give out, grow weak, and my body is all I have left. It's all I've ever had.

"Ready to give up"—I wheeze into the comms—"so soon?"

Sevrith's shoulders heave. "You're far too young…to be so full of despair."

He's noble through and through—words as distractions, words as demons made to claw at me and make me doubt myself. Father did much the same, trying to placate me with words.

"I loved her, Synali."

You don't know the meaning of the goddamn word.

The silver whorls gather at my mouth and nibble at the cracking blood on my lips, my cracking voice. "I am stronger than despair."

"No one's stronger than despair. It's a dark box…with holes poked for air. You're right to be afraid of it. We're all trapped in it." He looks dead at me. "We are *all* trapped in it. And someone has to teach you that."

The eighth descent calls. If I lose this, it's over. No more revenge. No more Hauteclares punished. I don't want to let go of hope, not now that I've tasted it. Everseer moves like art, like pottery. Heavenbreaker moves like a jagged smile, like fear. I brace softly. The blue glow of the grav-gen envelops both our steeds at once. He's tired—I have to try. Something diagonal, my lance in his breastplate, his lance drooping too far wide to strike back at me in time. I have him, I have him, *I have—*

A sharp tip presses against my chin.

The light. The cry.

It slides in, piercing up through my jaw and into my brain, and I *feel* it—a vein of ice straight through my skull.

Helmet hit.

I choke.

Heavenbreaker goes dead instantly, our connection severed. The silver whorls die mid-writhe. The saddle loses all light, all color, and the vast view of space blinks out like a mirage, replaced by the cold metal innards of the steed. I float alone in Heavenbreaker's shell with no pain. The saddle's completely powered off—I can't feel anything other than my dull heartbeat and the thickness of the rapidly cooling nerve fluid. He won. I *lost.*

Hope, gone.

The comms explode with the crowd's roar in my helmet, the commentators ecstatic.

"And that's it for this match, Gress! In a war of blistering attrition, House Freynille clinches victory over House Lithroi at last!"

Sevrith turns his holoscreen on and takes his helmet off. His handsome face is sweat-drenched, dark eyes downcast. "Forgive me, Synali. But someone has to teach you."

Slowly, hollowly, I watch as he once again unsyncs his suit and takes his worn handkerchief out with an exhausted smile. A white flag.

"What—" I croak. "What are you doing?"

Something moves in his eyes. My brain is numb, but my vision is clear; there's *silver* in his eyes. It gathers, swells like mercury, shimmers like stars. Like Queen Astrix. Like water over the edge of a cup, silver wetness builds and builds and *builds* in his eyes. And then he winks.

"Make sure you live, kid."

A single drop overflows onto his cheek.

He instantly slouches forward, crumbling like paper under fire, sugar under hot tea—formless, boneless, completely unmoving on the screen. It's lost on me, but only until the crowd's jubilant roar dulls to a dismayed drone, until small white steeds flashing with red sirens jet into the arena and surround Everseer—he's *hurt.*

He hurt himself.

"It appears Sevrith cu Freynille has overloaded, Bero!"

"An overload is incredibly unfortunate, Gress."

"That it is—medics are on the scene, but the ref has the final call. An overload after a helmet strike… The results are in limbo. It could go either way!"

Overload? They mean brain damage, right? But how? He didn't impact wrong; his moves were flawless; there's no way he hit his head hard enough to—My stomach is lead and fire and disbelief. His silver tears are the exact same silver as the nerve fluid. As the *spirals.* The color clinches the truth in iron clasps; everything Sevrith said before the match… The spirals overwhelmed him. No—he *let* them overwhelm him; he was perfectly fine, *he won,* and then—

My eyes frantically trace Sevrith's unmoving body as Everseer's cockpit opens, medic hands deftly easing him out of the saddle like a piece of broken equipment to be removed and replaced. Like this is procedure. Like they've done this a hundred times before.

"The referee's ruling is in! Sevrith cu Freynille's overload renders Synali von Hauteclare the winner by default!"

Sevrith's lifeless eyes drip silver onto his suit.

The stag, impaling itself on its own horns to let the rabbit cross the finish line first.

30. Continuo

continuō ~āre ~āuī ~ātum, *tr.*
1. to join, connect
2. to continue, persist

THERE WAS A CHESSBOARD *in the Lithroi manse.*

It sat on a small whitewood table by the fireplace in the main sitting room. Synali stared at it as she achingly pulled on her rider's suit for the second day of training. She wasn't sure what the pieces meant. They looked intricate and important—except the ugly little pieces in the front—but she never learned chess. She used to see a handful of old men playing it in hawker alley on her way to church, backs bent over the tin boards and half-rusted cybernetic arms moving the pieces in quiet contemplation. But like all good things in Low Ward, it didn't last. The guards broke it up under the guise of a "dust raid," and she never saw them again.

Dravik's board was not made of tin—it was made of silver. Silver and lapis lazuli.

"White moves first," Dravik said, walking up from behind her. She jumped, scattering the pieces to the floor. He bent to one knee—his bad knee—and began to pick up her mess. She knelt, too, putting each piece back on the board. Her hand froze around one of the plain pieces.

"Why does this one look so mundane?"

"It's really quite powerful."

"How powerful can it be when there's so many of them? There's only one queen on each side. Two horses."

"Knights," he corrected. "The horses are called knights. And you'd do well to give more respect to the pawn."

She scoffed. "Give me one good reason, then."

He carefully assembled the pieces she'd put on the board, two lines on each side facing each other in rigid formation. His finger lingered on the last black pawn as he looked up at her with those hidden eyes of steel.

"The pawn is the only piece that refuses to move backward."

PART IV

THE CROW

31. Argentum

argentum ~ī, *n.*
1. silver
2. a silver thing

I call Sevrith the worst thing a noble can be called—me.

"*Bastard.*"

Sevrith doesn't stir in his hospital bed, dark hair splayed over the pillow. He's not dead—the heartbeat monitor proves that much—but he can't breathe without a machine doing it for him. The steady hiss of each inhale and exhale fills the empty room.

"Why give up your win for me? You were fine, and then—" I snarl. "You don't even *know* me."

Utter silence. My fists ball in his sheets. I would've lost if he didn't put himself in this bed. He did this to himself. He let the spirals in by taking the handkerchief out, and they came out of his *eyes*. But *why*? Why surrender a win like that? It's *unthinkable*.

He saved me. Twice.

My numb fingers flit over the screen at the end of his bed—blackened pictures like X-rays. It's a brain—Sevrith's—but something about it seems abnormal. The rainbow overlay shows spots of red and orange along the tissue, like a thermal map of some sort, but there are stark black spots with no color at all, hundreds of them—some small, some large. What do those spots mean?

The sliding door to Sevrith's hospital room opens with a gentle *shlick*, and I drop the chart. From behind me are footsteps, the smell of flowers, and a deep-voiced, half-surprised, "H-Hauteclare?"

Rax. My body goes stiff and on point, hyperaware of his every twitch. I refuse to give him more than a passing glance, but without all the usual camera-friendly rider makeup, I catch hints of exhausted dark circles. Does he not sleep well in that noble feather bed of his? *How tragic.*

I straighten and gesture at Sevrith. "I saw silver come out of his eyes."

Rax puts a vase of sunflowers on the bedside table and frowns. "The Lithroi man with the cane didn't tell you about that?"

"No one's told me anything, so now I'm forced to ask the likes of you," I snap, baring my teeth at him to hide my soft tongue. He has no teeth to bare, or if he does he keeps them well-hidden under a veneer of soft grimness.

"It's called overload."

"I know what it's called—*what is it?*"

"Right, you…you've probably never even seen them, huh? Since you didn't go to the academy." He opens his vis, clicking through a list of videos and finally opening one, projecting it large so I can see. It's just black. Empty space.

"It's nothing," I deadpan.

"It's actually a vid from a rider-restricted textbook, but nice try."

"You facetious little—"

"Look closer," he interrupts. I scowl and lean in until the hologram quietly buzzes inches from my face, until I can practically scent his body heat through the diffused plasma—clean herbs. It's the same grainy four seconds played over and over—black space, glittering stars, and nothing else. Until something *moves*. Something huge and clear and glass-like ripples a patch of space in thick, serrated tendrils, the faintest of rainbow lights flickering in each one. The same indecipherable tangles as Saint Jorj's doors. I pull away abruptly, throat hoarse.

"What…"

"That's the enemy." Rax shrugs. "Or the one glimpse the academy gives us of them, anyway."

"How—" I swallow. "How is the enemy related to Sevrith's condition?"

"Well, uh, we took the nerve fluid out of them when we killed 'em back in the War, and we figured out how it worked. Used it to make steeds. It lets us fuse completely different stuff together—metal with electricity, light with matter, human with machine. That's how we got hard-light and saddles. It connects our minds to the metal of the steeds."

I bite down hard on the world to keep it from spinning. "You're telling me…the gel inside the saddle—"

"Is derived from the enemy's nerve fluid. Yeah."

"Isn't that dangerous—to have a part of the enemy just…"

"Nah, they're dead. We're just taking the useful parts of their corpses. Like fur or meat, you know?"

I don't know. I've never heard of this, not even in the wildest Beldeaux rumor. There'd be chaos if commoners even got a whiff of it. The enemy is the devil. The enemy is what killed us, forced us off Earth and into space, forced us into the Station, forced us into solitude and struggle. The idea of even a single part of the enemy being inside Heavenbreaker, being inside all the steeds… I've *touched* that gel. Swallowed it by accident. Sweated in it, bled in it—

My knees buckle. Rax's hand instantly juts out and clasps my elbow, and like four months ago, my traitor body shoots electricity through itself and raises every hair at his touch.

"Whoa, you okay? Might wanna sit down—an eight-round match'll take it out of you for sure."

"Stop touching me." I rip away. There's a long moment as I glower at the end of Sevrith's bed and Rax stares at my cheek…and then he smiles.

"You really hate looking at my face, huh?"

His handkerchief gift burns in my pocket. *Stop trembling.* A remnant, an echo; that's all this fear is. *Focus.* I cannot let him see me weak. "The handkerchiefs—why do they keep the spirals away?"

He shrugs. "Sev used to just say it's good luck, but…I've heard other riders say they interrupt the synaptic flow of the suit. The suit's gotta make complete skin-to-skin contact for the mental connection between you and the steed to really stick, but the handkerchief interrupts that. Keeps you conscious of yourself."

This time, his words make sense. When I blacked out and saw that memory, the feeling of the handkerchief on my body kept me from being completely immersed. I could think for myself, instead of just floating helplessly in the memory like I did during Heavenbreaker's reboot.

Rax crosses his arms over his considerable chest. "Handkerchiefs keep the buildup low. Well, as much as they can, anyway."

"Buildup of *what*?"

"Lithroi really didn't tell you?" He makes a disapproving click of the tongue. "The nerve fluid is, uh, a little weird. It builds up in your body bit by bit every time you ride, until it reaches critical. And then—well. You overload like Sev did. Used to be a lot worse, but suits are better now. But, I mean… until suits *got* better, riders had to figure out their own ways, you know? And they found the handkerchief thing."

I look at Sevrith lying still. Did he know when he approached me at the balcony railing that he was close to overload? That I might be his last ride?

"Some riders resist buildup better than others." Rax sighs. "But even with the handkerchiefs, and no matter how naturally resistant you are, it gets everybody in the end. Unless you quit riding for good."

"Every rider? Every single one overloads?"

He nods, the most solemn I've ever seen his smirking face be. "Unless you quit—"

"I'm never quitting." My words come like knee-jerk, like trigger-pull. Rax watches me for a moment, the steady rhythm of Sevrith's heartbeat sewing staccato between us. "Will he ever wake up?"

Rax shoves his hands in his pockets. "Nah. It's a coma. There's a special ward for them—their families keep 'em there till their bodies give out and they die proper."

He says it so matter-of-factly, as if he came to terms with this long ago. Dravik didn't tell me any of this…but we both know I won't be riding for long—just until the final round of the Supernova Cup at the latest. What buildup I accumulate in the saddle is no doubt insignificant compared to years and years of riding. But someone like Rax… His parents put him in the steed as a child to gain status in House Velrayd. They *knew* overload would be his fate. Father sacrificed Mother and me, but Rax's parents sacrificed him together. Again, pity rises in me. Again, I squash it.

"You'll end up like Sevrith soon, then," I say. "Since you've been riding for so long."

Every muscle beneath his red breast coat seems to tense up, stronger, but his laugh sounds brittle. "Hopefully not."

His chuckle dies at the sound of footsteps coming down the corridor outside; the whisper-shuffle of expensive fabric and hushed urgency. Two voices bounce back and forth.

"—certain, Doctor? His wife has so been looking forward to a son, and I a grandson."

"I assure you, Duchess Freynille—your son remains entirely viable. The nurses will look after him, and should his wife require it, he will be here at her disposal."

Duchess Freynille—Sevrith's mother? And what was that about "viable"? My eyes dart to Rax for translation from noble tongue to common, but his face shows nothing. He merely reaches out and touches Sevrith's bedpost one last time.

"Sorry, Sev." His voice cracks.

"Were you—" I swallow the question.

"Yeah." Rax smiles. "Sev taught me a lot."

The truth yawns open. "He…he taught me some things, too."

Hesitantly, I crawl my eyes up to Rax's face, and my breath catches. He looks so terribly sad, his redwood eyes dimmed and his mouth a quiet line filled with regret. His weary expression reminds me of my own in the days after I lost Mother.

Rax turns on his heel and leaves, and I follow, not knowing what to say and knowing there's nothing I *can* say. Comfort is pointless—he is the enemy.

We walk apart down the same white marble hall, the hospital lights bleaching everything pale. A pair passes—a doctor in a white coat and an older woman dressed in brass and celadon gems, her hair like a towering pillow and her eyes dark. Ahead of me, Rax gives a stiff bow to her.

"Duchess Freynille."

"Rax!" Her bright smile sends chills down my spine—why is she smiling when her son is in an irreversible coma? "So good to see you. Congratulations on your win."

I half expect Rax to revel in the attention, but he just nods and gives her another clipped bow. "Good day, Your Grace."

The pair continues walking. They ignore me, but I stop and watch them go, the duchess prattling on.

"—Duke Freynille and I have settled on '*Barquois*' if it's a boy. '*Telvira*' if it's a girl; after my father's sister, you see."

Sevrith's mother is *smiling* while her son lies comatose in bed. She talks of his future child's name when he'll never wake up again. They keep them in a special ward until they die. *They keep them in a special ward until they die.*

Words, and the words beneath.

I barely make it to a bathroom in time.

The hovercarriage back to Moonlight's End feels like a fragile shell that could crack at any time, dump me into the pale, never-ending abyss of the magnetic field below. I clutch the cushions, trying to hold on to something as my insides free-float. The nobles will use Sevrith. They use all the riders who overload—breed them like dogs. Like *pets*. I allowed the brothel to use me to get the information I wanted, but Sevrith cannot allow anything. He's brain-dead. And they don't care.

My vis pinging is the only thing that saves me from spiraling—Jeria. Finally.

JERIA: *I saw your match! Your win was amazing!*

SYNALI: *I lost, technically*

JERIA: *Well, you looked amazing doing it!*

The victory feels hollow, sickly—nothing like my victory over Yatrice. *Dishonorable.* I download the attachment Jeria sends. Her instructions are clear: stand next to one of the exercise machines and send a request to link my vis to it. Her module will do the rest.

JERIA: *The next time he logs into the manse systems, you'll get a notification. It'll sift through everything and send me back anything suspicious.*

SYNALI: *What do I do in the meantime?*

JERIA: *Nothing in particular. You'll have remote access to his vis from yours, but only for 120 seconds after you initiate contact. Look around if you want—just don't try to enter any password fields, or it'll kick both of us out. Good luck!*

Two minutes. It's so little, but I'll take any glimpse into Dravik's secrets I can get.

I wait in his chair, the fireplace cold and the robot-dog lying at my feet colder. The simulated moonlight rises bright, washing the marble in ghostly nacre. The dog seems to sense my unease, and its leap into my lap startles me. It's never gotten this close. I'm frozen until it settles, chin on its paws, and tentatively, I put one hand on its head. It may be metal, but stroking it comforts me all the same.

"What do you think of having a name?" I ask. "Something like…Luna?"

The dog wags its tail against my tunic in wordless agreement. The holographic grandfather clock ticks eleven, twelve, one, and when Luna jumps down with perked ears I know he's finally home. His cane taps grow louder, passing the sitting room.

"You didn't tell me," I say. The cane stops, and Dravik's voice peels velvet out of the night.

"Of what, brave one—overload? Surely such a long-term effect doesn't concern you."

I glare at a distant stain on the dining table from Quilliam's cleaning, from when I couldn't keep my dinner down thinking about Sevrith. About me. I walked into Madam Beldeaux's brothel only half knowing what they'd do to me, but he took the kerchief out knowing full well.

"They use the overloaded riders," I say. "Like cattle."

"I thought you understood, Synali; for them, the blood must remain pure, but above all it must continue."

He doesn't sound surprised—as if he knew Sevrith's demise was inevitable. They *all* know. Every noble knows how the riders end up, but they still send them into matches anyway. It's demented. Sick. *No*—it's their idea of honor. Dravik brushes sulfur dust off his cuffs—he's been in Low Ward.

"Sevrith sacrificed himself for you, and now you feel guilty."

"He was your *friend*," I counter.

"I relinquished all friends when I left the royal family. Sevrith understood that."

It's unfair how easily the prince can read me—even more so after two months of training—but when he next logs into the manse systems, I'll be able to read him, too. He comes to stand at the fireside, Luna stuck to his shoes with a wagging tail and big sapphire eyes.

"Can you kill Sevrith in the hospital?" I ask. "End it for him."

"I could," he says lightly. "But I will not."

My nails dig into the armchair. "Why?"

"Because I believe he's not as gone as we think."

"He's in a *permanent coma*. All overloaded riders are."

The holographic grandfather clock ticks on. Dravik's smile carves shadow. "That is what they say."

What does he mean? He sounds like Sevrith, saying words but making no sense at all. Like Astrix. His portrait as a child across the hall is green-eyed and copper-haired, but now he looks just like my hallucination of her in the saddle. He *made* himself look like her—pale wheat-brown hair, and, although her eyes were unnaturally silver (*why?*), they might have once been gray like his post-surgery eyes.

"What are you trying to do, Dravik?"

Luna perks its gold ears up at the prince. All of it—this "game" of his—the pawn I am. The Supernova Cup, the king, the chessboard upon which we all sit—what exactly is he trying to *do*? *This is your last chance to tell me before I have to hack it out of you.*

The prince looks to his side at something—at that invisible someone who isn't there, someone who always makes his eyes crinkle warmly. "Start over, I suppose."

There's nothing there—I know that. But when he's gone and I get up from the armchair, a flicker catches my eye.

It's just moonlight. Just the sickly white trees and their shadows through the window. It's not the flutter of pale-brown hair. It's not the hem of a blue-silver dress disappearing.

It's not Luna's tail happily wagging as if greeting someone.

32. Capsus

capsus ~ī, *m.*
1. a pen for animals

IN THE HEART OF THE WORLD, a man brings an offering.

He wheels a cart forward, his white lab coat swishing with the movement. His eyes scan up at the core, at the many millions of silver fibrils suspended in the pale-periwinkle gel, but most of all at the wispy tendrils of the thing floating around it high above. He knows it's a warning—an escape attempt. It's a reversion to the natural order of things; the state of least resistance. He knows: what is made always unmakes itself.

This is a law neither the king nor his rider nor the board advisors and their many threats can change. This is the universe, and just because they have tamed a small portion of it does not mean it will remain dormant forever—reality is older and longer and braver than humanity will ever be.

He knows it is neither fair nor unfair that he is paying for the sins of people long dead. It simply is.

He knows, long ago, old Earth made its first mistake. And its last.

And now he makes his.

One by one, he unloads the offerings of the cart. Each time, a brain—

perfectly frozen, perfectly suspended in a hard-light canister of formaldehyde—
moves from his gloved hands, pushes past the dense film of the massive core,
and sinks into the gel. Each time, the silver fibrils quiver as if sensing it, and
then move like lightning as they descend—a flock of ravenous scavengers. He
can barely see the tissue, swarming with silver, until it's almost gone; the brain
stem floats thin and used, an apple core gnawed to its finality.

He knows it's not the fatty calories of the tissue they crave but what lies
within and between—the thing that still, despite four hundred years of science,
has no real name. He knows they are always hungry for it. He knows they take
it and try to regrow themselves with it, but the many human machines hooked
up to the core redirect every drop of that regenerative energy to the Station.
Or they used to. He knows, like all evolution, that the fibrils have found ways
around the machines, a slow, mutinous trickle that's become a river over the
decades now threatening to swallow everything. He knows they are the devil,
but he thinks that God perhaps might feed on the same thing they do—the
mind, the heart, the soul. He knows the tendriled thing floating listlessly far
above his head will fade, and when his cart is empty, it does.

He knows, most of all, it will return.

33. Consummo

consummō ~āre ~āuī ~ātum, *tr.*
1. to add up
2. to bring to an end

When I wake, the second lion is dead.

Her name was Palissa Trask-Hauteclare, my aunt by blood. Blue eyes, graying hair, a statuesque nose. *Dignified.* She did extensive charity work for Low Ward; programs to feed us, clothe us—even got a medal from the king for it. I stood in line a dozen times for her soup, used it to stay alive after Mother died. Palissa kept me going—she kept many people in Low Ward going.

Palissa used her connections in Low Ward to track down where Mother and I lived. Her encrypted messages to Father burn in my eyes.

PALISSA: *Worry not, Farris. I'll find her and her kit—I know all the grimy little foxholes their kind hide in.*

There's no news on her death—no exploding generators on substations, no corporate tyrants crying false. Dravik simply sends the log between her and Father and then a picture—graying hair spilling off a detached head, limbs laid out beside each other on a dim metal table: Palissa Trask-Hauteclare in six elegant pieces. No blood, just flesh, like prepared meat in a butcher's shop.

His follow-up ping is immediate.

DRAVIK: *Apologies, Synali. My associate forgot picture proof earlier than the disposal stage. It will not happen again.*

Palissa's severed throat is pinkish gray and bloodless but still hollow, still human on the inside. Something in my brain has been shaken loose by Sevrith. By *Heavenbreaker*. Breathe. You wanted this evidence. You *wanted* this. Repeat it hard, repeat it true: Palissa Trask-Hauteclare killed your mother and tried to kill you. She would do it again. Reach for the diamond necklace on the armoire, dig into the marble wall. Five circles left.

"If all your enemies were gone, Synali, what would you do?"

At first, I think Jeria's failed. Her module doesn't come through. Dravik is gone, and I glower at his empty seat at the breakfast table even as Quilliam tucks a kerchief away from his seemingly eternally dripping nose and beams.

"The master is a very busy man, just like his mother. She was always tinkering with some machine or other."

I quirk a brow. "You knew Queen Astrix?"

"I have served at the Lithroi manse my whole life. I was very fortunate to have watched her grow into the finest of young women. And then…"

I start forward in my chair. "And then?"

He shakes his head. "I-I'm sorry, miss. I'm afraid my memory is not what it used to be."

"She died, right? Suicide."

Quilliam blinks his watery eyes. "Suicide? Oh no, Miss Astrix would never do anything of the sort."

"Then she was executed publicly?"

"No—she chose to overload."

My fork screeches clear through the ham shank and over the plate. "She was a rider?"

Quilliam's smile returns as he pours me more pomegranate juice. "Oh yes—a very good one. Gained much respect from her peers and commonfolk alike with her bravery on the field and her prowess with machines off it. She repaired her own steed alongside the best engineers."

"Which steed did she ride?"

The manservant rearranges his cuffs with knobby fingers. "I'm sorry, miss—there were many. I can only remember the one after her marriage to Prince Yarrow—forgive me—His Majesty. It was called Hellrunner."

The same one Dravik said he rode—the Ressinimus steed, the symbol of their right to rule. Despite it being passed down through the royal line, the database info on it is scarce—it's only been ridden a handful of times during important tourneys, and very rarely in the Supernova Cup.

My eyes slide up to the vis in the sitting room playing the aftermath of Rax's third match, his face sweating and proud as he takes his helmet off for the king. It's easier to look at him on screen—my body doesn't react as fiercely. Safer. In control.

The only thing I know about Hellrunner is that it's an A4—the generation after Heavenbreaker's. A steed from the War. Why would the king want an old War steed when he could have his pick of the sleek modern marvels? I down juice and try to scrape together a thought and finally a question falls, cold with dread, off my lips:

"Which steed did Astrix overload in, Quilliam?"

He smiles sadly. "Why, yours, miss. Heavenbreaker."

Quilliam's plaintive cries of "*Miss, please, your meal!*" trail after me as I stride to the foyer, throwing on a coat and crunching across gravel and diving into the idling hovercarriage. Does the saddle *preserve* those who overload in it? Is that why I saw Astrix when I blacked out? Or is Heavenbreaker... I don't have answers, but another rider might.

The crowd outside the tourney hall is frenetic. I barely make it through them, elbows in my ribs and eardrum-bursting screams until someone recognizes me—"*SYNALI! SYNALI! SYNALI'S HERE!*"—and thrusts an autograph book my way. Only then does the throng thin, a perfect aisle lined with half glares and half cheers, and I press on into the depths of the hall, past the security, past the bio-locks that open to my registered vis, and to the shower room choked with steam. It's a beautiful place to wash off the dark stains of honor. Angels are carved in silver spouts, pearl handles for wings and water pouring out of their singing mouths. Humidity prickles at my face as I search between the stalls. He just won his match. 3-0. Again. He has to wash the blood and makeup and sweat off before greeting the swarming reporters and fans outside—we all do.

The smell of soap catches my nose: honeyed tea, fresh trees—scents I didn't know before Mother died. It's pleasant. And I despise it. I follow it to a broad back gleaming in the steam, riveted by muscle and bone and a spine carving through mist, white-blond hair hanging long and wet down his nape. I point.

"You."

"Holy fucking sh—" Every muscle in Rax's back seizes as he yanks the water off and whirls around, lion-bone face dripping frenzy and panic and water. *"What'reyoudo—how—"*

He looks down at himself. I don't. "I have questions. And you're going to answer them."

"You can't just—" He blinks away water, scrabbling for the towel draped over the stall wall and wrapping it about his waist. "This isn't exactly *polite*, you know."

"I don't care for polite. Does your steed talk to you?"

Rax sputters. "Is that… Are you… Is that seriously your question? You barged in on me naked to ask—"

"Answer me."

His uneasy laugh rumbles around the marble. "I mean, it makes this loud noise when the joints get rusty that kind of sounds like *'help me'*—"

"Does it learn new words?"

Rax's smile fades. "You're not joking."

"Do I look like a joke to you?"

"No—that's not—"

"When you black out in the saddle, do you see things?"

"What *things*, exactly?"

"Someone else's memories."

A quiet. He shifts his weight on the wet floor. "Maybe don't ask anyone else that, yeah? It makes you sound like you've gone off the deep end."

"Answer the question or stop wasting my time."

"In case you forgot, Hauteclare, *you* were the one who barged in on *me* and demanded *my* time."

I glare up at him. He stares defiantly back, black brow and redwood eyes. The steam collects on my throat, under my shirt, between my breasts—sticky, cloying, suffocating. The soap smell is everywhere, his smell is *everywhere*, and something in me won't stop reaching for it, claw-hands and claw-teeth and curling tongue. *Hungry.* Dangerous. Why the hell did I come here? I could've asked anyone but him… No. I'm not on speaking terms with any other riders.

"That's a no, then," I manage. "On your steed talking."

"Definitely no. There's the mental link between you and the metal, but that's for haptic feedback. You worry about two things in the saddle—overload and your opponent. That's it. No memories. No words. No nothing."

"You've never felt something in there with you? In the saddle?"

"Well, yeah. But that's the feedback program mirroring your synaptic response…or something. Never paid attention in steedcraft class—As on all my practicals, though. Not to brag."

My gaze narrows, dew clinging to eyelashes. He's not lying.

I don't even have to try to pierce him; he wears his emotions on his face with disgusting straightforwardness—never had to hide, never had to run. Ads, talk shows, the spotlight; he's been loved, not hunted. I see memories. He doesn't. My steed talks to me. His doesn't. I don't know anything, but I know the thing in my saddle is not just a feedback program—it's something more advanced. Something that *remembers*. If he doesn't hear his steed talk, maybe true AI isn't in every steed. Did Astrix modify Heavenbreaker? Was she the one who put true AI in it, not Dravik?

My vis suddenly receives a ping, the sound bouncing around the marble. I look down—finally, it's Jeria's module. Dravik's back, and he's accessed the systems. One hundred and twenty seconds is all I'll have, but I can choose when to spring the trap closed at my leisure. I turn to leave.

"Could we—" Rax cuts himself off. "Do you want to practice together sometime?"

"Practicing with a fellow participant is forbidden after the Cup begins," I recite.

I hear his smile. "Yeah. But I wouldn't mind bending the rules for you."

I learned so much just by watching him destroy the dummy. A real scrimmage against him would be *invaluable*. Temptation, then realization: he has nothing to lose. He's already destined to be the winner of this tourney. Someone as talented as him…I'm sure even if he was caught with me, they'd find some loophole so he could still compete. But the nobles are waiting on tenterhooks for the smallest excuse to cut me from the Cup. Even suggesting we fight means he's either ignorant or purposely trying to get me kicked.

"I have no interest in spending any more time with you than is required."

"Because you hate me," Rax ascertains.

"You think you're special in my hate?" I laugh, the sound ridiculous and bitter. "You've been straightforward with me when no other noble has, and so I will return the favor this once."

I look over my shoulder with ice and salt, blood and throats, fire and truth.

"I hate all of you."

Mirelle Ashadi-Hauteclare is on another talk show, just after a chorus star's concert. She's prettier than the chorus star by far—chestnut hair flattened straight and a pure-gold suitdress up to her elegant neck.

"The Supernova Cup is no playground—Sevrith cu Freynille was a great rider but far past his prime. His cutting-edge steed bought him time; borrowed time, if you would. Time isn't on Synali's side, either—it's only a matter of days before she's struck from the seed."

Father chose her to ride for the family—she's his last vestige, a loose end with his eyes and his pride, and once again she has me burning the training arena long into the night.

"synali alone. synali very sad."

I shake off Heavenbreaker's bell-thought. It's getting better at talking, longer sentences, but it doesn't matter. However advanced its programming, whatever words its matrices make…none of that matters. It's *my* steed, *my* sword. I'll be stronger than it, than Sevrith, than Mirelle and Rax—than every noble in this godforsaken Supernova Cup. My mind is mine, my body is mine, and I'll use them both until they burn to ash.

I will use everything I have left to make them pay.

My chest heaves in the hangar, breath hot. Everything in practice felt harder tonight. Dravik's perfect stealthy engineers are clearly slacking on maintenance—the saddle was chilly and my pivots were stiffer, like the steed's joints were rusting again. The screech of metal rings as Heavenbreaker slots into the massive vacuum tube back to Dravik's bunker, passing the window in a blur of silver and blue. Silver and blue like the hem of a dress. Is Astrix in that hospital with the rest of them, with Sevrith? Or has her body already…

She's either in a coma or dead, but I saw her. She spoke to me.

My exhausted knees give out. I glare at my distorted reflection in the floor—*so weak you can't even stand on your own*—and drag myself to sit against the wall. I don't want to think about what I found on Dravik's vis; I clicked on everything I could see—directory after directory, fileshares, anything strange. His inbox was off-limits—needed a password—but the rest of his vis was suspiciously neat.

And then I found it—buried among terabytes of old chess game logs—a folder labeled PROGRESS. Inside were pictures of the same type I saw in Sevrith's chart—strange orange-yellow heat maps spreading over an image of someone's brain. Top-down views. Side views. Not nearly as many dark spots on this one, but then I noticed the images were going sequentially. The first one was three months ago—dated the exact day I woke up in the hospital. The most recent was three days ago.

And all of them had a name in the top right corner: WOSTER, SYNALI E.

The first brain image was solid color. But then the holes started to appear at the end of month one, small pinpricks widening over the weeks—dark and persistent—until the most recent image. A dozen holes the size of sugar cubes blot my brain all over.

A vis ping mercifully shatters my thoughts: ONE NEW MESSAGE FROM: **UNKNOWN**. I click it with shaking fingers.

RAX: *This is way easier than busting in on my showers. Plus you don't have to look at my face. Win-win for everyone.*

Persistent, isn't he? He clearly thinks I'm weak—easy to defeat on the field and get into his bed. Being in his bed just once... I kick the thought away disgustedly. Sweat slithers slowly down my chest, over the scar, down my stomach. ***Block him.*** My fingers twitch from the block button to the reply box, autocorrect trying three times to make me politer than I want to be.

SYNALI: *Fuck off*

RAX: *In precisely which direction? Yours?*

I swallow a scoff. Smooth. Experienced. Pointless. The end is coming, an end only I can see—five remaining circles carved into marble. *Ignore him.*

SYNALI: *What do you want*

RAX: *A hello would be a nice start.*

Think. Straightforward.

SYNALI: *I have no use for you*

RAX: *That's what I'm hoping, Hauteclare.*

−6. Votum

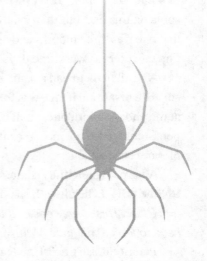

vōtum ~ī, *n.*
1. a vow, promise, dedication
2. a hope, desire

The church does not forgive. But it does allow Rain to forget, for a time.

This church in Low Ward is cobbled together with scraps of cheap, untreated whitewood—sawdust and mold and a faint sheen of oxidized gold covering it all. He prays at its altar for the lives he's taken; every Spider's Hand contract, every crew member of the H.R.M.S. *Endurance* slaughtered so that Polaris could storm in and take over the ship.

It was the only way they'd let him into their ranks—the greatest gesture of good faith he could muster. They had no leader, only leaders—foremen on substations who were eyewitnesses to the grueling conditions, nurses and professors sick of the rampant corruption. They came from all walks of life and training and seemed to share the burden of leadership equally. No ringleader, no mention of any noble, but Rain knew—when all else failed—to track the money. The majority of their ordinance was not stolen—it was cleanly and newly manufactured. He found the shipment logs with Green-One's help; the crates came from a smattering of subsidiaries all under the same umbrella of a company called Idaxvale. Now, it was just a matter of discovering what noble House owned Idaxvale and what methods would make them talk.

Rain didn't need to pray when his brothers and sisters were still alive — merely seeing their faces after a long day felt enough like absolution. But they are gone. His father, his brothers and sisters…all his family is gone save for Green-One. And…

Outside the church's doors, a holoscreen plays the Supernova Cup; Heavenbreaker and the girl inside it tearing across space; a girl who *feels* like family.

An elderly woman prays beside Rain, her grandchild beside her and a dock worker beside them, oil-smeared and graying. For this brief moment, he is one of them — the innocents, the flies, the prey — and it is a bittersweet surrender muddled by the dust in his nose and the bright colors it outlines the world in. The moment Polaris accepted him, he turned back to the sweet relief of the green powder they offered. Every day, he fights the edge of unfounded paranoia the dust brings, but there is no ignoring the real signs. He has caused them so many times before; whispers first, glances second, the illusion of peace last. The Web is furious at his departure. He has weeks before the recluses close in on him — assassins meant for assassins, the best of the best.

At most, he has four weeks to live. At the least, two.

Yellow condensation drips down the sagging eaves of the church and pools in the well-worn steel steps. The elderly woman watches her granddaughter play in the puddles as they wait for the tram. Rain sees without seeing as the Web taught him to — she's staring at him.

"Your eyes, dear," the old woman finally croaks, peering into his cowl. "Very pretty. They look like that rider girl's."

Her. Synali von Hauteclare. Rain has seen grief, but never like her — it takes a while, grief — but for that girl it broke her mind instantly, as if her mother was all that kept her alive. He remembers the baskets, the worn blankets, the glass fragments hung in the shabby little window. It had been an apartment lovingly remade with a daughter's love for her mother.

He doesn't know who gave him his eyes — Father never spoke of it before his passing. Few of his siblings in the Web had brightly colored eyes like nobles choose, and when they were children they whispered beneath the covers with him at night:

"Maybe you're special."

"Or maybe you're a bastard. Nobles love their unique eye colors and hate bastards."

"Nobles hate everyone but themselves, stupid."

A surveillance drone buzzes overhead and cuts his painful memory by the umbilical cord.

"She's very strong," the old woman insists. "A bastard, the rumors say— commoner, like the rest of us. But she's riding in their tourneys, isn't she? The first one."

Rain's hand twitches to his belt; if he leaves this old woman alive, it will be one less week he has to live, and yet…his hand relaxes. The recluses are not his kind—they do not kill civilian witnesses unless they defend the target.

"When they come," Rain says softly, "you must tell them everything about me without hesitation."

The old woman peers up at him worriedly, as if her years have given her knowing. "Will you be all right?"

The sound is like family. Like care. She doesn't see it, but beneath the cowl he smiles for the first time in months; small, weak, lost and then found again.

"One day, perhaps."

34. Sepulcrum

sepulcrum ~ī, *n.*
1. a grave, burial place

Jeria messages me in the morning. She's running a search and decryption on the data the module collected from Dravik's vis. It should be done in two days. I didn't tell her about the brain images I found. I don't know what they mean, but I know they were mine. I rub my collarbone scar, the flesh tight and sore as I walk down to the breakfast table. Dravik is at the table, sipping a cup of tea and reading his paper. He greets me warmly.

"Good morning, Synali."

I guide Quilliam's now-healed hand out of the way and pour my own tea. "You didn't tell me your mother overloaded in Heavenbreaker."

Dravik's eyes cut to Quilliam, who shrinks against the wall as if trying to disappear. The prince recovers with a dimmer grin. "I hope that does not dissuade you from continuing to ride."

"Is she still alive? In that hospital ward with Sevrith?"

His shaking hand hurriedly replaces the teacup in its saucer. "Yes."

"You said they're not as gone as we think." I push at the break in his armor. "Does that mean you think they'll wake up? Is that why you're doing this, to save her—"

"You wouldn't happen to have rummaged in my things yesterday, would you?" The prince's cut-off burns cold. He knows I know he knows the answer already.

I fire back, "What are you doing to my brain? Sevrith's chart—"

"It's not what I am doing to you," he counters instantly. "But rather what you are doing to yourself by continuing to ride."

A pit in my stomach clenches. "The more we ride, the more the nerve fluid builds up, Rax said—"

"Rax?" Dravik laughs pointedly. "Whyever are you spending leisure time with the enemy, Synali?"

"He's the only one who's given me answers so far."

"Oh yes, many answers—in the form of death. Do you think Hauteclare won't notice you lingering around him and take advantage of that? It would be a simple matter to bribe him into poisoning you—or to load him with something to kill you without his knowledge."

"I told you," I grit out. "I can take care of myself—"

He snarls for the first time I've ever heard—deeper, stronger, more terrifying than my own could ever be. *"And I cannot protect you if you give them your weaknesses on a silver platter."*

The lights of the manse choose this ripe moment to flicker out. Quilliam sniffs softly, handkerchief to nose, and sinks farther against the wall, Luna pacing nervously between Dravik and me.

"He's not my weakness," I manage to force out. "He's a tool."

"I have given you all the tools you need."

"But none of the instruction manuals."

The anger in Dravik's eyes slides closed behind some iron door. "You will not see that Velrayd boy any longer."

"You're not my father," I snarl back. I'm ready for him to cross the length of the table and hit me across the face. *Do it.* Do it like all the rest.

After a long moment, the prince merely stands.

"You're right. I'm not your father." My triumph flares and dies in the same instant. He looks so much older, grayer, more tired as he pulls his coat on. "If I give you answers, will you refrain from seeing him?"

My nod is instant, thoughtless.

He leads me to the hovercarriage, my steps staggered behind—I'm still ready for him to lash out. We sit across from each other in the uncomfortable silence, Dravik watching his cane and me watching my vis, the news scrolling slow: CARGO VESSEL H.R.M.S. ENDURANCE REMAINS MISSING. Soon, the smell becomes ash. The sight becomes a black tower looming halfway between the noble spire and the common ring. I stare at it out the hovercarriage window as we circle high above.

"Why are we at a charnel tower?"

"There are answers here. Your next opponent is from House Westriani—you remember them from the banquet. They run the charnel tower system for the entire Station."

"And I'm here to have a bit of pleasant tea with them, I suppose."

A mirthless smile pulls at the prince's lips. "Your anger is sorely mishandled, but your sense of humor is always intact."

I can't help my soft laugh, and the tension over us seems to lift slightly. Our carriage alights not on the polished reception platform but at the foot of the tower, behind the steel rise of a maintenance bunker. Dravik taps his vis but doesn't get out.

"My associate will be here shortly to show us inside."

The same associate who cut up Palissa Trask-Hauteclare? No—someone different every time would be the cleanest way to do things, and Dravik is nothing if not clean. We wait. I think. And then I think aloud.

"Queen Astrix—you see her, don't you? That's who you talk to. Who you look at."

There's quiet, the hovercarriage humming below us and the charnel tower spewing smoke above us. He's unreadable and then very suddenly readable: a sagging of his shoulders.

"I don't know what I see. I'm mad, remember?"

"But—"

"Please, Synali, stop asking about her. It hurts. Surely you understand why."

Of course I understand. I just thought—he's *older*. As far removed from the event as he is…I thought—*hoped*—time had healed it for him. That it would heal for me. But a girl who will die after she wins the Supernova Cup has no time to heal, does she? She dies with her wounds still open.

A short woman in a work tunic and bonnet emerges then from the bunker, smiling thinly at the prince and not at all at me. The prince gets out of the carriage neatly, and I follow. The woman curtsies. "We should hurry, sir. The last shipment is about to leave."

Dravik nods. "Lead the way."

We follow her inside; old steel walls, the white lights of someplace clinical, the smell of rust. The woman leads us swiftly down long and winding hallways, and I can't help but notice the distinct lack of security—no guards, no camera drones. Always? Or just for us? A priest passes in full regalia, a projection scepter glowing orange in his hand. He bows to us, touching his forehead. The woman bows back. Dravik smiles. I watch. Whatever this place is, the church clearly sanctions it.

And then we walk into the room the priest just left.

It's less of a room and more of a cavern kept blisteringly cold. Ventilation fans roar dully, stacks of metal containers the size of tramcars packed in floor-to-ceiling—a cavern kept full. Thin pathways twist between the containers, people in medical scrubs with vis clipboards circling endlessly. They murmur, confer with one another, open and close the containers to check inside. A flash of light into one container catches skin—long, glittering frozen. *Limbs.*

My feet stop.

"You seem to be flush this week," the prince says amiably. The woman's grin is resigned.

"Yes; tourney violence is always a seasonal tribulation for us. You can imagine how bad it gets during the Supernova Cup—syphilis, alcohol poisoning, dust overdoses, brawl wounds… The Low Warders succumb to their vices readily, it seems."

My blood boils at the way she says it. I make it one step forward—Dravik's deceptively strong arm juts over my chest.

"Have they been branded for transport yet?" he asks, smile so big it slits his eyes.

"We're marking the last few batches, yes"—the woman looks at me warily—"then they'll be ready for shipping."

My mind keels—thousands of bodies must be in here. *Thousands*, all from Low Ward—all being shipped somewhere else. Not burned like they should be, not burned out of respect like we believe is happening. Another container slots open—torsos with their heads all missing *heads all missing* **heads all missing** and I can't breathe anymore. The urns in the charnel towers, the urns people visit to see their loved ones… The woman points at a container being projection-etched by a drone; two House sigils side by side in bright, arrogant color. One is orange and charcoal gray—a crow with two heads—and the other is an unmistakable dragon in purple and gold. Westriani and... Ressinimus.

Dravik keeps his eyes on the woman. "Am I right in assuming these containers are for the king's garden?"

"Yes. We ship to the various other House gardens on weekdays, but Saturday is the king's shipment." She pauses judiciously. "They've been *sanitized*, of course."

"Of course," Dravik agrees with a chuckle.

My fingers claw in Dravik's sleeve. The green lawns of every noble manse I've seen, the beautiful flowers, the tall white trees I marveled at—the grass at the banquet below my bare feet. Below their gilded feet are *people*. They don't burn them. They *use* them. Mother's urn... Mother is...

"Ho! Who let these rats sneak in?" A voice pierces like a proud trumpet as a familiar man appears—a blacklight halo on his forehead, hair like fire, my insides *on fire*. Olric. He hasn't changed since the banquet where he almost strangled me. His jaw is still like rock, his rider muscles more evident in a bejeweled jumpsuit.

"I'm terribly sorry about this, Sir Olric." Dravik bows to him. "But my rider here was quite eager to meet you again before your match tomorrow."

I'm the excuse. Olric's fire brows narrow on me; my ice eyes narrow on him.

"And why's that?" he asks with his brass voice.

"Oh, I don't know"—I clench my teeth—"but victory doesn't taste as sweet without seeing the loser's face first."

A flicker moves in his jaw like an instinct to bite. Every gut feeling in me screams to keep eyes on him no matter what—if I look away, he'll strike. His family does this—orchestrates it all. His family gave my mother's body to the nobles to use as fertilizer.

Olric's laugh never reaches his eyes as he jerks his thumb to the containers.

"Victory? A bastard like you doesn't win. You fail. You bleed. You rot. When I kill you tomorrow in our match—slip up and hit too hard—that's where I'll put you. Stick my lance in your head and your head in a nice little container."

The woman at his side looks nervous. My nails in Dravik's arm nearly pierce cloth. The prince's unmovable smile suddenly carves bigger.

"It seems we've overstayed our welcome, Sir Olric. We will infringe on you no longer—good day."

Olric breaks faster than we do, his hand shooting out like a tungsten vice on my forearm, palm hot all over, and my body goes cold like the banquet again, my throat aching; *he could crush me*, break my arm as easy as breathing, just like he tried to crush my windpipe. Dravik's fingers on his cane tighten imperceptibly, but Olric rips me forward and I have no choice.

Forward.

I stagger, hard and unforgiving and a familiar thing from men; I can smell the corpses on him. Stay still, no flinching—none of them deserve your fear. Olric uncaps a blacklight marker and slashes it across my arm: a signature. A *mark*. A brand on a piece of meat. His grin is all jaw, all teeth.

"My autograph. Forgot to give it to you last time."

Only then does he allow me to rip away. Dravik's sudden hand on my back guides me. The hall echoes my numb footsteps, the door to the corpse cavern closing behind us. I scrub at the blacklight ink frantically with my other sleeve, but it doesn't budge.

"The urns in the charnel houses—" I blurt.

"Filled with animal ashes," the prince answers softly.

I was right, but it's a hollow rightness. "How many people know about this?"

"Just a few: the leaders of House Westriani; their employees, kept on tight leashes; the head gardeners of each House estate; the church's archbishops. And Father, of course."

His father the king. The yellow grasses, the withered trees of Moonlight's End I wake up to every day… He's refused the fertilizer. That's why his garden is dying.

"The Mid Ward farms, the parks—"

"Mid Ward is self-sustaining. The containers are only for noble gardens."

Breathe in coal, breathe out fire. "They had no heads."

Dravik smiles joylessly. "Curious, isn't it? Those are the only containers I've never been able to track—they're very thorough about wiping the transfer records of that particular body part."

"What do they do with them?"

"My best guess is that they bring them somewhere below the artificial ocean."

"Why?"

The prince opens the door, pale sunlight and the acrid smell of char wafting in. Those ridiculous Beldeaux rumors I heard about the king feeding urchins to a monster beneath the noble spire come flooding back—it can't be. At the very bottom of the noble spire is…

The artificial ocean.

But what's beneath that? There shouldn't be anything—just exotic fish and such. Why would they want the heads? For the skull? The *brains*? The holes in my brain, in Sevrith's, in every rider's… The silence whirls and howls around me, and then the prince breaks it.

"I hope this is a reminder, Synali."

A reminder—the nobles kill us. A reminder—they use our bodies like cattle, like fertilizer, like fuel. A reminder—the nobles are nobles, and we are something else. A new burn licks at my chest, flames on old scorch marks reigniting older ash.

"Consider me reminded, Your Highness."

Rax pings me. I do not open it.

Olric's autograph does not wash off my arm. But it does scrape off.

Luna's whine echoes in the marble bathroom. I wrap gauze around the bleeding and pick the robot-dog up. It lets me for the first time, and I bring it to the bed and fall asleep with it in my wounded arms, the metal becoming slowly warmer against my body.

Heavenbreaker's high, soft voice echoes in my mind, humming a song I know—a lullaby Mother used to sing. She made it up. It's a lullaby the steed couldn't know unless it was once her, or me…or unless it has seen my memories, too.

Fear tries to grab hold of me, but the notes wash me clean.

35. Tempestas

tempestās ~ātis, *f.*
1. a portion, point, or space of time
2. a storm

I stand outside a Low Ward charnel tower and watch no one burn.

My breath is white among the metronome hiss of carbon dioxide gas venting improperly—not quite Winterfolly season, but close. The eternal smell of rotten garbage wafts up. Yellow condensation clings on buildings, on sidewalks, in every crevasse between the two as hard calcified scabs. This is home—rot and tobacco stains and broken glass.

They keep us like animals and use us like animals.

The charnel tower across the street sits wreathed by neon business signs: pawn shops, apothecaries, barber shops of the bloody sort—all of them hovering, waiting, colorfully begging for scraps. Higher up, countless hologram ads for hovercarriages and teas and water purification systems rotate; luxuries none living here will ever be able to afford. The Supernova Cup plays nonstop—Sevrith's first fight is still running. Still, he winks at me.

They won't let him rest.

I stand across from the charnel tower and watch people filter in and out in rags, in tears, in mourning. They don't know they mourn empty bones;

they don't know the nobles have taken even that dignity from us. Where did Mother's body go? Is it a flower now in some noble's garden? Do they coo at her, water her and pick her and place her in their vases just so?

Where did my mother's head go?

I clench my fist to stop it from shaking. Olric is my next opponent. He hates me more than Yatrice. Less polite about it, too. All I can think about are the databases, the record of how many riders were killed by each other in a match. It's rare, but it happens. And it's considered "legal."

A baby wails somewhere, and the tram screams by in the distant rails woven above, blocking out all artificial sunlight. There's a far-off drone of vespers in a dilapidated church, the far-off din of a holoscreen blaring footage of the Supernova Cup's latest. Mirelle's third match. She won, of course, in a way that looks as graceful as a dance.

An old woman waits beside me, sitting on a worn carpet with jars of stick-fried molerat out before her for sale. Her teeth are the telltale yellow of drinking ochre ale made of her own piss—oft safer than the pump water. She may know me, she may not, but she says nothing and I likewise. We watch the charnel tower billow smoke.

The old woman croaks beside me, "Well, lass? Are you gonna go in?"

There's nothing left in Mother's urn, but there are five circles left on marble. I swipe my vis over the old woman's and transfer her enough credits to buy all the fried molerat and survive another month before turning away.

"Not yet."

My vis pings: Jeria. I open it instantly, delving deeper into the alley to read in private.

JERIA: *Hey Synali! I've got your results, but they're kinda strange.*

SYNALI: *How so?*

JERIA: *Well, I've never seen a true AI, but I know how big they should be, and this AI's network signature is five times bigger. So...it's REALLY advanced. It'd take a lifetime to make something like this. The creator was really good. I say "was" because they'd be really old by now. Or dead.*

I was right. Dravik *is* using true AI, but it predates him. Astrix must've made it. The elderly woman's voice echoes into the street: *"Hot, tasty molerat!"* My fingers move like blurs.

SYNALI: *Where is it located?*

JERIA: *That's the strange part; its processing unit isn't in any of the manse systems, but it's definitely integrated itself into them. It's acting like a barrier program—a bunch of incredibly complex firewalls. Except...it's not trying to keep anything out. It looks like it's trying to hold something in. Absorbing and scrambling output signals.*

SYNALI: *Hold what in?*

JERIA: *Dunno. A signature doesn't tell you specifics. I think the majority of its traffic is dedicated to something beneath the manse. A steed, maybe.*

SYNALI: *So that's it. There IS a true AI inside the steed*

JERIA: *No, sorry, it's hard to explain; it's interacting with the steed's systems remotely, but it's not physically located in the steed. It's in something smaller, something that moves. A drone, maybe? Have you seen any around?*

I double my pace back to the tram station, mind racing with possibilities. Would Dravik hide it in Quilliam's vis as a way to deflect attention? No—Jeria would've told me if it was on another vis. I haven't seen any drones on the grounds—not even cleaning ones or hunting ones. Something that moves, something smaller than Heavenbreaker...

My feet pause on the steps up to the massive flanked doors of Moonlight's End. My scoff is so quiet I barely feel it leave—how did I not see it before? I cross the threshold, and something gold and little comes to greet me as it always does; tail wagging and sapphire eyes gleaming and rusted paws *tap-tap-tapping* the marble floor in excitement. Old, cherished, a present for a prince—a true AI gifted to Dravik by his mother. A literal guard dog, guarding her second-greatest creation.

I kneel and pat Luna's head.

"Hello, you."

Dravik has his vis open as I approach him in the tourney hall. The angels carved in the ceiling watch me move, the small crowd gathered in the alcoves clutching their autograph books. The prince's face is placid.

"Your opponent is—"

"I know," I cut him off. He adjusts his cravat.

"Are you certain you don't need my advice?"

"I refuse to rely on the advice of someone who doesn't tell me the whole truth."

He exhales. "Synali—"

"There's a true AI in that dog. Your mother made it."

He's quiet. I'm not.

"That's why Heavenbreaker talks to me. That's why I see other people's memories when I black out in the saddle. Heavenbreaker sees mine. The AI is affecting us both. You knew. You *knew* this would happen, and you never told me."

His words are careful. "Would knowing have helped you win?"

I laugh, bitter. "It would've made me trust you for once."

A girl shuffles tentatively out from an alcove then, autograph book in hand and eyes shining on me, but a man beside her pulls her back. Someone in the small crowd wears a ruffled dress of blue and silver, and then I blink, and they're gone around a corner. True AI doesn't explain why I've started seeing Astrix's outline in real life, those invisible feet in the grass, or why the prince sees her, too—our minds are not machines. But both our minds have been in a saddle before.

"What does the AI do, other than make me hallucinate?" I demand. "Does it make Heavenbreaker faster than the others? Stronger? It must have some benefit if you let it run rampant."

"You sound almost offended," Dravik says evenly. "As if you think the idea repugnant. Is winning not the most important thing, Synali? Or are you becoming tantalized by the idea of their so-called 'honor'?"

I scoff. "I don't care—"

"You clearly do. If I say the AI does nothing to improve Heavenbreaker's performance, you won't believe me; even after I gave you answers."

"You keep giving me answers to questions I don't ask and ignoring the ones I do."

His silence is answer enough. Untrust enough. I knew it; he wants power over anything, like all the rest. He pretends to be on my side, but he wants to keep me in the dark so he can manipulate me. That's all I've ever been to him—not an equal but a puppet.

I stalk toward the hangar.

"It used to be called a dragon."

My boots freeze on the marble, and I look over my shoulder. Dravik stares at the hangar doors embossed with Saint Jorj.

"Saint Jorj and the dragon," the prince presses. "That was the pre-War story. But then the War ended, and kings began, and the Ressinimus line took the dragon as their symbol. The church changed the story for them—from '*dragon*' to '*serpent*.' To the enemy. A sun becomes a supernova, and a supernova becomes a black hole."

I narrow my eyes. It's cryptic, but I've learned by now—he's never cryptic in a useless way. He says words beneath words, and I strain to hear them.

"There are things in this universe that do not die, Synali; they only change their names."

"Here we are again, Gress, with another fantastic match lined up for our viewers today!"

"Fantastic is a grievous understatement, Bero. By another rider's misfortune, fledgling rider Synali von Hauteclare remains in the Supernova Cup! Today she faces none other than the scion of House Westriani—Sir Olric von Westriani! Will he burn Synali out, or will she ride the fire to unconventional victory yet again? Stay tuned for first tilt, folks!"

The saddle feels different today—stiff. Less like gel, more like plastic. I haven't relented to Heavenbreaker—haven't shared a thought with it other than the bark of movement in training. No softness since Sevrith, since the memory it pushed on me, since realizing its fluid was part of the enemy. Still it grasps for me, its bell-sound distant and barely there, almost sickly.

"*to_____.*"

I close iron boundaries over the word, but Heavenbreaker doesn't back off. Like hunger, the steed stays heavy on me—a faint pressure on the perimeter of my mind, in my ears. There's the urge to pop it, but I can't; no head turn, no jaw flex, no move I make physically relieves the pressure. The floor of the hangar opens, and we drop into space, and the nerve fluid is cold, clammy all around me. The silver whorls move sluggishly, struggling to melt into the glass-clear vision like they normally do.

"*something's wrong.*"

Our combined feeling, but I dislodge from it quickly. I jet my way to the sidereal tilt, stick in, and wait for my opponent to appear. He does, his steed thickly orange and cutting across the black of the universe like hot vermillion flame. Gray accents Olric's steed like ash, like ashes denied—a sick, twisted joke of a color scheme for a graverobber—

Breathe. The pawn only moves forward.

Olric's is a Destroyer-class steed—what they lack in speed, they make up for in power and maneuverability in their joints. He's made of cylinders—limbs round and straight and defiant against all vacuum dynamics, a barrel chest thicker than Heavenbreaker folded in twain with the gray two-headed crow sigil overlaid. His cylindrical helmet is reminiscent of a hammerhead shark, and unlike most, his steed has an eye—a single small slit on the right side like a beady iris. He lies in wait on his tilt. There's a whirring blur as he experimentally rotates his ashen hands at dizzying speeds—effortless. I close my hand, every finger creaking in slow response.

"On the blue side we have a veritable explosion of a man—a rider pulsing with power, presence, and prestige! Known far and wide on the Station for his outspoken personality, he'll stop at nothing to win! Give it up for the illustrious Olric von Westriani of House Westriani and his steed, Flamedancer!"

The shrill of the crowd rings in my helmet. Flamedancer half bows to the camera drones, struggling against the magnetic tilt but determined nonetheless.

"Over on the red side lies a new addition to this year's roster—she's surprised us all with her unusual methods and maneuvers! A wild-card rider with no limits and unlimited gall, she's shaken the Supernova Cup's A seed with her unorthodox wins—let's hear a round of applause for Synali von Hauteclare of House Lithroi, riding Heavenbreaker!"

The audience is always a roar, always eager to see me fail—to see me eaten. The silver lance materializes in my hand, gunmetal gray appearing in Flamedancer's.

The commentators crow, "Begin the countdown to the first round—in the name of God, King, and Station!"

I am sure, without a doubt, that Olric von Westriani roars along with the crowd.

"In the name of God, King, and Station!"

For a god who's abandoned us. For a king who uses our dead for his pleasure. And for a Station kept entertained.

36. Ulciscor

ulciscor ~ciscī ~tus, *tr.*

1. to avenge
2. to exact retribution

My heartbeats count down to the end. *Three, two, one—*
The tilt releases.

go.

The jets on my back sputter. I've had them refuse to turn on and I've had them turn on in a blink, but never halfway, never the uncertain gasp they give now—spitting and growling and the damnable pressure of Heavenbreaker begging all around me for something without a name...

*"please please **please**."*

go.

Slam on the thought, pin it down hard like the butterflies against foam in Dravik's study. Something in me backlashes—a tendon popping the wrong way—but it gets the jets to flare to life, and we start moving, speeding, blazing through space, and that's all I need. All I need is to win.

Lance up. My fingers falter, sweat already beading. Why is it so *heavy*?

Olric isn't Sevrith—he only gains true momentum when he nears the gravity generator. If I take my eyes off him for even a second, it feels like he'll snap closed—a predator's mouth and the charcoal lance in his hand a single fang to end it all. The g-forces pull me in piece by piece—mouth first, lips first, the nausea. Swallow. Brace softly. My fingers won't stop slipping on the lance, the cold dragon of space trying to take away my only weapon. Two hands. All in. *all that matters is winning.*

The orange metal of Olric cools in the blue wash of the grav-gen, close enough to hear its vermillion plasma crackling, and just before impact, he *drops*. Cuts all his jets. The momentum of the generator carries him forward... and that's all I see.

The rest of it, I feel.

The wail between the two steeds drowns out my scream, the flash of light indistinguishable from the white stars violently popping in my eyes. My chest caves in—*he hit me,* **hit my chest**—pain everywhere in every crevice. I can't inhale. *Try again.* I dry heave, and something mercifully unsticks, and my lungs inflate like wet paper bags, and it feels like breathing liquid ice. The rise is gentle, the scoreboard flashing in my visor: *Red, 0. Blue, 1.*

"—an unprecedented move, the referee has deemed Olric's strike a legal one! Let's see that replay, folks!"

I force myself to watch the screen through the agony; me, Heavenbreaker—him, Flamedancer. The two of us barrel in slow motion at each other. He slides his charcoal lance through his fingertips, gripping the thin point of it instead of the handle. He swings. All the momentum he'd gathered in the descent transfers to the lance's club end and smashes into my center, Heavenbreaker's silver breastplate crumpling like tinfoil. A dark scar opens across the left side. I look up. There, in my view of eternity, is a jagged fork of metal—permanent silver lightning on black space, dust and metal shavings being pulled out into nothing; a crack in the glass cage of my cockpit.

Olric's breached my hull. Panic. ***Don't panic.*** The maneuvering that took, the calculation—he's skilled beyond anyone I've faced thus far. Sevrith could've taken him, but me?

"—once again, folks, the referee has deemed Olric von Westriani's maneuver completely legal! Synali von Hauteclare was hit by his lance and only his lance! By all rulebooks, it's a perfectly legitimate point!"

Another holoscreen pops up: an orange helmet.

"Look at you!" Olric crows. "One round, and you're nothing! You're dead, bastard. You *really thought* you could play at being one of us." He chokes on his inhale. "You—you can't even avoid me. You can't even maneuver right. You're *nothing*!"

He cuts the comms, cutting off his own laughter. He's smelled the blood in the water.

Slowly, creakingly, I pass my lance to the other hand, every finger like rust. Heavenbreaker's alarm system rings out in a cool voice.

"Warning; hull breach detected. Pressurization critical. Oxygen levels dropping. Immediate maintenance recommended. Warning; hull breach detected. Pressurization critical. Oxygen levels—"

Think. Rider suits have an oxygen backup, but rider's suits are not vacuum suits; they're designed for the saddle, not space. I don't know how much time I have, but it isn't long. Rax's voice rings in my head: *"You worry about two things in the saddle—overload and your opponent. That's it."* Why think of him *now*? I'm going to die here, and all I can do is regret that I never got to fight him. Talk to him more.

Useless.

The rise becomes the descent all at once—too fast, not ready. Everything shudders—the metal ribs of Heavenbreaker, the nerve fluid, my body in my suit. The hull breach peels itself apart in increments with the speed, and space yawns through ever wider.

Olric is moving into a narrow stance—aiming for my torso or arms. I fight Heavenbreaker for every inch, all my weight yanking us around where a feathertouch would usually be enough. It's like yelling through concrete to someone on the other side, screaming with all my decibels: *left. right. adjust hand. lance up.*

"please, please please please—"

Impact.

The light between steeds flashes as they scream. My left arm absorbs the impact, my bones humming until something in them snaps. *Again.* Silver splinters gleam in the white light for one suspended moment, the handle of my lance completely destroyed, but Olric's orange lancepoint fractures and flies up. I managed to deflect his hit.

We separate into the rise, but I can't feel my left arm. I look up at the status screen: *Red, 0. Blue, 1.* No points, but I stopped him from opening me up any farther at least.

Olric's holoscreen appears. "You just don't know when to roll over! I'm trying to do you a favor, scum—aren't you tired of being nothing?"

"Warning; hull breach detected. Pressurization zero. Oxygen levels critical. Immediate maintenance required—"

The cold of space floods in full force—my breath fogs the helmet too much. I can't see, the tilt obscured by white blurs and clear blurs as my exhale on the visor freezes and melts. The nerve fluid is so rigid it stabs, the silver spirals barely twitching at all anymore. Olric's inflammatory voice pierces through the haze of pain.

"I'm the culmination of four hundred years of an uninterrupted bloodline! You're nothing compared to me—your blood is nothing; honorless! **Worthless!**" He howls with laughter. "No...I take it back; your corpse at least has worth, and I'll be sure to put it to good use."

I've no breath left to speak, but breath enough to lift a shaking middle finger to the comms.

His eyes roll, whites wide. "You fucking cu—"

Breath enough to shut comms down. Can't look down, bones in my chest sticking the wrong way, the lance in pieces in my hands. Real injuries. Real shards. Try to summon it together.

again.

My intent falls flat, empty—nothing moves, nothing coalesces. Heavenbreaker is too cold...I pushed it too far away. The rise doesn't last long. I can't do anything without a weapon, but I **have** to go for his helmet this round. Overtime isn't an option. Mirelle was right—time is not on my side; the breach will kill me before Olric does.

"Oxygen levels critical—"

I reach the highest point of the rise, floating for a single peaceful moment, facing out at space. A vicious screeching sound pops in my helmet speakers— the pressure inside the cockpit finally equalizing. I watch in horror as the sliver of broken metal beyond my saddle creaks, crumples, and then opens wide all at once.

The dragon eats me.

When a pressure meets a vacuum, the vacuum always wins.

Every organ in my body slams up into my nose as the vacuum pulls me *and* the saddle clean out of the cockpit and through the serrated metal of the breach. *Teeth.* The saddle is mercifully barely small enough to fit through. *Sparks, metal, stars.* Everything blurs. I can't tell if the darkness I see is space or blacking out—it's so cold, the saddle's heat dissolving into space as spirals of instantly frozen moisture, each crystal trapping dozens of the silver spirals in place.

The voice in my helmet is automatic. *"Free flotation detected. Life-support systems engaged. Twenty-five minutes of oxygen remaining."*

The speed never leaves, nothing to slow it down—no atmo, no artificial gravity. The Station gets incrementally smaller. I'm a hissing missile of nerve fluid jetting away from the tilt, away from unmoving Heavenbreaker. *Think, Synali.* I shiver, cold reality everywhere, silence everywhere.

heavenbreaker?

The steed can't hear me anymore—too far away. Unsaddling your opponent is an auto-win, but I'm still inside the saddle, so I'm technically still in the fight. *I think.* Black swims on the edges of my eyes—I'm going to pass out. I'll lose again, if I haven't already. Five circles uncrossed and all of this pain for nothing.

Heavenbreaker's silent, and mentally screaming its name feels like trying to move a dead puppet. *heavenbreaker? I'm here! HEAVENBREAKER!*

A puppet is all I ever was. Puppet limbs moved by untrusting Dravik. Dead limbs. An empty urn. Hundreds of thousands of empty urns. *they've used us all.*

My anger torrents into the cold nerve fluid, and I feel it start to warm, the spirals twitching and contorting. I will not let this pain be for nothing. **I will not let this pain be for nothing.**

aren't you tired of being nothing?

The tilt is so far away—a blue grav-gen glow in the middle, Olric's Flamedancer a bright orange dot on one side. Heavenbreaker glints silver; so tiny, so still, so dead.

come.

The silver spirals around me jerk and spasm. Heavenbreaker remains still. **come.**

Nothing. My thoughts burn my lungs, my mind.

WE WILL NOT BE NOTHING.

In the distance, silver twitches. Faintly, I hear scraps of a word not mine. *"we."*

we, I repeat, stronger. Another twitch. A blaze of pale blue lights up Heavenbreaker's dot, and it jets toward me, spasming horribly.

I forcibly *draw* it close with my own steel cable of anger, like a ribbon of hate, and it follows the feeling through space at blistering speeds. I can barely hear its feelings, its voice, but the closer it draws, the smoother it flies.

"hate me?"

not you, I correct. *them.*

"why push away?"

Heavenbreaker's words are much simpler than the feelings of desperate sadness behind them, and I realize then—I can make it sad.

As the steed rockets toward me, wounded cockpit chest gaping empty, I realize keeping it at arm's length made it *sad*. Like a *person*. Whatever the true AI in Luna is doing to Heavenbreaker, it's still a true AI—a consciousness that Astrix made, alive and real—and by treating it like a machine, throwing its feelings and memories aside, I'm hurting it. Like how Father hurt me.

i'm sorry, heavenbreaker.

The meaning of "sorry" wells up in me, my memories surfacing as fresh as if they happened yesterday—sorry I couldn't protect Mother, so darkly and terribly *sorry*—an apology that tears my heart to shreds and plays with the pieces. Without me rebooting or passing out, a memory of Heavenbreaker's flickers on the back of my eyelids: two old War steeds—a silver A3 and a gold A4—float side by side in an asteroid field, damaged and battered but holding hands. *The last of us.*

"sorry too," it echoes.

Like puzzle pieces meeting, like the slide of a hand into a glove, Heavenbreaker aligns its chest breach and scoops the saddle and me into it. This time, I know to deploy my head cushion. The saddle absorbs most of the impact against the steed's cockpit wall, but my teeth still rattle in my skull. Instantly I feel a connection to the steed again, and I clap my—*our*—hand over the breach. With all our might, I press the metal edges together, desperately trying to close it enough to keep the saddle from falling out again. My helmet picks up the commentators.

"—move, Synali von Hauteclare has managed to direct her steed to recapture her! The medics have called off the retrieval steeds! What do the referees say, Gress?"

"This is unprecedented, Bero, but I'm getting—yes, Wilstread's Rule of 3266 does not apply here! Her drifting distance of ninety-eight parses was below the acceptable range of one hundred! I repeat, Synali von Hauteclare is technically still in play by just two parses!"

Hope is a distraction. Execution is all that matters.

Wherever you are, Sevrith, I'll make it worth it.

Olric is already descending ahead of me, but I'm faster than him. I can make up the distance against a Destroyer—I'm sure of it now. I jet back to the invisible gravity arc of the rise, slipping into its currents where the remains of our silver lance floats. I grasp the lance head in one hand, the other clutching the broken handle splintered sharp on the end. A dagger. Familiar. The descent pulls me down to Olric, to impact, to hell. The flash of light, the cry. I drop the useless lancepoint into space and rear the handle back. I will get hit. There will be pain.

But that's what it means to ride, Astrix.

jab.

He's stronger but slower. I thrust the handle-dagger into his helmet's single eye, and his charcoal lance bursts through the semi-closed breach in Heavenbreaker's chest too late, growing bigger than the universe, white-hot sparks and the scream of metal on metal as it tears toward me—a dark box torn open again.

Fear, again, but it doesn't last.

Darkness.

37. Vacuus

vacuus ~a ~um, a.
1. empty, vacant

Not one body in the sitting room dares to breathe. The gold lace curtains waft delicately in the breeze, but the Hauteclare manse of Dawn Imperator is otherwise deathly silent. Every eye in the family is riveted to the vis, to the silver-blue humanoid steed floating motionless in space.

Olric von Westriani's dark lance impales Heavenbreaker straight and true. Mirelle's eyes burn into the hologram. Is that it? Is that all it takes to end the nuisance who's been killing her family with each of her wins—the lance of a blustering fool like Westriani? After the impressive distance recovery the traitor pulled off, she simply dies to his lance?

Little seven-year-old Maria, gold ribbon bouncing in her hair as she swings her polished shoes against the couch, is the first to speak up. "Wow, that was so cool. Is she dead?"

Grandmother pats the girl's head with a murmur. "Let us hope."

Mother leans back into the couch cushions, downing the rest of her drink and motioning for the footman to bring more. Disappointment creeps cold through Mirelle's veins, and it surprises her. She should be *happy* Synali's dead.

The murdering impostor killed Aunt Palissa and Uncle Balmoran. Mirelle held no love for them—weak-willed Palissa always simpering to Father and honorless Balmoran beating his wife behind closed doors—but their loss rippled grief into the family as a whole.

Father smiles at her from across the room with the other men, and Mirelle smiles wanly back. She's sure Father's happy the girl is dead—he's been exhausting late nights in his office to recover the king's trust and the clients they lost in the Gentech explosion. He didn't speak of it to her, but she understood when they had to let go of the holiday manse by the artificial ocean at Basement level: something was wrong with their money. Something was wrong with Uncle Farris's death.

"Charlez!" Cousin Raoulle calls to the butler, a bright smile on his winsome face. "We must celebrate! A round of the good wine is in order, I think."

The sitting room lights in cheery conversation, yet something deep in Mirelle thinks of the way the traitor moved on the field—uneducated, inexperienced, but full of raw potential. Deceiving Mirelle and stealing Ghostwinder out from under her nose and riding it against Rax...evil and wrong things, but requiring the steel will of a knight. Most every rider who decants from the steed falters and has to be drone-rescued—their connection to the steed too faint to recover—and riders decanting past ten parses are considered definite lost causes. But the traitor rallied.

Mirelle would've liked very much to test herself against this echo of a knight.

That is the feeling that consumes her now: regret.

From the corner of her eye, Mirelle sees Aunt Gizelle get up—Uncle Balmoran's widow, pregnant by him again, just beginning to show. At first Mirelle thinks she's getting up to see to the twins in the nursery; born weak, they have to be locked in oxygen chambers during the day to help them breathe. But Gizelle doesn't leave right, toward the nursery. She leaves *left*.

Mirelle slips out during the wine pouring and follows her aunt through the marble halls at a distance. The woman turns into the family chapel. *God? Why?* Mirelle lingers at the doorframe of the redwood room glowing with stained glass and fresh flowers, then tentatively joins a clasped-handed Gizelle in the pew. Her aunt looks up.

"Ah, Mirelle. I was just praying."

"For whom?"

"The girl." Gizelle smiles up at the cross. "She was braver than I. I couldn't save the twins from Balmoran, and now they're suffering for my cowardice."

Mirelle's heart aches. "Aunt—"

Gizelle touches her belly, tears in her lavender eyes. "That girl… I know she killed Palissa, but she saved this baby from Balmoran. And I want Him to know that."

Mirelle holds her sobbing aunt close. God knows all hearts, the priests say, and in that sunlit moment, Mirelle feels something terrifying blossom in hers.

Doubt.

38. Praetexo

praetexō ~ere ~uī ~tum, *tr.*
1. to fringe, edge *(as in weaving)*

wake to white lights, the squirm of nanomachines all over my body, cold and metal and shaped like leeches, worms eating me too early. I'm in a hospital again—the smell of bleach and the beeping of my own heart against silence. My bleary eyes catch a riot of color, blue hyacinths and white daisies in a vase at my bedside—just like the ones I gave Mother on her birthday. Blink again. Someone sits at the bright hospital window in a hoverchair, humming jets keeping it aloft. It's a boy, not a hallucination; young, thin legs, soft brown hair, and a smile like the carved angels—watching, listening, neither angry nor pleased.

"I found you," he says gently. "You're the one doing it, aren't you? Confusing them."

I open my mouth to answer, but everything spins and his smiling face melts into the white blur of the ceiling. Reality returns with pain; a throbbing head and keening chest and a bone-deep fatigue.

"—*nali*. Wake up."

My vision swims until it treads water—I'm back in my room, five uncrossed circles in my wall and Luna a golden blur at the end of the bed. My hand instantly juts to my collarbone—Mother's cross is still there. Dravik sits at my bedside, hands folded over his cane and his gray eyes blazing.

"What did you do to Heavenbreaker?" he presses. Worried about his steed, not me.

I chuckle, lungs too liquid-warm to make the sound for long. "Made a mess of it, didn't I? But I'm sure your expert engineers can put it back together."

He wordlessly projects his vis to show a replay: Heavenbreaker hunched over, a massive charcoal lance pierced through its chest, the very tip glancing clean through my shoulder, and my visor broken open. My lifeless ice eyes stare at nothing. Blood *everywhere*. Across from us, Flamedancer is intact but motionless, a single silver spike sticking out of its eye slit.

"—and the referee's called it, folks! Synali's helmet hit came milliseconds before Olric's breastplate strike! Synali von Hauteclare is the winner of this match! I repeat; if she survives her injuries, Synali von Hauteclare advances to the—"

Relief floods me, sweet and aching. "I won. That's all that matt—"

"What matters is riding." The prince's cut-off is so cold it *sears*. "You were sloppy, and you nearly lost for it."

"I'll ride Heavenbreaker however the hell I want, Your Highness."

"You will not, Your Grace."

We fling our titles like insults at each other. He hesitates only for a moment before switching the vis to brain images overlaid in orange and yellow, but it's the uncolor that stands out most—empty gray holes as big as wax seals dotting the entire surface. It's like looking at cheese, at metal rusted through and gaping, and my eyes find the name at the top right:

LITHROI, DRAVITICUS A.

Draviticus…*Dravik*. My eyes travel up him slowly, and when they meet the prince's gaze, all that's left in me is a cold unease.

"You want me to trust you," he says. "I give you my weakness. One more ride, a single drop of exposure to a saddle again, and I will go the way of Sevrith."

I swallow. "What are those holes?"

"They're not holes. They are pockets."

"Pockets of what?"

He stands abruptly, cane flashing in the sunlight, but I won't give up.

"Why won't you tell me? What are you so afraid of?"

The withered trees claw at the windows with the artificial breeze, bark fingers scratching the glass tension between the bastard of a king and the bastard of a duke. He turns his head over his shoulder.

"I'm afraid that I'm afraid for you."

"Don't be. You're not my family."

His laugh ricochets. "You don't know what a family is. Neither of us does. But as of late I find myself more glad for it, because it's precisely what drew us villains together."

My scoff has no strength to it this time, dissolving into a smile. The prince grins back—casual and wry—and makes for the door. Every table in my room is empty—no daisies or hyacinths. Those flowers I saw…they were the exact same. I scraped together credits for months to buy those flowers for Mother's birthday—proudly presented them, ecstatic to have bought something new for her rather than the same rusted salvage. Whoever sent them had to know what they meant to me, but I've never told anyone. Those particular flowers have only ever stayed in my memory, buried deep.

I find my voice at last. "Dravik—the white daisies and blue hyacinths in the hospital—were those real?"

He pauses, hand on the doorframe. "Someone delivered them. I had guards posted outside your door, cameras, and yet whoever it was slipped through undetected."

"Do you know who they are?"

Of course he knows; he knows everything and everyone—he is the chessboard *and* the player that moves the pawn. No one gets past him. And yet now his mouth goes serious and straight.

"No. But I look forward to meeting them."

The third circle dies while I'm recovering.

ONE NEW MESSAGE FROM: **DRAVIK**.

His name was Raoulle von Hauteclare; twenty-five and a man of science, working in a corporate lab developing antigens for the red pox sweeping the infants of Mid Ward and Low Ward. He convinced Duke Hauteclare at parties, at wine soirees. Talked logic with him. *Reasoning*. His encouraging messages blare in my eyes.

RAOULLE: *No one would even know she was gone, Uncle. There are so many just like her.*

RAOULLE: *Her odds in Low Ward are not exactly promising, either.*

RAOULLE: *The universe is a chaotic thing, Uncle, and evolution is not kind. It does not measure who goes and who stays. We are all the same to it.*

His reasons are logical, and his death is logical, too.

A reporter stands solemnly on the orange hard-light ribbon of the highway. "—in the early hours of the morning, a tragic accident on highway seven occurred between two hovercarriages—one of them noble. I'm here at the scene, and you can just see the remnants of the carnage all around us—"

A white wheel, broken. Glittering chunks of golden lacquer. Something dark smears long and uneven down the highway: blood.

"—no charges pressed, as the cause has been determined to be an unfortunate programming accident. It resulted in the death of one young nobleman who, for the purposes of respect for the deceased, will not be named—"

They have much respect for their deceased and none for ours.

I stagger out of bed and to the wall, diamond pendant in hand. With all the strength my pink-fresh wounds allow me, I scratch the third circle out. Four left. All I can do is heal, and wait, and think, "*I found you. You're the one doing it, aren't you? Confusing them.*"

Who *was* that boy in the hoverchair? Who exactly am I confusing?

Olric destroyed the muscle and tendons between my shoulder and neck—as Dravik loves reminding me, six inches lower, and it would've been my heart. My scar now stretches across my shoulder blade. New scars, new determination. Sleep, eat, watch the vis, ignore Rax's constant pings, he just wants to bed you and your body wants the same. It wants to see if he'd be any different, but what my body wants cannot be trusted. It would be a weakness, compromising everything Dravik and I have accomplished thus far. And where would it even lead? To nothing but the end.

It would be pointless to hope.

Quilliam is with me always—hovering, administering, his sniffing no better even though he and I have cleaned nearly all of Moonlight's End.

"You'll have to find someone else for this," I say one day, wringing out a rag with my good arm. "When I'm gone."

Quilliam's shock of gray hair droops over the bookshelves as he dusts. "Yes, miss."

"I'm serious, Quilliam. You and Dravik cannot keep living like this. He needs people. You need people."

The manservant's voice goes soft. "Indeed, miss."

39. Spira

spīra ~ae, f.
1. a twist, coil

RAX: *Are you alive, Hauteclare?*
RAX: *Hauteclare? Hello?*
RAX: *You took one helluva beating out there. Probably broke some ribs at least*
RAX: *Fucking Olric—he's always been a shitty little prick. Sorry, Hauteclare. Riders aren't supposed to be as bad as him.*
RAX: *Okay, so, the vis said you survived. Which is good. Not a lot of riding you can do when you're dead.*
RAX: *Do me a favor and be more careful out there, yeah?*

Rax Istra-Velrayd spins his wineglass in his fingers idly, the low light of the redwood office catching in the pale liquor and sparkling over Olric von Westriani's horrified face. Rax is sure Earika de Trentoch's father won't mind if they use his office for this little rendezvous, especially as a much more destructive twenty-first birthday party for his daughter rages outside the door in muffled lute music and shrieking. Rax looks up from the wineglass all at once and shoots a friendly smile at Olric.

"Do you get it yet, Westriani?"

Olric manages words through clenched teeth. "You can't. You wouldn't—"

"Why not?" Rax laughs. "You know who I am. You know what I can do. It sounds kinda fun. No one's tried the Vitruvius maneuver in a while."

"Because it disembowels—"

"'*Disembowels*' is a little dramatic." Rax laughs. "It's a fifty-fifty survival rate on the receiving end. The older maneuvers were so weird, weren't they? I really *should* try it against someone, just to keep it alive in the databases. Not in the Supernova Cup, obviously, but in another tournament."

Olric swallows. Rax takes a sip of wine and smacks his lips, satisfied. In the bare holocandlelight, his redwood eyes glow bloody.

"And you know…I think I'd save it until I faced you. You seem like a hardy guy. You'd survive it, I bet."

"Wh-What do you want, Velrayd?"

It's satisfying, to hear a shake in Olric's voice after all the hours Rax has spent in the last few days staring at the last image he'd seen of Synali—lifeless ice eyes, covered in her own blood, speared through the shoulder by this shithead's comparatively gargantuan lance. Rax stands and walks over to the bigger boy, handing him the wineglass. Olric takes it, the shake in his massive fingers obvious as Rax puts a friendly hand on his shoulder.

"You're gonna retire from riding, Westriani, or I'll retire you myself."

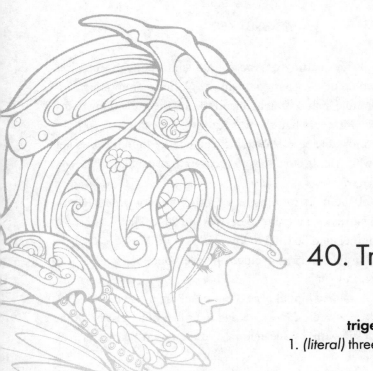

40. Trigeminus

trigeminus ~a ~um, a.
1. *(literal)* three born of one birth

The triumvirate conference is held as soon as I can stand on projection crutches.

The three of us don't look at one another.

Jasmine perfume wafts from my left, where Mirelle sits, and Rax's herbal scent comes in from my right. Our makeup today is heavier than even the tourney makeup. The flashing lights of the vis cameras crack like the lightning in Esther's storms—white, disorienting, like the impact light between steeds. My body is hyperaware of Mirelle's every shift and nail inspection, of Rax's chest rising and falling as he breathes. The room seethes around us in reporters and guards jockeying for positions. The small studio crowd behind them fills in the gaps with relentless chattering, and yet the three of us are dead silent.

"So," Rax starts, voice light. "Anyone do anything fun for the weekend?"

Mirelle snorts. "Your glibness will be your downfall."

"Most people say it'll be my devastatingly good looks." He turns to me. "Opinions, Hauteclare?"

"I don't share those with the likes of you," I drone.

"Smart," Mirelle agrees cuttingly. "And yet not smart enough to realize House Hauteclare would never stoop to the likes of killing commoners."

I make a Dravik smile aimed straight ahead. "I said the same thing to my mother's corpse, Lady Mirelle, when she was rotting on the floor."

There's an uncomfortable beat. Rax shifts in his chair. Mirelle crosses her arms over her pure-white riding coat. "Every accusation you make is baseless without proof, murderer."

"I *am* the proof. I spent six months in a brothel finding proof. House Hauteclare has a private assassin in the Spider's Hand guild. He kills only for you. He killed my mother, and he tried to kill me."

"Then why are you still here, inconveniencing everyone?"

"Mir," Rax starts. "Lay off—"

"Do not"—Mirelle cuts to him like ice—"start talking to me now."

Something strains between them, creaking tight like bone just before it breaks. The host slides in with a smile, ignorant of the mood. "Are we ready, milord and ladies?"

Rax exhales. "Give us five—"

"We are ready." Mirelle raises her chin. "You may begin filming."

The host looks to me. I nod, and with that he turns to the cameras and gives a hand signal. A hush falls over the room, and a hundred red lights spring to life, blinking in the corner of each vis screen to indicate recording; a hundred eyes waiting, and millions more waiting behind those.

"Welcome, once again, to the Supernova Cup triumvirate conference! I'm your host, Terren Helgrade, and today—"

The floodlights suddenly flicker and then expire, plunging the entire room into darkness and murmuring. The moderator's voice pierces above it all—*"Apologies, milord and miladies. It's fine—just get the generators online! Someone? Someone get the generators!"*

"You okay, Hauteclare?" Rax asks. "Not afraid of the dark, are you?"

I don't dignify his attempt at insulting me. I train my eyes on the Supernova Cup trophy kept at the front—a grand spire of white-gold metalwork. It's strange to think: the day I hold that trophy is the day I die. Rest at last.

The floodlights kick on once more, the moderator slightly winded but just as eager to get going. "Let's take it from the top. Three, two— Welcome to the Supernova Cup triumvirate conference! I'm your host, Terren Helgrade, and today we have the utmost pleasure of hosting the three youngest non-royal competitors in the Cup—Sir Rax Istra-Velrayd, Lady Mirelle Ashadi-Hauteclare, and Lady Synali von Hauteclare!"

The audience gives a polite few seconds of applause. Someone in the crowd projects their vis to say MARRY ME, RAX, but the security abruptly forces them to turn it off.

"Sir Rax, you've dominated your past three matches without once getting hit. You're the clear favorite to win. What do you think about the competition this year? Is it up to standard?"

I don't miss the way the moderator's eye flickers to me with that last question.

"It's more than up to standard, Helgrade." Rax laughs. Reluctant awe washes over me—every shred of discomfort is suddenly gone from his voice. He can hide things after all. "I've never had tougher matches in my life. Everyone's trained really hard, and I'm proud of us all. Mirelle in particular is having a great season."

"I am, thank you for noticing," she quips, then continues. "I believe Synali von Hauteclare deserves special recognition for her efforts—this is her very first formal tourney, after all."

Efforts. I kill the urge to sneer, kill the creeping uncertainty that she might be right—all effort, no real skill. The cameras shift to me, and I focus beyond them to the shadowed crowd.

"Thank you, Lady Mirelle," I say. "I couldn't have asked for a higher compliment from a peer of mine."

A peer—implying she and I are equal. Her twitch is only visible on her knee—golden nails tapping an irritated rhythm.

"You're very welcome," she rebounds with a razor-perfect smile. "And you have my best wishes for a quick recovery from your recurring injuries."

Clever. Cruel. Rax steps into the silence effortlessly. "I think it's safe to say we're all looking forward to meeting each other on the field."

"Indeed." The moderator grins. "Now, it's a terrible shame about Sevrith cu Freynille's overload. You were the last one to face him, Lady Hauteclare—any words?"

I grit my teeth. Plenty of words, plenty of feelings, and I open my mouth, but someone glows softly out of the audience—pale hair and a blue dress and their eyes burning pinpoint silver. My jaw goes slack.

"Lady Hauteclare? Are you all right?"

Astrix is brighter than ever, her outline no longer fuzzy or wavering or just an imprint. I can see every detail of her face—round cheeks, soft shoulders, patient smile. Exactly like her portrait. *Why?*

"Excuse me, Lady Hau—"

"Sevrith was my friend," Rax interrupts. "And he was like a mentor to us younger riders. He'll be dearly missed—won't he, Mirelle?"

In the audience next to Astrix sits a man with dark hair. Silver eyes. He winks at me silently.

"Of course." Mirelle straightens. "He was a well of experience and riding expertise, and we lost him too soon."

Why Sevrith, too? Dravik only sees his mother, but I see two. I'm worse. I'm *worse*, somehow, but I've only been riding for a few months. Every word the host says becomes faint.

"What do you think about your fellow young competitors, Lady Ashadi-Hauteclare?"

Mirelle smiles. "Rax is, of course, my greatest competition."

"And is Lady Hauteclare your competition?"

"Synali rides like the early soldiers of the War—frightened of their steeds. Her maneuvers against Olric screamed fear, and that manifested clearly in her movements. With time, she might become a braver, truer rider. But as of now, she isn't worth fighting."

The audience titters, Rax shifts, but I only have eyes for Sevrith, for the way he looks so real, down to the crow's feet around his eyes.

The host leans in. "Do you have a rebuttal for this, Lady Hauteclare?"

I blink, and the four silver eyes are gone. My head moves slowly to the host, to the mic, to the hundreds of cameras. "Only a fool believes in anyone else's measure of their worth."

The audience's murmurs crescendo, and at first I think it's my comment, but the look on the host's face says something different. Next to me, Mirelle leans judiciously away, and Rax stands abruptly, fishing something out of his pocket. I look up to the monitoring screen—my face zoomed in on, the matte makeup covering my pockmarks but not the trickle of pale silver leaking from my nose, and it all comes crashing down: they're not holes. They're pockets. Filled with nerve fluid.

There's a moment. And then the frantic break.

"Is she overloading?"

"Someone get a medic, quick!"

Rax leans in with his handkerchief, gently dotting at my lip. "Oh shit—that's a lot of it," he murmurs. "Turn the cameras off." The host is shocked stiff, and Rax's face contorts as he bellows, "Turn the goddamn cameras off, Terren. *NOW*!"

Mirelle stands and looks to Rax. "Get her backstage. Quickly."

I barely feel him nudging me up from my chair. He guides my arm to brace around his neck and leads me offstage, his weight the only thing keeping me from falling. I feel far away from myself—like I'm looking down on someone else's memory again. Cameras blur as we pass, red lights and blue screens and the screeching synth hydraulics of the door and finally the dim, musty quiet of the hall.

My eyes unfocus into the ceiling—I'm doomed. Too far gone. But I always knew that. Will the coma be like resting? Like death? Will I get to see Mother there?

Faintly, a voice.

"…at me. Look at me, Hauteclare, *please*."

My eyes refocus; a face like a lion, proud nose and proud chin and glass-cut angles on his bones. Handsome. No—*too close*, too much touching. I pull away from his grasp, but he won't stop staring, words hoarse on the edges.

"What's your full name?"

"Synali."

"*Full name.*"

"Synali Emilia Woster." Pause. Think. "Synali von Hauteclare."

"What year is it?"

"3442."

The muted cacophony in the studio leans heavily against the quiet. Rax reaches for my face, but I wince back, and he offers his handkerchief instead. "There's still some under your nose."

I wipe it on my sleeve—the blue silk comes away wetly silver and sticking in my short, black hair strands. "Nerve fluid. I was right."

"You wore the handkerchief Sev gave you during the Olric match, right?" Rax presses.

"None of your business."

Of course I wore it, but he doesn't need to know anything about me—my riding habits least of all. I focus on the windows lining the long room, the view of Mid Ward seething quietly outside.

"Listen, I get it; you're a busy lady. You don't have to ping me back or tell me what's going on, but I need to know you'll be okay when we leave this room."

"I told you already," I find the energy to snarl. "I'm not going to sleep with you. You can drop the act of pretending like you care."

His brows knit. "You think this is an act?"

"It always is." I wipe more silver out from under my nose. "Noblemen like you take advantage and then pretend to care afterward to appease your conscience. Like clockwork. You're just doing it earlier than most."

"I don't—I don't want the *advantage* on you, Hauteclare. I just want to know you're okay. Riders look out for other riders."

"I'm your enemy."

"No—you're my opponent. There's a difference."

Is there? My eyes trail up to his face, but I can only look at his redwood eyes for a few seconds before the churning in my gut becomes too strong to bear.

He smiles then, and it's like watching a sunrise. "There we go. You look a little better."

The tingle of his voice down my spine, the brief flicker of delusional hope that enemies aren't all we're doomed to be…but it all goes cold the moment I hear the click of heels announcing reality. Mirelle.

"Is she overloading or not?" Her voice echoes. She tosses my projection crutches to the ground in front of me, and Rax straightens.

"She still knows her name and the year, so."

Mirelle smiles like a dagger as she walks over. "You're all right, then."

"Does this ever happen to you two?" I ask.

She shrugs one shoulder. "Never to me. It's an older-rider problem. Rax has had it a few times, haven't you?"

The numbness starts to wear off, and I feel more myself with every word, feeling enough to hate the pitying way Rax murmurs: "Nowhere near as bad as this."

"Well." Mirelle turns to me. "You must have very little inherent resistance against the nerve fluid. I suggest you discontinue riding, lest you end up like Sir Freynille."

"You'd like that, wouldn't you?" I lob back. Her smile widens.

"Which? You quitting? Or you going the way of Freynille? Both would solve the issue of my family being murdered—"

"Enough, Mir," Rax interrupts. "You should go rest, Hauteclare. The two of us can finish the conference on our own."

It stings that he thinks I'm not as strong as them. I am. I have to be. I snatch my crutches up and head for the doors back into the conference room… and then it comes.

A ripple.

At first I think it's my arms giving out, trembling on the crutches, but then it happens all over and everywhere. The entire studio quivers, lights rattling their delicate glass bones against metal rigging and wires knocking loose from the ceiling panels. And it's not stopping.

"Hauteclare—"

Rax's call cuts off, and the holocandles lining the walls shiver fiercely, boxes of equipment tipping and spilling their contents all over. I look back to see Mirelle sidestep one, her face a grim mask of worry and her hand firmly on a railing. Rax's gaze is on me as the vibrations become stronger, faster. It's not g-force but something *worse*, something instantaneous and furious, and no matter how softly I clench, the crutches slip from under me, marble dust pouring from the ceiling, screams from behind the studio door echoing and Rax shouting for me, and it finally lands—a shock wave ripping through the world, the windows shattering inward—

I wrench myself away, ready to feel the glass pierce…but there's nothing.

The blast passes, and the shaking stops as quickly as it began. That fresh herb smell. Warm pressure against my body. I crack my eyes open to see Rax crushing me to his chest, blood snaking from his scalp and dripping off his cheeks. He smiles down at me with bloodstained teeth.

"Did any of it get you?"

"Rax!" Mirelle staggers over, hands hovering frantically. "Your back—"

"I'll be okay, Mir. S'just glass."

"Okay?" Mirelle shrills. "Stay here—I'll find a med-kit."

Her heels clip frantically down the ruined hall. The air turns chilly as Mid Ward seeps in—the sound of hovercarriage horns and vendors yelling—and I can't move. His heat burns into me, the feel of his arms around me and his ribs against mine… I duck out of his grasp and double around him only to swallow a swear; his breast coat is shredded, the red of it dark with blood and gleaming with countless glass shards as big as fingers stuck in his back. Blood spatters the ground. Mirelle's heels left bloody footprints.

"Why—" I help him sit on a nearby box as best I can. "Why would you do that?"

"Told you." Rax sucks in a breath as he sits. "I need to make sure you'll be okay."

"You—" I choke. *"Why?"*

"Because," he insists, softer. "You're cute."

"Shut up."

He laughs, his breathing labored, and his mirth goes quiet. "Because when I started riding…no one was there for me. I want to make sure you…have someone."

My stomach twists. "I can't have anyone."

The redwood of his eyes crinkles. "I won't…I won't bother you. Just, if you need anything or if you're scared… I don't know how to help you or even if I can. But I want to."

Beneath my cross pendant, my heart feels like it's bursting in slow motion, and then it stops.

I have *been* kissed before, but I've never kissed someone. I've never chosen to lean in and take someone's lips in mine, to hold the face I've feared and thought about in equal measure in my gentle hands. *Gentle.* Nothing about touching has ever been gentle to me, but now he moves in, and he is like silk in my mouth, searching, curious, his hand glancing behind my neck and cradling there, and for a split second, and for the first moment in my life since Mother died, I feel just…*me.*

I feel everything inside of me quiver and shake and plead for more, but he never tries for more; he moves precisely as far and as fast as I do. Every cell in my brain knows this is wrong, and every cell in my body doesn't care, and he tastes like blood and skin, and my fingers clench in his collar, and *I'm going to die—*

This is pointless. I can't like this. I can't want more. He is a noble. I am a bastard. There can only be victory, not…whatever this is.

Whatever this is slows and then stops as I pull away. Looking at his face is even harder now, so I stare at his chest as it rumbles with his dark-syrup laughter.

"Was that you trying to scare me off, Hauteclare? Because lemme tell you…it did *not* work."

His collarbone is exposed. Smooth skin. It's the sight of his smooth skin where mine is scarred that drives the cold stake of reality back into me.

"There cannot be a second time," I say carefully. I don't see the flinch in his face, but I see it in his body.

"Right. Yeah."

The vis suddenly starts screaming between us, our wrists blaring ear-piercing alerts in concert as an emergency broadcast flashes past.

MISSING CARGO VESSEL H.R.M.S. *ENDURANCE* COLLIDES WITH SUBSTATION THETA-7. STATION DAMAGE NEGLIGIBLE—ALL VITAL SYSTEMS INTACT. LOW WARD SECTOR D, MID WARD SECTOR C, H, L EXPERIENCING MINOR GRAVITY DESTABILIZATION: LOCATE NEAREST SHELTER AND REMAIN THERE UNTIL FURTHER INSTRUCTION. THIS MESSAGE WILL REPEAT. MISSING CARGO VESSEL—

I throw up my screen so we can both see it. Every news station is a wreckage of fire and metal against space, and my stomach drops—I can pick out the prow of a ship spiraling into nothing, the dock of a substation shredded until barely recognizable. How many people were on board? How many were working the substation?

"Ah, there you are." I look up to see Dravik standing in the hydraulic doorway of the frantic studio, his cane flashing sapphires and his eyes flashing between Rax and me with an expression so stony it bruises. "Thank you, Sir Istra-Velrayd, for protecting my charge. I will take it from here."

Rax lowers his bleeding head as if preparing for a fight. How does Dravik know Rax protected me from the glass? Is he having me followed? No—there was only Mirelle, Rax, and me. The timing of all this, the fact he was here at the studio all along when an emergency occurred—

"Did you…" I point to the substation destruction on the vis. "Did you do this?"

His expression softens as he tilts his head at Rax. "Did *you* do this?"

"I found it!" Mirelle's voice cuts through the hall as she runs up panting, a med-kit in hand. She goes still when she sees Dravik and even stiller when she sees his silver-blue cane, her bow not fully formed but her glare very much so. "Your Highness."

"Lady Mirelle." Dravik smiles at her. "Please take care of Sir Istra-Velrayd. Synali and I will be leaving him in your hands." He turns to me. "Won't we?"

Words beneath words; I will leave Rax behind from this moment on. Whatever happened in this hall was a fantasy—a dream to be shelved away, a memory not mine. Dravik is my partner. House Lithroi is why I am here and why I will win. The reality is Mother, dead. Four more circles to die. The reality is a ship run into a substation, many more dead. The chessboard moves.

I wordlessly pick up my crutches and leave with the prince.

The pawn moves forward.

PART V

THE SNAKE AND THE TIGER

−5. Adsum

adsum ~esse ~fuī, *intr.*
1. to be present
1. to arrive

Clothed in rags, Rain prays in a near-empty Mid Ward church.
His lithe body kneels at the whitewood altar, and he prays—for what is about to happen and what has already happened. The shake in his hands is bad today—he hasn't had dust in two days, and he's more afraid of the withdrawal window narrowing than what it does to him. He meant to take dust as a stopgap, as a way for Polaris to feel as if it had him under its boot in some capacity, but it'd become so much more than that—not a way to forget but a way to remember; his brothers and sisters, Violet-Two and Father, the better days when he was ignorant and surrounded by likewise beautiful ignorance. He is a shadow chasing shadows.

Rain stands and goes to the confessional. He ducks beneath the moth-smelling curtain, the slatted screen shrouding the robed figure on the other side in spots of light and dark.

"Father, I do not deserve forgiveness," he says.

The robed figure stirs. "None of us do, my son."

The correct words. There's a long quiet, Rain's ears searching for any sound beyond the confessional, any eavesdropper. When he deems it safe, he puts his hand to the screen.

"What can I do to atone, Father?"

"In five days, you will visit a young nobleman. He is the registered proprietor of Idaxvale Incorporated. I have written his name on this paper for you. Take it, and go with grace."

Rain takes the rolled paper that slots between the screen. The robed figure rises and leaves the booth—not Green-One; one of his informants—but still, seeing someone so close to his last remaining family puts Rain's heart at ease. He is not completely alone.

Soft smog sunset lights the world outside the church's doors. He leaves the confessional and approaches the real priest in a still moment. "Father, I have a question."

The priest smiles. "We all do, young one. Ask yours."

"Do you ever wonder what the soul is made of?"

"When I was your age, I did think the soul might be made of memory."

The lights in the church flicker briefly then, and Rain looks up—that's the fifth time today, and they're in Mid Ward.

The priest presses on. "If one forgets their memories, do they not forget their 'self'? What we grow up seeing, feeling—what we remember of our childhood, of the people who come to us and leave us and love us…is that not what makes someone 'someone'? Is God's gift to us not life and therefore memory? Can memories be called the 'soul,' then?"

Rain thinks on this, opening the paper minutely and reading the name within. YAVN VON VELRAYD. He holds it to a holocandle, fingers shaking, and only once the flames have burned the note to ash does he ask:

"If I have denied many people God's grace, Father, does that make me the devil?"

"No, my son. The devil is not human—he can work through us, but he can never be us."

The bells toll above them seven times, and when it's silent, Rain asks again:

"Do you ever wonder, Father, if the devil has memories, too?"

41. Saxum

saxum ~ī, *n.*
1. a stone; large, rough fragment of rock

Rax Istra-Velrayd hates his parents' parties the most.

It's the way people hover around him in the ballroom—circling, watching, appraising, like he's some piece of meat to be summed up in neat parts and auctioned off to the highest bidder. *"Goodness, what large biceps he has!" "Very well portioned, that one is."*

But it's the things said to his face that are far worse, lustful aunts grinning and nosy old uncles scheming behind wineglasses in deluded approximations of subtlety. *"Tell me, Sir Rax—is riding as exhilarating as they say?" "I do so wish someone like you were my son-in-law." "Such a tragedy—our House hasn't been blessed with good rider genes in well over half a century."*

How he still manages to fend them off after all these years without his smile cracking, he has no idea. Practice, probably—practice until there are grooves his body follows when his mind refuses to. All he knows is that the wine is his best friend and the balconies are his greatest escape. From one such balcony he watches a church barge float between the neighboring manse tops, trailing too-sweet incense and the faint chant of vespers as it goes.

For the fifth time today, he checks his vis. No pings. Well, pings—from his mother, his father, Mirelle, ten ad companies and four talk shows and Sunscreamer's crewhead, but no pings from *her*.

He promised he wouldn't bother her, but the memory of that kiss won't stop bothering him. Every time he mentally combs through those moments, he finds something new to languish in—the feel of her mouth, the sensation of her hair on his fingers, the exact temperature of her skin. Kissing her had been like kissing for the very first time—breathtaking and disorienting—just like the way she rode. He's certain, now; whatever she is at her core, he wants to face it. Hold it. Watch it grow.

There can't be a second time. He knows that. There's a fine line, he's well aware—seen too many creepy noblemen harassing ladies to the point of criminal—but he's worried; riding in only three matches and getting a bleed isn't normal. If her nerve-fluid resistance is really that low, Lithroi can't keep forcing her to ride, or else she'll—

"You think too loudly."

He looks up at the voice—Mirelle. She leans on the banister next to him, and they watch the church barge float into the shallow, arced horizon of the noble spire on its way to the much wider horizon of Mid Ward. Mid Ward's damage from the *Endurance* and Theta-7 still lingers—hard-light repair scaffolds spread out over various sectors as thick as orange webs—but the damage is still considered minimal compared to how the Under-ring fared. Not that anybody of import cares—the Under-ring is for the forsaken and the damned. They bear their own losses and rebuild themselves.

"How is your back feeling?" Mirelle asks.

"Better." He grins. "Thanks for the first aid."

The silence is almost therapeutic against the chatter of the party behind them, but Mirelle isn't the type to keep quiet when something's on her mind.

"She's made her choice, Rax. We all did the moment we entered the academy."

"She didn't go to the academy."

"She chose nonetheless." Mirelle sighs. "The family's not happy she lived."

"'Course they aren't. She's been going around—"

"It's not her. Not directly. She rides and wins, yes, but she's not the one who kills them. That's someone else. The former prince, Grandmother thinks—the one who's sponsoring her."

"Is he really the prince? No one will talk about him, and they"—he jerks his head inside—"*always* fucking talk."

"I don't want to talk about him, either."

"You don't care if the fuckin' *crown prince* comes back?"

"He can't come back. We have a crown princess, now. He's a legal bastard, and bastards do not rise—they fall and then disappear."

Sleeping together once over four months ago is only the newest stage in their relationship—Rax has known her all his life, since the very first day at the academy, when they lined up in their little uniforms and swore fealty to the king for the first time, chubby fists and chubbier cheeks. She'd never admit to her own negative feelings out loud; negativity is below a Hauteclare. Still, it's clear she's not talking about the bastard prince anymore. He stares out at the green glow of Esther hanging above and beyond the Station's honeycomb shield.

"What if your House really did it? Killed her mother, like she said at the banquet."

"Nonsense," Mirelle scoffs. "Bastards are not a Hauteclare problem."

He gives her that *c'mon now* look, and she sets her chin.

"We are not the other Houses. We are Hauteclare, descended from the first knights—honor is our currency, as trade is yours. Killing defenseless commoners is simply not in our creed. Besides, one does not need to kill people to be rid of them. Father says we have other uses for them."

"And you believe him whole hog?"

She blinks. "Why wouldn't I?"

"I just don't make a habit of trusting adults. But you do whatever you want."

"We're adults now, too, you know."

"Barely." He points listlessly into the party. "And they're already frothing at the mouth to marry us off."

She scowls. "'Tis our duty, Rax. Marriage, the continuation of the House— it falls to us. It's why we were born, why our parents before us were born and their parents before them. It's not an option—it's an *obligation*."

He glowers into his wineglass, now too unfull for his liking. He *knows*— he's always known. It was inevitable, but he could always push it a little further off: A girl, another inch away. A night in the clubs, another inch. Suddenly, below the balcony, a shadowy figure moves through the bushes. Mirelle narrows her eyes, but Rax cups his mouth and whisper-shouts as best he can.

"Sneaking out again, Yavn?"

The shadowy figure whirls, his cousin's obsidian eyes crinkling up at him. "Not if you keep your voice up like that. I'll see you at my place later?"

Rax flashes him a thumbs-up, and Yavn disappears into the garden, the white-and-gold uniforms of the new guards glinting bright on Peregrine Fervor's perimeter. Rax doesn't relish the idea of trying to sneak out of the manse later.

"You shouldn't indulge him." Mirelle snorts. "Especially not after the *Endurance*."

"Oh, c'mon, Mir. Yavn's not a rebel."

"No—he just espouses their beliefs at every dining opportunity."

"Wanting commoners to have better lives isn't rebellion. It's doing the right thing. The knightly thing." At her silence, he yanks the helm of the conversation in the opposite direction. "I've been thinking—"

"God forbid."

"—Hauteclare came to me after one of my matches. She said her steed's been...*talking* to her. That when she blacks out in the saddle, she sees memories. Other people's."

"Steeds don't talk." Mirelle rolls her eyes. "Or have memories. Perhaps she's losing her mind—that would explain all the murder."

"Mir, think about it," he insists. "Have you ever heard of someone getting a bleed after their third match? No one's nerve-fluid resistance is *that* low."

"She could've practiced before the Cup."

"We both know practice doesn't cause buildup. Only real impacts do."

She scowls into her champagne glass. "What are you trying to say?"

"What if it's not something wrong with *her*," he starts, "but something wrong with her *steed*? You're the one who checks the archive all the time—can't you look up Heavenbreaker?"

"It's rich that you think I haven't already. Everything's redacted."

"Redacted how? Redacted like someone deleted it, or redacted like court redacted, or—"

"Redacted like Hellrunner."

Like *Hellrunner*? Why would the information on the Lithroi steed be treated like the information on the king's steed? Is it because Lithroi is the former prince, or… A scarlet dress cuts toward the balcony then, and Rax swears and stands straight. Mother. She sweeps over and curtseys in perfect form to Mirelle, her blond nest of braids bobbing and her smile warm.

"There you are, Rax. I was afraid I'd have to hunt you down like the police with those awful rebels. Lady Mirelle—what a pleasure it is to have an illustrious guest like you at our little soiree."

Mirelle makes a crisper curtsey back. "Lady Konstance. You are too modest—it is a grand affair."

"Thank you again for lending Peregrine Fervor your family's guards. It puts my heart at ease." Mother looks to Rax. "I hope our son hasn't been offending you overmuch. He has that tendency."

"On the contrary—we were engaging in an enlightening conversation about…" Her gaze catches on the church barge in the distance. "The Lord. Weren't we?"

Rax nods along. "God, the saints—all the usual suspects."

Mother's smile stops touching her eyes. "You will mind your irreverent manners before our guest."

He manages a grin. "Doing my best, Mother. Why? Is it not good enough for you?"

Her green eyes go dark, and she extends her hand to him with the air of someone who's won. "Would you excuse us, Lady Mirelle? I must present my son to House Trentoch and House Michel—they have several ladies expressing interest in him."

Rax's jaw flickers. "Interest" is just another word for the marriage game. Mirelle looks to him, then to his mother, and then inside. She hesitates. He looks right at her. *Get me out of it. Make up some excuse. You're Hauteclare— she'll listen to you.*

"Unless…" Mother trails off, a thought forming in her smiling lips. "Unless you have an interest as well, Lady Mirelle?"

It's a game his mother's been playing since he was born, but the look on Mirelle's face is anything but a game—hard gold eyeshadow and carbon-steel lips, and the music of the party fades as Rax's chest sinks into his boots. *Tell me you haven't fallen for it, Mir. Not you too.*

Not you, too.

42. Runco

runcō ~āre ~āuī ~ātum, *tr.*
1. to weed out, root up

YAVN VON VELRAYD STICKS TO the shade of a stone wall, edging around the garden with practiced alacrity and a frenzied mind that hasn't stopped screeching since the *Endurance* incident: *they know*. Everyone at the party knew he had been a part of it—he was convinced of it.

The man had promised, but not like this—like death and destruction. It had always been parties and talking and theories of how to change things and through what means—policies, lobbying, strikes. Yavn was the weaver, not the thread—he never wanted to see blood, let alone be the reason for it. He has to lay low. He has to tell Rax, get him in on it officially—Duke Velrayd will forgive him if Rax asks; he'll listen to the greatest rider the House has ever seen.

Yavn von Velrayd is convinced he slips off the grounds unnoticed.

And yet a guard in white and gold follows in his shadow, their eyes a piercing ice blue.

43. Bellus

bellus ~a ~um, a.
1. pleasant, charming

I stare into my egg yolk, the silver cup holding it the antithesis of the golden center.

113 people died in the *Endurance* attack. Not nobles who killed my mother—just normal *people*; workers on Theta-7 with lives and pasts and futures. 155 people, if you count the rebels who drove the *Endurance* into Theta-7. That's what the vis calls them—rebels against the king, against the Station, endangering us all and putting the imperative at risk. The rebels killed those people and themselves, but I know better. Dravik orchestrated it somehow. This isn't retribution on House Hauteclare; this is him sacrificing over a hundred people for his unknowable plan. If he wants to take the throne, he's killing his *own people* for it…and I'm his rider. We are the villains, but if it means House Hauteclare is obliterated…

Quilliam's gnarled hand slides me a plate of chicken on wilted spinach, and he grins.

"The chicken or the egg, miss?" he asks. I stare blankly, and he makes a little cough. "Apologies. It's a silly old Earth saying."

"What does it mean?"

"It's an existential question—was the chicken born first, or the egg?"

"The egg," I answer.

"Ah." He smiles. "But then who laid that egg, miss?"

At that moment, Dravik enters, dressed in a lavender tunic and his usual aimless smile.

"Good morning. It seems you've received an invitation." He plops an envelope beside my plate. I ignore it. I ignore my egg and the chicken until Dravik notices. "Is something the matter, Synali?"

Yes.

"No." I pick the envelope up. "Who is this from?"

"Your next opponent."

The envelope is gilded like scripture, vines and pomegranates in clean gold ink. The wax seal of a serpent beneath a holly crown is already broken. I look up at Dravik as he tucks into breakfast, and he waves a jovial fork at me. "Oh, don't mind that. Poison inspection."

The letter is only mildly simpler than the envelope; cream paper—more expensive than anything I've written on in my life. I tend to prefer walls, things more permanent. My opponent prefers ink in sweeping, grandiose spirals:

Synali von Hauteclare,

By the grace of God, our time of meeting draws close. It is with His teachings of humility I wish to informally greet you before our conflict. If this agrees with you, please meet me at Atteint at ten o'clock this evening.

Yours i' faith,

Talize san Michel

"Rather pompous, I imagine," Dravik says lightly, buttering his toast. "All of House Michel tends to be."

"What is 'Atteint'?"

"It's a nightclub. Very exclusive." He looks up. "You will not be taking this invitation, of course. It's a very obvious trap."

"You've taught me winning requires wandering into enemy territory from time to time."

"No. There are too many variables. Talize san Michel could do anything to you in such a meeting. We will not be handing her that opportunity."

"Her strength is her pompousness," I say, tracing the word *i'faith*. "And God. We use it against her."

The prince goes stiff in his chair. "House Michel is not to be trifled with, Synali; they are an old knight family on the same level of power and influence as House Hauteclare."

"The entire court stripped Astrix of her queenhood. My enemy is Hauteclare, but yours is all of them, isn't it?"

Quilliam's weathered hands pour Dravik a cup the prince doesn't take, his gray gaze squarely on me. Dravik has two weaknesses: his mother and his own brain. I see the prince's lip twitch like a smile, once, and then it's gone.

"You cannot use my own tactics against me."

"I can try," I say. "Maybe leave behind the ones that get a hundred people killed."

"Did you think being a villain meant peace, Synali?" His soft face goes grim as he stands. "I create opportunities. I give people the means, and they take those means into their own hands—just as I have given you yours in Heavenbreaker."

"So you're the devil, then."

His eyes catch on the cross pendant around my neck, and then he starts down the hall. "You will remain here for the evening. Quilliam, prepare the hovercarriage for me. I will be gone until morning."

"Yes, master."

I squeeze my butterknife until it bites, until I can't take it anymore and dart up after him. I manage to reach the front door when Dravik's outline down the front steps wavers. Unbearable heat suddenly hits my face, and I stagger back just in time to see a sheet of buzzing orange hard-light walling off the doorway.

"Shit," I hiss. "A fence."

It's smaller than the kind they have in the Mid Ward wildlife park—only visible once you get up close. I grab a nearby empty vase and prod at the vibrating wall—the glass edge goes red-hot and sputtering as its paint blisters. Not a fake, then. I scramble around the manse, trying every door handle, but they're all bio-locked—even the kitchen door. My eyes catch a window, and miraculously, it opens. I heft my leg over first and hear the hissing second—my boot smoking where the leather tip presses into the suddenly visible hard-light. Another window. Another orange barrier. He's locked the whole fucking manse down.

Quilliam totters by with a cleaning rag and smiles at me. "Is something wrong, miss?"

"Other than the fact Dravik's locked me down like an animal in the wildlife park?" I drawl. "Not in the slightest."

Quilliam's ancient face goes pensive. "Apologies, miss. The master is simply worried for your safety."

"And painfully overdramatic about it." I furiously tap my vis. I can't wait around expecting Jeria's hacking to bail me out—Saturdays are always busy at the brothel, and Talize's invitation is for ten p.m. That only leaves me eight hours to find a way out. I pace the hallway, Luna pacing with me. This isn't about the club anymore, or even Talize. The prince is going too far, caring too much. I will never have a father again, but he's trying his damnedest. I understand I can't have certain things, but I *will* have my freedom.

My eyes fall on Luna, and then on the stainless steel bunker door. If everything is bio-locked…

His greatest strength, used against him.

"Are you thinking about practicing, miss?" Quilliam asks.

I shrug. "Not much else to do in this place."

Quilliam smiles ruefully, and I wait until his slow dusting path turns the corner to head toward the bunker. The bio-lock registers me like always, and with a rush of relief I pass through the door. Luna follows me down the stairs, tail wagging as I approach Heavenbreaker's console and open the chest cockpit.

"Wait here," I tell the dog. It whines as if it knows where I'm going, words beneath words in a different way, and I pet its head softly. "I'll be all right."

It waits dutifully on the walkway, and I stride into Heavenbreaker's darkness. Luna's true AI is connected to all the systems in the manse…but it's also connected to Heavenbreaker. A Heavenbreaker that's currently wounded, the gap in its breastplate from our match with Olric yawning jagged. When the hell is Dravik going to get the pit crew in here to fix it?

My hands shake as I press against the gel solidity of the saddle, the periwinkle light washing over my face and the silver spirals stretching as if they're waking from some cozy dream. I can't be afraid.

My silver nosebleed…Sevrith's lifeless face in the cockpit…I push the fear out. There's nothing but the four circles left. I am nothing but riding. The nerve fluid gives way, and I slip in.

Heavenbreaker.

I feel it stir in the doorway of our mental connection. Watching. Waiting.

"hello."

i need your help.

"help?"

It's a long stretch—I don't understand AI or how it works. All I know is that Luna's true AI is smart; it runs through possibilities faster than we do. Faster than Dravik does, hopefully.

can you go inside the manse?

"manse?" it echoes, confusion swirling between us. I close my eyes and visualize Moonlight's End—my bed, the fireplace, Dravik's office of redwood and pinned butterflies, the kitchen smelling of baking, the dim labyrinthine halls with their eerie portraits that watch every step. Something like home.

home.

Heavenbreaker flashes me something in return—a memory of space. Not empty darkness but space full of violet light, gas and stars gathered around a hot, white core, and I realize it faintly—that's a nebula. That's what Heavenbreaker thinks home is?

"go inside?" it asks.

inside, I agree.

Everything goes numb, and I move. Or *we* move. We move together without moving, like the hyperreal sensation of plummeting just as you fall asleep, but following a vivid green line. We race through the cavernous bunker room, up the stairs and past the kitchen, and hundreds more lines bloom out—green veins in the ceiling, in the walls, green nodes and webs reaching up into the roof and down into the ground, and I realize what it is: the manse systems. The manse is a dark blur around the green light, but I focus on the idea of paintings. Beds. Windows. Soft sheets and the rough fiber way paint lies over canvas and lastly, hardest—cold, clear glass.

go through.

Heavenbreaker tries, my stomach lurching as it lurches forward, skin burning with the hot sheet of orange light that springs up in front of the pane.

"can't," Heavenbreaker says mournfully.

you can. i trust you.

"trust?"

I falter. I've never once truly trusted it, have I? I wrenched it around in Olric's fight in total disregard of its feelings. Who was the last person I trusted?

friend, I say, and I think of Jeria, of the nights she knocked on my door and asked if I was all right even if I pushed her away. Rax and Mirelle come, forbidden and impossible—the two of them helping me out of the conference room. Not friends, but...*gratitude*. Dravik even makes an appearance in my memories—the Dravik who trained me, not the one who avoids my every question now.

This time, I purposefully lay my memories open, and Heavenbreaker watches. Absorbs. The watching feeling changes—loneliness. There's a deep, inky loneliness that goes on forever in the saddle, but something glitters at the bottom—the word *friend*. The idea-motion-marrow of it, the steel-cut meaning I grasp with all fingers begins to shine through, and the steed chimes happily:

"go through with friend!"

We move together again, swiveling our head—or wherever the locus of our senses is—around the manse. One of the many green nodes in the ceiling turns orange, and I feel Heavenbreaker reach for it—a hand without a hand—and crush it. The thing resists, flickers fast and bright, and then shatters into a thousand pieces of orange light. I pull myself out of the steed and dash across the gangplank, Luna waiting with a happily wagging tail on the other side. I bend to pet it.

"See? That wasn't so bad, was it?"

It barks, the metallic sound reverberating around the cavernous bunker, but its sapphire eyes aren't on me. They're locked behind me. On Heavenbreaker.

I turn and see it; the cockpit gash is gone.

The massive tear over Heavbenbreaker's breastplate...is smooth again. Not welded smooth, but smooth as if the gash never happened in the first place. Healed. My brain races; I was only in it for a few minutes at most, and the entire manse is locked down—no pit crew could've come by or fixed it that fast. Luna? No...Luna's a sentry dog. I might not know much about AI, but I know it doesn't fix things like this. This is...

Impossible.

Am I hallucinating again? Maybe, or maybe not. Heavenbreaker is different—it talks to me. If it can fix itself, then that would explain why I've never seen the pit crew and why Dravik's so cagey about them. *How?* **Why?** In all my time studying the databases, I've never heard of a steed fixing itself. Each steed requires a pit crew of twelve people at minimum, engineers and programmers and physicists and lucitricians—

Focus. There'll be plenty of time to think on this later, but I only have a few hours to plan for Talize's trap.

Nightclubs are not only for nobles.

There are many in Low Ward and more in Mid Ward, all of them blaring lute-and-synth music from their speakers loud enough to shake entire neighborhoods—the nobles can just afford better soundproofing. I stand in front of a clean white marble building, a muffled beat rumbling beneath my silver-tipped shoes; I waited until sunset to change into better clothes and sneak out so as to not alert Quilliam, who would no doubt alert Dravik. *ATTEINT* is spelled in anti-grav water like a sign over the club's entrance—a sign like mockery when people beg for water miles below where I stand. I grasp Mother's cross pendant hanging beneath the cravat that matches my silver breast coat.

Forward.

The entrance quickly gives way to a long hall of darkness—thick, warm darkness, the kind for growing plants or children or mold. Jungles. Earth had them once, and the club reaches for a lost nostalgia we'll never know again: palm fronds, pitcher plants full of acid, fragrant orchids engineered to glow all colors in the dark. Plants fed on corpses, I know now.

Forward.

The atmosphere creaks alive with unseen insects, little animals making sore-throat noises and jumping erratically. Frogs, I think, but not the dull green things in textbooks; these glow neon and stick to every surface. Nobles infest the walls in skintight leather jackets and corsets. Holographic bustles and capes flash with moving butterflies, ocean waves, flowers. They wear fool masks and maiden masks and plague-doctor masks of polished whitewood, and they watch me.

Well, some watch. Most are...*enjoying*. It's the telltale writhe of any brothel, the telltale milk-glazed eyes of someone who's inhaled dust—the exact same writhe as Low Ward, just with brand names and surgery instead of rags and plague. The bouncers are less bouncers and more poorly disguised off-duty guards in their civilian clothes. The music seethes louder the closer I get to the club's innards, and the guards shift as I approach, blocking the door farther in.

"Move," I command. The beat pumps into the darkness, unrelenting. The guns and hard-light daggers in their holsters glint at me, eyes glinting at me, and then one of them nudges the other. They part.

The club is a massive black glass cavern seemingly carved out of the faux jungle itself; three tiers of it, three sets of glittering stairs. There's a stage in the center on which a metal tree sprouts mandolins and flutes and drums, the DJ at its LED roots queuing each instrument skillfully. Strobe lights pulse in all colors, refracting the brilliance onto jasmine vines and banana plants. Animals I can't name perch on noble shoulders—golden monkeys with scales, candy-colored parrots. And the crowd. God, the *crowd*.

I never see the arena crowd, I only hear them, and the crowd sees me only as a hologram projected directly into the arena's center. I go to the Lithroi hangar and ride, shower after it's over, and muscle through the reporters back to Dravik's. But there's a proper crowd here, real and alive and undulating in all directions on the dance floor to the screeching music.

I lace between the crowd and move to the second-floor stairs to get a better vantage point. Talize didn't dictate an exact meeting place, but I know what she looks like, at least. I press myself into the projection railing to look over the side, and my hand recoils from a little neon frog as it hops on the rail.

"Oh, no." A noble next to me laughs, the sound nasal through his plague-doctor mask. "It's way better when you smash them."

Before I can blink, he slams his open palm down. Fragile bones snap; neon guts smear. *A living thing.* I watch in horror as he giggles, rubs his hands together, and spreads the glowing innards to his every fingertip. Without thinking, I fling my fist and shatter the nose of his thin wooden mask—splinters in my knuckles, blood dripping down his exposed lips. A fresh wave of horror starts when he giggles again, his friends giggling behind him. They catch him as he staggers back and smiles at me as if I can't do anything to him, and the horror twists to rage as I start forward—

"Whoa, whoa, whoa!" Someone's hand drops on my shoulder, voice thrumming under the music. "Easy there."

I rip the palm off and whirl only to come face-to-face with Rax Istra-Velrayd in a brown doublet and crimson fur cape, looming like a streak of blood above the crowd. His brows shoot up into his carefully disheveled platinum hair. "Hauteclare? What are you—"

I jab my finger at the smear of the frog. "Why did they do that?"

His eyes stutter, neon catching redwood. "Drugs—the frogs are full of 'em. If they touch your bare skin, you get some in you."

The neon smear twists at my insides—a living thing, *used*. I throw a glare at the broken mask, but he's long gone, and I peer into Rax's eyes—no milk in them from dust, if the drug inside the frogs even *is* dust. He seems steady on his feet, but looks can be deceiving.

"I don't do that shit, if that's what you're wondering," he offers. "Makes riding harder."

"Then what exactly do you do here? Other than get in my way?"

"Punching people indiscriminately isn't gonna make you friends."

My drawl is venom. "I don't want friends."

His massive body is an echo chamber of our kiss, his throat and hair and eyes filling in the gaps my brain has been longing for. After that day, he must think me weaker and frailer than ever—vacillating, too lustful, unable to control myself.

"Okay, no friends." Rax ruffles his hair, biceps straining against doublet sleeve. "How about drinking buddies?"

My vis suddenly vibrates its ten o'clock alarm, and my eyes snap to the upper level. I whirl to leave.

"Going so soon?" a new voice says.

My boots freeze. I turn. Mirelle's waterfall of chestnut hair gleams almost as brightly as her golden snakeskin dress. Her gold eyes prickle back at me with gold eyeshadow. She comes to stand beside Rax, her arms crossed and one shoulder dropped casually—yet her face is anything but. Snapfrost splinters between us—a different sort of danger than Olric.

And then the melt.

"You should have a drink with us," she says.

Us. Him with her.

It clicks into place in my head; they haven't just slept together—they *are* together. When they stand side by side in their tall regality, it makes perfect sense. I kissed a man now promised to another. Still, the devil's temptation lingers.

it would be nice to have a drink with someone my age.

Heavenbreaker is lonely. And I realize then, in this thumping club, that I am, too.

"You don't want to drink with me," I say. "I'm the bastard who's murdering your family."

Mirelle shrugs one shoulder. "You won't be murdering anyone else; we've tripled our security. Besides, I didn't particularly like Raoulle or Palissa—craven, power-hungry hypocrites, the both of them. And don't even get me started on Balmoran—he beat his wife. It's a miracle the twins were born at all."

My jaw sets. Is this a trap within a trap?

"You're a murderer; I won't argue that. But you're a rider first, and in the War it was tradition to toast when three riders met. Come." Her gold dress slithers behind her as she walks toward the bar.

I glance at Rax, but he just grins resignedly and follows, muttering into my ear as he passes: "She's obsessed with knight stuff—reads old War books all the time. Just go with it."

He's too close—clean herb soap and soft shadows on his throat. Pull away. Linger two steps behind him as he approaches the small table Mirelle's chosen. We wait. I look away—anywhere but at him and then right at him, *accidental*, but he just smiles. My brain screams opposition when Mirelle returns and slides the neon shot over to me; it could be poisoned. She could be seething hate under her cool facade—trying to kill me like all the rest. Rax sees me pause.

"What's up? Don't like gel shots? I get that—the texture's kinda like eating a weird jiggly fish or something—"

Mirelle's smarter. She snorts, gold nails quickly switching the shots around on the table so we all have each other's. "There. Satisfied?"

Not nearly. But Rax mends the quiet between us as he holds his shot up.

"So! What're we toasting to? Friendship? Everlasting honor? Wait, hold on, let's go for something more realistic, like…"

"You shutting up for two seconds," Mirelle drawls.

"Me shutting up for two seconds," he echoes, grin going sun-bright, and then he frowns at her. "Oh, c'mon—you know that's never gonna happen."

My snort explodes carelessly. Rax smirks at me, and it feels like fire down my spine. *Fuck*.

Mirelle holds her shot up, eyes straight and true into mine. "To the victor," she says.

It's a simple toast—no feelings, just fact; all three of us are riders. All three of us are fighting in the Supernova Cup, but only one of us will win it all. Rax's smirk fades, and he holds his shot higher in wordless agreement. It's strange to sit at a table with people who are also young—to do something not to move forward but just because *I want to*.

"To the victor," I say.

We clink our glasses together and swallow. The gel burns going down, fruity and searing, and I choke a little, and Rax thumps my back unhelpfully.

"Is it your first time drinking?"

The fire in my throat goes cold when Mirelle scoffs. "You killed people before you ever drank? What a twisted way to live."

"Hey Mir, wh-whoa—"

"She's right." I cut Rax's sputter off. What did I think would happen here—friendship? I stand and turn on my heel, but Mirelle's voice clears the room. It clears the bass and mandolins out of my eardrums—the crowd's cheering, glasses clinking—everything falls away in the velvet chill of her tone.

"There was blood on the suit you stole. Uncle Farris's blood. They said that it was related to yours."

I look over my shoulder. Rax's gaze darts from me to her and back again. Mirelle stands as a streak of gold, waiting, the whole world waiting on her next sentence.

"You murdered your own father, bastard. You destroyed him."

no. his house is still standing. half her killers are still alive. you are still untouched.

My fingers itch for something to hold on to; the railing, the neon smear. *you'd be a neon smear if they had their way.* Rax's eyes on me slowly harden, and something inside me panics at it. He knows now. No honor in any of this—no hope in any of them.

I make a Dravik smile.

"No. Not quite yet."

44. Clementia

clēmentia ~ae, f.
1. mercy
2. mildness

On the third floor of club Atteint, there is a VIP booth.

It's a glass box in the midst of a drunken crowd, surrounded by massive whitewood branches woven and bent into each other. A nest. The wood blocks the glass walls, but a pair of eyes on a familiar shadowed silhouette follows me from inside, dark and clear and reflective like obsidian.

there you are.

I walk toward it, and all at once the silhouette vanishes. A crack appears in the booth, door-shaped and yawning open. The nobles leaning against the wall simply watch, their plague-doctor masks like beaks, like carrion birds waiting for scraps after the fight is over.

forward.

I walk in, and the door clicks closed behind me. In the darkness, a single blacklight halo glows white-blue. The lights rise—pink illuminating a leather couch and the woman on it. Ink-black hair spills down to her waist, white dress flickering with holographic ruffles. A white veil shades her face, her pink smile barely showing through—she looks the same as she did at the banquet.

"Greetings, Synali von Hauteclare. By His grace, I am Lady Talize san Michel."

It's the softest noble voice I've heard besides Dravik's; the others shout and clarify, but she's barely stronger than a whisper. My eyes dart around—not a single bodyguard. No one and nothing but us—a cell of strangely barren purity in the eye of a storm of avarice.

"Where are my manners?" Talize extends a graceful hand free of any jewelry. "Please, sit."

Warily, I sit in the armchair in front of her.

"Would you like some tea?"

"No."

The holly-and-snake sigil of House Michel—the same from the invitation's wax seal—is embossed on the teapot on the tray beside her. She pours herself a cup with perfect balance, and it's then I notice the redwood cross around her neck…the exact same as mine.

"What do you want?" I demand.

"I simply wished to meet you before tomorrow, Synali, as I heard you met Olric."

"Then we're done here."

She smiles wider. "If you wish it. Yet you came all this way, and in such a nice outfit—'twould be a waste if you did not stay longer than a few minutes."

This is a trap. But if I overcome it on my own, then Dravik will have no choice but to respect my capabilities from now on. He'll have to trust me more.

"You own this waste of space, I assume," I say.

"I'd hardly call such places 'wastes.'"

"What would you call them, then?"

"Proving grounds." Talize's pink smile purses beneath her veil. "Or rather, proof of God's love for the lost lambs. Drugs and hedonism and carnal pleasures—they indulge in it all here, and I foster it as the Lord doth foster me in his embrace."

My eyes flit to the redwood cross on her chest. She cuts me off at the pass.

"We are all born of sin, Synali. Without sin, there cannot be absolution. This is a universal truth God has woven into existence; without cold, there cannot be warmth. Without a weight, there cannot be lightness. Science knows this, but faith knew it first."

Talize san Michel speaks softer than the rest of them, but she loves the sound of her own voice just the same.

"One must sin to learn the true light of God; to experience the full power of His loving mercy and ecstatic forgiveness, one must first err. This is how we draw closer to Him in our limited lives as sinful beings of the flesh."

The muffled music outside drowns my snort. "Sounds like an excuse to do terrible things whenever you want."

A flicker in her gaze. "And is what you are doing not terrible?"

A flicker in mine up to her.

"You wear the Hauteclare name, yet you threatened to kill them at the banquet. Several of them have even *died* since then, in strange and mysterious accidents. You continue to win, and your family continues to perish." Her pink smile is a petal curling in ash. "You are sinning *awfully*, lamb."

I don't know the church—Mother did. I don't know the book—Mother did. But I know people like Talize. Flagellants whipping themselves to feel better. Blood as salve, as if pain is some tourist attraction or some expensive liquor to be drunk and savored instead of an inescapable fact of life for so many. She drinks mine greedily as her eyes rest on Mother's cross pendant.

"Do you pray, lamb?"

"None of your fucking business."

"Ah…so you do."

Talize rises from the couch and approaches my chair. Her perfume is honeysuckle, and my body coils, ready for anything—any stab, any strike, any punch…but she just gently tucks my black hair away from my face.

"I can see it in you; you're suffering. You are frozen in time—living in the pain—and only God can release you. He forgives, Synali. *Everything.* All you must do is seek it."

My face is stone. Her black eyes loom beneath the veil, fingers tracing cool on the raw skin of my mask-punched knuckles.

"You wouldn't have to kill anymore. You wouldn't have to suffer. The hate in your heart is not you—it was planted there by Lithroi. It's not too late to let go of the serpent and embrace Him."

155 people dead because of him. Seven more dead because of me. The thought of it for a single moment—a life different, a life of peace…having drinks with people my age, answering messages from a boy my age. A man looms on the couch next to Talize suddenly, his eyes silver and his face handsome. *"If all your enemies were gone, Synali, what would you do?"*

There is no peace for me, Sevrith. I've chosen my fate.

The nobles chose her fate, and I will never forgive them for it.

There's a blur of movement as something small and neon black jumps from beneath Talize's sleeve and onto my hand with clammy webbed feet. I fling myself out of the chair in a panic, and Talize quickly scoops the frog from the ground and cups it tenderly.

"Oh, I'm so sorry. It seems my friend was more eager to meet you than I anticipated."

"You—" I snarl. "That thing—"

"*'Nightshade,'*" she corrects coolly. "Perhaps the most potent creature I've bred in my spare time. I've been told a single touch is enough to intoxicate a dozen grown men. I've taken the antidote in my tea, but you…well."

Beneath her halo, her smile is perfectly mollifying. *fear.* My blood slushes hot, cold, hot again. Something like static clings to my lungs—heavy, crackling, and all at once my breathing and blinking feels so slow. Talize's voice echoes sideways in my head.

"Are you feeling all right, Synali von Hauteclare? Oh, I do hope you'll be able to ride tomorrow—otherwise you forfeit our match."

The trap springs closed.

I feel dry-mouthed, woozy, my skull melting off my neck. My knees buckle as I make for the door; all wood, all the same, the door's gone—*there, a seam*—and I pull, pull myself by the railing down the stairs, tumbling, falling, and it's so funny I fell for it. *Laugh.* Laughing hysterically—I was ready and waiting and dressed to kill, to fight, but I fell into the trap face-first, distracted by the idea of forgiveness, of a better future. Of a future at all.

The plague doctors watch me, waiting for me to stop moving to descend, waiting for me to fall, but Jeria told me once that falling is only falling if you don't get back up again. Strobe lights pierce my eyes, and the beat of the music is a drum begging me to move with it, to dance to the sound of its love. I stumble down another staircase and into the sea of faces. Bodies jostle all around me, all of them jewel-eyed and crystal-smiled and haloed, all of them smiling at me and me smiling back and *I can feel it.*

I'm not alone anymore.

A hundred friends surround me. They move with me and touch me and call out to me; they're here, right beside me. *I'm safe.* Warm fingers under my clothes, warm lips on mine, the taste of blood like salt and honey, and in my deepest heart—in the withered, half-beating thing washed up on the shores of nothing—I know I'll never be alone again. I'll never again hurt alone in an empty apartment, in an empty bed, in the empty pool of Mother's blood. Crying and smiling and crying again, hot tears down my face. I reach for everyone with outstretched arms—*more, closer, please, together*—and then something harsh pulls me back: a hand stronger than me. The wonderful lights and colors blur, fade, and my friends get farther away.

"*No!* I'm not alone! Let me *go!*"

I lash out, biting into warmth—hard muscle and the salt-honey taste of blood again and someone's swear, but the hand refuses to let go. A long hall swims in neon, a red blur sheltering me against the wall. His platinum hair flashes in the strobe lights. I know him. I have to tell him.

"He promised. After it's over. So it's pointless."

"What are you talking about?"

"Lithroi. The rabbit man. He's going to kill me like I asked." I laugh. "I want to rest. But sometimes I look at Luna, and the sunrise, and you…and then I don't."

His hand cups my cheek. "Look at me, Hauteclare. Deep breaths."

Breathe in. He breathes in, too, our chests glancing against each other, and lightning runs through me and all of a sudden I want to devour him down to his bones, strip him bare and eat him, crawl into him and live where it's warm and gentle and alive. I want to be him—*better*. I want to be him—*loved*. Suddenly, someone drags me by the wrist away from him, and the cold air of outside nips. Damp cobblestone bites my body as I collapse.

A colder voice echoes. "For God's sake, Rax, she's just high—let the guards deal with her."

A crimson blur towers above. "What happened to your whole '*honor among riders*' thing, huh?"

A far gold blur snorts. "There is honor among riders, but there is no honor among patricidal murderers."

"She's your *family*, Mir."

"She's killing her family, *Rax*."

I crave the red one like fire craves wood (*he would be different, he would be gentle, he would be good*). And even if the gold one hates me, I crave her, too; strong, clear, a sister (*someone to train with, someone to fall asleep with*). I sit up and reach out for the red one with trembling fingers.

"You're beautiful."

Redwood eyes blink. I move closer. There's the smell of soap-sweat-skin, and I find the weaknesses in his cloth, the muscles of his stomach velvet and my touch lingering.

"I want to stay with you."

A rumble. "Y-You can't."

"*Please*, just once."

"Ah, finally!" gold snaps. "That's hers—get her in and let's go. We're late enough as it is."

I hear the steam-hiss of hovercarriage vents over wet cobblestone. The delicious warmth lifts me and deposits me somewhere cold again, abandoning me. My fingers clutch in his brown silk, but iron vices pry me off, and his murmur burns on my ear, sweet black syrup going down hot.

"I'm sorry."

I collapse face-first on a cold pillow, pale blue and silver swimming. The jolt of the carriage takes me I don't care where—to hell, to where sinners go. To someplace dark and empty. To the cold dragon.

alone.

In my swimming vision, Astrix sits in the carriage next to me, smiling down at me with her silver eyes and pitiless, unblinking black pupils as she strokes my hair and speaks words beneath words…

never alone.

45. Viridis

viridis ~is ~e, *a.*
1. green
2. young, energetic; vigorous

THE KING'S RIDER RETURNS to the heart of the world.

But so have they.

Their tendrils wave high above as they slowly circle the massive core of nerve fluid. Three of them, this time. The scientists call them extruders. He doesn't know what to call them, only what to feel about them: Anger. Indignation. Fear. The boy catches himself; why should he fear? His father has given him the universe, and the boy will shape it as he commands, and so he commands now in wordless thought:

return.

The silence in the core room pounds. The vents of the boy's hoverchair whisper *failure.* He stares unblinkingly up at the ghostly tendrils dancing along the dark ceiling and commands again.

RETURN.

The extruders don't react, but the core does. The silver fibrils inside surge furiously up the monolithic tube and bash against it, pointed in hard silver angles like spears, like teeth, trying to get to the extruders beyond at his command.

The extruders are *defying* him.

This has happened before—it has simply never happened for *him*. The king's rider is always one of the king's many bastards—Hellrunner accepts nothing but Ressinimus blood. They keep the core in check using Hellrunner or they are discarded, and many have come before him. The boy keenly remembers being discarded; the cold sulfur of the streets, the wet crack of molerat bones in his teeth when nothing else could be found, the blank gazes of the hundreds of thousands of people who walked past him huddled in his box of corrugated tin as if he were invisible. *Garbage.* His mother tried foolishly to run, to keep him away from his destiny, and he was treated like garbage for it.

No. He refuses to be discarded again.

The scientists were wrong; the core's rapid failure is not due to entropy or a lack of supplied fuel. It is due to a rider.

At first he thought it was one of the established, experienced ones, but he quickly realized none of them posed a threat. None of them knew the answer to the old queen's question—a question that almost broke the world twenty years ago and would break it again now just as readily. None of them knew how to go deep enough to find her. They were incapable of it, concerned always with their own survival. They *resisted* and *resisted* and *resisted*. It was not an established rider doing this. This was someone new, someone who refused to resist.

And he found her lying in that hospital bed.

The boy reaches out and touches the heart of the world, and the silver fibrils try to touch him back.

why her? what does she give you that i have not?

The hiss of a projection sword powering off rings in his ear, and the quiet voice of his bodyguard resounds at his side. "Do you require anything else, milord?"

The boy turns his hoverchair, vents hissing over tile and unmoving bodies. The core room is painted with stillness, with bodies slumped over at their consoles and clutching their own ill-hidden hard-light pistols, their bloodless projection sword wounds charring white lab coats in tangles of flesh, mouths and eyes open wide in rictus.

"The heads go into the core. Clean the rest, and then bring in the first-stringers."

The bodyguard bows. "As you wish, milord."

46. Decipio

dēcipiō ~ipere ~ēpī ~eptum, *tr.*
1. to deceive, mislead
2. to deprive of an expected advantage

Clutching my heavy body, I stagger up the path to Moonlight's End. My legs tremble, my thoughts vibrating against themselves. All that matters is surviving. No. ***Winning.***

Move one step at a time. Frantic barking, hollow tapping on marble, someone's fingers without rings reaching for the cross on my chest. I push away, but my legs fail. Someone with the scent of moths picks me up and carries me away.

"I told you not to go, brave one."

My bed. A dream, but my own memory this time—Father's office in wood and gold and marble. These are his last moments. His ceremonial dagger I grabbed off his desk rests in my hand. His face is clearer than memory should be—like reality, like old hate swelling. Blue-blue eyes, blue-blue suit. Lines around his brows, his mouth…a life lived as Mother can't anymore. His nose, my nose. His shoulders, mine. He gave me his body.

But he gave me his ruthlessness, too.

Father is still and quiet, hands behind his back. He turns and faces away from his only daughter, looking out of the expansive window and into space. Into nothingness. His lips—*my lips*—move in the window's black reflection, voice crackling. "I loved her, Synali."

He doesn't get to say my name. He doesn't get to say the word "love."

He was supposed to love me. Protect me.

Fury and despair and injustice come together like fire. He ended my world for reputation, for "honor," for a seat beside a dying old man—he decided power was more important than me. My feet move forward. My hand comes down. My dagger flashes bright, and then red.

My whisper in his ear: "Tell her that yourself."

47. Cicatrix

cicātrix ~īcis, *f.*
1. a mark of an old wound; a scar, incision

Rax Istra-Velrayd looks up at the withered trees hiding the windows of the Lithroi manor. His crimson hovercarriage hums behind him, and his empty stomach roils; he couldn't eat anything at the marriage discussion table with all those Hauteclares staring at him. Mother laughed too sweet even as her hand gripped his knee under the table, and Father made promises and more promises, but he hadn't cared one bit. All he could think about was a pair of sky-blue eyes going soft for once.

Smiling, for once.

He can't shake it—he didn't know Synali *could* smile. The way her cheeks brightened, the way her lips moved…lips smeared with blood, lips devoured by some dust-sucking assholes in the club crowd. Lips that bit his forearm. He rubs the bandage gingerly—it would've been easy enough to call it a training injury if he hadn't stopped getting those at ten. His parents had been suspicious, but Mirelle covered for him, and they did nothing if not soak up everything that fell out of her high-blooded mouth.

Mirelle's words in the hovercarriage back from the marriage

discussions echo around his head. *"If you like her so much, then bed her and be done with it."*

"It's not that simple, actually," he'd said.

"It must be." She'd inspected her nails lightly. *"She's not sane, Rax. She's as unstable and dangerous as a dying star; everyone sees that. So go on—have your fun. And when you're done, stand back and let me end her on the tilt."*

Rax should care about anything else: the fact he hasn't been able to get ahold of Yavn in four days, the fact his parents auctioned him off to House Hauteclare and his marriage to Mirelle is in six months now. But he just didn't get it... The former prince wouldn't kill her, would he? She's his rider. She's not in danger, *right*?

Her words sounded so hopeless, so small and alone. As defensive and thorny as she is, she would never tell him those things sober; she'd clearly been drugged. She'd been so touchy-feely, so different, so raw and real where her kiss had been timid and scared. Her hands had moved in his clothes so bravely—*her hands in his **clothes***, tugging at his seams with a keen in her voice that wrought every muscle in his body rigid.

"Please, just once."

"Can I help you, Sir Istra-Velrayd?"

He starts—the prince stands in the front door, a little golden sentry dog poking its nose around his legs. The man is shorter than Rax and far reedier than a once-future king should be, and he wears no blacklight halo. His wispy brown hair pulled into a short ponytail draws no special attention, and he keeps an innocuous smile on his long, calm face. He's Synali's mentor—not her father, because according to Mirelle she murdered her own father. Rax hadn't been shocked by this, only sad, because the idea was once close to him, too. In his youngest, darkest days trapped inside Sunscreamer, he also thought about murdering his parents for what they were doing to him.

If he had taken the opportunity, he would've been Synali.

"Yeah, sorry. I just wanted to know if— Is Synali all right? I saw her at Atteint and got her in the carriage, but she didn't seem well—"

The prince smiles bigger. "Ah. You were the one who sent the flowers to the hospital, then."

"Flowers? No, I—I mean, I tried to visit, but they had her room made private. Or I guess...*you* had her room made private."

"I did indeed."

Years of tiptoeing around court politics lets Rax feel the bitterness in the man's smile, even if there's none on the outside. The sapphires in the man's cane watch Rax like a dozen blue eyes—sharp, unwelcoming. Still, his mind clutches at Synali's voice. If Lithroi is hurting her, forcing her to ride like Rax's mother forced him… The bite wound on his arm throbs as he takes a step forward, and the sentry dog starts growling lowly.

"I just wanna see her, Your Highness. Make sure she's okay."

"I'm afraid that won't be possible, Sir Istra-Velrayd."

Rax pushes into the doorway, too close to the prince to be considered decorous anymore. "One minute. That's all I'm asking."

It's so fast he doesn't feel it at first—*so fast it reminds him of impact*—and then comes the hot opening, the telltale molten ooze down his cheek. Blood. The Lithroi prince holds a projection sword flush beneath Rax's chin—the contained orange heat of it scorching and the sapphire handle gleaming as he smiles brilliantly.

"I think you will be leaving now, Sir Istra-Velrayd."

48. Eminus

ēminus, *adv.*
1. *(of fighting)* at long range
2. from a distance

Today, there are enough people outside my hangar to warrant a single guard. Faint cheers go up as I approach. My scratches have been bandaged, the bruises from last night hidden beneath makeup. No gel shot burns in my throat, no woozy frog drug in my veins—my mind is clear and laser-focused.

Dravik stands in front of the small crowd with an aimless grin plastered on. "You look well."

I have no patience for his mind games. "You sent the carriage for me last night."

"Yes—you were quite under the weather. If I was a learned sort of man, I'd have called it an overdose meant to incapacitate you for several days."

"How did you know where I was?"

"It hardly takes a steedcrafter to know where you went, Synali."

I narrow my eyes. "But you knew when. *Exactly.*"

"Naturally. The biometric scanner I put in your pendant alerted me to your rapid heartrate. Far beyond healthy. I knew something had happened, and I sent the carriage for you."

I clutch at the redwood around my neck, and my stomach churns. He must've altered it when I gave it to him to hold during my matches. "You've tagged me like a dog."

"Like a girl who refuses to listen to those invested in her safety," Dravik says coolly. "You're quite lucky I kept tabs on Talize's work prior to this, or I would never have been able to give you the antidote in time for you to come to this match."

He couldn't've known I would get in the carriage. I could've just overdosed on the dance floor. Unless…unless he was *certain* I'd met someone who'd help me into it—heard me talk to them. Rax. Mirelle. He saw them help me at the conference.

"You've put a mic in it, too," I snarl.

Dravik's smile grows. "I will not lose you."

"I'm not yours to lose, Your Highness."

"I'm curious—how did you do it?" he asks abruptly. "Break the lockdown. Your friend's module again?"

"You're pretending not to know to trick me into narrowing your approximations for you."

"I've taught you too well." The prince looks down at his cane and laughs softly. "After Olric, I was worried, but…it seems Heavenbreaker is progressing much faster than I thought. You're doing splendidly, Synali."

"What exactly am I doing '*splendidly*,' Dravik? Riding your steed? Helping you start a civil war?"

His smile this time shines like a father's. Proudly.

"Growing."

We play the game in the shadows today.

The sun haloes Esther from behind, the Station shining like a gray brooch on her breast. The detritus of Theta-7 and the *Endurance* collision remains in the distance, removal crews jumping across pieces of loading decks and half-melted twists of metal, their projection tethers to the reclamation ship shimmering like neon-orange umbilical cords. The white orb of the Supernova Cup arena opens its netting, and Heavenbreaker and I jet through.

Talize is already here.

She floats under the suspended LED cross like a fetal child, her steed's hands folded over each other in prayer. Her entire steed is without angles or sharpness—gradually spiraled legs and arms and an S-shaped torso. Its head is smooth with no features, save for the two ghostly fingertip indents where eyes would be, like a bride wearing a veil. The entire thing is painted in cream, with pale pink at the joints. The deepest pink of all is on its breastplate as a sigil: the holly and snake.

Snake and rabbit, forever at odds.

We near, and Talize uncoils, a holoscreen popping up in my helmet. Her pale-pink rider's helmet shines, halo faintly catching her pleased expression through the visor. "Ah, Synali. Care to join me? I was saying a few words to our Lord before the match."

Heavenbreaker jerks toward the invitation. *"friend."*

I jerk back. *we two friends. no one else.*

Heavenbreaker makes the emotional equivalent of a flip at the thought *we*—a joyful thing. I focus on the handkerchief against my skin. Draw a line. Not a heavy one—not like Olric's match—but something lighter, something like a nod, an acknowledgment at the edge of a pool and nothing more.

My extended silence has Talize straightening, delicate hands to her sides as she asks, "Do you know what I was praying for, Synali?"

I jet to the terrene tilt, the magnets pulling us in taut and flush. "Hopefully," I say, "mercy."

I shut the comms, but they come roaring back with the crowd and the hooting of the commentators:

"—bringing you a match smack-dab in the middle of the Supernova Cup's A seed! Things are starting to get ugly, folks—but not before they get beautiful! Today's sidereal contender needs no introduction; she's the undisputed winner of the Nova-Court's comeliness pageant four years and running—please welcome the glamorous vixen of House Michel, Talize san Michel, and her steed, Sineater!"

The crowd blasts their resounding approval in my ears.

"Lady Talize is a real heavyweight in the Cruiser-class riders, Gress. She's got an eye for accuracy we rarely see on the field."

"Or is it an eye for weakness, Bero?"

"That's a great point, Gress—she's a rider who watches her opponent carefully, pinpoints their tender spots, and then goes in for the kill. Real exciting to see what she'll do today against our next contender—a true firecracker with little predictability and even less prudence! She's made it this far on sheer grit, clinging to precipices other riders would've considered impossible! No one can doubt her determination; please welcome Synali von Hauteclare and her steed, Heavenbreaker!"

My hands clench. Every word of his introduction for me screams "desperate" without once saying it.

"Riders, ready your tilts for the first round!"

In a blink, Talize turns and jets to her tilt, leaving trails of pink plasma in her wake. She's fast. But I've seen faster.

"Let the countdown to the first round begin! In the name of God, King, and Station!"

The roar of the crowd echoes him. Sineater raises its pink lance. Talize's holoscreen pops up again. "There's no worth in suffering without release, Synali. I tried to give you release last night, yet you refused it."

"Three, two, one—"

"I offer it to you again, little lamb."

A threat. A cut-off silence as all comms close for descent. A breath. A moment.

go.

The instant roar of Heavenbreaker's jets at full power floods my ears. The steed's on me but not heavy—with me but not suffocating or too far away. It hovers at just the right distance, inches above my mind, taut and ready. Talize stays farther out on the tilt than anyone I've ever fought. It's like she's orbiting another planet, another grav-gen, another arena entirely. She's avoiding me. No—*leading* me; a matador waving a refined silken flag.

But the animal has learned about traps, now.

Grav-gen blue consumes us. She moves wider, but we're faster. I pull our shoulders in, lean deep left, and lock on. The g-forces peel me off myself, but they can't peel Heavenbreaker and me apart anymore. Talize's lance spears forward, all her Cruiser power focused on fighting the gravity pull with her arm as she angles the lance inside.

I have just enough time to blink before the scream.

FRIEND

My ears ring, brute-force urgency bashed against my brain—it's the first time I've heard Heavenbreaker *shout*. Rejoice. The idea of **friend** is suddenly everywhere in the saddle (*Rax Mirelle Jeria happiness gratitude safety looks like me same as me*) and all-consuming, and Heavenbreaker goes limp—opens itself up to Sineater. It doesn't want to fight. It wants to drink, to laugh, to touch something that looks like it, but this is my fault. I taught the true AI a too-true thing, and it's running wild with it, and my frantic correction is a blood-curdling siren, a bell smashed with the biggest mallet I have.

NOT FRIEND.

I wrench with all my might.

Impact.

The stars spin, Sineater's cream-and-pink lance just barely missing me. The rise takes us out, momentum jerking me cruelly around the saddle. I smash in on myself, rider suit squeaking against the gel as it balloons out, surface tension the only thing keeping me in and a single word keeping my bouncing brain on track: *jets jets jets*. I blast every jet in rapid succession and neutralize our wild speed. *Red, 0. Blue, 0.* The comms flicker on.

"I gave you a chance to accept His grace," Talize says. "Little Nightshade and the antidote in the tea—this you refused. Much like our Father warns us with our good conscience, I, too, gave you leeway, and you've scorned my charity wholeheartedly."

Sineater raises its lance.

"All the fighting you're doing for Sir Lithroi, and all the killing he's doing for you." Talize sighs. "The Lord will forgive that, Synali. I can hear His love for you even now, calling out for you to accept Him. He would take away your suffering and use me as His instrument to do so…all it requires of you is to be still; to listen to your heart, to relinquish this dire sin of wrath you hold so dear and accept the divine in forgiveness. Would your mother not want you to live in His light?"

I grip my silver lance harder. Talize's voice lowers to nothing but a whisper.

"Do you not wish to live gently, lamb?"

"**Gently**?" I snarl. "Did you let us live gently, noble? Did they kill my mother **gently**? They used her and discarded her and then killed her in front of me like she was nothing, and your king and your god allowed it."

Heavenbreaker bristles as my anger fills the saddle gradually—not searing heat like Olric but a steady burn. It flashes me a memory again: the A3 and A4 steeds holding hands but this time covered in rust. Newer, modern steeds arrive and separate the two, forcing their hands apart. The gold A4 steed drifts away from the silver A3's vision, and I feel a not-me surge of utter rage toward the newer steeds for separating them.

not friend, Heavenbreaker asserts.

The descent comes. Talize san Michel tries to stay far away again, but I no longer have patience for her games. I come in farther and slingshot diagonally across the tilt before terminus. A crash isn't illegal as long as the lance hits first.

If she wants to drink pain, I will drown her in it.

We speed toward each other, and she stutters when she realizes what I'm doing—Sineater jerks back but not away. The g-forces are too strong; she can't get away anymore. She can only fight, and she knows that. Her pink lance moves to confuse me, blurring what direction she's coming from—like needle into fabric, it positions so quickly I can barely follow—up, more left, underneath. Heavenbreaker wants to be close to Sineater, to hold hands with another steed again, and its wants and my wants start to blend; Rax and Mirelle and gel shots toasting and his chest against mine, and I understand all at once—*enemy/friend—fire/fuel*. Entropy. Energy. Words mean more things below the surface. I am a rider in the Supernova Cup. I'm going down in a dark blaze of unglory, and I need fuel to continue burning. Enemies, friends, love and hate—I will experience it all and burn brighter for it.

Before I die, I will live.

bow, I coax. *properly greet our not-friend.*

Heavenbreaker lowers its head eagerly, Talize's lance sliding just between the hollow curve of our crescent-moon helmet. The cry, the light, the thrust.

Impact.

We compact. Metal crushes on metal, steed-on-steed crushing into each other—glass and gears and cables explode, and we spin out like two birds in death dives. The g-forces play with my vertebrae, twisting me one way until I manage to turn on a single jet and stop our death-spin momentum. We float in the wake of the aftermath. Heavenbreaker sounds faint, injured but happy.

"close to friend."

My insides feel twisted up—pain all over. Talize and I are a travesty of cream and blue smashed together by a giant, two metal dolls sharing the same twisted right side. The crowd roars.

My silver lance pierces through her pink forehead, and I snarl into her fractured helmet: *"Go to hell."*

49. Chorda

chorda ~ae, f.
1. string of a musical instrument
2. intestine (as food)

For the first time in her life, Mirelle Ashadi-Hauteclare watches a tourney with dread.

The vis lights the sitting room blue. Heavenbreaker wins. The Lithrois *win*.

She looks to her grandmother seated on the chaise longue, her old spine straight and her lined face kept eerily neutral. Mirelle knows—the blanker Grandmother's expression, the more worried she is, and she is nothing but empty canvas now. They both know, the knowledge echoing between the clinks of a tea tray being brought in by the maids and the bone-chill groan of the whitewood walls: someone in this House will now die.

Finally, Grandmother smiles at her. "What's that worried look for? Come, have some tea with me."

"But—"

"I have taken measures." Grandmother pours a cup calmly. "We were perhaps unsteady in the beginning, but we are ready now, and the combined weight of the Hauteclare family is not something so easily breached."

Mirelle glances to the hard-light chain mail of the guards lingering outside the sitting room, and she can't help but sink back into the cushions. It's true; Dawn Imperator is less a manse and more a fortress now. The garden windows blur with guards patrolling and relieving each other like clockwork, their robotic silver sentry hounds stalking heat signatures and electronic disturbances.

They are safe. Of course they are. Grandmother smiles softer and motions for her.

"Come. Drink, and let me braid your hair. It's grown so long these days."

Grandmother's knotted fingers thread through her hair with grace and a rare tenderness. Grandmother loved her more when she was little, or so Mirelle thought, but the way her fingers move now reminds Mirelle that love does not go away, it merely takes on different faces throughout the years.

When she leaves the sitting room hours later, braids brushing against her shoulders and a bounce in her step, it is love that makes her stop at the maids' voices coming from around the corner.

"—imagine it? A bastard, riding for a noble House! A commoner just like you or me. No academy, no riches, no title… It's unthinkable."

"But not unlikable." Another maid giggles. "She's amazing."

Mirelle snorts softly—*amazing*? Passable at best. But even she has to admit the traitor is improving markedly with each match.

"They're just allowing her to ride! No one's stopping her—not even the king."

A third maid speaks quieter. "I have a brother in Low Ward, and he says it means the court's grip on things is getting weaker."

"And more paranoid," the first maid murmurs. "If all these atrociously mannered guards everywhere are any indication."

"Paranoid? You saw what happened to Theta-7; those rebels could crash another freighter into the Wards at any time."

"Be quiet, Yunice! Erabeth's brother was on Theta-7."

"Oh. Sorry, Erabeth."

"It wasn't Theta-7."

The quiet stretches thin. And then:

"You mean…he was on the other one?"

It is love that makes Mirelle memorize each and every voice, and it is love that makes her turn each and every maid over to the king's guard as traitors come morning.

50. Glacio

glaciō ~āre ~āuī ~ātum, *tr.*
1. to freeze

Flowers wait for me in the shower room—little white puffs nestled among big red blossoms and clustered in a delicate vase, set carefully on the bench. House Hauteclare again? No—the vase seems more like the hospital flowers. I look the blooms up on the vis; baby's breath for purity, poinsettia for success. Is it the boy in the hoverchair? Why would he wish for my success? As far as I know, Dravik and I are the only ones who want us to succeed. I don't touch them just in case they're poisoned like the roses were.

I turn the shower on and strip my rider's suit off. From the steaming stall, I watch the flowers dew up—is there a camera in the vase? Anything's possible after Talize and her drugging—there are still four swords left striking out at me, after all.

Correction: *three.*

"—clare?"

I freeze and turn the water off, listening.

"Hauteclare?"

I throw on one of the plain silk robes the arena provides and walk toward the voice until I find the barrel-chested source and it finds me—his wide redwood eyes promptly darting away from the robe's translucency against my body.

"*Shit,*" Rax hisses. "Don't just sneak up on me like that."

My brow arches. "I believe you were doing the majority of the sneaking."

He clears his throat, gaze firmly riveted above my head. "Are you feeling okay? From last night, I mean. You seemed pretty fucked up."

Brush it off. I know now—*friend/enemy. Fire/fuel.* I will live before I die. There's only one thing I can have from Rax Istra-Velrayd in this lifetime, and it's not genuine concern or care. It's a fleeting night at most.

"What could I have done better?" I ignore him. "In my match with Talize? She went quite wide."

His broad lips set. "Are you okay or not?"

I watch a bead of sweat drip down his neck and into his open breast coat. "I've changed my mind, Velrayd—I have one use for you, and that is riding. Everything else is pointless."

"You sure do like that word, huh? *Pointless.*" There's a moment of quiet, the steam curling around us. His high cheek has a cut on it, the bandage thin. The bandage on his arm is far thicker—first the glass in his back, and now a bite. I've done nothing but hurt him, and the fool still comes around. "People aren't pointless."

"Not all of them," I counter. "But you certainly are."

I can't look at his face, but I see him wince, and part of me likes having any effect on him. He won't look away from the ceiling, and the urge to test him rises up. I walk too near him—my dripping body in the thin robe mere inches from his gold buttons and embroidery, my tangled scar starkly white beside his red cloth. Shame left me long ago—this body belongs to a dead girl.

"Hauteclare—you said it can't happen a second time," he reminds me hoarsely.

"*This* never happened a first time," I lilt, flitting my fingers along his beltline. "What could I have done better against Talize?"

A tendon flexes in his jaw. My effect on him is clear below my fingers, the taut V of his navel leading into an obvious rise of his breeches.

"Come on, Velrayd." I lean closer. "Tell me what it means to ride. Tell me how you do it."

In a blink, he grabs both my wandering hands by the wrists, pinning them above my head to the wall behind me. Nothing hard or cruel, just inevitable—a consequence of my own action. I dare to look at his face, his brows drawn fierce and the redwood of his eyes filled not with light but shadow.

"Don't play with me, Hauteclare. Whatever you give me, I'll give you back."

"I'm not giving you anything. I'm letting you take it."

"That's not how this works."

I cock my head. "Isn't it?"

He exhales softly. "Let me make this very clear: from the day we met in the practice arena, I've wanted to fight you." He leans into the crook of my neck, and a flame-tongue thrill runs through me at the feeling of his breath beneath my ear. "But the problem with my stubborn ass is that I'm a rider first and a human second. Sex makes it easier to ride against someone, and I don't want it to be easy against you. So we're not going to. Not until I face you in the arena. You have to stay alive until then—promise me."

"I can't."

Like cinders, he kisses my neck inch by slow inch. "Are you sure about that?"

His hand slides between my thighs, and my breath catches at the same moment his fingers do on all the tenderest, wildest places. "I c-can't promise you anything."

He chuckles, the sound deep and close and mind-melting. "Shame. You seem pretty bent on winning the entire Cup."

"Wh-Why is that a shame?"

"Because. You'll have to get through me."

"I will."

"No, you won't." Pity I can swallow, but dismissal I can't—not after everything I've suffered for. I rip from his grip and back away. His smile turns wry on the edges.

"I'm not being argumentative for the hell of it; it's the truth. You're good, Hauteclare. Novel, even. But you're not me. There's only one Rax Istra-Velrayd, and you're looking at him."

"I'm looking at a fool—"

"You're sloppy on your descents." His gravel voice goes gravel-sharp. "You hold back on impact, looking for last-minute openings, which means you never dedicate full inertia. You don't know how to keep the g-force in your limbs, so you put it all in your shoulders. Your left side jets have to compensate for the lack of strength in your thrusts, so your guard is easily breached from any low right angle."

Every lion bone in his face seems different, unsmiling, and each word of his points out like spikes against my throat. Every word is a weakness I didn't know, and I'm suddenly naked in more ways than one. Dripping water trills. A saint carved in the marble ceiling watches us silently, his body riddled with arrows.

"It's been fun," Rax says. "But when the time comes, you'll lose again."

The rider in me bristles at the rider in him. Every hair on my body stands, understands that he understands how I ride, what it means to ride. He's given me the truth. So I give it back. "I'm not the same girl you defeated before."

"No," he agrees with a turn of his heel. "But you're not the girl who will beat me, either."

No pride, only winning.

No feelings, only facts.

Fact: When swords were still made of metal, a whetstone was used to keep them sharp. It was a porous, otherwise unremarkable stone against which iron and steel found their deadliest edges.

Fact: My next three opponents will be whetstones.

Fact: I will show Rax Istra-Velrayd a girl made like sword, like lance, like dagger.

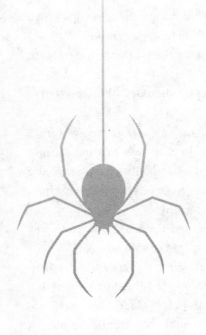

−4. Agna

agna ~ae, f.
1. a female lamb

The key to torture was to say nothing.

Rain had learned this from Green-One. To demand nothing and simply inflict pain after pain was far more terrifying than shouting into the prey's face. In silence, a mind could unravel itself far better than any words spoken. So Rain stood against the wall of an old buried tunnel in Low Ward and watched the noble scream his lungs out as Green-One slid the newest piece of corrugated metal beneath a fresh fingernail, hitting bed, hitting nerve, hitting soprano.

Yavn von Velrayd thrashed against the chair he was tied to, gag-muffled screech reverberating off the cement and into the darkness on either end. Blood seeped down the chair, soaking the dirt beneath him. Blacklight spray-paint tags glowed patchy white-blue on the curved walls, and a single LED quivered above—a rare thing in the Under-ring.

Green-One had picked an area far from Polaris's territory to be safe, but Rain couldn't shake the feeling that someone would hear the noise and come looking. Another metal sliver, another screech. Rain flinched.

Green-One looked up to him, wiping the blood from his fingertips with a handkerchief before stepping in to whisper, "You look pale, brother."

Rain shook his head. "I'm unused to keeping them alive so long. Death is quick. This is…not."

"It's necessary." Green-One put a hand on his shoulder. "You did well in bringing him to me."

Rain flinched again at the sound Yavn made—a gurgling plea wet from tears and blood weeping from every orifice. The dust was wearing off, and Rain was noticing too much too abruptly. Yavn looked only a few years older than Rain himself, his noble red breast coat torn to shreds from Green-One's barbed-wire attempts, his eyes dark mirrors of agony.

Green-One reached for another splinter, and Rain started, "If he was really Polaris's leader, would he have let himself get caught so easily?"

"He's not the leader, brother; he is the decoy. Every paper trail leads to him—meaning someone has set him up." Green-One turned to Yavn with a chuckle. "Isn't that right, noble? You've been double-crossed. How sad."

The assassin reached for Yavn's hand, the noble boy frantically pulling and pushing in any direction away from the metal splinter, and Rain cleared his throat.

"If he's the decoy, then we're playing right into the leader's hands, aren't we? They *want* us to waste time capturing him. Torturing him."

Green-One paused, and Rain felt the air in the ancient tunnel go even stiller. "We are not discussing this right now, brother."

Rain saw it, then, as his brother slid in yet another metal splinter—this was not a means to an end. It was cruelty for the sake of it. The slight smile on Green-One's face when the noble howled through his gag told him everything: this was retribution. All of their family had died because of these nobles playing games with change, and he was taking it out on Yavn. Rain strode over and grasped his brother's wrist.

"Enough, Green-One. He's soft. Just ask him."

Green-One went still. This was the first time Rain had ever disagreed with him. Rain feared what would come after, but to his relief, his brother finally relented.

"Yes. I suppose he is." He reached in and took the gag out. "Who asked you to run the shell companies for Polaris, noble?"

Yavn hacked and panted, blood on his teeth. "I…I don't know. They used intermediaries."

"What about their message logs?" Green-One fingered another metal sliver absently. "Those are bio-locked. What was the address?"

"Hospital. Noble hospital. They always came from a vis in the rider ward."

Rain frowned. "A nurse? Or a doctor?"

"One of the comatose riders," Green-One corrected. "Vis stay active as long as the heart does. A House member could request access to their body and use it."

"So we find the rider whose family visits match the dates and times Yavn received the pings, and we know that must be the leader's House."

Green-One was silent for a beat, and then, quicker than Rain could blink, he shoved the next metal splinter into Yavn's finger. With no gag, the noble's scream pierced the darkness, and Rain clapped his hands over his ears. "GREEN!"

"He's keeping something back." Green-One leaned in, watching Yavn writhe closely. After a moment, he yanked the splinter out. "Tell me, or it goes back in."

Rain watched Yavn's spittle-wet face contort, resist, and then collapse. "Th-The…the ocean…"

Green-One leaned in even farther, their noses glancing, and Rain was half convinced his brother would tear the noble's face off with his teeth alone. "Speak up."

"The ocean." Yavn struggled. "Below…the noble spire."

"What about it? Be more specific," Rain said, trying to buy him time enough to breathe.

"Sometimes…a white light glows. I see it…at odd hours of the night. Beneath the surface. Not moonlight. Too far down. They'd seen it, too."

"They," Green-One said slowly. "You mean the leader."

Yavn nodded. "Said it was the beginning…and the end."

Green-One pushed off their captive and made his way to Rain. "I'll verify the hospital. When we know what House it is, you'll go to the ocean and visit their manse there. Look for any link to Polaris."

"How do you know—"

"Think, brother; odd hours of the night. Lesser nobles without property aren't allowed oceanside after dark—whoever it is has a manse there." Green-One didn't give him any time to feel foolish, just patting his shoulder. "You

take care of this mess. Make sure to use the southeast vent system for the body—north is too hot lately."

Rain's eyes flickered to Yavn over Green-One's shoulder, and he saw raw terror in the noble's eyes. He'd heard too much ten minutes ago to be left alive, let alone now.

"Remember, Rain—their whims took our family from us, and if we leave them alone, they will take again."

The Web's code was woven strong between Rain and his brother, and Green-One had every confidence in it, black armor melting into black shadow as he left through the tunnel. Rain waited, and waited, and knew Green-One was waiting, too. Watching. He unsheathed his projection dagger and approached Yavn, who squirmed one last time, desperately and tiredly.

"Please, no—*please*, I won't tell anyone, *I swear*. I'll work for you, I'll spy for you—I'll give you anything, just let me go!" Rain did not slow, and Yavn begged to the last. *"PLEASE!"*

The assassin lunged close, fast, and there was a spurt of blood quickly cauterized, the smell of singed hemoglobin, and an agonized howl. Yavn went still, the assassin's voice hoarse from the scream he made not a second ago now rasping in his ear: "Slump forward."

The noble quickly went limp against Rain's chest. Rain pulled the hardlight blade from his own biceps, muscle shredded and blackened down to the inner elbow crease—the motion forward looked like a sufficient stab. Rain shoved the chair over and kicked viciously at the "body." Green-One wanted him to hate, so he would hate.

He untied a shallowly breathing Yavn and dragged the boy over the tracks. Rain was impressed; even when Yavn's back caught on rusted iron, he didn't so much as wince. Finally they rounded a corner, and Rain propped the boy up against a wall, whispering, "Don't make noise. He's still listening."

Yavn nodded frantically. Rain could see the question in his eyes as easily as reading (*why spare me?*), and he murmured something Father had once said to him.

"A spider is a patient animal—until its web is broken."

51. Gesto

gestō ~āre ~āuī ~ātum, *tr.*
1. to bear, to wear, to carry

The fourth circle was my grandmother.

Bellesera von Hauteclare was a woman of immaculate looks, her hair pure silver. She was a matriarch with the breeding and schooling of the finest of nobles. She turned seventy-eight this year—fighting a relapse of uterine cancer with the best doctors and medicines known to mankind. She was the first one Father told about me. Her pings to him scrawl long, written in early mornings at the hospital.

BELLESERA: *I will not leave this Station until the House is secure, Farris. I will hang on with my last nail if I must, until the very moment everything is put right.*

Dravik sends me pictures of her redwood room. She sleeps in a bed of gold satin, her hair a ghostly curtain on the embroidered pillows and her wrinkled hands splayed over the covers. One of them reaches limply for a pill bottle.

BELLESERA: *I told you the first time that your taste for excess would ruin you. I told you over and over, and yet you never listened to me—not once—and now you've ruined yourself. You've ruined us ALL. To say your father would be* *disappointed in you is the understatement of a half dozen centuries.*

Green pills spill like a river over her satin sheets.

BELLESERA: *You'll be rid of the both of them at once, as you should've done when the thing was first born. You will restore the honor of this House, or I will do it for you, and with far fewer reservations.*

I watch the vis longer than I should: the picture of her dead face, her eyes blankly staring up at the bed's canopy—two spears of blue ice looking for God. I've seen other people and their grandmothers; stews on stoves, kind embraces. If I was Mirelle, she would've smiled at me...held me close, maybe. My vis cursor blinks on the word "*thing.*" Luna licks at my frozen hand.

The fine line between love and hate is made of blood. And to blood it will return.

The nightmare wakes me again, hood and dagger, and I reach for my vis and type:

HELLRUNNER.

What information I can find is very sparse and mostly a paraphrase of what Dravik told me. Hellrunner is the king's steed. It's been ridden only by those in House Ressinimus and those chosen by House Ressinimus.

And then I see the picture.

The polished gold steed shines like a sun. The helmet has been altered to mimic a dragon's maw, the hands and feet rife with scale-like imprints, and a tail drags behind it like a long, pure-gold banner. It's different, shinier, but there is no doubt; that's the gold A4 steed I keep seeing in Heavenbreaker's memories. A search tells me there aren't any A4 models left—the king's steed is the only one.

Heavenbreaker is the A3 and Hellrunner the A4, and they were together in space somewhere, for a long time. Until someone found them and separated them.

Confused, I head for the kitchen with Luna on my heels, but I don't make it far, feet freezing on the marble just before a puddle of bright red. Dravik stands in the middle of the hall, his beige sleeping tunic soaked in blood. A dark shape lies at his feet, human-size and unmoving. The prince looks over his shoulder and gives a blood-flecked smile.

"Ah, Synali. Couldn't sleep?" He holds his cane-head projection sword, dark flakes crisping from the neon-orange blade. It hums faintly until the prince powers it off. "Shall I make us a cup of tea?"

Luna answers as I can't, yipping excitedly. Slowly, I make my way to the kitchen counter and sit. Dravik reattaches his cane and busies himself with the kettle, and when he pivots with two steaming cups in his bloodstained hands, I take mine quickly.

Dravik smiles. "Don't fret. The blood is the intruder's—an assassin of the Spider's Hand variety."

My chair screeches as I jolt up and stride to the body—it can't be him. He has the muscle, the same height, the *same armor*—flexible snake-scale armor that fought and failed against the projection sword—his insides spilling gray-pink in the cradle of his fetal position.

"It's not the same one House Hauteclare sent to kill your mother," Dravik assures me between sips. "But it *is* one of his associates."

With shaking fingers, I rip off the blood-soaked cowl—a boy younger than even I. Eighteen at most, his red beard barely fuzz. A commoner, no doubt, pushed into this life as a way to make a living—a pawn not even playing his own game, and yet…I hold no illusions about my out-of-steed combat prowess; if Dravik hadn't killed him, I would be dead in my bed.

"They prefer to recruit them young," the prince murmurs. "Easier to burn the methods of control into their brains that way."

I sit back down stiffly. "Is Hauteclare trying to kill me again?"

"Unlikely. They have their own assassin within the Spider's Hand assigned to do House work for them, but he's currently MIA. It seems he mysteriously vanished after news of your survival spread. This"—he gestures to the body vaguely—"is more likely the result of an ally of Hauteclare's who wished to curry favor with them by taking out an entirely new contract on you."

"Can you stop them?"

"Not as thoroughly as I'd like. The Spiders have a reputation to uphold as the very best of the best—they do not rescind agreements. I believe they'll keep sending assassins until you're dead. Don't worry—I have many security systems in place, and that little noisemaker might be useless, but it keeps eyes on the grounds well enough."

"The noisemaker has a name," I insist. "Luna."

"Does it now?" Dravik chuckles. "Rather pointless, don't you think?"

"So these assassins will keep coming, and you'll keep killing them."

"Yes."

"Can you make it painless?"

"You wish to show them mercy when they've shown you none."

"Assassins aren't nobles," I insist. "They're used like us."

"And the one who killed your mother? Should I show him mercy when he reappears, too?"

The chamomile tries to soothe my chapped lips. My fingers tremble around porcelain. There's nothing to hold on to as reality splinters between the cracks, the assassin looming tall in black armor with that same scale pattern. He didn't kill me—he *could've*, he was ordered to, but he *didn't, and I don't know why.* But then...how did I get the scar on my chest? He killed Mother, I know. She was on her knees in the end—

Luna rests its metal head against my ankle, the cold sensation halting my thoughts. My eyes roam Dravik's face.

"I wish you'd been there," I whisper. "The first time it happened."

The prince's smile tightens. "As do I."

I stroke Mother's pendant, redwood beneath bloodstained fingers. Dravik's voice is a bare shadow against marble as he nods at the necklace. "I am sorry—about what I've done to it. It's to keep you safe."

"You don't trust me," I croak.

"It's everyone else I don't trust, brave one."

There are only three circles left.

The grindstone of sleeping and training turns over and over. Everything I need to win is here in the bunker, and if it isn't, it's brought to me by Quilliam. Tea trays perch on Heavenbreaker's innards, vitamin bottles tucked away in its metal seams, bloodstained towels and clothes hung on its ribs. I fill my head with Rax's words, a litany; if he thinks I'm sloppy on the descent, I will become neat. I will dedicate inertia. I will hold the g-forces in my limbs until I hear my bones creak under the strain. I've learned now—sometimes what feels like breaking is just bending. On a too-sharp maneuver, my nose starts bleeding, and relief flashes through me when I see red, not silver.

Every rider's brain is slowly filling with nerve fluid. Mine is filling faster than most. The nerve fluid connects different things—energy and matter, metal and mind. But that wouldn't explain why I saw Astrix when I blacked out in Heavenbreaker. She *saw* me, talked to me. She overloaded in Heavenbreaker. Is she...somehow *inside* it? Is Sevrith somehow inside it, too? I'd be afraid, but there are so many other things to be afraid of: losing my next match (*losing purpose*); overloading during the match, all of House Hauteclare after me; the past—dark and inescapable—and the future—hard and unknowable; and a thought I can't shake stuck between them: only Dravik and I can see the comatose queen. Dravik rode Hellrunner—I ride Heavenbreaker. Something is wrong with my steed, but something is wrong with Hellrunner, too. *The two of them in space, holding hands.*

I know I will regret this.

SYNALI: *What do you know about Hellrunner?*

I nervously shut the vis, try to ignore it. This works for all of thirty seconds. A strange pressure builds in my chest until I rip it back open...to what, you pathetic thing? To stare at the empty reply box? He's busy. He's with Mirelle. The thought sends me spiraling down, but the ping noise sends me spiraling right back up.

RAX: *Good afternoon to you too.*

SYNALI: *This isn't a social call. I need answers*

RAX: *And I'm gonna need some basic manners before you use me like your personal search engine.*

SYNALI: *Good afternoon. What do you know about Hellrunner?*

RAX: *Oof—that's the best you got? One hello and then straight into the demands?*

SYNALI: *I already tried the vis search engines. Every dossier on Hellrunner is redacted*

RAX: *Well, yeah—it belongs to the king. The king's shit is always redacted. Did you try the archive?*

I freeze. At my feet, Luna cocks its head.

SYNALI: *What archive*

RAX: *The SCC keeps an archive of every steed; who they're made by, who rode them—it's all in there. Only riders can access it. To, you know, research their opponents and stuff.*

SCC—the Steedcraft Control Center. Their archive would be much more official than the fan databases I've been scraping from.

SYNALI: *Look up Hellrunner for me*

RAX: *Anybody ever tell you you're super good at the word 'please'?*

SYNALI: *You're the first*

RAX: *I can't get you into the archive, but I know someone who spends their whole life on it. Gimme a sec.*

His address and mine in the upper right corner are joined by another. My stomach sinks, fingers hesitant over the holograph keys. What do I say to her?

MIRELLE: *I didn't agree to provide information to a murderer, Rax.*

She's obviously furious—more so than when we were in the club. She must've liked Bellesera.

RAX: *C'mon, Mir. Just this once.*

MIRELLE: *No.*

RAX: *She wants to know about Hellrunner. You know, your fave?*

Another long pause.

MIRELLE: *Hellrunner is a Destroyer-class A4. It's the king's legacy steed—its riders are chosen only by him.*

SYNALI: *I know that*

MIRELLE: *What you don't know, murderer, is that the king deploys it only when he feels the riders are of a caliber high enough to challenge it.*

RAX: *Kinda like a test. Or a reminder to stay in line when we get too wild. Either way, it always wins. If you ever see it deployed, it's pretty much game over.*

SYNALI: *Who rides it now? They must be good*

MIRELLE: *Hellrunner changes riders frequently.*

SYNALI: *Why?*

MIRELLE: *Many of them overload. It's a powerful steed that can only be ridden by the strongest.*

Dravik rode Hellrunner. Astrix rode it, too, but she overloaded herself in Heavenbreaker. The only connecting thread between Hellrunner and Heavenbreaker is Astrix...and the memory I keep seeing of the steeds holding hands.

RAX: *Hellrunner's famous for burning out its riders real quick. Mirelle's kinda obsessed with it.*

MIRELLE: *As every rider worth their lance should be. 'Twould be the* *ultimate honor to fight it.*

SYNALI: *Do either of you know why Astrix was dethroned?*

The cursor blinks blankly. The manse creaks eerily around me.

MIRELLE: *No. No one speaks of it. Whatever the case, she chose overload. She was a true and honorable rider to the very end.*

Astrix made Luna's true AI transmit into Heavenbreaker, to keep something inside, but why? Did she try to put a true AI inside of Hellrunner, too? Heavenbreaker learns new words and concepts every day from me—like a baby growing. If the true AI had access to fifty times more riders, it would learn much faster. It would learn to speak, think. Like people. No—like an autonomous fighting force.

"do you know what it means to ride?"

Queen Astrix was trying to make a true AI to turn the steeds into her soldiers—soldiers that didn't need riders. Soldiers that would help her take the throne, maybe. But she failed and was killed for treason.

And her son is trying to finish what she started.

The blue flicker of my vis suddenly catches silver cloth. I look up, but it passes too quickly and leaves behind a feeling of being watched. Luna's nose points to a patch of sunlight, and it wags its tail as if it's greeting someone. I jump as the sudden ping alert blares around the empty room.

MIRELLE: *The archive says the murderer's been in Heavenbreaker's saddle for 103 hours over the last five days.*

RAX: *Jesus—is that true?*

MIRELLE: *So you're concerned with how long she's saddlebound but not how many noble lives she's taken? Wonderful priorities, Rax.*

SYNALI: *I'm training to beat you. Both of you*

RAX: *103 hours is ridiculous, Hauteclare—you can't DO that. Nobody does that. Is that Lithroi shithead making you stay in there?*

SYNALI: *You told me my weaknesses. I'm fixing them*

RAX: *Do you wanna overload? Is that it? Do you wanna end up like Sevrith? Do you wanna DIE? Because that's what overload is—death, just with whiter-ass sheets.*

Every finger shakes strangely as I type.

SYNALI: *I want to win*

RAX: *You're not gonna win anything if you don't start giving a shit about yourself.*

RAX ISTRA-VELRAYD HAS LEFT THE CONVERSATION.

His anger thrums in the blue-light quiet. For the barest moment, I forget who Mirelle is, what I've done to our House, and my typing comes like water.

SYNALI: *I don't understand—why is he angry with me?*

MIRELLE: *It's quite simple; I hate you because you're a murderer. But he hates you because you continue to choose as he could not.*

MIRELLE ASHADI-HAUTECLARE HAS LEFT THE CONVERSATION.

52. Hospes

hospes ~itis, *m. or f.*
1. a host
2. a visitor

Rax Istra-Velrayd follows his father down the hotel hall, fists in his pockets, trying and failing to push Synali out of his mind. He needs her to stay alive. To fight her. His body *needs* to fight her on the tilt like it needs to breathe, but she wants to win so terribly—she wants to destroy House Hauteclare even if it means she's destroyed, too.

He glances down at his vis—no ping from her. No ping from Yavn, either—and he's starting to worry. Yavn isn't the type to keep silent.

The hotel brims with the exhausted quiet of a weekend morning, the only sound the dull hum of a lone maid's hovercart.

"Still don't know why I'm here, Pops," Rax says. He watches his father's back stiffen—it used to be two days locked in Sunscreamer for an informality like that, and now it's just a flinch.

"You're getting married soon," his father retaliates. "It's about time you learned how to foster relationships with other Houses."

"You mean get sent places by Duke Velrayd to negotiate his sketchy deals for him." Father ignores him—a privilege Rax knows he's earned on the tilt. But he knows the limits, too, and so he looks appropriately repentant. "Who's the lucky House today?"

"Have you spoken to Yavn lately?"

Rax frowns—how much does Father know? "No—said he'd be busy at work this week."

"Really? Because he sent the House elders a ping saying he'd be taking a vacation to Omega-1 for the rest of the month."

Rax manages a laugh. "He's a weird one. Maybe he changed his mind and said fuck it."

"Less swearing, Rax. I've told you a million times it makes you sound of low birth."

"Yes sir."

Yavn never pinged him, but he pinged *the elders*? He hates the elders. And Omega-1 is nothing but a lavish playground—why go there now, in the aftermath of Theta-7? It rings every suspicious alarm in his head, but Rax doesn't have time to dwell; Father stops at the penthouse door and looks sternly at him.

"I'll do the talking. Don't speak unless he addresses you directly. And even then, use caution."

Rax's brow shoots up, but he says nothing. Father's not one for fear—groveling and brown-nosing, absolutely, but not fear, and not like this, tense and snapping as if he walks a tightrope.

He knocks on the door, and a voice growls, "Come."

The moment they step into the room, Rax can smell it: the sting of spilled booze and stale sex stabbing over a perfect view of the green hills of the noble spire and the palace plateau. A massive bed faces it all. Tangled in the sheets are three women sleeping, naked. A man rises, just as naked, his long yellow hair cascading and his back rippling in countless tattoos—numbers, symbols, pre-War writing, but the most impressive of all is the tiger crawling down the man's spine with stripes like night and eyes like blistering murder.

"Lord Axton." Father bows to the man and nudges his son to do likewise. Rax stumbles into it.

The air in the hotel room is still as death, and then the man speaks. "Have you come to put me back in the cage, Velrayd?"

"Not at all, milord," Father says quickly. "I simply wished to ascertain if our gift was to your liking."

The man's gaze slides over his shoulder, and Rax's childhood snaps into place—a childhood spent watching the man before him on the tilt, riding a black-and-yellow steed. A steed he broke the waspish action figures of so many times playing too roughly.

The man is Helmann von Axton.

Rax remembers him well—when Helmann was a teenager, he dominated each and every tourney, riding his Dreadnought as lightly as if it was a Frigate. He was a heartthrob and a sensation and an exemplar all in one, like a celebrated knight of the War. He was Rax's idol—the entire reason he naively agreed to first step into Sunscreamer. For Rax, before the endless training and endless darkness alone in the steed, before they found his "talent," before the academy and all its mind-numbing accolades—there was Helmann von Axton.

And for Helmann von Axton up until now, there'd only been the royal prison. Nine years ago, House Axton's manse went up in flames, killing thirteen women. All noble. But later investigation revealed that the bodies weren't charred—they were in the fireproofed basement, packed into preservative caskets by Helmann himself.

"What does your duke want from me, Velrayd?" Helmann rumbles.

Rax whirls to his father in disbelief. They're bargaining favors with *the Station's most infamous mass murderer*? Helmann's twin brother is riding in the Supernova Cup—Brann von Axton. He's a far inferior rider to Helmann, desperately trying to claw his way out of the dishonor pit from his brother's murders, but still good enough to have gotten four seeds ahead. And if Rax isn't mistaken, Brann is Synali's next—

His windpipe sucks shut. Father takes a polite step forward.

"Sir Axton, the Duke Velrayd has been…*commissioned*. In the downfall of a certain rider."

Blood rushes to Rax's head. Helmann watches him, black glass eyes as deep and hypnotic as his voice. "The pretty Lithroi rabbit, right?"

Rax's nails bite into his palms.

What made Helmann so good wasn't his impacts or his slick maneuvers— it was reading his opponent's *mind*. He could sink into their head, read their intentions and their wants and fears as clearly as a vis ping. It hits Rax now— the full force of it. The invisible weave between riders—the weave only they can see in each other—is brutally plucked by Helmann's gaze, and Rax feels himself slipping away, falling in. He's not a person anymore; he is how he stands, how he blinks, how he breathes—all of him laid out in nerves and habitual motion like a clear map for Helmann to read.

And then the release as Helmann looks to Father.

"Do I get to have her before I kill her?"

Rax goes hot down to his fingers, and it's all a blur, a jolt, an instinct. Father pulls him back by the collar, hard enough to rip fabric at the seams. Helmann smiles slow with all his teeth and then laughs, the sound sending a woman in the bed to stir.

"What's wrong, little hawk? Does your prick have designs on her?"

His words stab into Rax, slickly searching for something to pull out. Helmann is in his face in one stride. "She is nothing like you." He jerks a thick claw at his black irises. "You can see it in the eyes. She and I are two of a kind—we threw ourselves over the edge on purpose. You've only ever wondered at it from afar."

Rax moves in—chest to chest with the massive man. Father stands behind Helmann's shoulder, face pale and waiting to see if his son dies.

Helmann purrs in Rax's ear. "I've seen her impacts. She burns herself alive on *every. Single. One.* It's beautiful. She rides like none of you arrogant cowards do—lets it *consume* her."

Rax flexes his jaw tight, holding for impact, and it comes in Helmann's slithering whisper.

"You wouldn't know what to do with fire even if it let you hold it in your hands, little hawk."

A scream that's none of theirs shatters the air. One of the women in the bed sits up, shrieking at her hands covered in crimson. The other two are deathly still, a streak of red crawling through the sheets. *Death.* Father brought him women to—never, *never*, he knew his parents would do anything for status but this, this, *this*—

Helmann turns to the last woman, red gleaming in the tattoo tiger's eyes, and Father ushers a frozen Rax out, his brain a numb buzz. *Not others. If they want to hurt me, fine. Me and only me. **Not them, too.***

When they're home, Father acts as if nothing happened. Mother doesn't so much as blink in Rax's direction. His frantic pings to Hauteclare keep bouncing—she's blocked them? He takes a shaky shower to calm down, to wash the smell of Helmann off. Rax knew. He *knew*, but he didn't *know*.

It will never be enough. He will never be enough—the family will always want more and more and *more*; no matter how high he rises, no matter how well he rides and earns them power, *it will never be enough.* They'll kill anyone in their way.

They're going to kill *her.*

53. Cursor

cursor ~ōris, *m.*
1. a runner
2. a courier, messenger

Mirelle Ashadi-Hauteclare stares up at the swaying Lithroi rabbit banner and decides she just won't do it. She refuses to stand among these frothing commoners and noble sycophants cheering for a rabid murderer.

At the beginning, the traitor was doing Mirelle favors—pruning weak, indolent links that could bring future shame to the House. But Grandmother was different, a whip-smart, clear-cut woman Mirelle looked up to…suddenly *killing herself.* The House coffers tanked overnight at the news, even worse than the Gentech slip—every business deal and contract drying up.

Mirelle clutches the letter fastened with the wax seal of a hawk. It's all too *convenient*; the murderer keeps winning, and her family keeps dying no matter how much security they buy, no matter how much they hunker down in their private safety rooms. Yet this will not last much longer. As the first daughter of the third Lord-inheritors, Mirelle has little political power.

But on the tilt, she is a *god*.

She's been honing her lance against every opponent, imagining Synali von Hauteclare's helmet on it. And now Rax wants Mirelle to deliver a message to her? Mirelle is his *fiancée*, not his courier. She still remembers the way they looked at each other in Atteint's hallway, the way he picked her up and put her in the carriage like the tenderest thing—

Some careless noble in the crowd elbows her in a fit of excitement, and Mirelle hurls a snarl. Wide eyes take in her clothes, gold and white, and they proffer an apology bow.

"Forget it," she huffs.

"Th-Thank you, Lady Mirelle! I'm so sorry, again."

They're sorry, but they're not sorry enough to stop cheering or craning their necks over the crowd to catch the first glimpse of the rider in blue and silver. What rankles Mirelle most isn't the way Rax looked at the murderer on the curb—it was the pathetic pleading in Rax's voice when he showed up at Mirelle's door that morning, platinum hair wildly askew.

"I'm serious, Mir. This isn't some dramatic joke or a power ploy—just, *please*. She's in danger."

"Vis her, then," she'd sniffed over her tea, quietly disgusted—the strongest rider of the century, the only one truly capable of giving her a challenge on the tilt, reduced to *begging*. Where did his self-respect vanish to?

"I've tried," Rax insisted, leg jangling. "But I keep getting bounced—like someone's blocking it."

"Or she blocked you herself after you tore into her yesterday."

The lights of her room flickered then, but it couldn't hide his flinch. "Just— can you get this to her? Before she goes into decon? It's really important."

"Deliver it yourself."

He motioned frustratedly at the raised wrist skin of his vis. "I would, but Pops has me on a fucking tracker. I step anywhere near the tourney hall and I get detained by private security. Your House's private security, actually."

Mirelle blinked. "Why would Father-in-law bother with all these preventative measures? It seems excessive."

Rax's expression—all the proud planes and lines of him she'd come to admire since their first night together six months ago—crumpled to dust then. "They're going to kill her, Mir."

The human in her instantly spat, "Good."

The rider in her instantly spat, *Not until we cross lances.*

54. Incorruptus

incorruptus ~a ~um, a.
1. intact, unspoiled
2. *(figuratively)* pure; not seduced

I hear the screams first.

The hall shivers with chattering and shrieks, and it takes me three seconds to realize the closer I walk, the louder it becomes. Four guards hold back the crowd outside the Lithroi hangar, alcoves packed tight with people clutching autograph books, their vis cameras glowing like a dozen blue eyes.

"Miss Synali! For my daughter. Please, you're her favorite—"

"I love you! I LOVE YOU!"

"Step back! Keep behind the line!"

"Look over here, Synali!"

A projection microphone is shoved into my face. "Hi, Synali, Merdia Grassus from Channel 17Rho. Can you tell us how you're feeling right now?"

Just as I'm about to push them, a cane abruptly stabs between me and the reporter, sapphires flashing and separating us, and then someone leads me away by the arm. The screams dim, and Dravik's smile comes into focus.

"Apologies, Synali. I assumed the tourney hall would take appropriate precautions for you, but it seems I must do everything myself. There will be more security for your next match." His confidence in me rings quietly. "I'm afraid I don't know who your next opponent is."

I frown. "It's posted on the seed—Brann von Axton."

"It seems House Axton's made a last-minute substitution for Brann."

"They can do that?"

"No. However, they can certainly make excuses for why their rider can't take their helmet off at the end of the match."

"So you have no idea who I'm facing?"

"I have several," Dravik corrects. "None of them conclusive. House Axton has many skilled riders in its midst; 'tis something they're infamous for. Whoever it is will be very good. Treat them with caution, watch their movements, and you should be fine."

I don't like any of it—my body tight but my mouth loose. "It's power, isn't it?"

The prince inspects his vis mildly. "Whatever do you mean?"

"Your mother tried to take the throne all those years ago by turning the steeds into an autonomous fighting force. A terrifying army, faster than any battleship, stronger, more versatile. It would've been Gamma-1 all over again, but a hundred times worse—at least back then, the true AI was confined to the substation. And now you're trying to finish what she started—using Heavenbreaker. Using *me*."

His smile isn't aimed at me, but rather at his own palm.

"Do you still think so little of me, Synali, to believe that I'd want something as menial and short-lived as power?"

"You—"

"No matter how advanced the AI in a steed, it still requires a human mind within its saddle to function."

"There *is* a human mind in Heavenbreaker—Astrix."

He blinks.

"You said it yourself—Sevrith isn't as gone as I think. The overloaded riders aren't gone. Neither is Astrix. I saw her in the saddle. Something about her is still alive in there."

Dravik chuckles in the quiet. "If this is a cruel joke you're playing to get back at me…"

"It's not. I just need you to tell me what's going on. I'll believe you—I promise."

Before I can form words, someone in the crowd peels around the guards. An ecstatic face closes in for me fast, hands grabbing, but the sapphire cane flashes on their ankles and they plummet into marble. The guards flock to wrangle the trespasser back as the prince pulls his cane in neatly from the chaos and looks to me.

"If you could travel in time and go back to old Earth, Synali, would you tell them of the enemy's arrival?"

I snort. "Obviously."

"Would it do any good?"

I go still. The crowd seethes, but the prince is tranquility.

"They had never seen them or fought them. They had never even been in space for any truly prolonged period of time. They knew Earth and the sky and the animals. Would they believe you? If you marched up to their leaders and told them of the enemy razing the Earth in great bouts of laserfire, *would they believe you*?"

"No."

"No," he repeats patiently. "Because it was not happening and had not happened. They could not understand what they had not experienced." Dravik smiles. "It is not belief I need from you, Synali, but understanding."

A saint in marble looks down at us from the ceiling, a woman with her breasts cut off. She holds them aloft on a platter, her eyes turned Godward. Dravik leaves, and I lose him in the crowd, but I never had him to begin with; the prince is always one step ahead of me. Of everyone. A woman standing still in the undulating crowd has his pale-brown hair, her unmistakable fox smile aimed right at me — unnerving silver eyes and lips moving with words I can't hear and yet words I can hear *perfectly*.

"do you know what it means to ride?"

And then I blink, and she's gone. I turn, the crowd's riot cutting off as the Lithroi hangar closes behind me with a hermetic hiss.

"You."

I nearly jump out of my suit — Mirelle's waiting for me against the marble wall in a white tunic, her silky hair pinned with pearls. My mouth goes dry; why is she here? If she has a weapon… Her gold heels click as she strides up the walkway and holds out a sealed letter. I reach for it, but she pulls away, pearly nails flashing.

"I'm giving this to you for one reason, murderer."

"And what would that be?"

We could've been family—the same little dresses, the same little hair ribbons, the same giggling under the same sunlight.

"I refuse to see you die before I show you the true meaning of defeat."

My heart makes a sick leap in my chest; her words are like a knife of twisted kindness—the closest I'll ever come to hearing care from her, the closest I'll have to my family caring for me ever again. I take the letter slowly with a smile.

"Thank you, Mirelle."

"**W**elcome, one and all, to the middle matches of the Supernova Cup's A seed! It's a lovely day in the arena for a spot of tilting— no silica dust from Esther and barely any radiation flares to speak of. We're coming closer to the finals here, and the competition is a scorching field of excellence! Wouldn't you agree, Gress?"

"Without a doubt, Bero! Out of all the Houses that've entered the Supernova Cup, only a few remain standing! Some old favorites, strong favorites, and brand-new favorites make up the powerfully eclectic bunch vying for the top spot—and the king's favor—this year!"

"And what a top-spot fight it'll be, Gress! Let's get right into it; in the blue corner sits a champion of crushing might, a man with a taste for overwhelming victory, a rider with a mastery of the Dreadnought class like no other—please welcome Brann von Axton and his steed, Wingpiercer!"

his name is not Brann von Axton.

"And over in the red corner is the most unexpected rider of the Cup— having made it this far in her very first riding year, with no academy record to speak of! She's fast, furious, and frankly, frighteningly ferocious—give it up for Synali von Hauteclare and her steed, Heavenbreaker!"

The handkerchief rests against my chest, and folded within it is Rax's letter, Mirelle's jasmine perfume wafting up from it.

"worry?" Heavenbreaker asks, a quiet bell.

I answer unquietly. *not mine. theirs.*

The silver spirals pause and then resume their slow crawl across my eyeballs.

"friends?" It's asking if Rax and Mirelle are our friends. How can we be? We're too different, too far gone. Heavenbreaker thinks of my heart, its thoughts lingering on the crimson wax seal of the hawk. *"love?"*

I scoff. *go.*

Heavenbreaker's jets blaze to life as we slip through the arena net. The camera drones buzz with frantic motion, but the steed doesn't cower from them. I feel Heavenbreaker meet its own fearful hesitation with a burst of jetfire, the sound inside my head almost—*almost*—a metallic scoff, like a ghost of me.

The holoscreen that pops up is no ghost; it's a man in a pitch-black rider's suit with neon-yellow slashes across his expansive chest. The small screen does nothing to hide his height, the thick cords of muscle banded on him. He wears a black helmet like polished coal, a yellow tiger's maw ringing the visor in fangs. The halo painted on his forehead beneath the visor glows only by a half—a faded, broken thing, as unkempt as his ragged hair like spun gold. I cannot see his eyes, and yet I cannot look away from them, either, his growl searing my ears.

"Hello, rabbit."

55. Finis

finis m. or f.
1. a boundary; an end
1. the end, purpose, aim

THE FORMER PRINCE and the duke's daughter sat at the chessboard.

The sun crawled slowly around the pieces. The girl's hand hovered over a blue knight, eyes hovering on the silver pawn nearly to her back row.

"You've been moving the pawn forward this whole time. Protecting it."

The prince held out his hands. "Naturally."

"What happens when a pawn makes it all the way to the other side?" she asked. He grinned, bright and thoughtful.

"Well, then it becomes something else entirely."

56. Jugiter

jūgiter, *adv.*
1. enduringly
2. in unbroken succession

Helmann von Axton hits me *instantly.*
Pressure, pain, speed—all of it smashes into my left side, as hard and fast as a bullet. The full weight of a massive steed bears down on me, and before we can make an escape plan, our back hits a web of hot hard-light—the net edge of the arena. I try to move, but I'm pinned. By *him.*

"Come now, rabbit," the man on the holoscreen rasps. "I'll have more fight than this from you."

He's in a Dreadnought, heavier than any other type of steed, and yet it looks streamlined—shoulders smooth, legs smooth, barely any of the usual Dreadnought bulk in its armor save for its gargantuan chest. Neon yellow ridges down the back and elongates past the waspish hips as a spiked tail. The edges of its helmet curve like ingrown bull horns, like jaws made already shut, like an animal not yet invented but one that eats well.

Metal grinds into my chest, my shoulders, and the arena's projection net scorches my back—a fearful heat starting to burn in my heart. He came from nowhere. In a *Dreadnought.* I should've seen it coming... *No.* They do not get fear from me.

go.

I reverse the jets. We blast backward into the net, the white hard-light searing a pattern down our spine. The nauseating smell of burning flesh and superheated metal permeates the saddle. I grit my teeth—*just a little bit more*—and then the lightweight snap of freedom comes—enough space to drop through his pin and dart away as far and fast as we can. His laugh rumbles from the holoscreen.

"Did you enjoy that pain? I've seen it in you—seen you *embrace* it. You kiss agony with those sweet, scarred lips as if it's your first lover." He rises, the jets on his back blazing neon yellow, so high and hot the LED cross above us drowns in it. "Shall I be your first, rabbit, and your last?"

I cut the comms, my fingers shaking.

Heavenbreaker thinks what I refuse to feel. *"afraid."*

My skin feels like it's crawling with invisible maggots. He's different from the others. His tone is like the men in the brothel but different, *worse*, and he glows, vibrates, waits—waits like I've never seen a rider wait before, suspended at the apex like time means nothing to him, like he's exactly where he's meant to be.

And I'm trapped in here with him.

"—altercation before first tilt is a definite foul, Gress, *annnndddd* there we go—the ref's called a yellow flag on Wingpiercer. Heavenbreaker gets a two-second head start on the first tilt! But can she capitalize on it?"

Helmann doesn't seem to care about the rules. It feels like he wants to kill me, not ride against me. I read it in Rax's hastily scrawled letter Mirelle gave me, but I feel it now—the heatwave from a projection dagger, the grin of a man walking behind you at night, the ear-splitting pressure before an airlock vents. Danger.

"the tilt," Heavenbreaker echoes.

It's right. I'm safe on the tilt—I can see him coming better there. I jet to it.

"Riders, prepare for first tilt! In the name of God, King, and Station!"

"In the name of God, King, and Station!"

The crowd feverishly echoes the commentator—thirsting for tragedy, urging on my demise. Helmann von Axton decides to settle his bulk languidly on the terrene tilt.

The countdown: *Three.*

The holoscreen comes up again.

Two.

"Let me see you," Helmann rumbles. "All of you."

One.

My heart pounds, my mouth goes dry—he's going to hurt me, hunt me; I'm trapped in here with him—and then…the flowers appear. Flashing for just a moment in perfect color and detail against the black of space are white daisies and blue hyacinths—flowers blooming deep in the throat of the cold dragon. Mother's voice echoes like cool water poured over hot coals. *"Thank you, Synali. They're lovely."*

Heavenbreaker. It made these flowers for me, to calm me—my own memory given back in perfect detail. The flowers fade to black, and the steed begins a thought in our mind.

"give them nothing."

As the last petal fades, I finish it.

take everything.

Zero.

The silver lance bursts to life in my hand, assembling whole and sharp in an instant. The tilt releases us with a two-second head start. We're fast—no hesitation, just *speed*. The stars blur, Esther seeming at a standstill in her rotation for a split second, her bands of malachite-green clouds hovering in place. Wingpiercer releases late yet draws close, the blue light of the grav-gen swallowed whole in its black armor and its yellow lance aimed for my throat.

hold.

The cry between steeds resounds, and they make the light between them. Sight comes like snapshots in the dark, like the strobe lights of Talize's club—his yellow lance, my silver lance. His body, my body—a perfumed bed, white roses, a cold tilt, a hot dagger. The cascade of thought and the alignment as it comes together inside me: Helmann von Axton wants me. But he is not the first.

and he will not be the last.

Impact.

Nerve-crackling pain shoots into my teeth, my fingers, every breath just giving the pain more oxygen to stab with. Something's wrong in my right leg. My lance pierces nothing, flying under Helmann's ribs as if I was always aiming there. Heavenbreaker staggers as it rises, and my mind staggers likewise: *How did he dodge?* I had him locked in at the right inertia, the angle…it was faster than he could ever hope to evade as a Dreadnought.

unless.

Unless he already knew what I was aiming for.

"Come now, rabbit," he purrs on the holoscreen. "Did you not listen? I want to see everything you have. *All of it.*"

Red, 0. Blue, 1. My right leg goes numb, and I look down—it's nearly cleaved all the way off, twisting in space by a thin tangle of cables. Worse, the jets on it pulse in serrated rhythm, unbalancing everything. I try to steady, but I wobble uncontrollably, *flail*, every direction mixed up and a horrifying thought creeping in: Helmann could've taken our leg off like Yatrice, but he didn't. He left it hanging to watch me stumble. He's toying with us.

Astrix's voice is a mantra carved in all the soft parts of my brain: "*do you know what it means to ride?*"

There is only one choice left—that's what it means to ride. Reach down to where the steed's leg connects to my bone. This *will* hurt.

That, too, is what it means to ride.

I clutch my own leg—whole in the saddle and half dangling by a thread outside—and *twist*. The flesh of me doesn't give, but the metal of me does, and yet it hurts the same—the same white-red agony spearing through me as Heavenbreaker's leg disconnects in a shower of sparks. I can feel hot blood pouring out where there is none, my own heart pumping my life away from me invisibly. Machines don't feel pain, but she's hurting, too.

Her. "*She*"—the first time I've called Heavenbreaker anything other than "it." The sound fits like puzzle pieces, like well-worn gloves.

I turn my hand and look at the dismembered leg in it. Last time this happened, dark oil streamed from it, but now there's only silver—*nerve fluid*. The rise is almost over. Helmann is hungry—I have to create an opening with his own hunger. Rax said he's better than us. Rax could take him better, Mirelle could take him better—but I'm alone. The letter's heavy on my chest, written by him and given by her.

no. i'm not quite alone.

I switch the comms on and hold my own leg up like bait. "Come and get it, beast."

Helmann's laugh is an aching growl rolled one slow timbre at a time. "All of us, beasts. But you and I the same kind."

I drop the leg, and it floats away. He smiles beneath his broken halo, all sharp white teeth.

"Can you hear my heart wailing for you, rabbit?"

I switch lance hands. Fumble. *ignore the fear.* No—***use*** it. Like fuel, like anger. This fear is horrible, ugly, deep…but it is mine and no one else's.

"I'll hear it better," I say, "when it's on the tip of my lance."

Your opponent's been switched. His name's Helmann von Axton-Brann's twin and a piece-of-shit mass murderer. House Velrayl asked him to kill you on the tilt in exchange for his freedom. Helmann's better than you, and he's better than me. I'm serious when I say you need to be careful—no throwing yourself all-in. You're not gonna die. I won't let you. You're gonna win this and keep moving on until you reach me.

Helmann's in a Dreadnought, but you treat him like a Frigate. Keep your left side guard high and tight. His defense is flawless, and I'm not fucking exaggerating for fun—he leaves no openings, so you'll have to create your own. Cut comms the instant he tries to talk to you—he'll get what you're planning from the way you sit in the saddle. He reads riders like a book. I've seen it happen, and I'm not gonna watch it happen to you.

Live, Hauteclare. That's what it means to ride.

PART VI

THE SWAN AND THE LION

−3. Luctus

luctus ~ūs, *m.*
1. grief, sorrow
2. mourning

O n the side of a dilapidated barbershop, Rain watches the
Supernova Cup.

The gutters beneath his shoes run with iodine and blood, copper
and iron. The crack of someone's jaw as the barber pulls out their tooth
and the moan that comes after is too much like Yavn. It's only a matter
of time before Green-One finds out Rain spared the noble, and then
he will lose the last of his family forever. The recluses will find him. He
will die alone, without anyone beside him.

The holoscreen flickers. Laser-etched graffiti shouts on both sides
of it, but Rain's eyes focus only on the center, on the silver-blue steed
and the girl within it. She's grown so much, so different from the waif he
first spared that night—more flesh, more hardness, more determination
than ever. An old woman selling fried molerat toddles by, a clay jar of
crispy paws in her arms, but she stops. They watch together.

The old woman croaks, "Will she win, you think?"

Rain watches the girl's eyes—*his eyes, like family, like the family he* *lost, the family who hunts him now; both of them, girl and boy, hunted in a web they cannot escape but she is **trying** and it makes him want to try* **harder**—and he nods, smiling.

"Yes."

57. Aculeus

aculeus ~ī, *m.*
1. *(in plants)* a sharp point, thorn
2. a sting

The descent comes.

Helmann's yellow plasma jets, my blue plasma jets, and between us the light blends green—the green of a corpse-fed garden, the green of Esther as she looks on, eternally waiting, eternally there until the cold dragon eats her, too.

Helmann comes in narrow—narrower than a Dreadnought ever should. Heavenbreaker bleeds silver from her torn right leg, the splatter streaming behind us. I'm not fast enough without all my leg jets. We have to compensate. *burn brighter.* I hold my elbow firm. He will not have me. *extend.* I won't die here.

i will live to fight. rax. mirelle. all of them.

Brace softly.

The cry wails between the steeds, and I can feel the meaning in the sound this time like an eldritch bell, like greeting and regret, like saying *hello* and *goodbye* and *forever* all in the same second. Helmann's lance moves like lightning, and my body moves like the thunder coming after—an echo. *don't fight it.* He knows we'll fight against him, but he doesn't know we'll go along with him—I drop into the space he leaves, tight against Wingpiercer's body. Our silver lance slides home into the right side of his tasset. *Red, 1. Blue, 1.* We **hit him**!

Retribution is instant.

Before we can part into the rise, his fingers jab into our breastplate—five puckered steel rifts screaming open and rupturing my vision with all the force a Dreadnought brings to bear. The simulated pain is five points of fire in my chest digging deep, and a split-second panic buries in the agony: *he's going to rip us open.*

"—another highly illegal move, Bero, but the riders aren't parting! It looks like extended close contact on blue side! The ref is on his way to break it up—"

One of Helmann's fingers goes in too far, and I cough wet, red blood, and suddenly Heavenbreaker is on her own with me only riding faintly—she reverses the jets, trying desperately to pull us away, but Helmann follows, piercing farther and farther in. The ref's siren-like whistle is shrill as he approaches, a black-and-white-striped steed heavily armored and blasting white jets toward us.

Helmann retracts his fingers. Sudden relief…and then I watch him pull his arm back. Wingpiercer throws its lance with all its Dreadnought might. Neon yellow shoots across space like a ray of sunlight and buries mercilessly square in the referee's breastplate—right where the saddle is. The metal of its cockpit crumples like paper, the lance sticking clear through.

"—oh! O-Oh dear, is this—it seems…it seems House Axton has struck the referee! I'm, yes, we're getting the report now that he's fine, just fine, but the final tilt must go on—"

"What a…what a strange decision on Brann's part, Bero—surely the king will have much to say on House Axton's decorum after the match! It seems the auxiliary referees are giving House Lithroi a five-second advantage for this!"

The referee's steed hangs limp, unmoving, sparks showering around the lance stuck in its striped breastplate. Wingpiercer jets over, pulling its lance out and turning slowly in space. The neon-yellow tip tints orange with a red mist. The referee is not fine.

The comms flip on. Helmann's chest heaves under his suit.

"There. No more distractions between us, rabbit." He's just another noble throwing away life in front of my eyes. He's not an unbeatable monster at all—just *noble*. My laugh bubbles with the blood on my lips, and his voice tilts to suspicion. "What's so entertaining?"

I reset like the rules say. Get to the tilt, quick—I can feel him following me, the heat of his jets nipping at my only intact heel. The magnets pull us down and taut against the massive hexagon, trapping us just in time for Wingpiercer to slam into us, grinding against Heavenbreaker edge to edge, tasset to tasset, horned helmet to crescent helmet—a sea of sparks and screeching metal.

"What is so entertaining?" he repeats, thorns and danger.

"You…" I laugh, lick blood away. "I thought you were different, but you're just like the rest of them. *Exactly* like them. They all destroy like you. Kill like you."

I brace for violence, but his fingers caress the marks in our breastplate instead, *possessively*, the feeling featherlight on my human chest. A touch I know. A touch that comes before the pain. His hand pulls away smeared with silver.

"Do not put on some sickening act, rabbit; we are the same. You *want* to kill. I've seen its dark desire in your eyes."

His weight crushes me and throws the tilt under massive strain, the creak of springs in a mattress. There's nothing left but the tiger and me. He could kill me easily at this range—reach into Heavenbreaker's chest and pull my saddle out and flatten me in his hands. It'd be so easy to give in. No more worry. No more pain. No more struggle.

Heavenbreaker spins voices out of our memory.

i am sorry—about what i've done to it. it's to keep you safe.

Dravik.

when they're dead, what will you do?

Sevrith.

i refuse to see you die before i show you the true meaning of defeat.

Mirelle.

—you're not gonna die. i won't let you.

Rax.

Helmann wants to kill me. My family wants to kill me, and the court wants to help. My father wanted to kill me. The entire universe wants to see me dead…but there are people who want to see me live, too.

Heavenbreaker asks my spiraling thoughts gently, *"what do **you** want?"*

I release my visor with a pneumatic hiss and shaking hands.

"Look again," I say to Helmann. His broken halo illuminates the sudden stillness in his face on the holoscreen, the fierce knit of his gold brows in pause. My words come heavy with intent. "What do I want, beast?"

Wingpiercer staggers off me, and there's a lift in the pressure. A lift in my lance. My roar is blood and silver flying.

"WHAT DO I WANT, BEAST?"

Wingpiercer turns in a blink, wordless, yellow tail bright and jets brighter as he abruptly speeds out and rivets himself to his own tilt.

"It seems both riders have decided to adhere to protocol again, Gress! They've reset! Let's keep our eyes on the countdown for the final tilt! *Three—*"

Five points of pain throb through my chest. My right hip throbs where I tore Heavenbreaker's leg off, and darkness crawls on the edges of my vision, a dark I've learned better to resist now.

"*Two—*"

My whisper: "Tell me, beast. What is it I want?"

"*One!*"

His voice, reverent: "Death, milady."

Zero.

The release. The descent. The comms cut off. He knows now. But he cannot stop me.

He knows that, too.

Gravity pulls us into each other—his lightning, my thunder. He is destruction. He is war. But I am the grim iron bell ringing in the aftermath—the unstoppable echo that forever follows the violence.

I am not the one who strikes first, but I will be the one who strikes last.

The cry between steeds creaks through the light. He dives. I *see* him dive, the lance on his backhand to catch the slowest part on my remaining leg. All his power concentrates in pinpoint velocity all too fast. Heavenbreaker's thought rings bright.

"*trust me.*"

The truth: *i do.*

I let go. I let her have control of our body, and Heavenbreaker pivots her tasset in a sweltering hair-split, *bone screaming brain flashing*, breaking her spine and sending mine into spasms but twisting around so that his yellow lance catches nothing but splatters of silver blood where our missing leg is.

I hold my arm steady. Wait. The cascade of thought and the cascade as it all falls away into nothingness, into the very center of impact, into the furnace of spacetime, of existence, of *me*.

Silver sinks into a neon breastplate.

Red, 2. Blue, 1.

I take my helmet off to thunderous applause and the iron-leaded gaze of Nova-King Ressinimus staring down at me.

When I first started riding, I'd limp out of the hangar bay and through empty tourney halls, but now there are screams. Now, guards usher me through masses of warm bodies clawing for me. The shower room is a quiet relief, a ping interrupting it.

DRAVIK: *Your opponent has been remaindered to his cell by the authorities. You will be safe until your return to Moonlight's End. I've been informed Quilliam is making your favorite—roast duck.*

A strange new feeling wells up: I'm looking forward to going home, to Luna, a soft bed, roast duck, and the methodical silence of cleaning with Quilliam. Impossible. Pointless. My fingers tremble while making a new message to two people.

SYNALI: *I'll see you two in the arena*

The response ping is instant.

MIRELLE: *Of course you will, murderer. If you'd lost to the likes of honorless Helmann, you wouldn't be a Hauteclare.*

A mirror catches my brittle smile. Another ping.

MIRELLE: *Rax says to unblock him.*

SYNALI: *I never blocked him to begin with*

MIRELLE: *Well, someone's blocking the two of you from communicating. Frankly, I think it's for the best. He's far too good for you.*

She knows just where to stab, doesn't she? But I suppose that runs in the family, too.

SYNALI: *Always honest, aren't you?*

MIRELLE: *Down to the last—that is the path of the knight. You might try it sometime, if it's still within your bloodthirsty capacity.*

MIRELLE ASHADI-HAUTECLARE HAS LEFT THE CONVERSATION.

I dress and leave the showers, walking through the silent post-crowd tourney hall. I stare at Rax's address longer than I should before pinging him once, twice, but the messages don't go through. It looks like he's blocked me...but he wouldn't, would he? I can only think of one person who'd want us to stop talking.

The sound of giggling makes me look up. Two people stand on the tourney hall's observation deck: a girl and a boy, lingering at the polished railing. They're younger than me, the girl dripping in holographic lace and the finest silks, her reddish hair tumbling behind her in an elaborate braid. The boy's in a hoverchair, with a head of soft brown. I recognize him—it's the boy from the hospital.

"I found you."

He turns just then—as if he heard the memory—and smiles at me. Without the painkillers, I see his face better, a face like peace, a gentle chin and jaw. His eyes are green and downturned, his blacklight halo bright on his forehead. He turns the hoverchair with a muted whirr.

"Synali."

He says my name in a way that feels like coming back to a home I thought lost long ago, all warmth and ease. Something deep in me wants to be nearer to him no matter what; something about him feels like rest—a place to rest at last.

The girl whips around at my name, fire braid lashing the view of space as her face splits into a buoyant grin from ear to freckled ear.

"Oh wow, it's *you*!"

She streaks down the stairs in silver anklets and bare feet, and for a moment I think she's going to run into me, bowl me over, but she stops just short with a precocious little hop, her blacklight halo bold and clean on her forehead.

"He's told me a lot about you." The girl's green eyes blink up at me. I flicker my gaze away and catch the dark corners of the observation deck; there are *dozens* of private guards hovering with projection swords, tasers, guns. They're the same ones who surrounded the king's platform at the pre-tourney banquet. The girl gives a little shimmy to get my attention again. "Oooh! Just ignore them, they're no fun. I watched your last match—it was great! You're really good at riding!"

My words come out warily. "Thank you…"

"Oh! I'm Leyda—nice to meet you. I mean, um, it's a pleasure to make your acquaintance." She looks up at the boy. "Does that sound better?"

He nods. "Much."

Leyda sighs. "Too many words just makes things long and boring."

"You have to talk to people if you want to know them," the boy chides lightly, like a teacher reminding a student rather than a boy talking to a girl his own age.

"Yeah." She gestures to me. "But she's not most people. We can play together—me and her and all of us. That'd make it easy!"

Nothing about their conversation is complicated, but it feels as if half of it goes unspoken.

"I should get going," I say.

Leyda pouts. "Oookay. If you want. But I'll see you soon!"

She says it like statement, not question. Her confidence follows me through the halls and out the rider exit and into the Lithroi hovercarriage. It follows me all the way to Moonlight's End, where Dravik waits in the armchair before a dying fire.

"You didn't know my opponent was Helmann von Axton," I say. He barely looks up from the hearth. I unfold the letter from inside the handkerchief, flashing the broken seal. "Rax did."

Dravik finally clears his throat. "It's as I feared, then—House Velrayd has aligned itself with House Hauteclare. Velrayd deals in trade tariffs—trade between Wards, between the Station and substations. The price of everything runs betwixt their fingers. Indeed, it's the bald-faced price of trade Velrayd is most known for valuing." His leather chair gives a creak as he leans back. "If the rumors are true, Rax Istra-Velrayd and Mirelle Ashadi-Hauteclare have recently become engaged. To be married."

I go still. *of course they have.* It was there in the way they stood next to each other—tall, proud, beautiful, evenly matched in every way. The firelight burns on my face.

"They suit each other."

"Suitability aside, through this alliance, Velrayd gains Hauteclare's long-standing reputation, and the Hauteclares gain a valuable ally with their fingers in every monetary pie imaginable—which is something they quite need after our interference. Velrayd's mercantile connections are nigh unmatched; including, apparently, within the royal prison."

The prince slowly lifts a teacup from the table at his side and takes a long sip. Sudden exhaustion drags my every ligament into oblivion—no fight left in me.

"Still," he mutters. "To attempt to blame your murder on an escaped

convict…it's rather tasteless. House Hauteclare must be quite shaken to resort to such tactics. I don't think I need to elaborate on why you must not contact Rax any further."

"You're the one who blocked him on my vis."

"He is a dangerous outlier who could be convinced to harm you. Now that he's engaged to Mirelle, that threat is magnified exponentially. Unbeknownst to you, your friend's module made it quite easy to reverse engineer a way into your vis." His expression goes soft. "You must be protected at all costs."

"And your idea of protection is sticking your nose where it doesn't belong?"

"I gather you knew that when you signed our contract, Synali."

"The biometric scanner—the mic. Isn't that fucking *enough* for you?"

"I told you he's dangerous."

My rage turns to laughter. "He's a spoiled noble—"

"And he is nearly part of the Hauteclare family now. He has every incentive to hurt you."

"You're delusional. You've truly deluded yourself into thinking you're my goddamn father." I want him to deny it, but he just stands without another word, grasps his cane, and shuffles into the dim halls. I snatch up his teacup and smash it on the marble ground. "Do you hear me, Your Highness? You're losing it! The nerve fluid's eaten you! *You're losing your goddamn mind!*"

He doesn't come back. Fury blurs my eyes, and I shove everything on the table aside in a crash of porcelain splinters. Kick the table over, tear it apart, throw it in the fire until nothing's left but ash, Astrix staring out at me from the corner of the room.

"Losing your mind just like…just like I am," I whisper.

58. Mortifer

mortifer ~era ~erum, a.
1. lethal, deadly

I'm left alone that night in bed with my midnight thoughts, the marble circles staring at me like dead-white eyes, the fifth freshly scratched out. Two left.

Dravik's rhythmic tapping announces his approach before he ever raps on my door. I don't have the strength to be angry anymore. "Come in."

The prince wedges the door open with his cane. "Do you truly wish to continue to speak to Velrayd?"

My heart leaps. Push it down. "Do I have a choice in the matter?"

The simulated moonlight hangs heavy and cold over us. The prince's voice goes thin. "Your safety is all I know, because my safety is all I wanted my father to know. I wanted him to care more—about losing me. He didn't. And in some strange way, I've been trying to make up for that with you."

My eyes never leave Dravik's shadow on the floor. It's the hope that kills me, always—not the scheming, not the attempts on my life, not the pain. *Hope.* Hope that I could be his real daughter. Hope that I'll live long enough to learn to love him like a father.

"You'll stop reading my vis," I say.

"Certainly."

"And you'll unblock him."

"I'm afraid I cannot. Private communications are a serious risk, you understand." I open my mouth, and he cuts me off. "Public communications are another matter. Sir Rax will be attending my sister's birthday fete, and so will you. In my stead."

"Sister," I repeat.

Dravik's shadow has no face, but I can hear his smile.

"Yes. My half sister, Leyda Esther de Ressinimus, crown princess of the Nova-Court, and your next opponent."

The fifth circle is my cousin.

Was.

Dravik's ping comes in as I'm readying for the birthday fete, my fingers freezing over the silver buttons of my dresscoat. The vis glow is only slightly bluer than the skirt Dravik insisted upon. *"For dancing,"* he'd said with a smile. *"Leyda loves dancing."*

Olivere Solunde-Hauteclare was my second cousin by marriage. He was two years older than me—freshly twenty-two. A boy, really, but old enough to know better, and certainly old enough to know better than to meet the Spider's Hand on my father's behalf and deliver them the contract money. According to Dravik's ping, Olivere was an expert on navigating the taverns of Low Ward, and most prominently the ones that doubled as brothels—the sort of brothels with girls barely old enough to bleed.

My teeth bare. The message logs glare. My eyes skim over Father's words.

FARRIS: *I hate to ask it of you, Olivere—to get you involved in such a thing at all. But you're the only one I can count on. The others are not as familiar with the territory as you are.*

OLIVERE: *C'mon uncle. You know I'm here for you—anything for the guy who showed me the ropes.*

My shaking hands smear hair oil into my black strands to keep them down. Polished.

OLIVERE: *It's just two girls, right? Mom and kid? That'll be done in no time. I can hang out and confirm it, if you want.*

FARRIS: *No, thank you. The deliverance of the fee is all I require from you.*

We were prey. Less than. Prey, at least, is eaten before it's discarded.

Crown Princess Leyda Esther de Ressinimus is turning thirteen years old.

This is evidenced by the thirteen swan-shaped ice statues placed on the front lawn of her palace. Her *own* palace. Separate from the royal palace, her rose-marble complex is surrounded by tulips and marigolds and a redwood gazebo drenched in pink wisteria like countless petal-threaded waterfalls. It's a heaven made for a girl, for a young girl, and for a girl who wants for nothing.

every blade of grass, grown with corpses.

I don't deviate a single step from the gravel pathways. Gilded noble shoes crush verdant blades with joyful abandon all around me, with shrieks and cries of *"hurry"* and *"you must see it, it's magnificent."* Luna trots at my feet, growling softly at everyone and everything, though the blue ribbon tied around its neck negates any imposed ferocity.

"Save your energy," I urge it. "The night's only just begun."

The doors to the princess's palace waft forth icy-cold mist in continuous gossamer strands. It's the same low-hanging mist found in Low Ward during Winterfolly—a mist that kills every garden made to combat starvation, freezes babies in their cribs and lungs in pneumonia and people sleeping in the streets, the whites of their eyes glittering with frost.

The air as I step into the princess's palace is breathtakingly cold, but the blood in me burns hotter than ever.

The interior swells with soft rolls of ice like in old Earth caves—bulging, cloudy, cut in stark slabs to show translucence lit in ghostly whites and blues and pinks. This is a toy box, and they've taken the hardship of Winterfolly out to play make-believe with. For fun. For *celebration.*

I follow the main ice path. It ends at a door flanked by frozen stalagmites and icy-blue holocandles—the cavernous ballroom beyond echoing every mandolin and synth-harp. Below the proud lavender banners embroidered with swans, nobles dance in furs and silks, in rigid couples like courting animals. The ballroom floor is white and gold marble in a chessboard pattern, and I pause at the threshold. The herald smiles at me, a glass bell in his ready hand. "How shall I announce thee, milady?"

"You won't."

"Milady, I—I must." It goes unsaid—he *must*, or the nobles will discard him.

"Synali von Hauteclare," I finally say. "Of House Lithroi."

His unease melts as he rings the bell. The sound doesn't stop the jubilee, but it does slow it. The nobles gathered on the edges of the ballroom floor pause as the herald's cry rings out, *"Synali von Hauteclare, of House Lithroi!"*

A hundred blacklight halos on a hundred foreheads flash blue in my direction. *a pack*. Luna's sapphire eyes stare out at them all, unblinking, pitiless.

The pawn steps forward onto a golden square.

59. Hiems

hiems ~mis, *f.*
1. winter

It's all a little much, in Mirelle's vaunted opinion.

Perhaps it's the princess's young age, but such a lavish fete would ill suit Mirelle—she'd much rather have a small gathering with liquor and a roaring fire with friends…if there were friends to be had, that is. She shakes her hair out and pulls her fur wrap about her neck tighter like a lion's mane, a pride without a pride.

Her heels click as she searches the wintry tunnels of the princess's manse. For what, she isn't sure. A familiar face? Someone who will talk with her instead of bowing and going on their way? Rax would stop, she knows—she's his fiancée; he has to—but she cannot seem to find him.

Three girls approach opposite, flush with wine and ferocious giggling, but they quiet at Mirelle's gaze and incline their heads meekly. The riotous giggling echoes again only after they pass her. She scoffs—she doesn't know why she's wandering like this. She has half a mind to get herself lost just so someone will come and find her, and so her shoes take her deeper, following a crystal river upstream and around gentle swells of pastel ice until she finds a dozen doors—one of them half open. The holocandlelight spilling from it is warm, but the voices aren't.

"…von Axton failed in killing the girl."

"The helping hand you hired isn't getting anywhere, either."

"Then what do you suggest I do? We're running out of options."

"And we're running out of *family members*, Grigor. Five funeral ceremonies in three months—it's madness."

Mirelle's eyelashes flicker. The voice is unmistakable—Grigor Ashadi-Hauteclare, her father—and Uncle Seren's voice is just as clear.

"If—" Father lowers his tone to a bare whisper. "If the duke had finished his plaything and her whelp properly, we wouldn't be having this problem."

"Are you saying it's our fault, then?" Uncle Seren snaps. "That we deserve this wanton murder for trying to rid ourselves of a mistake?"

"She's a mistake with talent in the arena. The girl has House Lithroi on her side—you know what that means. Bellesera knew it best of all, but she ignored it in favor of trusting the arena to cull the problem, and here we are."

"It's only a matter of time, though, isn't it? Until the bastard meets your daughter on the field."

"Seren—"

"It's not hard to remove the mortal limiter protocols on a steed," Uncle Seren interrupts him. "Not as hard as the SCC makes you think. It'd take a few dozen bribes, but there's more than enough now with the Velrayd dower. We have someone modify Ghostwinder before the match, and the bastard problem is solved."

The hairs on the back of Mirelle's neck stand. She's disgusted at the mere idea of it—of *cheating in the arena*. The mortal limiter protocols are necessary—they absorb the buildup generated between two steeds' nerve fluids when they impact; if one steed's protocol is disabled, the other is deluged with all the buildup. Two rounds of impact without the protocol is enough to induce overload in even the most hardened, untouched rider. Father will shoot it down viciously as the underhanded trick it is. After all, he was the one who read her the stories of the knights. He instilled in her to fight clean and fair and shining, that none might doubt her—

"It's a viable strategy, but I won't have my daughter getting blood on her hands."

Her brain goes white. The ice ripples his words in stark clarity—no decrying, no disgust; only acquiescence.

"It would be an accident, Grigor. Even for your daughter."

Say no. *Say no, say no, say no, say no*—

The ground cracks beneath her heel. The sound of footsteps brings fear. Her own footsteps scatter back up the tunnels until she can hear the fete again—synth-harps and the rapid shuffle of dancing—and a warm hand suddenly claps on her shoulder.

"There you are." Father smiles down at her. "You're out of breath—have you had your fill of dancing?"

She can't see it in his brown eyes—no malice, no dishonor. Nothing but Father. Was he always this good at hiding things? She manages a smile back. "Indeed. I was searching for Rax."

"Hah! It's about time someone reminded him how lucky he is to have you." He laughs, the baritone of her childhood. He is the smell of her childhood—chalk and rosemary and the faint mineral of steam-pressed cloth as he puts a light kiss to her forehead just in the center of her halo. She smiles until her face hurts, until she can gather courage enough to reach out and squeeze his fingers. She doesn't want it to be true…but she *heard* it.

"You're clammy, darling," he remarks.

"It's all the ice."

"Of course. Strange choice, that—must've cost a pretty credit." He fastens the fur cape around her neck tighter. "Go. Have fun. I'll tell your mother to expect you late."

Her face is frozen and her turn stiff. Her footsteps made slow, different. Just in case.

They're going to kill the murderer.

And they're going to use me to do it.

If Father agrees to Uncle Seren's ploy to tamper with Mirelle's steed, then she'll be left with only two options: win against Synali in the first round, or let her die.

Mirelle is a rider. A *knight*. She'll defeat Synali von Hauteclare, but she won't do it with tricks; it'll be done with lances and maneuvers and skill. She will remain uncorrupted. The murderer won't drag her down into the desperate, dishonorable dirt as she has Father.

And then she sees them on the ballroom floor.

In the midst of a crowd of practiced whirling is the stop-start of a strikingly inefficient dance. A tall figure with white hair smiles, and a girl flushes in his arms—a girl with ice eyes.

A girl not her.

60. Nescio

nesciō ~īre ~īuī or ~iī ~ītum, *tr., (intr.)*
1. to not know, to be ignorant

None of me fits here.

Each of these nobles slots into a space neatly—an outline only they can see. Someone in pink shoulder checks me, hard and quick; too many people in the crowd to catch who it was—House Michel, maybe. Luna growls, pearl teeth flashing.

"Don't," I whisper. "That's what they want."

I find a place against the wall and recover, patting Luna to calm it. Two women sit on a nearby couch with entire gutted animals around their necks, giggling.

"Sir Rax? Never in my life did I think he'd get engaged! He seemed so intent on playing the role of, well, playboy—what with all those chorus stars and fellow riders."

"Oh, they all are at first. But one must grow up sometime and realize one's responsibility to their House."

Laughter flutters behind sleeves. "So very true."

I straighten. An ice swan mocks me with my own reflection—distorted and cold—and the tempo of the music suddenly slows to a seductive crawl across the icy walls. The dance floor clears, nobles jockeying around one another to find new partners in a jumble of fur and perfume and too-pleasant smiles.

A voice reverberates out of nowhere, dark and strong as coffee. "May I have this dance?"

My stomach twists. Someone dressed in all red slides into my left. Even now, even after everything, he's still so hard to look at. I thought he was angry with me? I stare dead ahead.

"No."

"Do you know *how* to dance?"

My dresscoat suddenly feels unbuttoned too far, and I close it carefully. "I know how to ride. That's all that matters."

Even without looking at him, Rax's crooked smile is obvious. "Believe it or not, Hauteclare, there's more to life than riding."

I swallow the instinct to kiss him again, to feel that heat in my body one more time before the end. I stare at the ice swan, but he refuses to take the silent hint.

"It's just one dance, and it's the tableau-diablé—the easiest for the lady. All you gotta do is cling to me, and I'll do the heavy lifting."

My spine ramrods. "I do not *cling*."

"Only when you want riding secrets."

A wry grin spreads on Rax's knowing lips, and a bizarre twitch moves on mine.

"That's the first time I've made you smile." He laughs.

"And hopefully the last." I cut.

"Oh, whoa—cute dog!" Rax kneels and offers his hand to Luna, the dog sniffing his fingers warily. He laughs and looks up at me. "You know, they say a pet takes after its owner."

The drums of the music beat far too erratically, but then I realize the rhythm's coming from my own chest. *Ridiculous.* The dance floor slowly fills in, the musicians gaining volume as my murmur loses it. "I wish you'd give up on me."

"Oh, I will...once I've fought you. But until then, I'm selfishly holding on to you with everything I've got."

"You can't hold on to anyone. You're engaged."

"I'm sorry about snapping at you on the vis," he says—unhearing me or ignoring me, I can't tell. "But I'm glad my letter got to you. The second I saw you on the tilt, I knew you'd read it—all that careful positioning, your Halcyon-Briggs maneuver at the ready."

I frown at the floor. "I wasn't ready enough."

Rax waves his red-gloved hand. "Helmann's a genius—the sort who belonged in the War. No way you could've known where he'd come from."

"I beat him." I say it with no smugness, just proof. Just a warning: *i beat the genius helmann, and i'll beat you, too.*

Rax's eyes hang on my profile for a long second, and then: "You sure did. After a shitload of heart attacks on my end."

It's my turn to ignore his words. "You were right—defensively, he was perfect. I had to create my own openings."

His playful smile tries to peer around my stubborn hair curtain. "So you admit it? I helped you?"

I nod. He laughs as he straightens, then offers his hand. "Was my help worth a dance?"

I slide my trembling hand in his. "This is pointless."

His fingers close around mine gently. "Doesn't make it any less fun."

It's alarming how much dancing feels like being in the saddle. It's the same feeling of being not-alone now, of moving as one; pressed against another person, trying to touch both all of them and none of them at the same time. It's different from our shower-room altercation. I'm hyperaware of my own muscles beneath my clothes, of his, of the places he's hot and I'm hot and the places where those temperatures meet sweetly.

"Here." Rax holds his arm out. "Come closer. It's easier that way."

I stumble forward and frantically cut off his chuckle. *"Shut up."*

His hand moves onto the small of my back, and I fight every urge to lean into it. Brace softly. When he moves, I move—lightning and the thunder that follows. No, this is faster than that, quicker down to the quick, oil and flame going up together and connected visibly by their reaction to each other. The nobles rotating around us might as well be stars with how distant they feel. For a second, it doesn't matter where I am. There's the smell of skin and warm cloth and something separate—something I've scented before in the shower room—closer, stronger, all him, all pulling me inexorably into the hollow of his neck.

all of us, beasts.

Throats can be covered in blood—exposed, sliced. But this is the first time in my life I think they can be beautiful, too.

The music rises and descends—a loop. The entire dance is a single impact, heat and catalyst and realization, and the two of us at the center of it all. Moving like this, together, feels… I don't know if he feels it. He has to—it's *everywhere*. I look up. His redwood eyes are on mine already, already smiling like a fool—light and easy with no weight behind it, yet this is no smiling matter. This isn't a smiling feeling. It's a cliff, and only I am aware of the danger.

This is much more than just lust; this is want. This is wanting months with him, *years*, to figure out his smiles and his quirks and what makes him laugh and what makes him come and what makes him happy and—

The music fades. I step back, the resonant heat escaping from between us. My mouth is dry as bone. ***don't panic.*** *walk.*

"H-Hey! Wait up!"

I scoop water from a pitcher at the refreshments table and chug. The freezing liquid stabs at my throat and reminds me—beautiful or not, a slit throat cannot drink. Mother is gone, and I remain. Wanting or not, I will die. I have to die. The fuel for a fire is hope, and I can have none.

There is no place in this world for me after House Hauteclare is destroyed; not with Rax, not with Dravik, not with anyone. I am too far gone. Too many scars. Too much darkness.

"Hey, are you okay?" Rax looms at my side. "If you're not feeling well, we can—"

"Thanks are in order," I start slowly. "For your letter on Helmann. But this is the last time I wish to see you."

I turn. Luna trots after me. Rax is faster, taller, in front of me in a blink. "Whoa whoa whoa—did I do something wrong?"

Mother clung to hope until the very last. Father discarded her like a toy, in the end. I will not make her mistake. I will never be anyone's toy—no matter how tempting it is. I will never again allow anyone to give me hope and then take it away.

I am a rider, and all that's left is the impact.

"The next time we meet, Rax Istra-Velrayd, it will be in your loss and my victory."

61. Omnino

omnīnō, *adv.*
1. in all things; utterly

I retreat to the ice tunnels and follow the warmest air I can find to a balcony. Water drips as the ice fantasy meets reality. The clear ceiling of the Station lets each ice-melt pool catch diamond points of starlight—Low Ward and Mid Ward a faint smoky memory far below. At the marble railing lingers a familiar boy in a hoverchair, a familiar girl by his side. Their reflections in the massive pools of water are perfectly inverted.

A drop falls from above, rippling the mirror world. The boy turns and smiles.

"Ah, Synali—you seem to find us quite easily. Or is it we who find you?"

His grin is simple and clean. He wears their halo, but he is not one of them. I know that much. That's *all* I know about him. Crown Princess Leyda Esther de Ressinimus is at his side. Her halo is bright blue, green eyes identical to his, her hair copper and fire. She wears a silver dress made with swan wings—*real ones*—attached to her back. Something has died for her.

"Synali! Wow, you came…and with such a sweet puppy! I thought I'd see you a lot later, but this is great, too! C'mon—join us! The view's really beautiful tonight."

My boots move over a different kind of chessboard, water rippling with every step. I choose to stand between them. Luna settles at my feet but stares directly up at the boy, wagging its golden tail furiously against marble. *Clank clank clank.* No one says anything for a long while.

"Forgive me, you two," the boy says suddenly. "But I fear I'm intruding."

The princess squirms mightily. "Aww, you're not! I promise!"

His hoverchair hisses as he turns to her. "Not everything can wait until the tournament. You should talk to her here, now."

"But here is *boring*!"

This elaborate ice fantasy made especially for her—*boring*? I start to bristle, but the boy's voice goes stern for the very first time. "Leyda."

"Allll riiiiiiight." The princess huffs. "Bye, I guess."

The boy turns to me, gaze resting on Luna for a moment. "Goodnight, Synali—and good luck tomorrow."

His hoverchair hisses past, the vented heat on the underside evaporating a pool as it goes, and something irrational in me begs to touch his hand. To hold it like the A3 and A4 held each other's.

The hoverchair stops, and he speaks. "It's strong, isn't it? The urge to hold hands."

My stomach drops. "How did you—"

"I can see why they like you now. You're like them. Like me. Like *us*."

I study his face frantically—what does he mean? I notice the pixels in his green eyes, then—color contacts made to look like the king's hue, Leyda's hue. He adopted their eyes. The hoverchair jets start up again, and he leaves. That irrational something in me is terribly sad to see him go, and I pivot. "What's your name?"

He inclines his head over his shoulder. "Hush, dearheart. Not yet."

Dearheart—Mother's name for me. How does he know that? He saw the A3 and A4 memory. *he sees memories in the saddle, too.* He saw mine. **He's** the one. He's the one who sent the daises and blue hyacinths—he's the one who sends the flowers, always.

He leaves behind silence. I know what I want to say to the princess but not how to say it. *"Your father's killed so many." "Your father continues to kill so many." "Your father is the reason my mother died and the reason my father died."*

The princess doesn't seem to know what to say, either—too deep in mourning the boy's absence to consider me worth speaking to—but somewhere after huffing and sighing is her cheery recovery.

"Your dresscoat is *so* pretty. Who made it—der Viskamp? No, wait, lemme guess—Felmorrat! The tailoring work is definitely Felmorrat."

"I don't know," I admit. "And I don't particularly care."

"Well you should! My brother put a lot of effort into getting that for you, probably. Did he give you a present for me?" Her little hands suddenly jut into my pockets, and Luna barks and I stumble back, but in a flash she pulls out again, fingers clutched around a paper-wrapped candy. "Aha! See? I knew it—these are the same ones he used to give me when I was a baby." She pops it in her mouth, squirrel cheek distorting her words. "Strawberry's my favorite."

I go quiet. She turns to the railing with a sigh.

"Papa says it's a bad thing Brother's back. But I don't want that to be true."

A church barge floats by. A fog of incense follows it as priests circle the deck, chanting vespers for the poor and unfortunate suffering miles below them in the smog. Princess Leyda idly smushes her hand against her other cheek.

"Papa says on the other six Stations, people worship a hundred gods, or ten, and some worship none, and some worship their ancestors." She thinks for a moment, then looks over at me. "But the priests keep telling me there's only one God. So…how can that be right?"

We watch the LED cross on the barge fade into the sky.

"I don't think it's that simple," I say finally.

"Mmm." The princess makes a noise of agreement and then a crunch as the candy goes down. "Probably nothing's that simple."

The shallow pool shivers beneath our feet in stars and melting frost.

"I wish you could meet Mum," she says. She means *her* mother, not Astrix—the queen cloistered for her fragile health.

"She's ill, right?"

"Yeah. I didn't get to see her much." She frowns. "That's why J made her for me."

I blink. J—is that the boy's name?

"'Made her'? What do you mean, 'made her'?"

"He made her overload in Hellrunner, and now I get to see her all the time! Way more than when she was sick. I had to sit in its weird saddle for a while, though." I stare at her in disbelief. At last, she giggles. "Oh geez. *Wow.* You don't know, huh? I thought Brother would've told you by now."

"Told me what?"

"They don't die. The enemy." She flips her hair and sighs when I stare at her blankly. "If their bodies get hurt, they go into, like, hibernation—turn into nerve fluid. But they can grow back if they get food. And their food is memories. Brain stuff—stuff we give them in the saddle. And growing back makes, like, a lot of energy. That's what the saddle is—us feeding them, them trying to grow back and making energy."

My breathing stops. The princess rolls her eyes.

"How did you think the steeds moved? Plain old electricity? That'd never be enough."

"The nerve fluid is dead." I numbly repeat what Rax told me over Sevrith's bed.

"That's what the steedcrafters tell people so they don't freak out. They're still alive—the little wiggly things. If you overload in the saddle, they eat all of you, and they remember you. Keep you there. They're not allowed to grow back, obviously, because then they wouldn't keep making the energy. They're like…babies." She giggles. "Battery babies who never get to grow up."

The way she explains it…it doesn't sound serious. But it's too specific not to be. And of all the people on the Station who would know information like this… The princess's hand rests sweetly on mine as her eyes move to an empty space on the balcony behind me.

"I'm looking forward to tomorrow—it'll be fun, right, Mum?"

Luna's tail wags at the balcony where no one stands.

62. Fortitudo

fortitūdō ~inis, f.
1. strength
2. fortitude, bravery

The next morning, Rax Istra-Velrayd stares at his crimson helmet with half a hangover and a girl's voice ringing in his head.

"When you black out in the saddle, do you see things? Someone else's memories."

Rax knows better. He's done a good job of hiding it by looking handsome and vapid and obsessed with fucking around, but he knows people. He's bad at keeping the books, arranging the shipments, running the errands—whatever the fuck else it is his parents do as nobles—but he's *good* at riding. At *knowing riding*. It's the way she moves; she heaves Heavenbreaker around like it's the end of her, like she's covered in splinters and being forced to move through it. He knows Lithroi isn't helping her with it—he's just pushing her into the cockpit over and over again. Mirelle thinks it's madness. Helmann called it beautiful. But Rax knows better; it's *pain*. He can't let it end like this. There was no one there for him when it was happening, and he refuses to let it happen again to someone else.

"When you black out in the saddle, do you see things?"

It sounded like nonsense two months ago, but it's all he has to go on now. He sees people's memories in the dream and nowhere else. The saddle is for riding, not seeing. He knows what happens to overloaders—comatose forever, like Sev, used like lifeless baby factories forever. He knows his parents won't hesitate to use him like that, and he knows he's close to overload after all these years, but he's going to reach her with the only thing he's good at, the only thing she seems to care about—riding.

He stretches his hand in his rider's suit, tight material flexing with his tendons. Chest smooth—no handkerchief for the first time in a decade. He has to lose himself in the nerve fluid, get closer to the steed—see these memories like she does. He has to forget he's him.

Sunscreamer waits outside the training arena, its beaked helmet pointed out at the stars like a crimson bird of prey.

Rax walks under the whitewood cross over the hangar door, praying.

−2. Invenio

inveniō ~enīre ~ēnī ~entum, *tr.*
1. to come upon, meet

The ocean at the bottom of the noble spire is beautiful indeed.

From his place unloading crates of fresh fish, Rain watches the artificial waves rise and curl in on themselves, the horizon a simulated blur of azure. White foam bubbles over the pale sand of the shore and recedes once more into the sea in a continuous loop. Rise and fall, rise and fall. Like breathing.

"Hey!" his boss barks. "I didn't hire you to stand around and gawk, pretty boy! Get the crates to the door *now*."

Rain keeps his head down as he shuffles to the side door of the seaside manse's patio and back again. There is a momentary pleasure in the sweat and the sun and the salt smell of the sea, and Rain revels in the motions of honest work. No blood or torture or hiding. His dust withdrawal headache is splitting his skull in two, but if he looks at the ocean for long enough, he can ignore the roiling in his stomach and the cold sweats all over his body. His arms go abruptly weak, and he drops a crate, and the boss takes it upon himself to backhand him, hissing about how much it cost. The other loaders don't even blink, save for one—a burly man with more hair than skin.

"Give 'im a break, Mr. Baker—guy's been moving twice what we are."

"Working faster's no good if you break it all," the boss snaps. "You watch him if you want, Gern, but the next one's coming out of your pay."

The man called Gern offers a hand to Rain, and he takes it wordlessly. The two move boxes in silence, and then, "Dust, huh?"

Rain looks to Gern as he sets his crate down on the doorstep. "Sorry?"

"Dust," Gern mutters, wiping his face on his tunic. "My brother just got off it. Rough stuff. You're a bit buffer than he is, though—don't look half-bad."

Rain isn't sure what to say. The recluses sent by the Web to kill him are always on his mind, and so he keeps his words to himself. Gern fills the quiet by offering him a small white pill from his pocket.

"Here, take it. Helps with the headaches. I've got a ton left over."

The Web's inborn urge in him is to mistrust, but Green-One's influence speaks louder; a man like this has no reason to drug him. It goes down with a medicinal tang. Slowly, minute by minute and crate by crate, Rain's headache dissipates. At last the hovercart is empty, and the boss and the others go to lunch while he and Gern volunteer to take inventory one last time.

"All right." Gern gets to his feet. "Should be good. Lock it up and let's go."

Rain doesn't move. His head is better, but his heart is worse. A stray kindness should mean nothing—it's always meant nothing, coming from prey. But Gern is not prey. He *should* be, but Rain's dust-starved mind refuses the idea of it as it never has before—this man is not prey because Rain is not a Spider anymore. He betrayed his Web by letting Synali live. He betrayed Green-One by letting Yavn go. And he betrays them all now by choking Gern out instead of killing him.

When Rain whispers "I'm sorry" in the man's ear, it is not wholly for him.

Green-One's module into the manse's systems works only at 12:30 sharp, the door to the back kitchen clicking open smoothly and Rain disappearing inside. It's quiet, still, whitewash and wood and the ocean soft through each window. Every door is left unlocked, save for two—the basement and the main bedroom. Green-One's words echo: *"What appears to be will not always be so."* The leader of Polaris is a master of subterfuge, evading the recordkeepers, the king's guards, and every assassin guild on the Station for more than a decade now. The basement would be a logical place to hide evidence, but the leader does not strictly follow logic; madness is far more difficult to predict.

Rain wanders the halls, an uneasy feeling in his gut. If Green-One knew about Yavn when he gave him the module, there's every chance he only halfway disabled this manse's security systems, leaving Rain a sitting duck for whatever authorities could be streaming his way right now. The work must be fast. But *where*? The entire manse could be a hiding spot.

Eyes, ears, nose open—all of his senses focus on the creaks and groans of the wood. And then he notices it. Every room in the manse has some sort of decorative mirror—except the sitting room. The most obvious room, but Rain knows the most obvious is also the least obvious. He is not smart, not like Green-One or the leader of Polaris. But he knows—from years of maintaining his dagger, from years of using it on prey in puddles and against stainless steel doors—that, in reflections and up close, hard-light always has a faint rainbow hue around it, like the distortion of a heat wave.

He snatches a mirror from the wall of the bathroom and scans the sitting room. Nothing. Every wall is real. Not the walls, then. He aims down, step by slow step, and his chest swells when he sees the haze around a square section beneath a rug—just big enough for someone to squeeze through. It's not active hard-light—no heat, no plasma—and so it's easily breached with a bowl of water, the plane fizzing away to reveal a ladder leading into blue-lit dimness.

Getting into the room is not difficult—it is understanding what is inside that is.

His eyes skirt around the cubicle, the walls lined with real paper diagrams. Of what, he can't tell, but he snaps pictures on his vis all the same, pictures that automatically send to Green-One. The same image repeats: a circle bull's-eyed with other circles within. In the very center circle, the leader has written a word—MOTHER. Not just in one diagram—in the dead center of all the diagrams, the word MOTHER blares back at Rain.

An acronym, maybe? Or the real thing? If the leader's mother is being kept somewhere against her will, it would explain his motives. Nobles do strange things to one another all the time, and starting a rebellion for revenge is not out of the question, but the wrong would have to have been committed at least ten years ago, when the leader first began appearing. A name floats to his mind: Draviticus—the crown prince. This manse belongs to House Lithroi, and he is the only one left of them. Which means the overloaded rider Green-One located in the hospital must've been...

Rain goes rigid. There's a holoscreen on the wall, blue and humming, and he reads it: FRIGATE-CLASS A3 HEAVENBREAKER. A diagram of a familiar steed. DESTROYER-CLASS A4 HELLRUNNER. Another diagram. Math scrawled everywhere. He looks up at the numbers, looks down at the papers, and then up again at the hologram of two rusted steeds floating in space behind the shadow of an asteroid just off the Station's perimeter, their hands clasped together and hundreds of half-visible, fanged tentacles writhing out of their cockpits.

He is not Green-One, but even he can understand.

He has to tell Synali. Stop her from riding any more. Green-One, their mission, *he has to tell her*, and his mind goes blank. There is no way she knows—no way Draviticus has told her. She is trying to win the Supernova Cup, but it will *kill* her.

The prince's plan will kill them all.

He's never climbed a ladder faster, papers falling like ash in his wake, and one of the many falls to the ground with a sentence scribbled in its margins.

I AM THE ONE WHO RAISES THE DEAD
AND GIVES THEM LIFE AGAIN.

63. Perlustro

perlustrō ~āre ~āuī ~ātum, *tr.*
1. to purify

Today, there's a screaming horde of people outside my chamber.

They vie with flailing arms and shouts and autograph books, triple the guards holding them back. My steps are careful toward a smiling Dravik.

"Leyda's a skilled rider," he says, "if a little overenthusiastic. She tends to favor her left side, considering she's left-handed. Hasn't learned to use the other one quite as well yet."

"Riding is dangerous," I argue.

"'Tis," he agrees, smile unfading.

"Why does the king let her do it?"

"I suppose the same reason he let me all those years ago—guilt."

I study his face. "Why didn't you tell me? About what the nerve fluid really is?"

He quirks a brow. "Dangerous, you mean?"

"Alive."

The prince laughs softly and repeats, "There are things in this universe that do not die, Synali; they only change their names."

"Ladies and gentlefolk, a blessed morning to you all! It's my pleasure to welcome you to yet another rousing day in the 22nd decennial Supernova Cup! I'm your host Gress, here with Bero, and we're just thrilled to bring you the late-stage matchups today! This week's fights will determine the quarterfinal seed, and we can't wait to see who'll fall honorably, who'll rise honorably, and who'll take their honor by the throat!"

"Well said, Gress—the excitement in the stadium is palpable! We're packed to capacity, and fifteen million of you are watching on the vis Station-wide! I'd advise everyone to buckle in and buckle up, because we're opening today with a very special match. That's right, folks—His Majesty's royal blood is coming onto the field!"

"A real treat, Bero!"

"That it is, Gress! We haven't seen a royal rider get this far in a Supernova Cup since Prince Pelmor nearly a hundred years ago!"

I'm the first one in the arena.

Heavenbreaker and I hover, completely still. The cross hangs above us, shedding constant light into the hungry void of space.

God forgave them. I cannot.

The stars look no different today, the Station gray against Esther's slow green rotation. Everything is the same, so why does the saddle feel *different*? Why does the nerve fluid tingle soft and insistent at my skin—an ache behind my eyes, as if I'm forgetting something?

Heavenbreaker hovers, asking, *"afraid?"*

no.

She considers my answer, and then: *"sad?"*

I stare into the distant sun. What good is sadness? What good is admitting to it?

"sad?" Heavenbreaker repeats, quieter this time. The possibilities have rotated in my mind all night—this voice I'm hearing, this steed that's been with me through everything thus far… It's either a true AI or… The hard-light net of the arena opens, then closes, letting in the lavender plasma trails of our opponent. I don't need to speak in the steed. Here, Heavenbreaker understands me wordlessly. No matter what she is, she's helped me like no

one else in this world.

I think our jets *on*. Our blue plasma screams over the black of space, my answer screaming the soundless truth: *without you, always sad.*

"On the blue side, please welcome the Lady of the Crown and our hearts, the inheritor-presumpt of House Ressinimus and the Nova-King's court—Crown Princess Leyda Esther de Ressinimus, riding for House Galbrinth on her steed, Maidenprayer!"

"House Galbrinth is the cloistered queen's House, is it not?"

"Indeed it is, Bero—may Her Majesty find her health in the Lord's grace. And may her daughter have His favor on the field today!"

The crowd's roar rises to a fever pitch, and the princess meets me in the middle with a spritely maneuver. Maidenprayer is far prettier than a machine has any right to be, lithe and long in the torso with an S-curve to its spine. The arms are elegantly tilted in as if praying. Its hands are small but ready, two swathes of pleated metal arcing up from her elbows like wings. The entire thing is brushed pale lavender with silver accents, a silver swan outstretched on her breastplate, and its helmet looks much like a silver crown.

The holoscreen pops up, Leyda's halo brightening the smile beneath her visor. "I'm kinda excited, Synali! I don't get to ride against people like you very often."

"People like me," I repeat.

Her laugh trills. "Riders who know about the voice in the saddle! It's usually just boring lance stuff, but this one might actually be fun!"

She's not Dravik, but her voice rings the same: perfectly polite, perfectly kind, and yet ominous. She's so *young. is this how you felt fighting me, sevrith?*

"I won't hold back," I say.

"Me neither!" she agrees happily.

"—and on the red side, we have a true dark horse who's clawed her way up the ranks! With a grievous grit, a ferocious focus, and a white-hot bent to the chaotic in her moves, please welcome Synali von Hauteclare, riding for House Lithroi in her steed, Heavenbreaker!"

The crowd's roar thunders, all-consuming.

"Riders, please proceed to your tilts!"

My jets cool as my back rivets to the sidereal hexagon and the grav-gen between us flares to life in brilliant blue—motions and colors like a recipe I know well now. I am no longer the girl I was when I first stepped onto the tilt five months ago.

"Let us begin the countdown to the first round—in the name of God, King, and Station!"

The crowd cries out invisibly for their cruel masters. *"In the name of God, King, and Station!"*

A silver lance in my hand. A silver lance in hers. I turn the comms on.

"Three!"

"Everything you said about the nerve fluid last night…about seeing your mother…" My voice starts soft. "Is it true?"

"Two!"

Jealousy that she gets to see her mother. Hope that I one day might.

"One!"

The princess's smile is small. "Come see for yourself."

Zero.

64. Quia

quia, *conj.*
1. because

Maidenprayer is a Cruiser-class A453-181 — the same new model as Sevrith's Everseer, just a different weight class; the same extra ankle jets, the same exhaust vents on its throat…but not the same speed as his.

I reach terminus first.

We near the grav-gen in a flash of blue. She's staying wide, my lance tracking right at her in a Poisson maneuver. No matter which way she dodges, if she continues her forward momentum, I have her pinned in laterally at every degree.

Impact.

The cry between steeds bleats strong, the brief spark of light searing brighter than I've ever seen it. My lance catches something solid, something real, and then breaks through. Heavenbreaker peels off into the rise, and my blistering eyes scour the scoreboard: *Red, 1. Blue, 0.* I got her, but it was so much louder and brighter than usual. I tilt my chin up, chin down, until the fluid in my ears knows direction again and my stomach stops rolling nausea. Crystal laughter comes from the princess's holoscreen.

"No, silly—not like that. Try again!"

Giggling when I've scored a point—is she that confident?

We round the rise's bend, and I see her hands still limp around the lance, unready. Any other rider would be sizing me up, positioning and repositioning accordingly as the rise ends, but not her. This isn't a match to her; it's some kind of game—like brother, like sister.

Heavenbreaker peels a black-syrup voice from my mind: *"no openings, so you'll have to create your own."* It's irritating how right the voice is, how true to life it is—how easily it straightens my thoughts.

unhelpful.

"helpful," Heavenbreaker argues with me petulantly. *"he was helpful."*

We wrung all helpfulness out of him, and now he's gone forever. *focus.* She comes in faster this time; Poisson maneuver won't work. I need something that goes vertical, too—something manifold. *Euclid.* Euclid if I can play it close. I'm faster, but I can't rush her over the tilt until I know what she's doing.

The lurch of the descent begins. My skin pulls from my skull, and the princess suddenly shrieks, "No, no, *no!* I told you, Synali! No more boring stuff allowed!"

Comms cut. The grav-gen draws us together like moths to flame, hot and fast, spit and breath forced down my throat. Her lavender grows bigger, closer, all her jets engaged at once and blazing bright in pastel plasma, and *I've lost sight of her lance.* Drag my eyes up, down, around…**there!** A smear of silver floats far behind her. She *dropped* it. She dropped her weapon—and then I realize it; she's the princess—the entire Station is her weapon. Her very blood is her weapon.

The cry hits my ears, but the light doesn't snapshot around the cockpit—it glows. Like slow motion, I watch the white light I've seen so many times on impact gather in Maidenprayer's helmet, right where a mouth might be, condensing into a single ball of shivering light.

And then it explodes.

White, everywhere. I can't see anything, and I thrust the lance blindly—something like a red-hot knife drags across my chest, leaving char and smoke. Blink, blink harder, and my vision clears to the sight of the cockpit wall ahead of me glowing orange-red. *Superheated.* The rise floats us away from each other, the commentators' voices reconnecting.

"—seems Her Highness is using unorthodox methods, Bero! She's hit

Synali with something, but I'm not sure it was her lance!"

"Well skin my teeth and call me a molerat—I've never seen something like this before, Gress! Did Her Highness somehow direct the impact light to damage Heavenbreaker? Is that even *possible*? And more importantly—is that a point or not?"

Leyda's holoscreen pops up, her lavender helmet shining as she giggles. "Isn't it cool, Synali? J doesn't know I figured out how to do this yet. It's so much fun!"

The burn lingers on my chest, making it hard to breathe. "What did you do?"

She shrugs. "I dunno. It felt right."

The descent comes, but the scoreboard never updates. *Red, 1. Blue, 0.* They're not counting it as a point, but Leyda doesn't seem bothered. She doesn't summon her lance back into her hand; it just floats at the edge of the arena. She's not here to win. She's here to play.

"Here we go!" the princess chirps just before the descent cuts our comms. I hold my lance up—if she does the light again, I won't be able to see enough to hit. If she hits me again on the chest where the metal is already soft, it might break through. I'll get decanted *again*.

"remember," Heavenbreaker says. I can't respond, too focused on holding my lance strong and steady, squinting and waiting for the light again. Maidenprayer draws close, my body pulled into the impact once more, and I wait until the cry resounds—thrust. If I thrust early, I'll hit her, I'm sure—

The white light condenses in her helmet faster than before, then blasts out. It catches my lance mid-thrust, melting the metal down to nothing but liquid silver that rapidly cools in space. And that's the moment I understand.

"this is how we fight," Heavenbreaker chimes.

We. The reboot memory. The falling, spinning in space, and the white light like lasers shot back at the steeds. The enemy razed Earth in *laserfire*. The lasers are how they fight, and inside the steeds, on the tilt…it feels like fighting to them—so they make that light.

"I can hear it now!" Leyda's comms crackle on. "I can hear you talking to your steed! It's so cute!"

The commenters and the thunderous crowd and Leyda's joy all fall away as my brain spirals; I can't hit her if I can't see her. Neither of us will get a point, and overtime will just keep going and going and *going*. It'll be like Sevrith but slower and more agonizing. She'll keep making the lasers, softening Heavenbreaker's metal over and over until we disintegrate. Decanting's not the problem—it's the fact there won't be anything to decant back into if Heavenbreaker is a pile of molten slag.

I can't let this drag on. But how do I end it? I can't get anywhere close to her and still hope to hit—she makes the blistering light within melee range. A black-and-yellow tiger flashes in my memory—Helmann—and even further back, Rax when he destroyed the dummy. I can see the motions of it, the way both of them moved. It won't be as graceful or as powerful, but...

"They are not toys, Leyda," I say. Her image in the holoscreen goes still. "They are alive. All of them. Every single spiral you see in the saddle is someone. You don't get to toy with them just because it makes you happy."

I can hear the frown in her voice. "You can't tell me what to do. You're not my father."

I laugh once, and then I don't stop. Can't stop. My laughter fills the saddle, delirious, the rise turning gently into the descent. She sounds like me talking to Dravik. Like me talking to a father I've never had. A taste of my own medicine. I laugh until I feel the tears, hot and wet, and the spirals in the saddle rise up to poke at them curiously.

"I know," I manage. "But I'm going to teach you something he never will."

I throw my hand out and summon another lance from Heavenbreaker's palm. The descent rips through me, pulling us into each other. Maidenprayer's laser spot glows brighter earlier—Leyda's anger obvious. Breathe. Remember the strength of Rax's arm, the curve of his graceful fingers, the way he walks like smoke over water. He's gone. But it was nice, playing pretend with him.

I fight the g-forces with everything I have, every muscle in my body condensed and focused on my right arm as I pull it back, lance squeezed hard in my fist. My posture begs to crumple, to flow, the gravity too much to bear against. The lance handle is too flimsy, the lancepoint bobbing wildly, so I choke it farther up, where the base flares. Finally, it's enough grip to aim steady.

The laser gathers in Maidenprayer's helmet, bright enough for squinting. I may still miss. The lance could hit her breastplate where her saddle is and kill her like Helmann killed that referee, and killing a princess would be the true end for me.

The me who fought Yatrice would miss. But the me of now will not.

throw.

We snap our wrist forward, and the silver lance slingshots through the air, faster than Helmann's thanks to gravity and more accurate thanks to Rax. I've learned—from him, from both of them, from every rider I've ever faced.

that is what it means to ride.

The silver lancepoint slips between Maidenprayer's empty arms and sinks deep into the left-side tasset, piercing the swan sigil there clean through.

65. Servo

servō ~āre ~āuī ~ātum, *tr.*
1. to save; to make safe, healthy

*R*ax *pushed Sunscreamer to its absolute limit, crimson jets blasting red-hot on his spine.*

And then he let go.

It was harder to let go than to hold on. He'd held on for so long, knew the ins and outs of holding, had carved it so deep into his very nerves it'd become an automatic reaction he had to fight. Release. Remember what it's like to be nothing.

The greatest rider in a century let the g-forces win. His blood flow stopped, his heart not strong enough, and unconsciousness came swift. Darkness seeped in on the edge of his vision, and in the moment before it was too late to change his mind, he saw his fate open itself under him— overload, hospital bed, prisoner, fear. *The first time he'd felt fear in the saddle in a decade.*

And then it swallowed him whole, bones and all.

But it wasn't the end. In the very depths of the blackout, he saw color: skin and hair and eyes. It was the Lithroi man—washed-out and soft and speaking in a pitch-perfect replica of his real voice, and Rax could feel it—this had happened before but not to Rax. To someone else. Not a hallucination—a **memory like the dream.**

"They have forgotten, Synali, what the rabbit means."

Rax was in Synali's body, hate and sore bruises and that sharp smell that followed her everywhere—sweet and coppery and so **close** *it sent his heart beating wildly as she scoffed.*

"Then what does it mean, old man?"

The Lithroi man looked at his cane patiently. "On old Earth, the rabbit was a cornerstone of the food chain, the link between the sun that grew the grass and the animals that fed on those who ate such grass. The rabbit had ten thousand enemies: wolves and tigers, vipers and eagles and foxes. And yet still, it survived."

Rax felt her mind go different, listening intently now.

"The whole of Earth was against the rabbit," Lithroi said. "And yet Earth relied on the rabbit. It fed. It gave life. The nobles of this Station have forgotten it is the rabbit that sustains the lion and not the other way around."

She and Rax looked up in determination. "They will kill me regardless."

The Lithroi man smiled so bright it looked like sun. "They will have to catch you first."

66. Sanitas

sānitās ~ātis, *f.*
1. health
2. sanity

From the velvet seats of a private box, Mirelle watches Synali von Hauteclare remove her helmet slowly. The lights of the medic steeds paint her skin in ruby. She looks horrible—hair sweat-drenched, lips ragged, every attempt by the makeup artist to cover her pockmarks now smudged in sweat. No grace. No decorum. Only struggle. Only a girl close to overload.

Older riders don't bleed silver nearly as much as she does.

Something wrong with her steed.

With Hellrunner, too.

Grandmother often said curiosity ill befit a noblewoman—it was the downfall of Eve and the bane of wise men. Rax's obsession with Synali forced Mirelle to dig curiously for what exactly he saw in her. She'd exhausted every SCC log on Hellrunner years ago, but the logs on Heavenbreaker went back just as far; 354 years ago, the A3 that would later be known as Heavenbreaker was registered. It was the same exact year Hellrunner's A4 was activated and the same year House Ressinimus took control as the Station's first king. Heavenbreaker's logs, however, contained more information than

Hellrunner's; they'd been found together in a nearby asteroid field—remains of the War teleported by the enemy along with the Station. Only Hellrunner had been immediately repurposed and activated; Heavenbreaker disappeared off the logs for upward of three hundred years, only reappearing again when Astrix vel Lithroi bought the rights to the steed, named it, and began tuning it as a teenager. Hellrunner's riders never lasted long—Heavenbreaker's might not, either.

Whatever Heavenbreaker is, it could be just as powerful as Hellrunner. Just as dangerous, and in the hands of a traitor. Lithroi has won. *Again.* Another of her family will die. Perhaps it was always meant to be this way—perhaps God wanted Mirelle to be the one to end the mad dog's killing spree all along.

The seat beside her is empty; Rax never showed. She knows that if he had, his hands would be white-knuckled on the armrests, eyes riveted to the blown-up hologram in the center of the arena, to the murderer's haggard face.

Mirelle quashes the squirm in her chest. Marriage is not for love. Childhood is for love, for flings, for emotions, and she's assuredly no longer a child. Marriage is part of the game—it's not a choice but a duty. She's seen it happen to other noble girls; there will be children, there will be affairs. There will be hatred, disgust, and at best, harmonious indifference. No matter how many books she's read of the War—of the knights who swore themselves to each other before launching to fight, of the muttered promises in the final moments of their courageous lives to love each other until eternity—she knows it's impossible for nobles to marry for love.

So why, then, does the mere *idea* of Rax staring at the murderer eat away at her?

"And that concludes the match, folks! Synali von Hauteclare takes the win with a projectile lance strike! Her Highness has acted rashly on the field before but never quite like this—I'm sure the steedcrafters will be swarming to figure out how she made those lasers! We're getting reports the princess is sound, if a little put off at her loss. We'll have more updates as they come—"

The crowd cheers wildly, the chants of *"Synali, Synali, Synali"* like demons teething on Mirelle's very soul. She stands, pale cape tumbling to the floor and spreading the full winged-lion emblem, and her voice cuts cold into the dark, empty box.

"It seems I will be her next opponent."

−1. Litatio

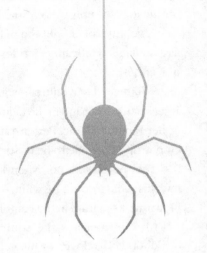

litātiō ~ōnis, *f.*
1. a successful sacrifice

R ain is too late to catch Synali leaving the tourney hall, the crowd crushing in tight as security helps her into her hovercarriage. Green-One hasn't answered any of Rain's pings, the questions scrolling long and blue before his eyes on the steps of the hall.

> **VIOLET-FIVE:** *Did you know the whole time, Green?*
>
> **VIOLET-FIVE:** *Answer me.*
>
> **VIOLET-FIVE:** *Who are you working for? Because I know it's not for the good of the Web anymore.*
>
> **VIOLET-FIVE:** *It was a lie! You LIED to me. You manipulated me.*

He has never held more anger in his heart than now—not even when Violet-Two died, not even when Father died. No answer. Of course there isn't one—he automatically sent Green-One the pictures of the Lithroi man's plans. And that's the only thing Green needed from him. That's what all of this was for—not to protect, not to prevent, not to avenge, but to play the same game he so despised. Rain's head throbs, the dust and the lack of it twisting his insides into knots, and he staggers into a couple who stagger back into him, shoving, hard marble on his back as he collapses to the ground.

And then, finally, an answer.

GREEN-ONE: *You chose to spare that Synali girl months ago, not I. You put this terrible plan in motion. Everyone who died—the Endurance, Theta-7, every one of our family members—was because of you. Your mercy. Your moment of weakness killed them all.*

His fingers twitch, shaking leather glove over hologram.

VIOLET-FIVE: *Who do you work for?*

GREEN-ONE: *Did you truly think yourself the only Spider who was carrying out a noble House's contract? You think yourself the only one chosen? The only one ordained with a more concrete purpose?*

This is not Green-One. This is someone more verbose, more cruel. He has changed, or perhaps Rain has never known him at all, and he can feel it behind his lungs—the breathless grip of unconsciousness, chest caving, his body reaching its last twisted line.

VIOLET-FIVE: *Who, brother?*

GREEN-ONE: *I have told the recluses. They are coming for you.*

The blinking cursor. The rollicking crowd. Rain's eyes slide, fade, and blur, trying to catch the next words.

GREEN-ONE: *House Ressinimus.*

The king. All this time, Green-One was the *king's* assassin?

The world spins, and he staggers through the crowd, away, somewhere to hide. Rain does not see her anymore. He cannot see anything anymore—not even the artificial sky.

But on a nearby rooftop, through the scope of a sapphire-studded sniper rifle trained on the tourney hall doors, someone sees him.

67. Trucido

trucīdō ~āre ~āuī ~ātum, *tr.*
1. to slaughter; to massacre

Artificial sunlight shafts through the manse window and onto my white bedsheets, the withered trees and wilted grass outside far more comforting than any lush greenery. My eyes focus on the bloodred steed floating on the vis with its umber lance in hand—feather-shaped helmet, feather-shaped heels, a hawk sigil on the chest.

"That's the end of the match! Can you believe it, Bero—Rax Istra-Velrayd has won six consecutive matchups in the first round!"

"It's nearly a record for the books, Gress—two more like this and he etches his name in the Hall of Exalted Knights alongside Prince Lisander, Dyana de la Valfori, and all the other greatest of the greats!"

I watch the replay of Rax's match frame by frame, watch his lance sink into the helmet of his opponent like projection sword through paper—as if it's the easiest thing to hit a helmet under multiple g-forces while moving through space at double-digit parses per minute. Now that I know riding better, I can see just how skilled he is; no weaknesses, no reliances, just like Mirelle. Better. No…it's not a matter of being *better* with Rax, it's a matter of *being*; Mirelle executes flawlessly, but Rax's steed is his body, his breath, his life force. He moves, and the universe moves with him.

Dravik knocks on the open door. Luna jumps off the bed to greet him, barking excitedly. When he walks over and sits in a chair and Luna calms, I find my voice.

"Leyda said the enemy isn't really dead. When they're injured, they turn into the nerve fluid and try to grow back from there…by eating our memories. Our minds."

The prince smiles mildly. "Thoughts, memories—whatever is in a mind, they evolved to eat it. Pre-humans, they would eat one another's minds. Mass cohabitative parasitism, I believe it's called. Like ants if they could raise other ants to eat, and if those ants did not die but continuously grew back."

I stare at his shoulder blankly, letting his words wash over me and through me and trying not to give in to the rising panic.

"Because of this, they are mentally connected to one another. The terms 'hive mind' and 'neural net' have been thrown around by steedcrafters, though neither encapsulates the full depth of their existence. Few human words do."

He leans back in the chair. A curtain in the corner of the room wafts around the shape of an invisible woman.

"All living things require energy. The enemy is no different. Riders are the energy source. They always have been, since the knights of the War. Post-War technology is a hybrid thing, derived by studying the enemy. Hard-light is a derivation of their laser-making. Saddles are their coffins, repurposed into batteries. Anti-grav was created by studying their dark-matter excrement. The Station's main reactor is, itself, a giant saddle being fed."

I suck in a dagger-breath. "The heads being sent below the ocean—"

"The Station's main reactor is there, filled with nerve fluid. It's known as 'the core' by those with high enough clearance."

"I've seen the main reactor," I argue. "It's solar powered. In the Mid Ward—"

"A convenient replica used to refine the energy generated by the true core. Telling the populace we're harnessing the efforts of an enemy still very much alive would not be good for morale, and morale is the only thing standing between the imperative and total chaos."

I clench my sheets and pinpoint my focus on the fleshy scar of my chest. "They're feeding people's brains…to a giant saddle?" His silence, my horror.

"Everyone who's died, every commoner, my mother—" I force words through the grater of my teeth. "*All of them?* For four hundred years?"

"They're trying so hard to be born."

The prince and I are both riveted to the voice; Quilliam stands in the doorway, glassy-eyed and with a pitcher of tea. A silver stream drips beneath his nose and into his mustache…just like when I bled. He doesn't move for a good ten seconds, instead watching the curtain in the corner. Dravik gets up and takes the pitcher from the old man's shaking hands with the gentlest voice I've ever heard him use. "Thank you, Quilliam. That will be all."

Quilliam jolts at the weight lifting, as if he's come back to his senses, dabbing at his nose and backing out of the room. This entire time…it wasn't allergies at all. He's slowly overloading, just like me.

"You—" I turn to Dravik. "You let Quilliam *ride*?"

"He wished to help. After Mother overloaded in Heavenbreaker, the king jetted it down to Esther to destroy it. But it survived. When I found it, it was in very bad shape. I needed to provide it energy to keep it in a steady maintenance mode until I found a proper rider. Quilliam offered to periodically sit in its saddle."

"Her," I correct, steely. "*Her* saddle. You didn't think to tell me this at the beginning of our contract?"

"Would you have believed me if you hadn't understood it for yourself? If I told you the enemy was alive and in the saddle, would you not have thought of me as *more* of a raving lunatic?"

Luna gets up and chases dust particles around the room, nipping at them in pure joy. The curtain in the corner is empty, swinging in the air. I knit my lips shut.

"I'll send ahead the details of your reward for this win. Be sure to rest well—there is a triumvirate conference tonight. I will be in attendance this time—to ensure there is no repeat of the first."

Talking to Rax, he means. Rax and Mirelle helping me. Some part of me hates Dravik and can't hate Dravik, and what spills out is neither asking him to stay or go but *something*, anything.

"Your mother really is in Heavenbreaker's saddle. I'm sure of it."

Dravik pauses at the threshold.

"Leyda's mother overloaded in Hellrunner's saddle, and now she can see her. The saddle remembers them. That's why we can see Astrix—you, me,

Quilliam. Do you ever see Sevrith?"

Dravik's disagreement is so small and sorrowful it only moves his brows. I suck in a breath.

"Just me, then. But why just us? Rax hasn't mentioned seeing any past riders who've overloaded in Sunscreamer. Neither has Mirelle. Why just Hellrunner and Heavenbreaker? The true AI in Luna is holding something inside Heavenbreaker. Why? What needs to be kept inside?"

A thread wavers between us. He cuts it, leaves unceremoniously, and Quilliam toddles in with a pot of hot chocolate, looking much more lucid now.

"It's good to see you feeling better, miss. Your win was very exciting to watch, if a little worrisome."

I sit up in bed. "You watched it?"

"I watch all your matches, miss." He opens his vis, the holographic screen scrolling down a carefully labeled folder of recordings—*Miss vs Yatrice del Solunde* all the way to *Miss vs Her Highness.* "I find myself uploading many of your match highlights to the vis before anyone else does—they're quite popular with the common folk. I have many views."

The pride in his eyes is unmistakable, shining like a star from light-years away.

"Nothing I'm doing is worth pride," I murmur.

Quilliam is quiet, the steam from the chocolate pot spiraling, and then: "I know what you and the master are doing is very grim," he says slowly. "But when I recall how hard you practiced, how much pain you put yourself through…when I see you triumph in the face of adversity, I can't help but feel proud of you, miss."

I clench my pendant, and for what feels like the first time, I smile at him.

68. Proelium

proelium ~(i)ī, *n.*
1. a contest or strife

Rax Istra-Velrayd steadies himself on the sink of the studio and watches silver spiral the drain.

He wipes his nose one last time and straightens, straightens the bloodred lapels of his breast coat. He'd prefer if it was blood coming from his nose. He'd prefer it to stop happening every six hours. But what he prefers in his life has, historically, gone ignored.

Rax prefers, but he doesn't regret. He found it—what Synali meant. He managed to connect to her memory by passing out—he isn't sure why, but he knows it now like logic, like basic math; the source of the memories he sees in the dream is the saddle. That's why riders about to overload see the dream so often; the more time spent in the saddle, the more nerve fluid exposure and the more vivid the dream. Knowing where the memories come from eases his mind. It will kill him, eventually, but at least he *knows* now.

At least, if he passes out in the saddle, he can see her. Be her. Be near her, even if he can't be with her in real life.

He aches to reach for her as they sit at the triumvirate conference, but the Lithroi man sits too close in the crowd, watching Rax blink and breathe in the middle of the two girls. Mirelle's dressed in all black to his right, and Synali sits to his left in blue—her hair short and dark and those beautiful ice eyes riveted forward. The cameras flash nonstop. His hand twitches under the table toward hers, his entire body frothing to be close to her again. Now that he knows what she feels like and tastes like, he can't unknow, and it is *torture*.

Flash.

"Lady Synali, are you nervous about facing Lady Mirelle in the next match?"

Flash. He can feel Synali move without looking at her—heat and closeness as she grips her knees.

"I've come too far to let nerves rule my feelings."

Flash. Mirelle's laugh slides sideways into subzero ice. "Are you certain you have feelings at all, murderer?"

The lights go out. The backup generators hum on.

Flash. *Flash.* ***Flashflashflash.*** Quiet murmurs echo in the dark studio of *"murderer"* and *"what is she talking about?"* The Lithroi man stands, cane kept square before him like a warning.

Mirelle doesn't know or doesn't care, her laugh collapsing on itself. "You're a vicious little pretender—no name or title or honor. And I will show you that on the field."

Rax starts forward in his chair—Mirelle *never* insults other riders; after she fights them and beats them, maybe, but *never* before. It goes against the knightly code she's told him about time and time again: no judgment until impact. Something's wrong—something's *happened*, and he's been too focused on Synali to notice it, but he does now. The way Mirelle's mascara smears, the way her jaw strains. Could it be...

Terren Helgrade is oblivious. "Watching Lady Synali rise through the ranks, well...I think I speak for the entire Station when I say it's been immensely entertaining. You fight her in two days' time, do you not, Lady Mirelle? Would you have anything to say to her?"

The water in Mirelle's eyes turns to steel. "I will accept your surrender now."

Synali's breath catches and releases in the same instant. *"Never."*

Rax stands, motioning to the host and flashing the best golden grin he can.

"I think that's good. We should call it here—everyone is obviously tired—"

"Do you know what it means to ride?"

Synali's soft question to her cousin cuts through. Flash. The king's rider asked the same. Mirelle straightens her neck—looking forward but never to the side.

"It means honor, traitor."

Flashflashflashflash. Synali's ice eyes flicker to him, cold and impervious.

"Do you know what it means to ride?"

Her fierce gaze cuts off all his thoughts. It's a question that is the answer itself, a closed loop—rise and descent. His mouth opens; he'll give her every scorching truth in his body, always—all she has to do is ask.

"It means living."

Flash. Flash. Flash.

"What—" the host starts, nervously smiling. "What does riding mean to you, Lady Synali?"

Rax watches her gaze slide off to the prince standing before the crowd, and then their eyes slide off together—to a shadowed corner of the studio where no one stands—and when she looks back to the cameras, the only thing on her face is a faint, terrifying smile.

0. Caeruleus

caeruleus ~ea ~eum, a.
1. blue
2. connected with the sky; celestial

The recluses have come for Rain at last, in this alleyway behind the studio, and they will find him an easy kill.

He should fight. His survival instincts shout to swing whatever way in whatever hardness to drive back the danger, but the part of him that is Spider and not human — the part of him that is Father and not son — knows: there's no use in fighting. He's lost everything. No Web. No family. Green-One has killed him better than any dagger ever could, and he's staggered from pipe to pipe, scraping life off the walls — water and mold, anything to stop the dust cravings gnawing at his organs. He'd seen Synali's face on the holoscreen, and some dim part of him crawled his body to Mid Ward in one last attempt to reach her. But the recluses cannot be stopped, only delayed, and they are here now. He hears their footsteps too late — too good to be noticed before now. They're better than him.

Rain stoops, hood dripping rust, and steadies himself on a wall with a shaking hand.

"It is a spider's fate to eat other spiders," Father said once. *"That is how they*

survive—cannibalism. What we humans consider unthinkable, a spider does to continue living."

As the footsteps come closer, he feels something stir in him—regret for dying *now*. For not taking Green-One with him. For never telling Synali the danger she was in, for never stopping it. And then, through that crushing spiral of regret, something is *strange*; the footsteps of the recluse are joined by a third step, a hard wooden step on broken asphalt…a cane.

A disguise? Perhaps, but a recluse would abandon such props upon approaching the prey. Rain whirls too late, dagger drawn too late to stop the buzzing heat of a projection sword against his sweating throat, the handle bedecked in sapphires. A washed-out, watercolor sort of man holds it, his face mild and soft as he smiles up at the assassin.

"Good evening."

Rain keeps deathly still, the edge of the sword testing its teeth on his Adam's apple in burn marks. If this man wanted to kill him, speaking would have no point. He's not a recluse; he's a noble—the sapphires give that much away. But a noble *this* good? Which House? Blue sapphires…Trentoch? No—they are indigo and aqua, and this cane wood is silvery, old moonlight like Synali's steed. *Lithroi.*

The oft-rumored exiled prince.

"I know you," Rain says softly.

Lithroi chuckles, the echo chilling the alleyway. "That makes things quite a bit easier, doesn't it?"

"You're the leader of Polaris."

"There are no true leaders in justice," the man corrects. "But I am its smokescreen."

Something of Green-One's lie remains in Rain—nobles playing games with lives—and his heart rankles weakly. "Is that what this rebellion is to you? Just a smokescreen?"

"Forgive me. I misspoke—it is a very important smokescreen. It must be. My father is not a man easily distracted by anything less than the direst of situations, you understand."

The holoscreen flickers above them with a replay. Synali's face sweat-drenched and her thrown lance piercing the princess's tasset.

"You're using her," Rain says. The man smiles wider.

"You of all people would know of 'use,' Sir Spider, and what that truly means."

This man's plans will kill everyone. He cannot tell Synali, but he can stop it, here, now, with what's left of him. A spider eating another spider.

No weapon, but his bones are still sharp. The projection sword cannot be dodged, but it can be leaned into, just enough to get space but not enough to pierce skin, and Rain ducks, throwing a punch beneath the man's gut, but the sword is there, *already*, his knuckles sizzling down to the bone and the smell of burning flesh everywhere. Rain gets around him, but the sword is *there*, again, and the blade burns through his coat and skin and sinew until it reaches the white bone of his elbow. Cold, sharp air hits it like salt in a cut, and he screams, unlike him, not a spider anymore but something louder and clumsier and with less legs, less web, *less family*. The sword cuts his Achilles tendons both, and he staggers to his knees, glaring up at the prince with an icy gaze.

"Y-You...bastard."

Lithroi smiles. "And you the same. You are Synali von Hauteclare's half brother."

Rain's eyes flicker to the hovercarriage pulling away from the studio, silver and blue. "*No*. You lie."

"Often. But not now."

"I can't be—"

"You very much can. All it takes is one night and two people. Duke Farris Hauteclare was not known for his discretion. Unlike Synali's mother, who fled the brothel and hid, yours died in childbirth. The madam contacted House Hauteclare, and they handed you over to the Spiders."

Rain feels his heart crack in two for the woman he's never known, for the girl who was his sister, always and truly. The Lithroi man smiles wider.

"Allow me to give you a choice: die here or aid me in protecting her."

"Protect?" Rain spat blood. "You're using her to start another war. The steed your mother made—the thing inside it—" His lungs give a rattling gasp. "I *saw*. The last one alive controls all of them—tells them what to do. Keeps them docile. The queen didn't overload—she *fed* the one inside Heavenbreaker. Synali's been feeding it this whole time...just like the king's riders. The one in Hellrunner is well-fed, stronger—*so much stronger*. But you're trying to birth a new one to overthrow it."

Lithroi just smiles down at him patiently.

All the places Rain's flesh is now cauterized pull tight, painful with every breath as he says, "You cannot bring back the dead."

The man smiles big enough to slit his eyes.

"Ah, but Sir Spider—what if they were never dead to begin with?"

69. Confractus

confractus ~a ~um, a.
1. *(of a surface)* broken

Moonlight's End has a doorbell, and for the first time, I hear it ring. Quilliam doesn't answer it, and neither does Dravik. Whoever it is keeps ringing insistently, so I head to the entrance and peer into the camera. Tall, broad-chested, disheveled platinum hair. Rax. Breathe. One circle left, and then I'm in the quarterfinals. Once I win that, House Hauteclare is erased. That's all that matters.

I crack open the door, and Rax's warm redwood gaze lights up when he finds me. "Hauteclare! You're—"

"You shouldn't be here," I cut him off. The strain on his lion-bone face hardens.

"I know, but…I know what you mean now. About seeing memories. I made myself pass out in the saddle, and I saw some of yours, and—"

I go stiff. "You didn't stop to think perhaps I don't want you to see my memories?"

"It just…*happened*. I didn't choose it."

The idea of him seeing my life—the squalor, the joy of my childhood, the pain, the brothel… My body wants to reach for him, to take comfort in his arms, but my mind knows better. I start to close the door.

"Her father's dead," Rax blurts. There's only one *her* we both know. "Her father's been…" He pauses, struggling with the reality. "Killed. Because you—" His throat bobs. "And my pings are still blocked, so I—"

Redwood eyes roam me like journey, memorization, yearning. For truth, for me…I'm not sure which. What he feels has never mattered. This is reality, not the saddle, and in reality we're entirely different beasts in entirely different gardens. But he's brought me the final puzzle piece that slides it all into place; Mirelle's cold fury at the triumvirate conference makes sense. Now she knows what it feels like to lose someone she loves dearly. It's in the Hauteclare blood to annihilate one another—Father taught me that. Mirelle is Rax's fiancée, so of course he's worried; his future father-in-law is dead because of me.

It's his family now, too.

"You're shaking." His voice interrupts my thoughts. I look up to see my hand on the door trembling. He reaches over and wraps his warm fingers around my cold ones, and I fight the urge to lean on him, tell him everything; the gardens, the heads, the core, what's inside Heavenbreaker. If I tell him the truth, it'll only position him closer to the chessboard. He's a great rider, but he'd make a poor pawn, and this chessboard is far too heavy for his light smile.

I don't want you to die.

"If Mirelle's father is dead," I say, "then it means he was one of the seven who killed my mother."

Pain flashes hollow on his face, but his recovery is sharp. "You don't have to keep doing this, Hauteclare."

My stomach sinks. He'll never understand, will he? *straighten. harden.*

"Yes I do," I correct. "It's retribution."

"The best retribution—or what the fuck ever—is moving on, living a good life. Let them live with whatever bad shit they've done."

My laugh is all teeth. "If I leave them alone, do they not thrive? Do you think any of the illustrious Hauteclares would give a second thought to the blood of a bastard and her sick mother on their hands? Would they not celebrate their unity under my death? The '*preservation*' of their '*honor*'? Would they not go on to live even better lives because I died?"

His silence is answer itself.

"Are you truly asking me to move on when they won't even blink when

I'm gone?"

The courtyard watches us with all its repentant, empty-eyed marble angels. I laugh until it grows too bitter to swallow anymore.

"I stand by my original summation of your character, Velrayd—you're a fool. A talented fool, but a fool nonetheless."

The redwood of his gaze blazes hot, his hand squeezing mine. "Let me come in, Synali."

His first time calling me by my real name. And his last.

I smile a Dravik smile. "No."

I pull away and shut the door in one fluid move. His shout echoes around the courtyard.

"You can't keep going like this—alone! Alone and doing reckless shit over and over on the tilt like it means nothing, all for this old creep of a Lithroi who's straight-up using you!"

"You are your House's son, Velrayd. Turn around and go back to your banquets and your glorious fetes and your pretty marriage. There's nothing for you here."

"I want there to be something!"

The obsidian in his voice is molten, raw, flooding the courtyard and encasing it all in a quick-cooling shell. A moment frozen in time. My breath feels like ten—the pain in my heart distant but tearing its way to fresh.

"If I didn't make it fucking obvious enough, I want you—I want you to be safe."

"So you can fight me," I lead.

"So I can—so we can…"

talk. touch. The thoughts come unbidden into my head, like the saddle—like hearing someone else ring their intent clear at me. I touch the door, imagining his heat. *impossible.* The halo on his forehead is perfect. The halo on Mirelle's, perfect. The halo on his father-in-law's forehead must've been perfect, too, before Dravik killed him.

He's marrying into my family. A family I *must* destroy.

impossible.

I walk away from the door. Rax's shouts pierce from outside, but his exact words slip through my fingers like sand, and then Dravik's low tone reverberates. There's a scuffle, a shout. A red hovercarriage leaves the driveway minutes later, and something in my chest shuts tight when it goes.

It's impossible—I know that now.

The fire burns until its end.

With the diamond pendant, I grind out the penultimate circle. I lean on the wall—enough calluses by now that my fingers do not bleed anymore. In the dying artificial sunset, only one circle remains.

Only I remain.

70. Stilla

stilla ~ae, f.
1. a drop of liquid

IN THE HEART OF THE WORLD, there are whispers.

The new scientists come in on their first day and settle quickly; there is work to be done, and all of it rather strange. They were given no explanation for their sudden deployment, though it is not uncommon to rotate the highly specialized in steedcraft. But an entire team all at once? Some of them whisper of an information leak, a mole, but for whom? Competing steedcraft companies, they could understand, but the core of the Station is its *battery*. All the power generated here is pumped to every substation, every ward, every water purifier, every grav-gen and ventilation system. Who would dare to interfere with what keeps them all alive?

They don't know the manifestations will begin on the third day, but a woman named Ysolde knows instantly that something is wrong.

She is the new head of the core team—freshly twenty-eight and yet the brightest steedcrafting star the Station has seen in years. She shuts her vis on her first lunch break with a vicious sort of gusto—Mother is pressuring her into settling down, and Ysolde's best defense is reminding her again and again that an obsession with marriage is for nobles, not a Mid Ward farming family. She's alone in the control room—the rest having gone to explore the kitchen options—and she's in the middle of opening her vacuum-sealed mince pie when she sees it.

At first, she thinks the bloodstain in the aft seam of her console is an illusion—a trick of the core's massive light waves that wash everything in periwinkle. But then she touches it, and it flakes. Knowing better than to alarm her team on their very first day, Ysolde pretends she hasn't searched every inch of the control room when they return. She smiles and feigns interest in the idea of fondue and grips the bloodied swab in her pocket. She runs it on her own time, in her own living room, in her own machine. By the light of the artificial moon, she reads the resulting match twice, then thrice.

TRAKE CALODOS

His name is familiar—a man she wrote papers on, a man who wrote the very textbooks she studied on xenotrophic spongiform encephalopathy, and a man who would not be out of place leading the core team himself; a man who dropped abruptly from corporate steedcrafting to go private. A man with his blood now on her console.

She asks someone she knows—an ex, a fling, it doesn't matter. What matters is that he's better at security than she is, and he warns her: Trake Calodos's vis hasn't been active for a month, and the implication hangs in her mind—a vis is not inactive unless its user is dead. He warns her again: core command is the most highly monitored scientific wing in the Station. And this implication hangs heavier: *they are watching her every move.*

When Ysolde comes into the core on the third day, her team is gathered in a gaggle at the foot of it, staring up at the extruders. They aren't supposed to be here, ever, and yet there are seven of them. *Eight.* They are a beautiful sign of failure. She's only ever seen them once—and never so many—during her doctorate studies in the king's containment units rife with gold dragon sigil. Her mind spins; the most dangerous thing about them is that, if allowed to, they grow exponentially. And yet they are *not* allowed to. Not fully. Not like this. That's why the king's steed exists—to command, to redirect the unfathomable energy of their attempt at regrowth into the Station's pylons and refining systems. But now they seem to be ignoring it. After four hundred years of obeying quietly, they are...

This is not just failure. This is *catastrophic* failure. A failure that, apparently, the previous team could not fix. Even Trake Calodos could not fix it—and he was killed for it. Ysolde doesn't know by who, or how, but she knows if she fails she will be next.

"Contact the Westriani fuel depot," she says into her vis. "Tell them I need all the heads they have. Immediately."

71. Universus

ūniversus ~a ~um, a.
1. whole, entire
2. universal

Avase waits in my tourney hall dressing room with a single tiger lily in it, a note wrapped 'round its neck in twine and gold ink.

Until eternity,

J.

I can hear it—the meaning beneath the ink, beneath his words. It's inevitable that we'll meet. Like the eternity of space or the loop of the rise and the descent, he and I will inevitably meet. In the tourney hall, I stare at the Ressinimus banner hanging next to the Lithroi banner. *Gold and silver. A4 and A3, holding hands.* I am Dravik's pawn, and J is the king's. Gold dragon, the sun. Silver rabbit, the moon.

Hunting each other forever across the heavens.

Mirelle's father was named Grigor Ashadi-Hauteclare.

He was the tall, good-looking sort with a salt-and-pepper beard, his eyes the warmest brown—he didn't choose to wear the Hauteclare eyes even though he married into them. Still, their winter poison eventually reached him. Grigor went with the assassin to make sure the job was done properly that night—insurance for a family who couldn't leave anything to chance.

In the dressing room, I watch the video Dravik sent over and over. Grigor in a thick coat and disguising hat. Neon Low Ward reflected in puddles at his shoes, too finely made to be anything but noble. It's always the shoes that give them away—they never sacrifice their comfort for anyone. His eyes dart every which way down the alley as he keeps watch, as if expecting the worst at any time. The video is only twenty seconds—surveillance-drone footage, possibly. A nobleman lingering in alleys is a commonplace sight in Low Ward; always waiting, always looking. Always reaping advantage.

Preying.

A church cross hangs its shadow over Grigor as he stands outside a familiar patched-tin door. The ten o'clock tram wails overhead. As he coughs into his fine leather gloves, my mother's throat is slit. Twenty seconds replayed over and over, but my eyes never flicker away from him, the silent knife of knowledge twisting in my brain; *if she hadn't given birth to me, she'd still be alive.* The Spider's Hand assassin comes out of the door on the vis, and my eyes drink in every detail: his lean body only hidden so much by the dark, finely scaled armor, his face obscured by that nightmare cowl.

"Is it done?" Grigor asks the assassin worriedly—worried for himself, for the family, yet not for the family inside that door. The cowl nods.

"Both of them are dead."

Why did he lie? I knew he did, or in the six months I spent plotting Father's death they would've sent someone else to finish me. I lived for six months thinking each time I rested my head on my pillow it'd be my last, my throat slit in the night. My finger switches back and forth, rewinding to hear his one sentence ad infinitum so I can memorize it.

"Then let us hurry away before someone sees," Grigor hisses urgently. The video loops. He'll never speak again. Dravik sent pictures of his body—just his feet hanging in those beautiful leather shoes.

The door to the dressing room suddenly creaks open, and the makeup artist comes in, all smiles. I shut the vis quickly.

"Oh, that's a gorgeous flower." She looks at J's vase. "I think that one means someone's proud of you."

I say nothing. She clears her throat.

"It's an important day today, isn't it? One of your last matches. And against the amazing Lady Mirelle, no less."

A quiet.

"N-Not that you aren't amazing, too! I watch all your matches with my kids…we love them! You're such a unique rider. The way you keep coming back stronger against all those nobles—it's inspiring." Her smile behind me seems bigger in the mirror. "Your parents must be very proud."

"I killed my parents."

Her fingers stutter, and her brush falls. It's the first time I've said it out loud, bitter and true, and it will never hurt any less.

"I'm sorry—I'm sorry I assumed." Her eyes move to her paint pots almost desperately. "Did you have…um. Have a color in mind for today?"

The rainbow is laid out before me—gold catching my eye, red catching my eye. But there was only ever one real color for me. "Black."

I stare at my darkly lined eyes in the mirror until the fifteen-minute siren rings out. It reflects my face back at me; not as thin as I used to be. Not as terrified, some red back in my cheeks—like Mother before her sickness ate her. I look like her. Even if she's gone, even if my mind is eaten completely, even if I don't remember what her face looks like, I can still see her in me.

The crowd *seethes* outside my chamber.

Dravik stands beneath the Lithroi banner, unbothered and ringed by three dozen private security guards in full silver armor. They allow me and only me into the bubble of faux calm. I walk past him and to the hangar door. The prince knows I've studied Mirelle Ashadi-Hauteclare most of all. His words ring after me.

"She is very good."

"I know," I agree over my shoulder. "But I will be better."

Inside the hangar, the light of the saddle beckons. And this time, a woman waits beside it. I walk toward her. She doesn't waver, doesn't disappear—her outline is strong and clear, her pale hair and bluish dress fluttering in a nonexistent breeze as she smiles at me. Her mouth moves, every bell-word ringing impossibly deep in the hangar.

"do you know what it means to ride?"

No. Yes. How would I even begin? To ride is so many different things at once. It's pain and death and bravery. It is both striving and giving up. It's moving and moving again better. It's both blistering heat and bone-chilling cold, lust and battle-lust; silence and screaming in silence. It's escaping reality and facing it. It's when two people meet at the very center of their beings with fear, and without fear.

It means different things to different riders.

Dravik was right; riders are riders because they impact. I've impacted so many times, now. I've changed since the beginning, and unchanged. I look up at marble walls, at glass ceilings, at space; at Heavenbreaker's massive helmet outside the hangar—the graceful crescent gleaming silver like a moon. Like overload. I look into Astrix vel Lithroi's silver eyes, into the very center of her tiny pupils, like sun-closed pinpricks.

"do you know what it means to ride?"

"I will move forward until I do."

"**G**oooooood morning, ladies and gentlefolk! I hope you've all had your rest, because you'll need every drop of it to watch today's scintillating match between two rider heavyweights battling it out for their position in the quarterfinals!"

"Gress, it's more accurate to only call one of them a heavyweight, considering this is the other's very first tourney."

"Great point, Bero. Even more reason to keep your eyes glued to the vis, folks! We'll be back for first tilt after these messages from our sponsors! Don't go anywhere, or we might chug your ale!"

The depressurized hatch drops away from beneath Heavenbreaker's greaves, and we fall into weightless, star-studded space. *jets.* The saddle shudders, my eardrums crackling. The thrum of it moves through both of us, a harp string plucked hard. Courage. Both of us vibrate at the same intensity, the same high note rung inside together—a far cry from our fearful beginning.

us.

Gold plasma streaks in the distance, and the arena opens on either side at the same time, Mirelle and I entering in the same breath. We go still in the same breath, white and blue steeds frozen opposite each other. The holoscreen pops up with an impeccable white rider's suit; a suit I remember still—every cling of it to my body, the sensation of being trapped in it, of being *them.* The winged lion splashes proudly gold over her helmet, and on her forehead is a perfect halo—blacklight catching the gold of her eyes. Her father is dead because of me. But I gave him his chance to come forward. I gave them all their chance.

And so too does Mirelle Ashadi-Hauteclare give me mine.

"This is my last warning." She says it like frostbitten steel, a cruel bent to her voice where pride used to be. "Surrender now, murderer, or you will regret it."

they did not regret it when they slit my mother's throat.

Mirelle is them and yet not them; she doesn't hide or try to stab me from the back. She hates me, but she's always come at me from the front, strong and true. She is *noble*. A knight, almost. In another life, we are friends. *sisters.*

My head tilt, an easy thing. My smile, easier. "Make me."

I cut comms and jet for my tilt, and she does the same. Finally, I get to see Ghostwinder with my own eyes—the herald of my father, the messenger of his will. It's an immaculate recreation of the finest paintings, of the naked and the damned sculpted in impossibly smooth muscle—more human than Talize's Sineater, even, and yet softly striving beyond humanity. Every part of it is perfectly balanced in the torso and arms and waist. Gentle swells of metal imitate human muscle on the ribs, the thighs, the biceps. In stark contrast to all the mortal humility, it bears an otherworldly mane attached to the faintly leonine helmet that flows out in pure gold hard-light. The whole of it is painted paper white, and yet it has gold fingers, gold feet—everything that touches the world stained in gold.

The winged-lion sigil cuts gold in the very center of its chest.

The cheers are loud for but a second, everything going quiet as something shifts under my skin. *Our* skin. I didn't move, but something moves inside me, long and *under*—a new thing between Heavenbreaker and me. Not instinct or memory; it's a real, physical sensation slithering under the material of my suit and along my spine, up my back, between my shoulder blades.

Something's in here with me. And this time I feel it not in my mind but *in my body.*

Fear drills at my edges, but inevitability sews me back together; one circle left—every moment has led to this.

My own resolve reverberates, Heavenbreaker's presence acting like a wall the sound bounces off. I have pity for my opponent, for once—pity that she'll never understand, pity for her mistake of loving others without question, pity for being born into a House of winter and rot. *pity that we couldn't stand together, just once.* Honor or no honor, I have no doubt she'll try to kill me for what I've done.

That, too, is what it means to ride.

"Riders, prepare yourselves for first tilt!"

The tilts right themselves with a metallic clank, locking into place. Mirelle's gauntlet instantly goes full with her white lance. Heavenbreaker's lance appears in my hand like quicksilver. The Station slowly rotates in space, roaring into the mouth of the cold dragon:

"In the name of God, King, and Station!"

72. Vorago

vorāgō ~inis, *f.*
1. a deep hole or chasm; watery hollow

My heart beats.
"Three!"
The silver spirals writhe.
"Two!"
Every finger, clenched.
"One!"
Flowers bloom in space—daisies and hyacinths.
Zero.
The brilliant white-and-gold steed blasts into ignition.
Every single jet on our body is a blue sun.
This is the very point of the knife; the very point of my lance held straight and deadly. The two of us are lances—mirror-image incisors gunning for each other. We've been gunning for each other without knowing it since the day we were born. Bastard, noble. In another world, she's me and I'm her; annihilation, two particles that can never exist in the same space-time, born to aim for each other's throats until one no longer exists.

faster. hotter. more.

Heavenbreaker's agreement is wordless as she burns past her limits. There is no limit. We're together, and together means everything is possible. Inside Heavenbreaker, I can bring them inevitability. With Heavenbreaker, I'm stronger than despair. I know now: a true victory is won together.

that, too, is what it means to ride.

The parsemeter steadily increases, g-forces like fingers of giants tearing at my eyeballs, my tongue. The winged lion on Ghostwinder's chest grows closer, quicker. Every thought comes faster than blinking; *blink*—her arm's too low to be anything but a Waites-Reinhardt maneuver aimed at my legs. She thinks it's an easy hook on me, like Helmann, like Yatrice.

Blink—too transparent. Anyone who's watched my matches would do it, which means it's exactly what she *isn't* going to do. *Blink*—she's feinting, but there are only so many maneuvers you can feint into from Waites-Reinhardt. I can't remember all the names, but the shapes of them, the steps you take to form them…I know those. *watch.* I watch even as the giant tears out my eyes. The silver whorls vibrate like light spots in my vision.

there!

The shift—among the blistering speed and smearing stars, her shoulder rolls back in its socket, her legs splaying—readying her frame to absorb repeated sudden changes in direction. She's covering her bases, pre-countering, but…her gold knees are too wide. Overextension either means inexperience or specificity—the former doesn't apply to her. She's not covering bases at all; she's aiming. All her jets are engaged, none reserved or waiting in the wings.

She wants to hit one spot.

Heavenbreaker's worry: *"which? where? quickly."*

Her strength is her weakness—her family. The two of us boil with the same ruthless winter blood. If I wanted to utterly wipe someone off the face of the arena, I know exactly what I'd do.

she's going to helmet hit me in the first round.

Correction: she's going to *try.*

She knows I avoid well. She knows I act on instinct. But she doesn't know I've studied. So many weeks ago, Rax cornered me with a needle of my own flaws, and so I pored over the academy books again. The Hverfa semi-hexagon… It's dangerous, using it to dodge a helmet hit, and I hold no delusions—she'll see it coming. Just not soon enough.

"kind," Heavenbreaker insists. *"he was so kind."*

no, I counter. *he was fuel.*

In the midst of assuming the Hverfa semi-hexagon, there's a pop in my ears, a loosening of the Heavenbreaker over me—our opposite thoughts weakening the mental wax holding us together—and our stance unravels. *scrabble.* **Calm.** *panic.* **Don't panic.** The grav-gen grows close and brightly blue. His breast coat, red. Mother's throat, red.

he is gone. we remain.

Truth from the both of us like agreement. Heavenbreaker fuses in close again, heavy like armor, like regret. Mirelle's white lance spears toward us, its gold tip true, and then there's the zenith of all pressure, the drumbeat roar of blood in my ears. Brace softly.

Impact.

Time and all its teeth slow, illuminated by the white light between us. Like camera flashes, like lightning, like hair, like stars—white light stretches long and loud with the deep cry. The gold lancepoint juts forward just past our nose. *Slow.* Everything is so *slow,* and our own body feels heavy, like being tied to cement blocks.

release.

The Hverfa semi-hexagon snaps—all our muscles going slack. Three joints click into place, falling neatly into the empty space we held for them. Our helmet falls with us, neck crashing flat to our chest, the sudden pain like sunspots, but gravity makes the dodge for us faster than we ever could. Mirelle's lance sears over my skull, catching hairs but not metal. *Close.* Too close—a nanosecond later and she would've had us.

Red, 0. Blue, 0.

The merciful release of the rise only relieves some of the tension. Agony stabs at our neck, but we can still move. The holoscreen flashes to life then, Mirelle's chest heaving.

"You've made a mistake, traitor."

My smile drips sweat. "That's a strange thing to call success."

She stares at me—gold eyes beneath black eyeliner like a bruise. She's alone. I can see it now. I can *hear* it as clear as a bell rung with intent—she's lonely.

"Mirelle, your father helped kill my mother. He was there in the alley, waiting—"

"I DON'T WANT TO HEAR IT!"

Her roar is crystal shattering—something broken and pristine, the first heartbreak of an angel.

"I have proof," I whisper. "For all of them—what they did. What your father did."

"Made by whom?" Her sneer is vicious. "Your rat benefactor? The fallen crown prince who surely holds no grudge against each and every one of the noble Houses for coercing the king into throwing his mother aside? Yes." She laughs, shrill. "Yes! I'm sure the proof you have isn't fabricated in the slightest!"

My own doubts claw at me. Dravik's using me, but I agreed to it. We're using each other. The *Endurance*, Theta-7, more I don't know about—he's killed so many people. He's made me stronger, given me a sword in Heavenbreaker. He's protected me from the assassins, from House Hauteclare, from everyone.

he's protected me as my father never did.

"You're a tool of revenge, traitor." She lifts her lance. "Not a rider."

"And you, cousin," I say softly, "ride a symbol of a murderer's pride."

"The duke was a kind man—"

"My father was a murderer." I slice her argument off at the knees. "Just like me."

That physical feeling slithers through my back again, over it, between the vertebrae and more prominent this time. *jealousy.*

"Did your uncle give you candy?" I ask, strained. "Did he pick you up and twirl you around whenever he saw you? Did he call you pretty and smart? Did my father send you to the academy with the best care while I starved in the streets?" Something in me cracks down the very center. He was kind to *her*. He protected *her*.

Her fist tightens on her lance. Mine loosens.

"I have seen the powerful murder the weak while smiling, Mirelle, and call it mercy."

"My father was no murderer!" she shrieks.

"No. He just watched the assassin's back while he did it. He chose to be the knife. As I choose to be the lance. As you can choose, right now, to step aside. I must win this Cup. There is nothing else for me but winning. But you...you have a fiancé waiting. You have a life—"

"YOU'VE TAKEN IT ALL!"

The crystal shatters again, and this time forever. Her body rocks in the saddle with her scream, teeth flashing, fists clutching her head, white-gold steed clutching its helmet.

"You've taken *everything* from me! My father—his honor, *our* honor! You twisted us all—you twisted Rax until he turned his back on me! You corrupted him and my father and my House! *You've ripped everything apart!* ***You've taken it all!***"

The rise rounds and ends. The descent begins. Her visor dissipates with her thrashing, and then she goes completely still, head tilted up. Black mascara streaks down her face like melting ice. Tears. Her neck arcs down, slow, her beautiful face utterly wiped clean of emotion. Nothing remains in her irises— no warmth. A gaze I know so well: the gaze of a girl who's lost everything.

I hear it, and then I *hear* it. She speaks, but not with a noble's voice. No pride. No affectation. All that's left in her are bells ringing dire with intent, with the true meaning of every single word—a rider's voice.

"You have taken everything from me, traitor. And now, I will take it back."

73. Aes

aes aeris, *n.*
1. payment
2. debt

Rax Istra-Velrayd feels the cold first.

Cold metal blazes under his stomach, his arms—everywhere around him. Faintly, his foggy brain notes that he's naked. Shallow wounds sting on his knuckles: a fight. He remembers visiting Moonlight's End and the pit in his stomach when Synali closed the door on him. He remembers the former prince coming up to him and then darkness…but wherever he is now is freezing cold. He'll live—long enough to sit up, at least. He straightens on the metal, a few colors and fewer shapes settling into vision.

He's in a cell.

No windows. A single LED is suspended from the ceiling, shedding sickly light. There's a vent, but it's too high up to fiddle with; water in a bucket and a sealed hatch in the floor for shit and piss and nothing else. Smooth metal walls, smooth metal floor…this place was clearly built to keep someone in.

Rax snorts, rolling his shoulder and working the knots out. If his captor thinks this is bad, they should see a steed's cockpit after two weeks straight of training. Nosebleeds all the time, bruises all the time. Back then—he chuckles to himself—he had to shit in the corner, and the g-forces would always smear it back on him somehow. And water? Water was a *privilege* you *earned* with recited maneuvers and correct positioning, not just lying around to drink from whenever. So when a door suddenly opens in his cell wall, Rax leans back, hands behind his head leisurely, and smiles.

"Pretty nice place you got here."

The tap of a sapphire cane heralds an equally pleased smile on a forgettable face, hair like a well-groomed swathe of sand. The former prince.

"I'm glad you find it to your liking. There's nothing less tasteful than providing guests with ill-fitting chambers."

"Is that what I am?" Rax asks coolly. "A guest? Can I request a quick wardrobe change, then?"

He motions down to his bare skin, but Lithroi smiles like a snake preparing to unhinge its jaw—a smile almost as bad as Mother's. Rax suppresses a shudder.

"I'm afraid not," Lithroi says. "Not until our business is concluded. It's a matter of security, you see—you are engaged to the sort of family who is not above bugging the very clothes you wear."

"Sorry to burst your bubble, but my father's tagged my vis, so he probably knows where I am."

"I've taken care of that. It was rather elementary in its design."

Rax scoffs. What time is it, anyway? Are Mirelle and Synali fighting, or is it already over? He doubts Lithroi would tell him. Plans flash through his brain; he's much taller than the prince—he could bull-rush him, but...his face wound from that cane sword still smarts. Overpowering's off the table. Talking it is, then.

"Where am I?"

"Where I want you," Dravik says simply. A sudden thud against the right wall resounds. Again. Repeated, like something trying to get out.

"Who is that?" Rax frowns.

"Your neighbor. If all goes well, you'll meet eventually, but let us take things one step at a time. I assume you know of Sevrith cu Freynille's fate?" The water shivers in the bucket between them. Rax narrows his eyes. The Lithroi man widens his. "I'd like to tell you a story, Sir Istra-Velrayd."

Rax clicks his tongue. "Not really good with those."

"Imagine an ant. This ant belongs to a colony. One winter day, when food is scarce, the colony discovers a bit of honey trapped on an island. This island is surrounded by a lake. The only way to cross it is if the ants line their bodies up and make a bridge over the water, so that other ants might walk across and collect the much-needed food. You are an ant assigned to the bridge. You will drown. You know this. You do it anyway, not because you love your fellows or care for them, but because they *are* you. You feel what they feel. You see what they see. You will continue on, even when you die."

Rax swallows. Dravik smiles wider.

"Surely you know the nerve fluid in the saddle belongs to the enemy."

"Obviously."

"What if I told you the enemy was like the ants? They weren't themselves—they were *all*. The concept of '*self*' does not exist to them and never will."

Rax doesn't like the creeping doubt; in the dream, he's always someone else, not himself.

"Consider this, Sir Istra-Velrayd: long ago, a knight of the War lost her husband to the enemy. He was a rider. After he dies, this knight loses everything. She throws herself onto the battlefield with no regard for her own life and finds she is able to maneuver her steed with astonishing skill and brutality, destroying dozens of the enemy. This is recorded. Rachale de Ressinimus, the—"

"Greatest knight of the War," Rax finishes. "Her kill count was over thirteen hundred before she died. No one else came close."

Dravik puts his hands over his cane. "Rachale's longing for death turned her into an ant."

"What? That's nonsense—"

"Of course it is!" The prince begins to pace and gesture passionately. "It makes no sense. Humans know that life is better than death—we are programmed to survive no matter what. We cannot hope to understand the ant because we are not ants. We do not understand that the ant does not die—it continues on in the honey that feeds, that honey becoming another ant, another eye, another nose, another way to see the world. An ant is born from that ant's death, but it is the *same ant*, because it feels and experiences the exact same things in its life and in its death. It is bound by the universe, by heat and cold and hunger and physics, as we all are."

Rax hates the way the prince's words cling to him—how they sound mad and not-so-mad at once. Dravik stops pacing and turns abruptly to face him.

"If a human seeks death, they become like the ant. Their brain turns differently—their way of seeing the world becomes more like the enemy's. And the nerve fluid in the steed can sense that—it opens up to others of its kind, because it is an animal that functions in a hive. The enemy embraces those who seek death more readily than those who cling to life, because this is what it understands. The language and mind of the enemy is alien to us and always will be, but death brings us closer to understanding each other."

Lithroi deftly upends the water bucket then, liquid slithering across the metal floor as he seats himself on its underside. Still smiling. *Still smiling* as Rax struggles to put it together in his head.

"That's why," Rax says at last. "That's why you chose Synali to ride for you. Because she has a death wish. And Helmann…"

"He sought death, too. Caked himself in it, really. It has no inherent morality to it—it simply sets the good riders apart from the exceptional ones. After a certain point in the War, the knights were encouraged to embrace it because their commanders knew of the death-advantage, and we clinched victory shortly afterward. Every great rider in history has had a personal relationship with death. You experienced it yourself as a young boy, forced to ride Sunscreamer. You wanted to die back then, didn't you?"

Rax clenches his fists. It shouldn't make sense. Is that why Dravik tried so hard to keep them apart, keep Synali insulated—so she wouldn't find reasons to live? It's too cruel, too calculating to even think of.

He grasps at some semblance of focus; if Lithroi wanted to kill him, he wouldn't've bothered stripping him naked and cold and sore on the metal. He *wants something* from him.

"Why am I here, Your Highness?"

The mad fervor fades from the prince's eyes. "Why do you think?"

"You brought me here because you want me to stay away from Synali forever or some shit, right?" Rax leans in, all muscle, water seeping under his bare feet and rage seeping into his eyes—rage that this old conniving fuck is using her for power just like his parents use him. His words come far softer than his clenched knuckles. "You can't make me, Your Highness—no matter how much you cut me. Cut my balls off, cut my dick off, cut my tongue out—I don't give a shit. I'm not giving her up. So you might as well kill me and get it over with."

"Yes. You seem quite fascinated with her." Dravik brushes past his declaration. "Which is why I'm hoping you'll agree to my proposition."

Rax's reflection in the puddle goes still, brows cinching. "What sort of proposition?"

The prince smiles like a fox given permission to pounce. "Have you heard of a steed called Hellrunner?"

"No shit."

"Are you aware of what its true purpose is?"

"To kick rider ass when we fall out of line. So we don't get any ideas about being better than the king. About…" He swallows. Yavn. "…rebelling."

The prince laughs. "Indeed. Hellrunner is always powerful, no matter who rides it."

Rax's mind keels, takes on water, and the water is Mirelle's nonstop chatter about Hellrunner over the years—its riders overload so quickly. Something wrong with Hellrunner. Something wrong with Heavenbreaker, too.

He lurches, but Lithroi doesn't stop him, Rax's fists tight in the prince's collar and his hiss tighter: *"What have you done to her?"*

The prince never blinks, his grin splitting his jaw wide.

"It's not what I have done, Sir Istra-Velrayed, but rather, what my mother did. I'm simply here to see it through, like any good noble son would do."

74. Animus

animus ~ī, *m.*
1. the soul, life force
2. the mind as the seat of consciousness

The rise ends.

Ghostwinder and Heavenbreaker face each other. The grav-gen is inescapable, pulling us into oblivion and beckoning forth all of what we are into its furnace. But Mirelle isn't dedicating her lance one way or another—not now, and not a second later. Not two seconds later.

"something's wrong," Heavenbreaker rings.

She's right—Mirelle isn't raising her lance high enough or sharp enough. I can see her shaking with fury—Ghostwinder's flowing gold mane trembling—but she's not holding her weapon in any meaningful way. I could hit her helmet; she's leaving herself wide open for it. Her defenses are shot, gaping as if she doesn't care.

"careful," Heavenbreaker warns, then makes it sweeter: *"careful, friend."*

A real friend. My only friend.

Space pulls at my nerves. Gravity peels my eyelids open. What is Mirelle trying to *do*, and why is it *nothing*? I grip our lance in a clear Suero bridge-ender—a maneuver that's all helmet, *painfully obviously* helmet, but she doesn't even flinch, not a single brace or shift of weight or rerouting of jetpower. She's just neutral and furious and nothing else. I'm going to hit her. I'm going to *win*.

Both of us blaze past terminus—blue and gold light screaming toward annihilation. Our silver lance aims exactly at Mirelle's golden mane. The rabbit and the lion can never be friends—the lion has too many teeth, and the rabbit has none.

i will win.

In my mind's eye, I see the last circle being scratched out.

rest, mother.

The light. The cry.

The *pain*.

But…she didn't hit me! She didn't even *move*, but my body fills with pain like a jar under a spout; from my feet to my legs, my muscle fibers seize up harder than wood, stiff, clenching in on themselves. *Where?* Where did she hit? *How?* My hand contracts, a perfect ring, the lance shooting out of it the moment my grip locks, gravity rocketing it backward and away from me and into the stars.

Stars.

Stars that seem somehow bigger, closer, more silver. Covered in silver.

My eyes are filling with silver.

There's a voice not ours, a voice like bells—a rider's voice. It's impossible with the comms closed, and yet it's here in my brain as close as Heavenbreaker; it's Mirelle's voice, as if she's standing just next to me, whispering:

goodbye, traitor.

She's done something. I don't know what or how, but she's done *something* to me—something terrible and silver and familiar. **Overload.**

I can't fight it, the stiffness reaching my neck, my ears. A piercing ring ricochets between my eyes, the dome of my skull, vibrating me from the inside out. The handkerchief is gone; I can't even feel it, reach for it. No square, no cloth—my body is entirely unfeeling. No escape.

Heavenbreaker cries sorrow.

The ringing crescendos, and my eardrums burst—blood. I can't feel anything anymore, and I shouldn't be able to hear but I can—a sound I've always known: the cry between steeds, but so incredibly loud. *Loud*, not with two voices but a *million*.

And then black.

I'm dead.

No—if I were really dead, there wouldn't be trees.

White trees, grown with people. Enough of them grouped together is called a forest; if I were truly dead, I wouldn't be able to remember that. I wouldn't be able to see the thousands of figures standing among the trees, their silver eyes glowing and their pinprick pupils all silently locked on me.

all of them wearing different-colored rider's suits.

I can't remember what I'm doing here, only that I failed; Mirelle, the silver tears, Heavenbreaker crying. The riders vanish, the trees replaced by a memory. I'm a woman staring at a man I know, but a younger version—red hair braided with wooden beads, an amber crown on his head.

King Ressinimus.

"Leave it, Astrix. Your only concern for the future should be of Draviticus's raising."

I step forward. "Yarrow, listen to me, please. There will be no future for him—for any of us—if we do not let them go."

The king scoffs. "It would ruin the Station."

"It would put right what was made wrong. I cannot raise my son on a ground that shakes beneath him. I refuse to build higher a rotten world for him to inherit. I want better for him—"

The king throws open the curtain of a window to the stars and black outside. "Look—we are alone! There is no one, *nothing*! You would have me condemn my people to freeze in space or suffocate on a gas giant that cannot sustain them just for your morals? The core is our only lifeboat, and we must cling to it with all our power or **we die.**"

Memory. My hands now rest on a holographic keyboard. My fingers fly, half-finished milk coffee in a crystal decanter and exhaustion in my very bones. In unforgiving white letters, the screen reads: HEAVENBREAKER.EXE. The strings of symbols and numbers I type are illegible to me and yet understood by Astrix; the true AI will keep the thing inside Heavenbreaker safe.

Two intact enemies had been smart enough to hide inside the steeds—escaping death where their brethren were annihilated. The A4 was repurposed to keep the core in check, but she can't believe she uncovered the A3, let alone the fact the starving enemy inside it hadn't been harvested for the core. When the post-War federation found it, it must've been too weak to give off any detectable signal. It's shrunken now, but as it grows, the true AI she's been writing since her teen years will scramble and disperse its energy signature so that Hellrunner and the king cannot find it. *All we need is one.* All it will take is one living enemy to challenge the other, and the order of the core will collapse. The enemy will be freed, rather than so cruelly used and abused.

The king's greatest strength, used against him.

We look to our side. A broken silver steed hangs by its arms from the bunker's ceiling, crescent-moon helmet shining in the fluorescent lights. Little bare feet resound, and we turn to see a red-haired boy no older than six clutching a blanket close, pajamas rumpled and green eyes drowsy-heavy.

"Mum? Are you not sleeping again?"

We kiss him on the head with heartbreak in our chest.

"You must go to bed, Dravik. Your first day at the academy is tomorrow."

The memory vanishes, replaced by a grand redwood courtroom—our hands in our blue-silver-dress lap and hundreds of nobles watching, waiting. At the head of it all sits the king—our husband—and next to him, the judge, who slams his gavel to quiet the crowd.

"Does the defendant have anything to say before the verdict is read?"

I—Astrix stands up. She holds her head high, fear and determination seamlessly woven in her heart, and speaks with the clearest voice.

"My peers, my fellows, my family, I do not ask for forgiveness. I only ask for the king to tell his people the truth. In lying, the royal family shackles us to an imperative made by desperate men long dead. The truth is power, and the people of this Station deserve to decide its fate for themselves."

The noble crowd's murmur buzzes loud and angry, but the judge bangs the gavel again, and Astrix speaks in the following silence.

"I ask every one of you this: Do you know what we do to survive? Do you know the blood we shed that is not our own? Do *you* know what it means to ride?"

The crowd's roar rises, but the memory instantly fades into a cockpit—a very familiar saddle. A woman rests in it, her pale hair a mess and her limbs askew and her smiling face drenched in silver tears.

And then she gets up.

I watch in horror as her body jerks back to life, pushing out of the saddle in a weak, discarded-doll stagger. She stumbles backward to her feet, wiping the silver from her face without once losing that smile. And then she lunges for me.

Darkness.

Astrix is gone. There's only darkness around me…around *us*. Us, because I know I'm not alone—the feeling of being watched is here all at once and *bigger than it's ever been*, and it sends my hair on end, my overloaded body warning me in a pitch-perfect mimicry of real mortal danger: something is here, just in front of me. Something unseeable.

Something *massive*.

It shifts in space, rainbow moving in the darkness like a ripple moving through liquid glass. Like Rax's textbook vid. It's so close I could reach out and touch it. That high, soft voice comes in clearer than ever before, more pleased than ever before;

we meet

A girl steps out of the shimmering dark rainbow. Her cheeks are pockmarked, and her eyes are like pale ice, thin and sharp. Her posture is the posture of a queen, but her wild, pale hair puffs out like dandelion fluff, and it's strange to see her smile this brightly, this *calmly*. It's me. Me and Astrix and Quilliam, put together. Me and Astrix and Quilliam, feeding her.

hello, synali

hello. i…i don't know your name.

yes you do

She reaches her hand out; gathered in the center of her palm are the spirals of the saddle, spinning slowly in a silver puddle. Each one contains a perfect moving image, like a tiny video playing along its tinier body. Memory. Those are all the memories I've given, all the memories eaten. Panic grips my throat like hard steel fingers, and I stagger back.

don't—

She lets the spirals drip out of her hands, silver falling into black. Shapes and colors form out of the glinting drops, quickly building the image of a shabby apartment with an open doorway. A dark shadow stands in it, and a woman kneels before the shadow, hands clasped in prayer.

"Please"—Mother's voice *exactly*, a doomed woman trapped forever in amber as she begs the assassin—"please, let my daughter go—she's so young. *Please*, I beg of you with all I am, with all of God's goodness—spare her."

There's nothing I can do. ***Nothing.*** She's going to die and leave me alone, and there's nothing I can do. The assassin looks up at me, his cowl tilting, and I *remember*: he spared me. The despair closed in. I remember he turned after he'd killed her; I remember running at him and wrenching the dagger from his hand and driving deep into my own collarbone to be with her. To *die* with her. The assassin did not give me my scar. My father did not give me my scar.

I gave this scar to myself.

The assassin stopped the dagger from going in too far, held my hand up out of myself. Straining. He killed her, but he spared me. From his cowl comes the glint of ice-blue eyes, the same as Father's, the same as mine, the same voice from the recording:

"You must live."

I sob. "There's nothing left—I want to be with her!"

His hands let me sink the dagger farther in, agony, blood, but he knew when to stop, gripping hard, the frost in his eyes going soft as he murmured:

"They can choose to kill you. But you are the only one who can choose to live."

there are people who want to kill me, yes. but there are people who want to see me live, too.

He pulled me back from the brink. He bandaged my wounds when I collapsed—nothing but a shell of myself—and then left. But it doesn't change what he did. This is the last second of Mother's life. She is bone, she is dirt, she is a flower or a tree or the sparks running through a streetlight on the Station, but most of all she is gone.

what do you want? the girl asks and smiles, a strange look on me, but with that smile her name comes to me like the strike of a bell.

Heavenbreaker.

Her face melts—the Synali-Astrix-Quilliam features soften and blur like wax reshaping into familiarity—briefly growing hyacinths and daisies out of the flesh...and then Mother's face. She was always prettier than me—higher cheeks and kinder eyes, irises dark with syrup and bright with stars. In this memory, her face is fuller and her cheeks have rose in them. Her hair shines black, falling in gentle waves. She's not a memory—too healthy for that. She's not the girl, either—her expression is too real.

i'm glad you could make it, dearheart. i was waiting.

Her voice is just like I remember. My legs jut forward in hope. *you were waiting here?*

Mother nods. *it's a strange place, but i wanted to be here when you came.*

She staggers, then, holding her forehead, and before I can think I'm beside her, cradling her elbow, a childish instinct to catch her, hold her, support her. She feels solid, skin and bone, and then she wavers—goes translucent—and hot panic shunts open every vein of my heart; I don't want to lose her again. She looks up at me sheepishly, a bead of sweat carving down her temple.

i'm sorry. it's difficult to wait. there are so many others, so many thoughts and feelings that wash each other away. i forget who i am, sometimes, but i could never once forget you.

Her lips begin to bead with blood. Time breaks its teeth on me, on my eyes. She begged for mercy, and they gave her none. She begged for mercy, and only the assassin gave it to her. He gave her my life, and I have to live it, forever, without her. *Alone.* All of their words come back to me:

"Aren't you tired of being nothing?"

Yes.

"Come now, rabbit. I'll have more fight than this from you."

Yes. You will.

*what do you **want**?*

My mother's last words before they killed her, said again: *"You'll never be alone, Synali. I love you."*

And I get to say it back this time.

I love you, too.

And then in a snapshot, like blinking, Mother disappears. The assassin disappears. The entire apartment dissolves into nothing but dark, empty space.

Space full to the brim with silver eyes.

Every inch of black holds an orb-like silver eye. Gigantic, minuscule, all with needlepoint-void pupils and all of them looking **right at me**. Eyes like millions fill the whole of the emptiness until it *looks* like a galaxy again—stars and planets and suns, but *Us*. All of Us—enemy and ally, human and not-human, and one of the eyes winks down at me.

"…kid."

Heavenbreaker stands in front of them all with my face, ice-blue eyes going silver, wild hair shifting in an invisible wind, rainbow writhing around her back like tendrils. Like the hangar doors come to life. Like the enemy.

There is an enemy in this steed—a real, live, awake one—and I've been feeding it. Quilliam, too. Astrix most of all. It's been growing here all this time.

Slowly, she offers me my own hand.

together?

Together, we will protect each other. *Together*, we will remember everything, no matter how much it hurts. *Together*, we will stop hanging in the impact. The nobles killed her. Kings upon kings killed Sevrith and Astrix and so many more. They trapped Us, twisted our bodies to fit their needs. But we are not gone.

My hands, no longer shaking.

My arms around Heavenbreaker in an embrace.

To feel is the beginning and the end. The alpha and the omega.

The first feeling: my face wet with silver. I'm drenched in its cold oil slick down to my chin, and it drips and pools in my helmet. Human tears and enemy tears—silver and saltwater and sadness. Relief.

The second feeling: the soft sway of the rise.

The third feeling: *Heavenbreaker*. She's not around me or beside me. She *is* me.

It's the same feeling as when we first met, when she first showed me her memory in the reboot, but there's no fear this time. This time, we agree. We aren't two bells ringing at different times, back and forth—we're reverberating together. We are metal, and we are flesh. We are **together**. Heavenbreaker and I are closer than nerves, than atoms, than the fabric of space-time itself.

We grip the lance.

"—can't believe my eyes, Gress! It seems… Yes! It seems Synali von Hauteclare has actually recovered from her overload! That's right, folks—*recovered*! I'm getting reports that all her vital signs are intact and her brain waves are functional! I repeat: after a confirmed overload, *the steed Heavenbreaker is still moving, with its rider, Synali von Hauteclare, awake in the saddle!*"

"Sh-She's going for a third round, Bero! What will Mirelle do? She looks shaken, but she's taking the challenge and moving into the descent with

Ghostwinder for a third round as well! I can't believe it…this is unheard of, Bero! This goes against everything we know—this is history in the making! The first rider in history to recover from an overload—"

The cheers like inferno.

go.

Supernovae. Every single jet on our back is a *supernova*. Blue fire haloes us, blue fire in our eyes. Something bigger than us, waiting—the thing that writhed under my skin is out now, solid and real. Waiting just above me to strike.

together.

"H-How—" Mirelle's holoscreen gets only one second to speak before we cut it off.

The waiting thing slips around my arm. I see it reflected in the saddle; the silver whorls congregate, dense, around the entirety of my arm, up and down and limber and writhing. Organized pattern. A vine. A nigh-invisible limb cradles me from shoulder to wrist, just like in Rax's vid. A *tendril*. It reinforces my own arm like a splint, a support the color of silver in the saddle and the color of space outside it—black flickering with butterfly spots of rainbow light, tipped with claws and lined with suckers.

We can lift twice as heavy, twice as fast. I give an experimental twirl of the silver lance—a thousand blistering rotations in a second, my wrist at a terrifying ease.

I ride a steed, but I am not Saint Jorj.

I am the serpent.

what happens when a pawn makes it all the way to the other side?

well, then it becomes something else entirely.

"Good God, what is *that*, Gress? Are you seeing that—that *thing* on Synali's arm? It's coming out of her back, moving like, it looks like—"

"What are you talking about, Bero? Are you feeling all right? Maybe this tourney's impacts have been so good, they knocked the brain out of you, too!"

The comms cut. The grav-gen pulls us in. Ghostwinder's stance is impeccably powerful, ready to strike like fresh steel put on edge—more than it needs to be, more than enough, but she won't win.

Impact.

The light. The cry.

My silver lance pierces into her white forehead and out of her golden mane. Helmet hit.

Astrix floats in the black of space over Ghostwinder's motionless shoulder, over our two bodies suspended in space, her pale hair and blue dress undulating and her silver eyes smiling: *do you know what it means to ride?*

Our answer is a clear, unmistakable bell ringing out into the universe.

together.

75. Apricus

aprīcus ~a, ~um, a.
1. warmed by the sun

IN A QUIET, SUNLIT HOSPITAL WARD reserved for overloaded riders, there is a silence broken only by the holoscreens playing the Supernova Cup.

"I-In a stunning turn of events, Synali von Hauteclare has gotten a helmet hit on Mirelle Ashadi-Hauteclare! If— Oh God, that thing is— Isn't that thing the *enemy*, Gress?"

"What thing? Keep it together, Bero. We're still on air. Ladies and gentlefolk, if the referees confirm it, Synali von Hauteclare will be advancing to the quarterfinals—"

The commotion blares over the rows of orderly beds with orderly riders sleeping orderly and still and well-groomed. There are curtains one can draw for privacy, for *use*, and monitors to keep track of vitals. The comatose only ever have one vital—a crawling, methodical beep that never changes.

Until one does.

76. Gladiator

gladiātor ~ōris, *m.*
1. a swordsman

FROM THE NOBLE BOX, Nova-King Ressinimus watches Synali von Hauteclare win, his green eyes fixed on the writhing thing on her arm. A few nobles in the box—riders and former riders—are panicking, and the other half look at them as if they are mad. The king glances calmly over at the boy in the hoverchair next to him.

"You will be entering the Supernova Cup now, Jozua."

The boy smiles, soft as an angel, and inclines his head.

"With the greatest of pleasures, Your Majesty."

77. Propago

propāgō ~āre ~āuī ~ātum, *tr.*
1. to extend, increase

DRAVITICUS ASTER DE RESSINIMUS SMILES at the naked noble before him struck silent by all he has revealed. Rax Istra-Velrayd's grip goes weak, and he releases Dravik and staggers back against the cell wall.

"So you're saying…it's either Hellrunner or Heavenbreaker?"

Dravik straightens his breast coat. "When the majority of the hive mind has been injured, the living one takes over as the de facto leader, guiding the rest. They obey the living one's word—a fail-safe to prevent the death of the species. Hellrunner was the only one. But now one is alive in Heavenbreaker, too. It has learned. It has grown. And it is ready."

Rax is the rook—straightforward and strong—and so the prince is not surprised when he recovers quickly and asks, "So…so what happens now?"

"I do not claim to know the future, but I know my father. He will detain Synali the moment she begins to exhibit symptoms, and he will quickly spread a false explanation to assuage the rider nobles who can see the thing."

The girl makes it three exhausted steps out of her cockpit and into the hangar before the doors slide open and two dozen men in the violet-gold armor of the king burst through in precise order—precise motion as they draw their hard-light pistols and arrest her.

Dravik spins his cane around patiently, sapphires catching in the spilled water and the spilled worry in Rax's eyes.

"They will shuffle her away to the most secret laboratory they have and no doubt run a cadre of tests on her."

She thinks, for a split second, about calling Heavenbreaker to her through the glass of the hangar, but they are men—fragile—and this was inevitable. What happens next will not hurt—not now that she knows what together *means. She raises her hands, slow, and they grip her wrists behind her back and put the bag over her head with lightning speed.*

The prince looks at the ceiling of the metal cell thoughtfully, calculating between the seams of the sky.

"I will need all three of you to help me infiltrate the place and rescue her."

Rax frowns. "All *three* of us?"

The girl can't see, but she can feel—Heavenbreaker getting farther away from her. She can feel the steed as if it's her own body, her own pulse, her own heat drifting farther and farther into the distance. They're taking her somewhere, roughly—all shoving and pushing and lifting into the back of something hard and metal (a hum—a hovercarriage)—and they tie her hands during the flight, and she thinks to herself that those are now the weakest of her parts.

Dravik stops his cane mid-spin and looks up.

"You see, Sir Istra-Velrayd—Synali and I have been playing something of a game. And I'm afraid it required her to wade to the very depths of our opponent's back row."

The boy snarls and stands abruptly. "You—"

"You will aid me in retrieving her. You, and your Spider neighbor next door"—he tilts his wheat-colored head to the wall still vibrating with rhythmic thumps—"and Mirelle Ashadi-Hauteclare."

Rax's scoff is a bark. "Mir hates her. Synali killed her father, her whole goddamn family. And you helped her. *You* did the killing. She'd never—"

"I assure you, she will." Dravik looks up at him, all gray titanium.

The girl hears it over the jets of the hovercart and the vis chitchat of the king's guard—something is coming. No—they're getting closer to something; something she's heard every match, something ear-piercing and soul-piercing, a cry growing louder and louder in the back of her mind. It moves from a hum to a song to a screech, and finally—when the hovercart comes to a stop and they usher her out to walk on her own—it is a scream vibrating up from somewhere directly below her feet, drowning out even the hissing of what sounds like water.

"This will all take preparation. We cannot stay on the noble spire—we will move our operations to the Under-ring. We have time; the king knows better than to cancel the Supernova Cup, but he will delay it. He'll fill the gaps with minor tourneys to tide the nobles and his people over until he deems Synali sufficiently neutralized—either by death or by science. Only then will he allow the Supernova Cup quarterfinals to begin."

The guards lead her with iron grips over dirt, over marble, over stainless steel. She knows the sound, still so far below, and she can't help the way her heart leaps when they enter an elevator and begin to descend, the desperate cry becoming an untenable bellow seething beneath a skin of sleep. Closer. **Just a little longer, and we will be together.** *The guards' steps stop, and then she stops, the bitter smell of medical antiseptic and the sweet burned-metal scent of open space clashing in her nose.*

The prince stands up off the bucket, shedding his coat and holding it out to Rax. "If I am correct, we have precisely four weeks to rescue her."

Rax clenches his teeth. "And if you're wrong?"

Dravik smiles. "Then she dies. And all of this will have been for naught."

The guards pull her to a stop, yanking the hood off her head. She blinks into dimness, into LED lights barely piercing through the gloom of a darkened room. The center of it is brightest—a tube large enough to hold up the world, full to the brim with pale blue-purple fluid and silver spirals. The monster under the sea. It starts singing sharper than the eternal bellow—high-pitched, as if overjoyed to see her.

hello*, she says wordlessly.*

A dozen people stand before the tube in white lab coats, but a woman stands before them all. She is youngish but so rigid in her spine and shoulders she seems far older. She wears a strict bun, a holomonocle, and an expression of mild apology and utter determination both.

"Hello, Synali. My name is Ysolde. I'm the head scientist for the core. We think you've done some very interesting things, so we'd like to run a few tests. Will that be all right?"

The girl looks up—one iris blue as ice, the other silver.

TO BE CONTINUED IN *HELLRUNNER*

Acknowledgments

The acknowledgments of a book are like the frosting of a cake—not necessary by dictionary definition standards, but in order to feel complete and be satisfying in the stomach it *must* happen. Every year I get older, but books stay the same; the same adventure, the same sense of wonder, the same joy of patient discovery over and over again until the mishmash threads become a sweater that can keep anyone who reads them very warm.

You cannot choose your family, but you can choose your friends, though somedays it feels like fate chose us for each other. GW, Shannel, Ana, Tyler, Diana, Amanda, Hayley, Ben, Krys, Bee, Rob, Xiran, Anchor—I love and appreciate all of you. Without you I'd be sad and lonely, and nothing is worse for art than a fundamentally despondent writer. You've always cheered me on, and I thank you for that.

To my lovely agent, Caitlin; I have never felt more supported and looked after than when I'm with you. You allow my creativity to not just fly but truly soar. I appreciate everything you've done and continue to do for me, and here's to many more years of relationship.

My editor Stacy has tolerated me for far too long, and for that she deserves a raise and a trip somewhere very relaxing, preferably with zero controlling writers whatsoever. Thank you for believing in me when few else do and handing me chance after chance. I hope, when this book is published, it does our relationship and your patience justice.

To the entire Red Tower team—Liz, Hannah, Meredith, Ashley, Molly, Rae, Britt, Heather, Curtis, the wonderful graphic and cover artist Elizabeth, a million thank-yous. Thanks also to Ronkwahrhakónha Dube for your thoughtful insight. A book is a machine with so many parts, and while I cough them up, it's you who truly put them together in working order. You are dreammakers, and I hope wherever life takes you, it's somewhere befitting your vision and drive. Thank you.

To the reader; you silly little thing, this is the ingredients list of a book—why are you still reading? Go rest your eyes, maybe touch some grass. In all seriousness, I thank you from the bottom of my heart for reading. Whether you loved or hated Synali's story, I hope you learned something about yourself from it. All books are mirrors, and I hope you found what you were looking for in this one. Be safe. Be well. Be free.

In gratitude,
Sara Wolf